W9-DEI-135

UNSPOKEN

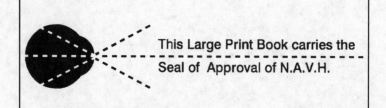

This Large Print Book carries the
Seal of Approval of N.A.V.H.

UNSPOKEN

DEE HENDERSON

THORNDIKE PRESS

A part of Gale, Cengage Learning

GALE
CENGAGE Learning

Detroit • New York • San Francisco • New Haven, Conn • Waterville, Maine • London

GALE
CENGAGE Learning®

LIBRARY OF CONGRESS CATALOGING-IN-PUBLICATION DATA

Henderson, Dee.
  Unspoken / by Dee Henderson. — Large print edition.
    pages ; cm. — (Thorndike Press large print Christian fiction)
  ISBN 978-1-4104-6259-6 (hardcover) — ISBN 1-4104-6259-5 (hardcover) 1.
Kidnapping victims—Fiction. 2. Large type books. I. Title.
PS3558.E4829U57 2013b
813'.54—dc23   2013031914

Published in 2013 by arrangement with Bethany House Publishers, a division of Baker Publishing Group

Printed in the United States of America
1 2 3 4 5 6 7 17 16 15 14 13

UNSPOKEN

PROLOGUE

I never talk about what happened.

There are reasons, good reasons, but I keep those to myself too.

I'm told the cops dealing with my case are wrapping up the last details, the task force dispersing back to their prior jobs. They seem relieved, the ones who have stopped by the hospital — relieved to see me alive, and they are tired. I have dominated their every waking moment, and the stress of the case has been enormous. They are glad I'm alive, and they are ready to move on.

My sister has hired me a bodyguard. Someone to keep the press away, along with the gawkers. There are newscasters vying for the first interview, and photographers trying to sneak in to get first photos. The bodyguard is talking to my nurse down the hall, and I can hear his voice — low-pitched, determined — and the way he says ma'am I can hear his still-fresh military background.

He hasn't tapped on my door to introduce himself yet, but that is coming soon. I think I'm ready.

I hope I don't see too much pity in his gaze, or too much seriousness. I'm alive, not dead. I'd like a smile occasionally, or even a laugh, rather than more of the grave intensity I see in everyone around me.

A tap on the door has me looking up from flipping pages in a magazine. I see a guy in jeans and a casual shirt who looks like a college student. Lanky, tall, nice blue eyes. I notice the hands in his back pockets, and the quick scan he's giving me.

"Ruth, I'm John Key." The voice puts him as the soldier-now-bodyguard I've been waiting to meet.

I decide I like his smile.

"I'm thinking about changing my name." I have no idea why that is my first sentence, but apparently he's better at social skills than I am because he merely nods before walking into the room and taking a seat on the edge of the bed, crowding me, but in a nice way, not trying to not make contact.

"Don't make it Margaret. And I don't like Shelly," he offers, taking my suggestion seriously.

"I was thinking about Jessica. Or maybe Charlotte."

"I could learn to like Charlotte."

I decide on the spot I'll be Charlotte. The person I have been, Ruth Bazoni, needs the space to rest, and even, maybe, to be forgotten. Charlotte . . . Charlotte Something — it feels kind of interesting to think of starting over.

I think it's his voice that I like best. The sound is different from the voices I've feared. John is young, but the voice is old. His eyes are old too. There's experience there that seems out of place. But I understand it. This man has seen war. He only looks young. I wonder if my eyes look the same. A young face, with ancient eyes.

"Your sister hired me, but my job description is so vague it's got no boundaries. To keep it simple, I'm going to tell people I'm your boyfriend, and then tell them to go away."

I nod, as if it's not that big a deal, but it's a big deal. The fact he would make the suggestion, would look past what's happened in order to make it, is an act of deep kindness. I've never had a boyfriend, and I know I'll be single for the rest of my life, but I can pretend if he can. "Could our first date be pizza and somewhere that is not this room? I'm hungry. And I'm bored."

His laugh is nice. "I'm good for pizza."

He stands. "If we're going to spend the next few weeks breaking the rules, we might as well start now. The elevator is close by. I can find a place in this hospital complex with at least a view, and a good pizza can get delivered. Think you can get dressed on your own, or should I invent a reason for the nurse to come help you?"

"I'll manage."

He nods and steps away, lets the door close behind him.

I know I am much too thin — nearly all bones. I'll probably manage just half a piece of pizza before becoming full. But I can see a day when those will not be the facts, and I want to get there soon.

I change into black slacks and a university sweatshirt, being careful of my aching wrist, and struggle to slip my feet into tennis shoes. I am sweating when I'm done, wondering how foolish I'm going to feel when my strength runs out before I can get back to my bed. I push away the thought, open the door.

John is leaning against the wall outside my room, and he nods to the wheelchair parked beside him. I settle in the chair and spread the blanket he hands me out across my lap. I notice my nurse is gone from the center station. "You told her we were leaving."

"What she doesn't see, she can't testify to."

He tugs a chain with dog tags and two worn keepsake medals off his neck. "Wear these. They brought me good luck. You could use some too." He slides them over my hair, lets them fall into place, then steps behind the wheelchair and begins pushing me toward the elevator.

I finger the metal, still warm from being against his skin. I blink back tears. I managed to get a guy who is genuinely nice. I hope he stays, at least a month or two.

"What kind of pizza?" he asks.

I smile, my first real smile in four years. "Supreme, please."

■ ■ ■ ■

PART ONE:
BRYCE BISHOP

■ ■ ■ ■

ONE

The day his life changed forever didn't announce itself; it just arrived.

The winter sun set early, and by the store lights against a dark night Bryce Bishop walked the display cases in his store, visually noting the changes from yesterday. They had done a steady business in old silver — Morgan dollars, Standing Liberty half-dollars. The end-of-day report Devon had generated would give him the exact numbers, but he could see it had been a profitable day.

In ten years he might be buying back what they had sold today. He was in one of the few retail businesses where the merchandise would never again be created and was rarely destroyed — it only changed hands. Most of the high-end collectible coins in the Chicago area eventually came through his store — Bishop Chicago — to be appraised for insurance purposes, to be sold, to be

15

photographed for an upcoming auction. There was good money to be made in old coins if you knew how to buy and sell wisely. He did. He had been doing so for more than a decade.

Bryce polished a spot off the display glass with his shirt-sleeve cuff. He was bored out of his mind, but the business was profitable and gave good jobs to ten people he liked. He could hand the keys to Devon and be an absentee owner. The store would be in good hands. But walking away from his life wouldn't solve his problem. He reset the security for the showroom floor and pushed down the restless desire not to come in tomorrow.

"Have a safe night, Mr. Bishop," the security guard called from his desk.

"You too, Gary."

Bryce walked around to the back of the building to the parking lot. Snow from the prior night still dusted the pavement. He tugged out his keys. It would be good to get home. No one was waiting for him, and maybe that was part of the problem. But his extended family was important to him — sisters, brothers, parents, cousins, the next generation of kids beginning to look to him for baseball games, movie afternoons, vacation trips — and he had friends who would fill the evening if he wanted to see someone. He was mind-numbingly bored, and it wasn't a good reality. But it was something he could change if he could just figure out what he wanted different in his days.

"Bishop."

He turned to see a woman leaning against an old truck in the far corner of the lot, her hands buried in the pockets of her jacket.

"You're about to get a call. You should answer it."

Silence hung between them, and then the phone in his pocket began to ring. He watched her as he listened to the sound, and she didn't move. Neither did he, as he considered what might be going on. Robbery, with a threat to his family to get him to comply? A kidnapping, demanding a ransom? He could see no one else in the parking lot, but the security lights only illuminated the surface and cast shadows — someone else could easily be sitting in a vehicle watching.

"Nothing bad has happened. It's simply an introduction." Her voice floated across the parking lot, faint but clear.

He pulled the phone from his pocket, eyes still on her. "Bishop."

"I don't know the lady, but I know who is vouching for her," Paul Falcon told him, the familiar voice a relief to hear. "This is highly unorthodox, but it's solid. You can trust what you're about to see and hear."

"Thanks, Paul. Call you back." He slid the phone back in his pocket.

"All right?"

The director of the FBI's Chicago office was vouching for the woman. He nodded. She pushed away from the truck, walked toward him. "Ten minutes, Mr. Bishop. You'll have your questions answered."

"Who are you?"

"Charlotte Graham. We've not met before. We do share a few friends." She was a woman about his age, her hair worn loose and long, the jeans and jacket neither new nor worn. "I have something to show you. That red security door over there" — she pointed — "is the back entrance to the storefront next to yours. Come in with me, please." She walked over to the door without looking to see if he followed and unlocked it.

He knew the store. A clothing boutique had moved out in an abrupt bankruptcy, and the lease on the property had been snapped up before his company had been able to put in a bid to buy the space. The retail spaces shared a common brick wall, and it would have been an ideal expansion.

18

The front windows to the storefront were still frosted over, with no sign indicating what kind of business was coming in, but workmen had been going in and out for a few weeks.

"Please watch your step," she cautioned, switching on lights. "The carpet for this back hall was laid a few days ago, and doorway finishing boards are still to go down." He followed her through the well-lit hallway. He could smell fresh paint and also good coffee.

They entered the shop proper. Walls had been removed, opening the space into a large showroom. Display cases were arranged in two melding arcs, with comfortable seating, private tables, good lighting, excellent artwork — a nice flow to the space. Tall vases filled with fresh flowers stylishly arranged caught his immediate attention. He'd been to enough store openings to know when a place was one turn of the key away from being ready to open. This was retail in the final finishing stage.

"Please, have a look around. You're the only customer tonight."

His first impression was *jewelry store*, for the showroom had that feel of elegance. He walked to the first case and looked inside. Gold coins. His breath settled wrong. He read the discreet sticker prices. He thought about turning around and walking out, but it wouldn't change what he was seeing. He began at the first case, and he took his time looking.

Charlotte chose a bottled water from the drinks offered near the coffee bar and watched the man prowl the store. Not a man to say much when ticked off. That was useful to know.

Bishop finally slowed his review and turned to look at her. "I see you plan for us to be competitors." The anger was there, hot, controlled, but his voice remained cool. "Your store is next door to ours, with a layout and elegance similar to Bishop Chicago. Your prices are lower, and while our inventories don't appear to overlap much, your coins will appeal to the same customer we've worked years to attract."

She screwed the cap back on the water bottle. "These aren't all the coins. We overlap. I was simply selective in the first inventory I chose to display."

"We can't match your prices." He pushed his hands into his pockets, and she saw them ball into fists. "Was that the purpose of this meeting tonight? To show me what was coming?"

She had expected the anger, planned for it. He was seeing a threat to his family business, and she'd chosen to make it an in-your-face event. She could cripple his business selling at these prices. She knew it, he knew it.

She set aside the water. "I don't want to open this store, Bishop. I want you to buy it."

She watched him as that statement sank in, as suspicion and confusion edged into the anger.

"You want me to buy it."

"The inventory, not the store itself. I rather like how the remodel turned out, and I'm going to keep the property."

"If you wanted to sell me some coins, Charlotte, you could have walked into Bishop Chicago and said, 'I've got some coins I'd like to sell.' "

She would have laughed at the dry remark, but he wasn't in the mood for amusement. She settled for a small smile. "This is more dramatic, don't you think?"

She poured a cup of coffee and pushed it into his hands. "If you want to keep me out of your business, Bishop, you're going to have to figure out how to buy my inventory. I'll give you good prices, I won't be unreasonable in the volumes I ask you to deal with, but I'm ready to sell some coins and I don't plan to take forever to get it done."

She ran her hand across the top of a display case she had filled and neatly priced. "You buy what's here in the store, I'll give you thirty days, and then I'll show you this store filled with more coins. We'll do this again, round two. You can buy the coins, or I'll open the doors to the public and become your competition. And after round two, we'll do round three."

"How many coins in all?"

"Let's take this one decision at a time. Buying what is here will give you thirty days of me not being your competitor." She moved briskly across the room to the desk and retrieved the inventory sheet. "Become a dealer to other coin stores; raise money from investors to buy the coins, store them, and sell them over a period of years — however you want to deal with them, but the condition is that you buy everything in the store. Tonight."

He scanned the list. "Why such low prices? You're not only underpricing Bishop Chicago, you're below wholesale on many of these coins."

"Sharing the profit means the people I do business with come back and do business with me again."

He looked over at her. "You've done this before — the store setting, the surprise invitation."

"I targeted Hamilton-Grice in London for the European coins. You should feel flattered I chose Bishop Chicago. I was considering Cambridge Coins out of New York."

"I'm not sure 'flattered' is the word I would use. Who are you?"

She smiled. "Charlotte Graham."

"Collector? Dealer? Fence? I haven't seen coins at these prices in over a decade. For all I know, the coins could be stolen."

"Hence the introduction from the Chicago FBI director. The coins are mine to sell."

"I need to know how you came to be in possession of them."

"My grandfather liked coins. He died recently."

"I'm sorry to hear it."

She nodded. "Do we have a deal?"

Bryce looked around the store, then back at her. "Do I have a choice?" He walked over to the desk and initialed each page of the list. "I'll buy your inventory, Charlotte. Where do you want me to wire the money?"

"A check will do fine."

Bryce put a security firm on a background check of Charlotte Graham on the drive home, headed upstairs to change out of the business suit, and called Paul Falcon at his home number. "She's selling some coins, and she has a very unorthodox way of doing it. Who vouched for her?"

"I can't say, which in itself should tell you something. Are you buying the coins?"

That answer told him another cop was behind the introduction, someone Paul deeply trusted. Bryce pulled off a dress shoe and tossed it toward his closet. "I'll make thirty percent on my money, but I'd like to be able to say no as it feels like I'm doing business with the mob. She's got me as confused as anyone I have ever met." He was trying to be charitable and give her the benefit of the doubt. Maybe she hadn't intended her dramatic approach to be so in-his-face offensive, but the anger caused by this evening was like a bad toothache. *Confused* was the most polite word he could come up with for what he was feeling.

"She's legit, Bryce," Paul replied, sounding amused. "And while I've never met her, from what I know *of* her, I would be inclined to like her a great deal."

"Okay." That was worth something.

"She really turned you the wrong way tonight."

"She did. I've got Chapel Security doing

a full background check."

Paul was silent for a while. "I'd be curious — professionally — to hear what they come up with."

Bishop realized the undercurrent. "Charlotte Graham isn't her real name, is it?"

"I'll owe you a favor if I can see the report."

The other shoe landed in the closet. "This night is just full of unexpected surprises. I'll share the report with you. She said her grandfather passed away. Any estate disputes going on, lawsuits, problems with provenance, or any other mess I'm walking into?"

"Not that I'm aware of, and I'd be aware. On that front you're fine. The coins are hers to sell."

"Wonderful." Bryce kept his tone noncommittal as he pulled off his tie and turned the conversation to his immediate problem. "You want to buy some coins for an investment?"

"How much are we talking?"

"I spent one million six tonight on five hundred coins, and it sounds like I'll be buying more. She's got some nice gold — an 1835 Half Eagle, a 1912 Indian five, a couple of gorgeous 1799 tens. I can put together a package of fifty for two fifty and be far enough below market your annual security-clearance review is going to wonder if it was a payoff."

"I'm interested."

"I'll send you photos and prices. And to think when this evening started I was bored and restless. Ann back home yet? She'll enjoy seeing these coins."

"Ohio for another two days. She wants me to invite you over for dinner. She's got someone she would like you to meet."

"I like your wife, and surprisingly like her friends, but we've determined I'm not matchmaking material."

"You're simply . . . choosy."

"That's one word for it. Sure. Tell her I'll come for dinner if she can give me some notice. It's going to be a hectic month." He would need the break, and it would be useful to see what else Paul might tell him about Charlotte Graham if pressed. He wondered idly what her real name was. "Anything you can tell me about why Charlotte's got cops vouching for her?"

"No. I got a call, made a call. I was surprised to hear she was in Chicago."

"Wish she hadn't been."

Paul laughed. "Now I'm curious to meet her just because she rubbed you the wrong way. Don't make a quick decision about this one, Bryce. She's not all she appears to be."

"That I've figured out. Talk to you tomorrow, Paul."

Bishop hung up the phone, tossed it on the dresser with his wallet, then tussled with a stuck cuff link. The woman was going to be a pain, no matter what her name was. He set his alarm for five a.m., his mind already formulating a strategy for the next few days. He had cash to raise, his staff to mobilize, clients to contact. He pulled out jeans and a sweatshirt, then headed downstairs to get dinner. He was no longer bored. He'd give her some credit for that.

"I wish she'd let one of us go with her." Ellie Dance set aside the background check on Bryce Bishop and moved over a glass paperweight — a gift from Charlotte — to hold the pages.

John Key, leaning against the doorjamb of Ellie's home office, ate another pecan from the handful he held. "She'll be fine. He's a good guy."

"A bit conservative, on the edge of stuffy, but yeah — a good guy. Did we talk her into Bishop because we didn't want her to head to Atlanta or New York?"

"Probably." John smiled. "Don't rethink it, Ellie. The decision is made. You spent months gaming this out. This will work for her. She needs to keep a low profile when in Chicago, but she's been doing that for the last decade. She'll be fine."

"Then why am I as nervous as a new mother?"

"You like protecting people, organizing things. It makes you a good business manager for Charlotte and an even better best friend."

Ellie glanced at the photo on the desk. Sixteen years of friendship, fourteen in business together — they knew each other's darkest secrets, and they both had some very difficult ones. Charlotte had been calm when she left, mentally ready, but she hadn't eaten. Under the calm had been a fine layer of nerves. She'd be hungry when she got back. Lasagna was baking in the oven. It wasn't much, but there would be a meal ready. "I've been doing some more thinking on her final options. I'll have something on paper for her to consider in another six weeks or so."

"The final deadline is three years after her grandfather's death. She's still got time before she has to decide."

They heard the back door security chime as the code to Ellie's home cleared. John glanced over his shoulder and straightened.

"She's back earlier than I expected."

Ellie shut off the desk lamp and found her shoes. Charlotte would want a few minutes to settle before being asked about the evening, so neither one hurried to meet her. "Take Mitch some dinner since you've got him posted for security tonight."

"Noticed that, did you?"

"You said low profile and we would be fine."

"Think I'd leave anything to chance?"

"No. I'm guessing you also had Joseph discreetly tailing her since she said you couldn't." Ellie paused beside him, slid an arm around his waist. He'd marry her in a minute if she'd let him, had made no secret of that fact over the years. "Glad you're here."

John dropped a kiss on her hair. "So am I."

"What's she going to ultimately decide, John?"

"She'll turn it down."

Ellie sighed. "Yeah. I think so too."

He ran a comforting hand across her back. "You want her to say yes even given the condition?"

"I think she'd be happier if she did."

He thought about it. "Maybe she would be. But this has pushed her enough outside her comfort zone there's not enough safe space and time for her to come to that conclusion."

"I need to figure out a way to create that safe space while there's still time."

"If that's possible to do, you'll find it." He shut off the office lights and reached for her hand as he turned them toward the kitchen. "Did Charlotte give you her latest sketchbook?"

"The Shadow Lake sketches? They're lovely. I'll be at the gallery tomorrow getting the best of them framed. I'm going to raise her prices again this month."

"She winces at the prices you charge for one of her sketches."

"Which is why an artist needs a business manager, someone who can price a work appropriately for the market."

"I heard a rumor there's a new Marie painting coming."

"A thirty-six by forty-eight-inch canvas — *Rolling Hills at Sunset*. Probably a few weeks yet."

"If she hasn't already told you," John said, "Charlotte would like to buy it. She's never been able to afford one before."

"I'll show it at the gallery for six months before setting the price, but it's going to be multiples higher than Marie's last painting."

"It will be worth every penny. I'm planning to make a trip back down just to see it." He stopped them in the hall just short of the kitchen. "Relax."

"I wish Charlotte's grandfather had never found her, wish none of this was being asked of her. If we got this wrong, John —"

"If we did, we'll adjust." He squeezed her hand. "Elliot Marks out of Atlanta could work. I just like Bryce Bishop more."

"So do I. Okay." Ellie smoothed a hand down her dress and took a deep breath. "We're going to get her through this. No matter what else happens, she's got us."

"She always will," John promised. "Whatever she says about tonight, simply say 'we can work with that.' "

Ellie laughed and tightened her hand in his. "Let's go see how the evening went."

Two

Bryce let himself into Charlotte's shop using the key and security code she had given him, found the lights. He carried the box he had brought into the showroom and set it on the desk.

She had built a beautiful store. In the early morning light he was even more impressed with what she had accomplished with the space. This was formidable competition.

Bishop Chicago had a leg up with their website, the eighty years of history and reputation, knowledgeable staff, and a deep list of clients. But quality and price were the cornerstones of the coin business. Charlotte could poach his sales staff for their expertise. If she added a three-year buy-back guarantee to what she sold — and she could afford to do it at these prices — sales at Bishop Chicago would virtually stop. In the light of day the decision to buy out her inventory was not only the right decision, it was his only decision. She hadn't hesitated to go for the jugular on this deal. He wondered where she had learned that ruthless bent, might even have cautiously admired it if she hadn't targeted him.

He slipped on white cotton gloves, entered the security code to open the first display case, and picked up one of the coins. He turned it over to study the details, confirming what he had observed the night before. She was both under-grading the coins and pricing well below market. The woman was going to make him some serious money if he could survive her method of selling.

He put the coin back, studied the rest of the display, and for the first time since this began let himself relax and simply appreciate the sight. The coins were his, at very good prices. In a business where the initial purchase determined much of the final profit, he'd made a good decision. He'd been forced to make it, but the decision itself was solid. The risk was not in the coins, but in the scale of the deal.

He took a seat in a very comfortable chair, pulled out a pen and paper, and started a list.

He'd spent one million six keeping this inventory from hitting the market. He wanted to have four million in cash on hand before she showed him the next group of coins. There was a high probability he had seen the best coins she had with this collection, yet he wasn't going to make the assumption the next lots of coins would cost him less. She'd show him another group of coins, and another after that. So four million in liquid cash in thirty days. Careful decisions. Nothing stupid. But he had to be ready and able to say yes.

With inventory purchased at these prices, if he could absorb all she had to offer, if he could keep her out of the business as a competitor, he could nearly guarantee Bishop Chicago would prosper for the next decade. He just had to navigate the cash flow when he wasn't sure how deep he had to plan.

He heard the back door open with a soft chime and glanced at his watch. She had said seven a.m., and she was a few minutes early. She came in dressed much the same as last night, jeans and a sweatshirt from a university in Texas this time. She had brought her own coffee.

"Breakfast is on the desk if you're interested," he mentioned.

"Poisoned, perhaps?"

He half smiled. "Not until I've bought all your coins."

A beautifully brushed Irish setter had walked in beside her and now sat looking at him. He held his hand down, palm out, and the dog got up to come over. "Beautiful animal."

"Princess is the regal one in the family. Her sister Duchess is very much the mischief-maker." She helped herself to a bagel and cream cheese. "I'm on my way out of town. Anything you need to ask before I leave?"

"Insurance and security."

"My insurance will continue to cover the coins until they leave the premises. I'm now listed as custodian of the coins you've bought. Your security firm is already monitoring this storefront." She shrugged. "Seemed simpler as you would know who was best for the job."

"I need a phone number where I can reach you."

She pulled out a business card, added a number to the back, offered it.

The front of the card was simply her name.

"When will you be back?"

She opened an orange juice. "A few weeks."

"I'll have the coins moved from here by then."

"No problem. Codes and locks have been changed. You and I are the only ones with access to this place." She perched on the arm of a chair. "Still mad?" she asked around a bite of the bagel.

He had to smile. "More just curious. Why me? Why not Cambridge Coins out of New York?"

"You're a Christian, a teacher at your church. It offends your God if you steal. That's useful to me."

He felt a startled surprise. "You're serious."

"I don't believe like you do, but it's an interesting fact that you do. Family businesses thrive or die by the ethics of the guy running the place. Bishop Chicago is profitable — has to be to keep the doors open. But you don't cut corners to get there because you also have to sleep well at night. I bet you reimburse the business for postage when you use a stamp for a personal letter."

He felt like he was being complimented and insulted at the same time. "I'm more comfortable following the rules."

She laughed. "I could also say it was easier to haul the coins to Chicago than to take them to New York." She pushed off the arm of the chair, and the setter went to stand beside her. "I want to make the tollway before traffic picks up. I'll get out of here, let you get to work."

"Drive carefully, Charlotte."

"Plan to. Oh — one last thing. Would you carry the flowers next door before they die? Your staff might enjoy them."

"I'll do that. You set quite a display for a single customer."

"This was practice."

"For what?"

She just smiled. "See you in a few weeks, Bishop."

Two blocks east of Bishop Chicago was Falcons, a restaurant whose owner and head chef was Paul Falcon's sister, Jackie. The restaurant opened at ten thirty for the early lunch crowd, but those with a longtime friendship with her could get breakfast and a quiet place to have a meeting. Bryce qualified, and he spent twenty minutes reminiscing with Jackie in the kitchen while she began cooking their breakfast, then walked into the dining room and chose a table in the empty room. He pulled the list out of his pocket and added more notes while he waited for his key staff to arrive.

"Hey, boss." Devon pulled out chairs for Sharon and Kim and took a seat between them. "Glad you called."

"Nice you were all free." Bryce passed across a basket of hot blueberry muffins just out of the oven.

Two waitstaff appeared with filled plates, followed by their waitress. "It's a pleasure to have you back, Bryce," she said.

"This looks wonderful, Amy." She poured coffee for the four of them and left them to their breakfast meeting.

"So, boss, what did we do to earn this?" Devon asked, reaching for cream for his coffee.

"It's what you're going to do," Bryce replied, sampling the crepe and nodding his appreciation. Jackie laid out a nice breakfast. "Remember how we used to dream about the big estate find? The one that would put Bishop Chicago on the map and make us all rich?"

Devon put down his muffin and looked at Bryce. "The one that would let me afford to marry Sharon?"

His wife made a face and elbowed him in the ribs for that quip.

Bishop smiled. "That's the one. It dropped into our laps last night."

"Seriously, boss?" Kim asked, setting down her orange juice.

He turned his attention to her. Kim Leonard was the best salesperson he had, and the success of his plan rested in large part on her skills. "Kim, I'm going to hand you five hundred coins to sell, mostly gold, 1810 to 1880, all high grade, and I need you to move half of them within a month."

Kim's hand trembled against the glass. But Bryce saw the gleam of excitement in her eyes and gave her a slight nod. She worked on salary plus a three-percent commission, and he was offering to make her a very good year. "Have your best sales staff on the phones to contact customers, plan an auction, travel to show the coins — whatever you decide will work best. The first of the coins are going to reach Bishop Chicago this afternoon. I've already laid some ground with Paul Falcon to take a package of fifty for two hundred fifty thousand, so you can work that possibility as one of your first sales."

"I'll wow him," she promised.

Bryce looked over at Sharon. "The two photographers you like to work with on the auction catalogs — I'll make it worth their while to come to the shop and work for you for the next couple of months. You're the best I've got for presentation, so how to display the coins — in the store, the catalog, on the website — is going to fall to you. I'm raising you to double on all overtime plus a percent commission on these coins. Anything I can do to free up your time — hire a housekeeper, keep your husband out of your way — just let me know."

She smiled and nodded. "Thanks, Bryce."

Bryce looked at the man he trusted most with the business. "Devon, grading the coins and getting them into inventory will be on you and your staff. Let's batch them through in groups of twenty-five, with at least an hour break between groups. I need careful work as much as I need fast work."

"We can handle it, boss."

"I'm counting on it. I want you and Kim to go over the coin prices and bring me a list with your recommendations. I'll make the final decision on what price we'll bring them to market."

He glanced around the table. "Devon grades the coins and gets them into inventory, Sharon photographs, Kim sells. And while you all are doing that —" he paused, enjoying the moment — "I'm going to find us the cash to buy more coins from the same estate."

He sampled the sausage puff pastry while his speechless staff stopped eating. Jackie wouldn't appreciate plates coming back with food untasted.

"There's more?" Devon asked for all of them.

Bryce reached for his coffee. "I'm told there is."

He'd been working the numbers in his head most of the morning. "Devon, I'd like to take everything we have in present inventory down in price to our cost plus eight percent. It will move inventory, raise cash, and give us much-needed vault and display space. But that's going to put enormous strain on the website business for processing orders, packaging, and shipping coins. I need you to go back through the employment records, look at those we have employed on a temporary basis to help at auctions, at coin shows, select those who are careful, who work well with minimal supervision, and staff us up to handle it. As soon as you have enough staff on hand to provide quality service, take down the prices."

"I can think of several possibilities without even pulling the files."

"They'll be temp positions, but at least four months of steady work." Bryce considered the problems he had identified. "Depending on the pace of sales, managing the vault space is going to be one of the squeeze points. We're fine for the first five hundred coins, but it's the group after this one that starts to get interesting. So for now, Devon, I'm going to take back on my plate all purchase decisions on new inventory."

"I've got no problem with that, boss. I imagine cash flow is going to be interesting for a while too."

Bryce nodded. "I broke my piggy bank this morning and told my banker I was putting another slug of personal cash into the business. When you see the coins over the next few days, you'll understand the gamble. I think we have the potential to secure our profitability for the next several years if we manage this carefully. We need to expand vault space so we can hold more inventory — I'll be focused on fixing that."

Bryce settled back in his chair, his coffee in his hand. "One last thing. I'm not going to tell you much about the estate, or the lady selling. She's got some sting to her."

Devon appeared to think about that. "Sounds interesting."

Bryce laughed. "Oh, she is that."

He finished his coffee, then the last of the crepe. He hadn't enjoyed a breakfast meeting more than this one in ages. He glanced at the time and made a decision. He set aside his napkin, pushed back his chair. "I'm going to let the three of you enjoy your breakfast and plan the details of this while I go get the first hundred coins. I'll meet you back at the shop in, say, an hour and a half."

Sharon smiled at him. "I don't think you're bored anymore, Bryce."

"Not so much."

"We'll be ready for the coins. It's going to be fun," Sharon promised.

To his surprise Bryce found that Sharon was right about the fun. With Charlotte out of the picture for a couple of weeks, he could focus on what needed to be done and was enjoying the work. He arrived at Bishop Chicago the third day just after nine, carrying yet another box of coins. The store was humming with activity. The front window display had been changed, photographs of coins in the vault were strategically placed, and fresh coffee and donuts were set out. Kim, on the phone, looked over, smiled, and held up two fingers.

Sharon had the center display case open, and Bryce stopped beside her to see what had just sold. "Kim placed the 1866 Gold Liberty ten and the 1880 Gold Indian three," Sharon told him, moving the coins into archive-quality sleeves and placing them into sales boxes.

"Two of the best coins in the group."

"And priced accordingly," Kim said, smiling as she hung up the phone. "Jim wants to see anything else we get in Indian threes."

"I'm carrying another four."

Kim did a bit of a dance. "I love sales days."

Bryce laughed. "Where are we at, total?"

"Twenty-nine sales, and strong prospects on the others we have graded and photographed so far. Current clients should absorb the first hundred coins without much problem. Devon thinks he'll have the grading finished today."

"I'm carrying the beginning of the second hundred. It's going to be a good day. Find me if I can help you with anything."

He left the coins with Devon and headed to his office. He wanted every coin Charlotte planned to sell. Four million in thirty days was his goal, and his plan on how to get there was coming together. Selling current inventory, some of the estate coins, adding another equity slice of his own personal cash were pieces of the answer.

The final piece was to put together a group of buyers for the coins so their cash was available if necessary. He planned to buy aggressively for Bishop Chicago. But the one thing he could not afford was having Charlotte go into business next door. Having a syndicate of buyers as a backstop would mitigate that risk. Bryce opened his address book and picked up the phone. He'd be ready within thirty days.

"Bryce, this got couriered over." Kim caught him in the hall to hand off a package.

"Thanks, Kim."

The package was from Chapel Security. Bryce took it back to his office, slit open the envelope inside, and pulled out a single page.

Interesting request, Bishop. Charlotte Graham is the owner of Graham Enterprises, Trust, Wisconsin. It's the third largest transportation, warehouse, and storage business in the country. She inherited ownership of the business from her grandfather, Fred Graham, who passed away in May of 2011.

Fred Graham never married, but the grandfather/granddaughter connection has legal standing. It appears Fred Graham had a daughter he never acknowledged. The connection is through Charlotte's mother. I've got threads that suggest Charlotte changed her last name to Graham in 2006.

Charlotte Graham owns residential property in Silverton, WI, that she bought in 2007 and paid for with cash. The truck she drives is registered to that address. She leased the storefront using the law firm of Baird, McRay, & Scott out of New York. All bills related to the storefront route to that law firm.

Before 2006 the picture is murky. Looks like Charlotte's from Texas. Age unknown. Marital status unknown. Birthplace unknown. Prior name unknown.

Eric Chapel had added a handwritten note.

She might be the sketch artist CRM. Serious talent if I've got her pegged right. More as I find it. Call if you have further specific questions.

Bishop thoughtfully folded the page. It wasn't what he expected. The art in the shop next door had caught his attention, and he wondered if he'd find something with those initials. If she was more than just a passive owner, was now running the transportation and warehouse company, he doubted the business was something she found easy to do or that it gave her much time for her art. He had some sympathy for her situation. The fact she'd inherited a company and the responsibilities of it, along with some wealth, had a familiar ring.

THREE

Paul Falcon leaned against his wife's work-table and waited for her to stop typing. Ann had lifted a finger when he walked into their shared home office to signal she needed another minute. He had no idea what story she was working on — she was stingy about giving out details before it was done — but she would work the hours to write it, and he would enjoy the book when it was done. Black was leaning against his knee, and out of habit Paul shared a pretzel from his handful with the dog.

"Thank you. Done for the day." Ann glanced back at the screen. "Or at least for the next hour."

Paul leaned over and kissed her.

She offered a smile and kissed him back as her attention fully shifted away from the story to him. "Welcome home."

"It's late. I brought work home with me. Dinner smells good."

"Jackie said put the crock pot on low and leave it alone. I could do that."

He smiled. "We'll both enjoy it."

"How was work?"

"Decent day." Though she had been out of law enforcement for a while, her security clearance was still higher than his, so he told her the details while she worked his tie loose. "Someone might be studying security around the former Sears Tower, and it's got me worried. On the good side, we finally busted that shipment company moving cash around for the Madoni family. Didn't net as much cash as I hoped, but it sent a message."

"How much?"

"Sixteen million. I think we hit their supply of fives and tens, so it might at least annoy them a bit."

He nudged her toward the couch in their office so he could sit and put his feet up for twenty minutes. "Sam and Rita are out on a date tonight. They don't think I know, but give a boss credit for being a good sleuth. Dinner at Porchello's followed by music somewhere I didn't manage to nail down. Probably not *the* question tonight, but it looks promising. That was my day. How was yours?"

"Pretty quiet. I slept in, read a book, typed

on a story. Your dad called — he said you should call him back. Boone wants to buy an ice-skating rink. Your mom said yes for lunch tomorrow here, and we're going to go shopping afterwards. Black and I discussed a play date with Jasmine."

Paul glanced down at the dog, now looking up at the sound of his name. "Budding romance is getting serious, is it?"

The dog slapped a tail against the floor, then leaned over to pick up Ann's shoe and disappeared toward the bedroom.

Ann watched him leave. "The problem is he only puts one of them away."

Paul laughed, and relaxed for the first time since the day had begun. He was normally on the way to the office by seven a.m. For security reasons a driver and bureau car were provided now that he ran the Chicago office. He started his workday in the back seat, reading the overnight brief that came to his home by secure fax. Catching half an hour of normal time with Ann when he got home each night was something he treasured.

"What cold case did you bring home?"

He curled a strand of her hair around his finger. "What makes you think I did?"

"We solved the last one."

She might be a retired homicide cop, and

he'd managed to get himself promoted too high for the rewards of hands-on running a case, but they both could keep their hand in. He dropped a kiss on her hair. "Baby Connor."

"I wasn't a cop yet, but I remember it, the funeral."

"Of the cases I considered, this one stood out for its sadness. A three-month-old baby boy taken from a stroller at a shopping center, the note left says *We'll be in touch.* The father gets a call on the fourth day from a local pub telling him how to find where his son is buried. The case needs solving. I brought a copy of the call home with me. The audio guys cleaned it up with today's equipment; they were able to separate several of the background conversations."

"Anything useful?"

"A busy pub on a Wednesday night."

"I'll enjoy working on it with you."

"Nineteen years old. It's ice cold."

"We enjoy a challenge. It's open. That's what matters."

Paul reached into his shirt pocket, pulled out a small archive-quality, clear plastic sleeve. "I also stopped by to see Bryce for a couple minutes. He thought you might enjoy this one."

The coin inside was a silver-capped Bust

half-dollar, one of the 1834s she favored. Paul knew she would enjoy it, and Bryce had assured him it was in better condition than most Ann had handled during the years she had dealt coins.

"You've got good taste," she said, turning the coin over.

"Bryce helps with that. Have you heard anything more about why Charlotte is in town?" Ann's sources were better than his on some matters.

"Her business with Bryce is simply selling the coins from her grandfather's estate. Probably where this one came from. But the rest of it — she's got the kind of deci-sions ahead of her I wouldn't wish on anyone. I touched base with John. He seems . . . well, not worried but cautious, watchful. She really needs a quiet few months."

"After seeing Bryce, I phoned the office to have them pull the Bazoni file."

"You'll need a big room. Look at how it ended."

Paul smoothed hair back from her face. "Know something?"

Ann simply shrugged.

"Yeah." The two women shared a history of having been snatched. Ann would know Charlotte's story. "I think she's got Bryce a bit flustered," Paul mentioned.

"Really?" Ann smiled. "There's a first for everything. I've never seen the man flustered." She tucked the coin back in his pocket. "Ginger Nyce said yes to coming to dinner."

Paul was pleasantly surprised at the thought of Bryce and Ginger together as a couple. If they clicked, it would be a very good fit. "Ginger Nyce. That's an interesting choice."

"She'd be good for him. Going to go running with Bryce this weekend?"

"If the weather cooperates."

"Mention Ginger likes to travel and shares his taste in music."

Paul smiled. "I'll see if I can work it in."

Black came back carrying his dinner bowl.

Ann leaned down to take it. "Black, you had dinner."

Her dog dropped his head on her knee.

Paul watched the quiet conversation between the two of them and let his wife up when she gave in to Black's plea. He could remember the days he didn't have a wife and dog, but he wouldn't trade anything to have those days back. This was simply too entertaining. "You're a pushover."

"You share your breakfast. And I saw you give him a pretzel."

"Didn't say I wasn't one too. Has he gained weight?"

"The vet says he's lost three pounds. I'm jealous of our dog."

"I'll fix our dinner while you fix his second course." Paul stopped to open his briefcase and get out the baby Connor summary so Ann could read it while he worked on the meal.

Paul opened one eye as Ann's elbow pressed into his rib cage from her side of the bed. Her light was still on.

" 'Baby Connor Hewitt, three months old, was abducted from a stroller at the outdoor Lincoln Square shopping center,' " she read aloud, " 'when his mother stopped to assist a girl who had fallen and skinned her knees. It happened at 6:14 p.m. July twenty-first, a Saturday night, when the shopping center was crowded with foot traffic.' "

She was rereading the summary file at . . . he tried to make out the time on the clock, then conceded reality and closed his eyes. He'd married a woman who was as much a night owl as he was a morning lark. For her it wasn't the middle of the night.

" 'Interviews with those in the shopping center and the parking lots produced no direct eyewitnesses to the abduction, but a consensus formed of two young men, one carrying a child, jackets, jeans, ball caps and gloves, getting into a white panel van.' " He heard the folder close. "Question."

"Okay," he murmured, both eyes still closed, but listening.

"Do we think two guys took baby Connor? Or were the witnesses giving us simply an innocent family out shopping? People try to be helpful when a cop asks them a question like 'Did you see anyone walking toward the parking lot with an infant?' "

They both knew the odds the consensus was wrong. "At least two people," Paul replied. "One to hold the baby, one to drive. Not sure I'd take a baby, though, if I'm a guy. What do you do with it the next day? And the one after that? Better to grab a child who can sit at the table and eat a sandwich, follow directions, already be potty-trained."

"Someone took an infant and wasn't worried about what the day-to-day details would be like."

"This probably wasn't just two guys," he noted. "And babies cry. Though that might explain why baby Connor was shaken to death within three days. I think we're looking for a family with money problems. Brothers maybe, drag in a wife to handle the day-to-day of caring for a baby."

She thought about that. "Thanks." She shut off the light. "I bet you get odd looks when guys ask what kind of gifts you give your wife, and you say old coins and cold cases."

"Only from those who don't know my wife." Whoever had taken baby Connor was enjoying their last months of freedom, they just didn't know it yet.

"You can sleep now."

"Going to."

The room grew quiet enough Paul could hear the dog breathing by the foot of the bed. He wrapped an arm around his wife. Life was good.

Paul paused in the kitchen on his way to take Black for his morning walk. Ann was writing on a pad of paper and drinking coffee, and she wasn't one to particularly like coffee. "You're up early. What's got you puzzled?"

Ann handed him the coffee mug. "Listen to the baby Connor call again." She cued up the recording.

"This is not the ransom call you are expecting. Your son died yesterday. I got asked to bury the child and declined.

The FBI is tracing this call so you know I'm at the Dublin Pub in Meadow Park. The bulletin board by the pay phones, on the back of a photo of Mrs. Leary's lost cat, you'll find a map to where your son is buried. They did the job themselves after arguing with me for a bit. If the information is good, leave ten thousand with the bartender and I'll consider calling back when I have more to say."

The tape went to static. Ann shut off the recording. "We'll talk about the call itself another time. It's not the call that's got me puzzled. It's the Mrs. Leary's lost cat. It's like the inside joke of Chicago, Mrs. O'Leary whose cow started the great fire of 1871. It feels like a tongue-in-check reference to that."

"Somewhere in the notes they figured it out," Paul told her. "The name on the photo was actually Mrs. Cary. He altered it. I suspect our caller drew the map, played with the name while he thought about what he wanted to say on the call, stuck the photo back on the bulletin board, and dropped his coins into the pay phone. Which reminds me — make a note to see if anyone thought to check for fingerprints on the coins. He wiped down the phone and the photo, probably didn't think of the coins." Black was leaning into the back of his knee to move him toward the elevator. Paul ruffled his ears in apology.

"Cops spent much of the subsequent investigation trying to find the caller and probably had his prints on the change if they had thought to look," Ann said.

"It happens." Paul picked up a piece of bacon to share with Black and leaned over to kiss her. "Sure you weren't up early because you're nervous about my mom coming over for lunch?"

"I might have wanted to make sure I hid some of my clutter."

"Don't make her too uncomfortable with everything in its place. She's more disorganized than you."

"I knew there was a reason I loved your parents." The phone rang and they both ignored it.

"The Harbor guys are nervous. Lots of dignitaries down at the pier today. You might want to avoid that direction when you and Mom go shopping. And whoever is casing the Willis Tower has both my attention and the Chicago PD's. Plainclothes cops might get skittish when they notice the fact you're carrying."

"We'll stay off Wacker Drive too."

"Appreciate it. Try to spend some money."

She smiled and pushed him toward the elevator. "Go walk our dog and then go to work. Chicago needs you running that battleship of an FBI office."

He stole another kiss. "Yes, ma'am."

FOUR

Bryce walked back toward Bishop Chicago. He liked Ann's friends as a rule, and tonight had been no exception. It had been an enjoyable dinner with Ann and Paul Falcon, along with their guest, Ginger Nyce. So why had he not asked Ginger for her phone number?

He had spent a perfectly pleasant evening talking with her. She was an interior designer who specialized in kitchen remodels, they shared friends and some interests, she'd fit nicely into his life, and he'd merely said good-night when the evening was over. He knew Ann had been hopeful they would hit it off, and a bit disappointed when he had not pursued it. He should have been interested — that was the problem, and he couldn't sort out why he hadn't been.

Work was under control. His staff had risen to the challenge and were doing an exceptional job with the estate coins. The cash he needed to raise was well under way. He'd even found himself with enough idle time that he had been watching for Charlotte to reappear. She'd said she would be back in a couple of weeks, and it was now three. He told himself it was because he didn't want the surprise of her arrival catching him off guard again, and that was true. But part of him wondered if she would return or if she would simply vanish one day as abruptly as she appeared.

He'd geared up for a big change in the business, and now he was simply waiting. Asking for Ginger's number would have been adding a new personal interest, and until he knew what was going to be happening with his professional life, he didn't want to start something significant in his personal life. He relaxed at his reasoning. Starting a relationship and immediately shortchanging it for time wasn't his style.

There was an outdoor concert coming up in a couple of months. If he wanted to get to know Ginger better, that would be a reason to call, and by then life should be more settled. He liked the idea and made himself a mental note to buy the tickets. He could always gift them on if he changed his mind.

He'd left his car in the lot at Bishop

Chicago since Paul and Ann didn't live far and downtown parking was always at a premium. He dug out his keys. It had been a good evening, but it was time to call it a day.

Bryce slowed and slid his keys back into his pocket. Heading home appeared to be on hold. Charlotte was leaning against his car.

"I figured you were around," she offered by way of a greeting.

"I had dinner with friends." And the rationale he'd just settled on for not pursuing Ginger bumped into reality. He was looking at the reason. Ginger was pleasant and comfortable, while Charlotte was dangerously unpredictable. Bishop felt his sigh deep in his chest. It was not a good thing to be attracted to what could be dangerous, but he had to admit that was part of what was going on.

"Group two is here if you would like to help me unpack them."

"You don't want to wait until tomorrow?"

"I'm not in Chicago tomorrow."

He decided if she wanted to work tonight rather than sleep he wasn't going to waste his time trying to change her mind. He'd help her get the job done. "As long as I don't have to actually buy them for another ten days, sure."

She unlocked the back security door, punched in the code, and preceded him inside.

White shipping boxes were lined up along the hallway wall. He counted as he walked toward the showroom. Thirty-two of them. "What's your plan?"

"Open a box, put them in a display case. Rearrange after I see what is here."

"You don't know?"

"It's been a busy few weeks. I gathered what was interesting, wrapped it in bubble wrap, and put it in a box. You're not the only storefront I'm filling, Bishop. I've mostly dealt with the odd collectibles these last couple weeks. I'm the proud owner of about fifty hurricane lamps, Hershey memorabilia, sixty-year-old Coca-Cola bottles, and enough empty old cigar boxes that I lost count at two hundred."

Bryce found a knife and opened the first box. "How did your grandfather die?"

"Old age."

He looked up at her, saw the first flash of true humor on her face.

"He did his own thing, Bryce, and lived life like he wanted to. I doubt he saw a doctor more than twice in his final years. If he was in pain, he never said. The official cause of death was a heart attack while he slept. He was ninety-two."

"Nice way to go."

"He would have thought so. I didn't know him well. I didn't know he was my grandfather until six years ago, and it's hard to bridge a generational age gap even when you're both willing to try. But I liked what I knew of him, even if he never did acknowledge my mom while she was alive."

Her mom had passed way. Bryce tucked away that information along with the little else he knew about her. He tugged at the tape around a ball of bubble wrap. "You have an interesting way of wrapping things." He finally freed the coin inside and slid an 1820s gold piece onto a display tray.

"There's a story to the bubble wrap." She didn't bother to tell it, just slit open another box.

"We're doing well selling the first group of coins."

"Bishop — no offense — but I'm really tired of coins. Got anything else interesting to talk about?"

"Your interesting, or mine?"

She laughed and handed him back the knife. "You open the boxes, I'll deal with the bubble wrap."

She sat down on the floor and pulled an

open box over to her side, picked up the next wrapped ball.

He started a new subject. "Where are your dogs?"

"John's got them."

He glanced at her hand. The way she said the man's name sounded like more than just an old friend, but she wore no rings.

"Always liked Irish setters?"

"They're friendly, normally quiet, and they like to keep you company. I prefer big dogs to small ones."

"I had a collie growing up, but cities are hard on dogs. I don't have one now."

"Cities are hard on people too." She set a Carson City Morgan dollar on top of a box with a casualness that had him reaching for gloves to properly pick it up and set it on the display tray.

She took the time to pull on white cotton gloves. "Okay?"

"Thank you."

She nodded and picked up another bubble-wrapped ball.

"You said you've got other storefronts besides this one."

"Three. The furniture deal is similar to yours. I set up shop next to an expert and let them sell the antiques for a share of the profits. The other two are my employees, selling odds and ends, at the stores and online. One is in St. Paul, the other in Cincinnati."

"How long have you been doing this?"

"He died in May of 2011. I'm just now getting up to volume with what needs to be sold. Probably another year, but that's being optimistic. I don't like estate auctions. I think items go for a fraction of what they should, and I'm not one to leave money on the table."

"You're doing that with me."

"Bishop, these are chum."

"Chum."

"A fishing term. When you put bait in the water to draw in larger fish."

"You're selling me coins below market price because you want me interested?"

"Basically."

"Interested in what?"

"I've got a lot of coins to sell." She held out a shotgun roll. "You might like to buy these."

He took the paper-wrapped roll of Wheat pennies, glanced at the date and mint, and nearly dropped them. He sat down hard on the floor beside her. "Don't do this to me, Charlotte. I'm too young to die of a heart attack."

"He had it in one of the cigar boxes. I

think it's an old forgery rather than the real thing."

He gingerly turned the roll in his hand. It was paper-stamped as Mint issued, and those were 1909-S vdb Wheat pennies showing at the ends of the roll, still a brilliant copper red. "A forgery?"

"He had it in a cigar box on his desk, not in the vault."

He studied the paper. "It's hundred-year-old paper."

"How can you tell?"

"I handle a lot of it. How much do you want for this? Side deal, unrelated to our bigger deal."

She unwrapped another ball. "A hundred twenty-five thousand."

"A single 1909-S vdb grading MS-66 sold last year at auction for seventy-eight thousand."

"I know. I looked it up. But what are the odds that really is a Mint-issue roll? My grandfather certainly didn't treat it as priceless. And most 1909-S vdb's in solid grades will sell around three thousand. It's rare to get a truly exceptional coin even in a fresh roll."

"You could open the roll and know."

"I could, but no. I'll sell the roll unopened. It's the potential of it that makes the price interesting. Is it an old forgery, or the real thing? Is there a spectacular coin among the fifty, or simply several solid-grade coins? Open it and we both know. I'm a gambler by nature. Besides, the market can only absorb so many at that high a grade. If it's real you'll have to hold the coins for several years and sell them slowly to get their true value."

"One twenty-five, against the potential of five hundred . . . or a substantial loss."

"Yes."

Bishop studied the roll of coins. Maybe he was a bit of a gambler by nature too, but experience told him this was the real thing. He shook his head. "You should ask for more, Charlotte."

"One twenty-five is tangible — reasonable enough that if you find the inside of that roll is full of nineteen twenty-eights, I won't feel so awful I'm tempted to give you the money back."

He smiled. "Will you take a check?"

"Sure."

"You've got a deal on this one tonight."

She offered the coin she had unwrapped. "This one is more certain."

It was a Carson City Morgan in excellent condition and easily worth seventeen thousand.

"The unopened pennies are more interesting." He wanted to open the roll and know but forced himself to leave it for later. He tucked the shotgun roll into an empty piece of bubble wrap and laid it by his jacket. He pulled over another box to open.

"It's going to drive you crazy wondering about it."

He almost chuckled but said instead, "I need to learn some patience. I'll get a trash bag for this loose bubble wrap, but don't toss out the sack until we go back through it and have made sure a coin didn't get tossed by mistake."

"Sure." She tore at the tape on another wrapped ball.

"It's like a Christmas party in here, Charlotte."

"I'd rather be opening things I could play with."

It took three hours to get the coins unwrapped and into the display cases. Bishop stood looking over the range of gold and silver she had brought and realized it was a step up in rarity from what was in group one. "I count four hundred eighty-nine coins."

"Sounds about right." Charlotte brought the coffee mugs she had washed out back to the beverage counter. "I'll price them when I get back to town in a few days, give you a figure for what is here. Next Thursday evening work for you?"

"I'll be ready. Where are you heading? One of your other shops?"

"No. Not a safe topic, Bishop. No offense."

"None taken then."

She pulled keys from her pocket, glanced at him.

He nodded.

She turned security for the showroom back on, and they walked through to the back of the shop. "I appreciate the help getting them unpacked. Going to open your roll of coins tonight?"

"Tomorrow morning, first thing. I've waited this long, I can let my expert do the unveiling for me."

"I hope you find your treasure."

He closed the back security door for the shop and saw the security camera move. He lifted a hand to whoever was watching.

"Can I drop you off somewhere, Charlotte? I can give you a lift back to your truck in the morning."

"I'm tired, but roads are reasonably clear this time of night. I'll be fine. We finished that pot of coffee."

"I can feel the caffeine down to my toes," he replied, oddly hesitant to say good-night. "Drive careful."

"I will. See you in a few days, Bishop."

Bryce waited until she backed her truck from its space before unlocking his car and settling into the driver's seat. She was selling off the estate of a man who had lived a life with the habit of holding on to things — some, like the coins, valuable because of what they were, other items like the cigar boxes worth something now simply because they had not been thrown out years ago. Graham Enterprises, Trust, Wisconsin. The third largest transportation, warehouse, and storage company in the country. Bishop wondered how much of that storage space Fred Graham had used for his own personal things.

Charlotte hadn't been difficult to deal with tonight, but he still felt off-kilter with her, like there was a layer of truth beyond the layer he could see. Two of the framed sketches — both penned drawings capturing a group of kids having a friendly snowball fight — were signed *CRM.* He should have asked her about them. He should have asked where she was from, what she did for a living, why Chapel couldn't find much of a history for her. Instead he'd asked nothing important, and learned very little.

John. That name had stuck in his mind. She trusted whoever he was with her dogs. Yet another piece of the puzzle that was Charlotte to wonder at. She was a wealthy woman who drove a beat-up truck, didn't wear jewelry, not even earrings, and drank her coffee black. He wondered how many other holes in the picture he might get filled before she disappeared from his life. She'd be gone as soon as she had sold him the last of the coins. But based on tonight, maybe that wouldn't be as soon as he had thought. This wasn't likely going to end with three groups of coins.

Devon cleared off the worktable. "You really have a Mint-issued roll of 1909-S vdb's? I've never seen one before."

Bryce set it on the table and pulled over a chair. "Maybe."

Devon laid out cloth, pulled on gloves, and picked up the roll. "Now this is a beautiful sight."

Sharon took several photos of the roll, both end coins, the stamp on the paper. "Okay."

Devon looked at Bryce. "You sure, boss?"

"Let's open it and see."

Devon carefully peeled back the paper,

unrolled it, and laid the coins across the cloth in rows of ten coins. "Second row, fourth coin," Sharon said softly, and Devon turned it over.

"If that isn't a sixty-six I don't know what would be."

Devon turned each coin, taking his time, and finally leaned back. "I'm at four thirty-five, conservatively. What did you pay?"

"One twenty-five."

"A Bishop deal. Send flowers."

Bishop laughed. "Or something. These are gorgeous coins." He leaned back in his chair. "A really nice chum."

"Chum?"

"Her description of these coins. Makes me wonder what else she's going to be selling."

"I think you can afford to take us to lunch."

"I'm thinking the company needs a free delivered-lunch policy," Bryce replied, sharing a chuckle but serious about the idea. "You know those five hundred coins we've been having a delightful time selling? There are four hundred eighty-nine more coming right behind them, which, as a group, are a step up in rarity."

"Will you have enough cash?"

"I'll borrow some money against my

home, and I'm working on a few more ideas."

"You . . . no offense, boss, but really?"

"Would you pass up on these coins knowing the profit margin in them?"

Devon looked at the coins and then at his wife. "I'd sell everything up to our first-born."

Sharon snapped his photo. "We're having kids?"

"Bishop makes us wealthy enough with this deal, we might be able to afford to have one or two."

Sharon set aside the camera and grabbed Devon's tie. "There's about to be fraternizing in the office, boss." She planted a kiss on her husband. "I want two."

"Okay."

Bishop picked up the camera and snapped a photo of the two of them. "Sharon, he's going to be a great dad. Just remind him of that when he's complaining about the lack of sleep."

"We should celebrate or something. Your coins, not us having a baby."

Bishop laughed. "That's got merit too. We'll come up with something nice where we can include friends and family once we get all the estate coins dealt with. Devon, let's send all fifty of these to PCGS and get them officially graded and slabbed. I'm thinking two of the better coins we auction ourselves to feel out the market price, and then auction the best coin at the national summer show."

"You don't want to hold it for a few years?"

"I'll still have forty-seven more to sell."

He got up from the table and from the shelf picked up one of the Indian Head pennies they had sent to PCGS last month that was now waiting to go back to the showroom floor. The hard plastic case protecting and displaying the coin, the label officially grading it as an MS-63, the barcode assigned by PCGS giving it a traceability across buyers — it made storage and safeguarding of a rare coin easier on the buyer.

Devon did an expert job on the grading, so the cost of the PCGS service wasn't normally worth the expense, but for this roll of coins it would be useful. He'd keep a record of the barcodes given for the fifty coins in Charlotte's roll and for his own interest track them over the next decade to see where they ended up in various collections. "Have Kim find me when she gets in. I'm going to give her a hunting license to sell the lowest fifteen Wheat pennies once we know the official grades."

■ ■ ■ ■

Bryce met Charlotte at her shop Thursday evening. He didn't take her flowers, but he did take her chocolates. "These are for you," he said as she walked in.

Charlotte took the ribbon-wrapped box with enough caution that Bryce laughed. "And to think I'm the one who's wary. You sold me some very nice coins, Charlotte."

"I'm about to sell you some more if we can agree on a price."

"We'll get to that." He had his checkbook in his pocket and cash in the bank, but found himself oddly not in a hurry to get to that bottom line. "What's with the rental car? Your truck having problems?"

"I just came from the airport. I smell good coffee?"

"I brought the rest of a pot from next door, and the remains of a cheese tray we had set out for customers."

"Thanks." She crossed the room and poured herself a mug. "I've got the inventory list, but it's still handwritten."

He settled in a chair so she would stop prowling and settle somewhere herself. "If I can read your handwriting, it will be fine. What are you thinking?"

"One million eight."

He steepled his fingers.

"What, too high?" She perched on the arm of a chair and ate some of the cheese slices.

"Two million two would help me sleep easier at night. There are five outliers. The 1841 Liberty Proof in particular."

"I saw it. It's a nice coin."

"There are only a handful in existence that grade higher."

"I'll split the difference with you at two, so you can sleep."

"Thanks. You don't look like you've slept much."

"Bad day." She took a deep drink of the coffee. "I was in New York." She dropped into the chair with an abrupt move and leaned her head back against the wall, her gaze still on him. "I've got a twin sister. We had words."

There were two of them. He found that knowledge oddly terrifying. "Sorry to hear it."

"John's sorting it out."

He waited a beat, but she didn't elaborate. "He sounds like a good friend to have."

"He's good at damage control. Not that this one is going to get stuffed back in its bottle, but he'll handle what can be handled."

Bryce realized suddenly she looked raw. Someone had sucker-punched her, and it was barely below the surface. "Family words can be tough."

"Let's change the subject, Bishop."

He racked his memory for topics. "We do okay talking about dogs."

She laughed and nearly choked on the coffee. "They are probably on a sugar high about now. This time I left them with Ellie, and she's a soft touch when they both decide to sit and watch her fix a meal. I'll pick them up tomorrow on the way home."

"Where's home?"

"Don't tell me you haven't checked me out, Bishop. I'm not that naïve."

"Graham Enterprises, Trust, Wisconsin. You've got a place in Silverton."

"Small place, but nice. I'm not there as much as I would like. I've been camped out at Fred's place while I empty out the rooms."

"Your sister hasn't been a help?"

"Not named in the will."

"Ouch."

"My sister married a good man, but a man with a serious flaw, like a rupture in a nice diamond. He's addicted to gambling, and no matter how many times he gets his life straightened out and his marriage back

78

together, he hits a stressor and falls back into his pattern. Fred told me I'd have to handle the problem, that he wouldn't name my sister in the will. I think she had laid down the law with him and insisted she not be named so as to protect her husband from the weight of it.

"She's cut me off from helping them financially — it's her marriage and who am I to say what she needs to do. I can help with her girls' college fund, be lavish with the birthday and Christmas gifts, pay for a nice family vacation in the summer, but that's it. Her husband knows there's some money. He has no idea of the scale of it.

"I made the mistake of visiting while I was in New York on business and walked into another crisis. Made a second mistake of offering to help. Made it only to Tabitha when I knew he wouldn't overhear, but still got slammed back hard. Money doesn't solve the problem, and having more of it only makes matters worse. Like I don't already know that." She turned the coffee mug. "Like I said. Bad day."

An understatement, if he had ever heard one. *Jesus, what words might help here?* Bryce thought the quiet prayer while waiting to see if Charlotte wanted to offer anything else about her day. When she said nothing more, and no words came to mind that might help, he shifted the conversation. "What's John going to do?"

"Get Thomas back into Gamblers Anonymous as a condition of paying off the debt, tell Tabitha after it's done."

"I'm sorry."

"It's grace, and another chance, which is what he needs. Tabitha would like the justice of the consequences to fall this time. But I think I understand how close Thomas is to giving up. He loves his wife and kids, and he's getting to the point he's going to decide leaving is the only thing he can do for them. Not a good outcome. My sister loves him, and he's a good husband and dad when he's not being an idiot trying to reach for the moon for his big win."

"You like him."

"Yeah, I do. He was there for Tabitha when she needed someone in her corner. That matters to me. So I'll let John handle what can be handled, and keep my distance once again."

She sighed and briefly closed her eyes. "Been through too many of these days lately." She leaned forward and set aside the empty mug. "Every sister relationship is different — some are close, others like rivalries. Tabitha and I, we were close — really close.

But some things in life can be destroyed if enough pressure is applied. Life ruptured for us at sixteen, and not by our choice. There are fragments of our relationship we both have worked hard to carefully glue back together, but what shattered isn't ever going to be repaired. It's not like a smashed piece of glass that can be remelted and reformed. We love each other, but we've basically stayed apart for the last ten years. Talk every Sunday afternoon, but otherwise don't get together. My mistake for making the visit. The estate I have to deal with now, it's just another source of pressure."

"It shouldn't have to be a mistake."

"Maybe someday."

"Who's the oldest?"

She half smiled. "I am. By a few minutes."

"I could have guessed that." He got up and retrieved the coffee, filled a mug for himself and refilled hers. "I've got a brother who is an astronaut, and another who is a submariner."

"And you sell coins."

"Dad's always appreciated the laugh in that. Families are strange, no matter how you look at it. One sister who works in the production side of movies — finds the advertisers, the props — another who runs a car-repair shop with her husband. I'm the middle-child businessman."

"You're all close?"

"Yeah. But I know the ugly feeling of having had words with a sister."

"Mine was named *People* magazine's Model of the Decade. My sister."

He smiled at the way she said it. "Pride. Now *that* we do share. She's family, and family you brag on."

"If I had to compete with her in looks, it would have been a rivalry. We got spared being identical twins." She got up to pace. "You need anything before I disappear for a few weeks?"

He wondered how much of the restlessness was nerves. "No, I'm good. Looks like I've got plenty to do."

She put the handwritten inventory list on the display case.

He wrote her the check that made the coins his.

"Thanks."

"How many more coins do you have, Charlotte?"

"That's a conversation for another day. Will you lock up?"

"Sure."

"Thanks for the chocolates." She pulled out her keys, picked up the gift-wrapped box, and disappeared down the back hall.

He heard the security door chime as she left. A twin. There were two of them. He felt immensely grateful he was only dealing with one.

"Has Charlotte told you much about herself?" Paul asked, turning over one of the coins he had bought.

Bryce paced Paul's home office. "She likes Irish setters."

Paul laughed.

"She's told me a bit," Bryce expanded. "Graham Enterprises. Lives in Silverton. Details Chapel had already given me. She's got a twin sister, Tabitha, in New York, and a brother-in-law, Thomas, who gambles. Chapel is now certain she's the sketch artist CRM." Bryce turned to look at his friend. "Would you be interested in confirming that?"

"I'll confirm it because she's not made it a secret," Paul replied. "She'd tell you yes if you asked directly."

"We haven't had the kind of conversation that lends itself to the question." Bryce forced himself to settle in a chair. "She met her grandfather for the first time about six years ago, got to know him a bit before he died. She's selling things from his estate at several storefronts — antique furniture, collectibles, odds and ends. She's sold me about a thousand coins, and has more to sell."

"So another layer of the puzzle." Paul set aside the coin.

"I've got the feeling you know the whole story, Paul."

"I do now that it's become of interest to me."

"What else can you tell me?"

Paul studied him. "She'll tell you what she wants you to know."

"Which is probably why I feel off-kilter every time I'm around her. I'm aware I'm seeing only part of the truth, and it is annoying, not to mention frustrating. She's mentioned John a couple of times. Would you know who that is?"

"John Key. An interesting man. I've met him more than once."

"Can you tell me more without crossing into what is private?"

Paul thought about it. "John was her bodyguard for a few years, back when she was twenty."

"There was trouble?"

"The kind most people don't survive."

"You don't see that when meeting her."

"From what I hear, there's a lot to admire about the lady. I know cops who worked the case. They were surprised to hear she was in Chicago."

"She's what, mid-thirties, forty, now? Would I find an answer if I went back looking for one?"

"Probably. Would suggest you don't. You'll feel like you're standing on hot bricks if you know the story. She doesn't need that."

"It's history for her."

"Don't know how much of it's forgotten history, but I'd say she left it behind a long time ago."

"Then I guess I'll find out when she decides to tell me." Bryce got up to pace again. "She's interesting, Paul, in an oddly *she's-dangerous* kind of way."

"Ginger is easy to be with, Charlotte is not."

Bryce walked over to the bookshelf and thumbed a book. "Yeah."

"Don't start planning a future. I think she's already got one."

"She's not my type —" He turned when Paul laughed. "Seriously, she's just this unfamiliar aberration that has turned up in my life, and I can't easily take my mind off her. And John Key — she doesn't wear his ring but you can hear it in her voice. They're close." Bryce stopped pacing and returned to the chair and the point of the visit. "You said you wanted to talk about the buyer syndicate."

"Talking about Charlotte is more interesting." Paul held up a hand to stop the reply and went with the change of subject. "You're pocketing cash commitments for six months?"

"I'm buying with my own cash first. But if I need more cash than I've got ready at hand, I'm willing to make a buy for a syndicate. I've bought three million six, and she's still got more coins. She hasn't said, but I'm beginning to think she's got the full spectrum. I'd like to be ready for whatever she has.

"If you want in," Bryce continued, "the commitment needs to be liquid and able to be wired. Any U.S. coin pre-1964 — it might be ten-dollar gold pieces or it might be Buffalo nickels and Mercury dimes. If I think it's a good deep value, I'll buy it. If I deploy the cash, it's locked in with the coins as the collateral. I'll sell them however seems best to maximize their value. Cash distributes at the end of each year based on syndicate share."

"The upside being you're buying coins at incredibly good prices."

"That's the plan. The bulk of the profits are locked in by the initial purchase price.

But it's likely to be illiquid for a number of years."

"I'll talk it over with Ann and get you a number. Dad wants in."

"You were showing off your coins?"

"Oh, yeah."

Bryce smiled. "The nice thing about you having a wife who used to be a coin dealer is you can tell me yes to fifty coins for two fifty and not get a lecture about diversifying your investments."

"Ann wanted to buy another hundred and flip them. I told her it would be impolite to go into business against a good friend who was selling you the coins in the first place."

Bryce laughed. "I like her instincts. It confirms my own. I marked the coins up to make a nice profit on my buy, and pros are still circling wanting to seize the opportunity for the value. Hence the reason for the syndicate. If I let what Charlotte is selling make it to the market, I'll miss the biggest profit opportunity I'll probably see in my lifetime."

"She's leaving value on the table."

"She calls these coins *chum.*"

"Charlotte used that word?"

Bryce nodded. "Makes you wonder, doesn't it?"

"How deep have you had Chapel dig into

who her grandfather was?"

"A lot of newspaper articles about Graham Enterprises, but only a few lines about the man who owned it. He wasn't known in his community for his charitable donations to civic causes. I think he kept what he earned during his ninety-two years, had a place to store it, and just let it accumulate."

"He built a nice collection."

"I've floated his name to other dealers, and no one has a record of doing business with him, either buying or selling. Eventually one of these coins will be rare enough a dealer will remember the actual coin, know who bought it, and I'll have the name of at least one of the straw buyers he was using."

"Makes sense. These are raw coins, not slabbed, which suggests he built his collection long before the internet and professional grading became the norm for higher-end coins." Paul thought about it. "Charlotte knows what she's got to sell. The estate inventory for tax purposes would have seen to that. She's had that in her hand for over a year. If these are chum, it makes you wonder — are you going to see a large volume of coins, or are you going to see a few of the whales?"

A whale was one of the rare coins that came to market only once in a generation, which began at six figures and often kept going at auction to seven figures. Bryce pondered Paul's question and then voiced his private worry for the first time. "Paul, I'm afraid I'm going to see both."

FIVE

Paul leaned across Ann for the remote as the ball game entered a rain delay, muted the volume, and set it back on the table. They were trying to share the couch in the den, but it wasn't working particularly well, both of them encircled with loose papers and open files. He stuck his pen and calculator into the insulated cup holder, looked through the snack options on the table, and opened the can of peanuts.

"What do you think of the ice-skating rink?" Ann asked, setting aside the file she was reading.

"I think Boone wants to drive around on a huge ice-resurfacing machine, a Zamboni they're called. The numbers are fine. He can turn around the business easily enough if he converts the front part of the building into a pizza restaurant and staffs it with families of those who have kids coming to practice or have a hockey game. Nothing to say a two-hour shift waiting tables the third Wednesday of every month won't be a popular and easy job to fill. He only needs extra help when the stands are full anyway."

"We should plan a visit to see it once he's got his kid's hockey team wearing Falcon jerseys."

"I'll let you and Vicky set it up. Tell Margaret to put it on my calendar."

"What did Bryce have to say last night?"

Paul hesitated.

"What?"

"What do you think of Bryce Bishop and Charlotte Graham?"

Ann sat up, startled. "No way."

"I'm just reading the tea leaves, but I tell you, she has his head turning."

Ann picked up a pillow and covered her mouth, laughed, lowered the pillow enough to ask, "How much, one to ten?"

"Sevenish. He's intrigued. He doesn't know what to do about that, but it's got him thinking."

"She's a very nice woman, Paul. Top-ten-caliber nice. Wow. The idea of it is enough to set your head spinning. It's not going to happen, not in a thousand Sundays, but the idea of it . . . they *would* make very good friends."

"It's going to be interesting to see that

develop."

"She won't tell him. I mean she will, but not directly. The security is too drummed into her thinking by now. But she'll give him the road map if he wants to pick it up."

"He's the one kind of guy I think about with Charlotte Graham and think . . . yeah. He's another John Key in his own way."

"Oh, you bring interesting news tonight, Paul. I'm sorry I wasn't around to hear it in person."

"Right now it's just her selling Bryce some very nice coins. We'll see if it goes further. I'm wondering if you want to go out to the Dance and Covey Gallery this weekend, see what new pieces she's drawn recently."

"I'd love that. I wish she'd sell *Lava Flows*. When you realize it's just colored pencils, you wonder what God was thinking when he handed her that gift. She's good with simple mediums."

"She's stayed with pen and pencils, and that may be part of the gift. She had the wisdom to learn her tools and stay within them even as the art progressed."

"Bryce and Charlotte . . . Give me a few days for that to settle in."

"If you hear anything on your grapevine, share the news."

"I will."

He nudged the folder she had been reading to shift the subject. "Your story or the case?"

Ann got more comfortable on the couch, crossing into his space. "Baby Connor. Got a minute for an idea?"

"Sure."

"From the summary report, the child was found buried near the walk path in the park. The boy was wearing a clean diaper and clean night sleeper. He was wrapped in the light-blue blanket that had been with him when he was abducted. The blanket was over his face, held closed with a small butterfly pin — the size of something you might wear on a lapel. The pin was not something the Hewitt family had seen before. The autopsy showed the child was a victim of 'shaken baby syndrome,' had died approximately three days after he was taken." Her years on the force couldn't keep out a slight tremor in her voice as she finished. Ann lowered the page. "I'm back to sorting out the clues about who we are looking for. Shake a baby to death suggests a guy not accustomed to being around a crying infant."

"Agreed."

"Someone bought diapers, baby clothes. Someone had a butterfly pin — the kind of thing a woman, or more likely a young girl, would have around. It was something lying around the house that was picked up and used after the baby died. Cops should have been looking for a home with other children in it, but I'm going to guess they didn't realize that early in the investigation."

"A useful observation."

Ann sorted through the photos and offered two. "The clothing is new. So there wasn't a very young child in the house with a sleeper already around that could be used. I would have guessed the clothing would be bought before the crime, but notice the sleeper is the right size for Connor. That's either a lucky guess or someone was comfortable going out clothes shopping after the child was taken. The diaper's correctly put on the child, the sleeper, the butterfly pin — those point to there being a woman somewhere in this picture. A wife with a girl six to twelve years old, maybe."

Paul shook his head. "Other kids in the house old enough to talk, you'd better have a good cover story for the baby. It's one thing to say you're baby-sitting for a few hours, another when the baby is there for days. Kids talk.

"We might be looking for a grandmother," he offered. "She would handle the diaper properly, dress the child correctly, would care to use a pin to secure the blanket to cover the child's face before burial. A granddaughter's butterfly pin could easily be lying around the house. A grandmother, a couple sons, money trouble in the family. 'We'll take an infant, he can't tell the cops about us. We'll get paid fast, and we'll give him back quickly. A week, we've got our problem solved.' I could hear that conversation around a kitchen table."

Ann set aside the pages. "I like working cases with you. A grandmother. I don't think I would have made that leap. Now how are we going to work that idea nineteen years later?"

"First question — did the people we are looking for hold the child, and bury the child, in a place familiar to them? If they did, we need to look in the neighborhood where baby Connor was found and where the Dublin Pub is located — specifically at Meadow Park."

"The media attention on the crime, the speed with which they buried the child after he died suggests they might have made the mistake of burying him near where they had held him. They went out at night, probably with that particular park, that specific destination in mind. It's decent odds."

"Baby Connor's father, Henry Hewitt, spent a lot of time trying to find who killed his son. After Henry died, those files went to his brother. What we don't have in our case files about the neighborhood and who lived there nineteen years ago, we may find in his."

"We should ask if we can see them."

"When we've gone as far as we can ourselves. I don't want to raise the family's hope of solving this without cause."

The ball game came out of rain delay, and Paul put aside the papers and the Falcon family business to watch the game. As heir apparent to the business empire, his job was to keep an eye on the overall picture while others in the family managed the various businesses. He enjoyed the role and would be ready when his dad decided to step aside.

"They never made a ransom demand," Ann mentioned, still studying the file.

He rubbed her ankle. "First timers. They take the child, they have a plan to call with their ransom demand, have a plan for where to collect their ransom money, but the police and media arrive in larger force than they planned for, and they panic. They're trying to rethink how to safely get their ransom money, days pass, the child dies.

They bury him. If they had walked away at that point, the cops would have had no leads, and they would have gotten away with their failure. Instead, they call."

He waited for it.

Ann poked him with her toe. "They called."

Paul smiled. "Wondered when you would get to that obvious fact."

"They had a falling out. No way I buy the caller is some third-hand person they asked to help bury the child. He was one of the original group."

"The person who drew that map and made the pub call is probably not the one who killed the child but the partner who lost the chance for a ransom because the child died," Paul guessed. "He's sitting at the bar having a drink, brooding over the turn of matters, says stuff it, and decides to make the call. A nice falling out between kidnappers. Otherwise, why call? The cops have no leads on the case, the child is dead, has been successfully buried — walk away and no one is ever the wiser. But you're angry you didn't get paid, and it's the other guy's fault. So you'll leave your map and get some cash."

Ann slowly nodded. "I won't give my partner up because he can implicate me in the kidnapping, but I'm sure going to collect something for my efforts and not share the cash with him because he's the one who ruined our payday."

"It plays. We should look for murders in the neighborhood around the pub and, say, the surrounding ten miles. Maybe this dispute escalated even further after the kidnapping goes wrong. You're angry your partner killed the child, he's angry you called the father to get cash. Cops are crawling all over that bar, and they have your partner's voice on tape. You kidnap and kill a child, it's not much of a step to kill the guy who might turn you in." Paul thought about it. "Actually, I'm going to be surprised if that isn't how this resolved itself. The caller didn't call back a second time because he's dead."

Ann was making notes. "He got paid ten thousand for a phone call. When the money ran out, he would be thinking about how he could safely make another phone call. It's very easy money. Nothing says he wouldn't have been able to make a phone call from, say, Montana, and asked to have the money mailed somewhere. He's already proven he knows what happened. He knows the father would have sent it."

"The father would have paid just on the

hope of learning the names of those in-volved." Paul settled back on the couch. "The money is too easy and the risks too low not to make a second call. So, he was dead before he spent the first ten thousand. Even if he was cautious about spending the money, I'm guessing ten thousand would last no more than a year. We look for people murdered within a year of baby Connor, and I bet we find one of our kidnappers."

Ann nudged further into his space. "This is almost too easy, at least in theory."

Paul tossed a few more peanuts into his mouth, his eyes on the game. "The snag is out there. Cops never put a name to the voice of the caller on that tape. I have a feel-ing that's going to be where we smack our heads too."

Six

Charlotte's store now had a radio so Bryce could listen to the sports news or a game while he worked. His staff didn't yet know this store next to theirs held the estate coins. He simply arrived at Bishop Chicago each morning with another box of coins to hand off to Devon. Part of the reason he hadn't told them was the fact it wasn't his property, and Charlotte deserved the extra security that the privacy would bring. Part of it was the fact he simply enjoyed being able to work in a shop where staff weren't feeling like the boss was in the showroom observing their work.

Bryce heard the back security door chime. He wasn't expecting anyone, and closed the display case out of habit, flipping the lock that sealed the glass and activated the internal security beam. "Charlotte?"

"Yes." She came in sandwiched between two dogs.

He crossed the room to take the large box she carried.

"Your sister who does movies, would she be interested in old movie stuff?"

"Probably."

"Then this box is for her. Turns out Fred, or someone in his family, was around when they went from making silent films to talking ones, and liked going to the movies. There are a couple of autographed movie posters in there that might look nice framed and a bunch of movie premiere artwork and photos. If I try to sell it, I'm just going to get hassled for where I got it and do I have more. I'd rather just pass it on."

"She'll appreciate it. Thanks."

"That's my excuse for stopping by. I see empty display cases. You're making progress?"

"The last two weeks have been enjoyable and productive. We're about halfway through grading group two."

"I gather from that pleased expression they are proving to be easy coins to sell."

"We had our first bidding war break out yesterday over an 1850 Charlotte five — Charlotte being the place where it was minted."

"Got that reference. There are coin guides burning into my tired brain at night to go along with the antique and collectibles guides."

"I know buying and selling are always different sides of the ledger, but I promise to be fair if you need an informed opinion on a coin."

"I always figured you would be." Charlotte leaned against the display case, her hand on the glass. Bryce winced, and she smiled when she saw the direction of his gaze. She rubbed at the print with her sleeve and mostly wiped it off. "You are instinctively a shopkeeper — I do admire that."

"Only an uncle for a boss can make you appreciate finger-print-free glass. My first job in this business was cleaning windows and the glass display cases."

"I shall try to remember and be kinder about where I leave prints." She studied him. "You asked how many more coins I have to sell."

"Yes."

"Why don't you come and see." She pulled over a piece of paper and started to draw a map.

He put his hand over hers. "Why don't I just ride along?"

She looked over at him. "Afraid I'll change my mind?"

"Yes."

She laughed and pointed. "I've got the dogs."

"And I'm guessing not your truck if you brought them both with you."

"The dogs get a yearly visit with the vet who owns their mother. I borrowed John's SUV."

"Good. The dogs can share the back seat."

"It's close to a five-hour drive. Route 90 to 39 north, past Stevens Point."

"Figured that." He smiled at her confusion. "You threw the chum. I bit. I'd like to see the coins enough I looked up where you might have them stored."

"How do you feel about being the driver?"

"Much better than being the passenger."

She handed him her keys. "I could use the drive time to get some work done."

"Hey, our first compromise. We should practice and get good at it." At her smile, he pocketed her keys. "Give me ten minutes to tell my staff I'll be gone for the day."

She placed a hand on his arm. "How are you going to get home?"

"I'll rent a car. That's going to be a minor part of this trip, Charlotte. Back in a bit. Remind me to get the sunglasses case out of my car."

Bryce checked the rearview mirror and

moved over to the left lane to pass a construction van. Whatever he had been expecting from this trip, reality had turned out
better. It was a quiet, pleasant, peaceful
drive. He hadn't heard more than twenty
words from Charlotte, and they had been
on the road over three hours now. The dogs
were sound asleep in the back after a short
stop to let them run.

She had been serious about using the time
to get some work done. She'd hauled a
briefcase into the front seat with her and
used the surface as a desk. She had system-
atically worked her way through a deep pile
of paperwork, writing replies in the margins
of pages, signing others, and most of the
time simply checking the corner of the page
before setting it aside.

She'd started writing letters when they
reached the second hour on the road. He
glanced over. The stack of envelopes,
stamped, ready to mail, was growing. She
had her checkbook out now. Food pantries,
animal shelters. She was writing out checks
to nonprofits. From the list she was working
from, a lot of checks.

She caught his look. "Have you ever been
hungry, Bryce?"

"Not like you're implying."

"I have. I'm going to get to every food

pantry in the country before I'm done, and several overseas for good measure."

"It sounds like a nice way to use some of his cash."

"Better than keeping more of it than my sister and I need."

She licked an envelope, sealed it, added it to the stack. "Where would you give some money away if you had extra?"

She asked it as a serious question, and he took his time before he replied. "My church, because I know the budget and the fact the money is spent carefully. Organizations like World Vision and Samaritan's Purse. They can stretch the impact of the dollars given by partnering with companies donating goods. Some of the micro-loan programs that work with individuals directly can use a few hundred dollars to expand a business that will help support a family."

"Give me a list."

He glanced over at her.

"I'd like to give some of his money to churches and religious charities, but I don't know how to evaluate who does a good job and who doesn't. So do me a favor and help me out. Give me a list."

"Okay, I could do that. How much?"

She thought about it, then shook her head. "No. I'm not going to tell you how much.

I'd like you to give me one piece of paper, your best ideas and the amounts you would give. If I can give to everything on your list, I will. Otherwise I'll ask you to prioritize and scale back what is on the page until it fits what I want to give."

"You might be surprised at the list."

"Probably not. I bet you're as cautious with my money as you are with your own."

"I like to give."

"Really?"

"I am cautious about spending money, but giving it away? I figure God gives it back again eventually. Either in more cash or simply in things that don't go wrong in life that would have needed that cash. I give, God makes life work out. That seems like a fair deal to me."

"Ever tested that?"

"Every time I put a gift in the offering plate." He glanced over at her. "Generosity is a good thing. So is grace like you offered to your brother-in-law."

"Don't make it sound like I'm nice, Bishop. If I could buy my sister out of her troubles I would spend the money in a heartbeat. The problem with gambling — money is the problem, not the solution. I'm sure Tabitha's right, and I just made matters worse."

"You did it with good intentions."

"I've done a lot of things with good intentions and most have badly messed up my own life."

The interstate sign for upcoming exits listed Lincoln, Madison, Route 4, Graham Enterprises. It was Bryce's first clue something bigger than he had pictured was up ahead. Semitrucks began to pass him on the right, and one came in behind him, filling his rearview mirror. "Charlotte."

He looked over to make sure she was awake. She'd stopped working after the last stop and closed her eyes. "I want Exit 9?"

She sat up, looked around. "Yes."

He took the exit and in the rearview mirror counted five semis with turn signals blinking, slowing for the same exit.

A fifteen-foot-high fence paralleled the four-lane road. All Bryce could see on the other side of the fence were rolling man-made berms with neatly mowed grass. The posted speed limit was twenty-five mph, and he understood why as the road widened from four lanes to eight. They had arrived at Graham Enterprises' main gate. Semis were slow-rolling through the entrance lanes, and two were on their way out.

"Stay in the left lane going north," Charlotte said, pointing. "We'll use Gate C and bypass the truck traffic."

Bishop nodded and followed the van making the same choice. He kept his speed down, expecting to see Gate C coming up ahead, but there was only more high fence paralleling the road. Charlotte opened her briefcase, pulled out her planner. Bryce began to see the occasional warehouse on his right when the berms were low enough.

Five miles on the road going north and Charlotte was still flipping pages and occasionally marking items off. "This is a big place," he mentioned.

She smiled but didn't look up. "*Huge* is the word you're looking for."

"This is all Graham Enterprises?"

She slipped the pen into the cover of the planner. "My grandfather's family acquired the military base when it closed back in the fifties and doubled the footprint of Graham Enterprises. We don't use all the land for warehouses."

"I'm relieved to hear it," he said dryly.

She laughed and pointed. "Gate C is coming up on your right. Follow the rock drive past the parking lot for the company's sales office, and pull up to the gate. Security will recognize the vehicle."

He made the turn. The security guard

lifted a hand in greeting, then raised the gate to let them enter.

"We'll stay on this road for about two miles and go to the admin building."

The road took them toward what he thought might be the center of Graham Enterprises. Warehouses began to materialize on both sides of the road. Cross lanes were busy with trucks, and he realized there were two kinds of roads — those designed for cars, and wider, deeper roads designed for the heavy weight of loaded trucks.

"These warehouses are leased to companies needing overflow space. The next section is our own storage and distribution. Graham Enterprises buys in bulk and ships in smaller quantities, mostly dry goods, paper products. Beyond that is long-term storage, and the rest is Graham family land. All of Shadow Lake is on our property. There's good fishing this year. Guys have been pulling out nice-size bass, bluegill, and the river feeding the lake has yielded some good-size catfish."

Charlotte reached back and ruffled the fur of the dog closest to her. They both were awake now and moving about, occasionally whining softly, no doubt recognizing home. "That warehouse with the green horizontal stripe — that's the freezer. Costs a small fortune to cool it, and we charge accordingly, but it's nearly always full. It's the newest building on the property.

"We're a countercyclical business. When the economy is good, nearly all our space gets leased out by other companies, and we essentially become security and not much else. When the economy softens, the warehouses empty out, and we go on buying sprees picking up liquidating inventory, equipment in bankruptcy sales, anything tough to store that is selling for pennies on the dollar. We store it away until the economy begins to recover, and we can then sell it back into the market for multiples of what we paid. We're only about half full at the moment, which tells me the economy is beginning to soften, but there hasn't been much merchandise up for sale at prices we like yet."

She pointed ahead on the left. "You'll want the blue building."

Bryce parked in the lot on the south side of the admin building. The nearly empty parking lot had three cars, one of which was Charlotte's truck. He glanced at the time. 3:17 p.m. Right at a five-hour drive with the three stops.

Charlotte let the dogs out, and they stretched, then loped together across the mowed grass and rolled for the pleasure of it. "So much for the good brushing." She tossed their trash from lunch into a barrel near a picnic table.

Bryce stopped beside her to watch the dogs.

"I let them run loose here. They'll be fine. Everyone who works here considers them their dogs. When I want them to come back, I ring that bell by the flagpole. They can hear it over most of this end of the property. Once they've worn off their energy, most of the time they just decide to follow me around."

"It must be dog heaven, all this territory to call their own."

"I like to think so."

Charlotte led the way up the walk.

The door opened before they reached it, and an older lady stepped out, held the door for them. "I thought I saw you on the gate video. We're at 134 and 97," she mentioned to Charlotte.

"Pickups?"

"52."

"Who —"

"Christopher."

"Thanks."

Bemused, Bryce looked back and forth between the two women as they carried on their abbreviated conversation — about what, he had no idea.

"John's hunting for you. Best not be found."

"I didn't drive. He did." Charlotte nodded toward Bryce.

The lady laughed. "Better hope John buys that. The 47 is coming in at top of the hour, and 9 is free. Full crew scheduled plus two extra on page. 82 and 12 have come and gone. You want a late lunch for your company?"

"I'll take him by the diner later."

"Then I'm late for getting my hair done. Call if you need me."

"Will do, H."

Charlotte watched the lady head to the parking lot. "Bishop, that was Henrietta Scoop. She runs Graham Enterprises, even if she keeps the title of secretary. Unpacking that conversation for you, there's a train due in top of the hour, dry goods, so warehouse 9 for the unload. We've had 134 incoming semis add their cargo to storage, and 97 semis' worth ship out. 52 pickups of partial loads, and Christopher managed to draw the short straw as foreman for the night shift. I now know as much as if I'd been here to see the paper and take the calls."

"Busy day?"

"Average to slow. Three trains today. The only thing that didn't happen was much buying, as Fred liked to do most of that himself, and I inherited the job."

It suddenly clicked. "The bubble-wrap story."

She smiled. "I bought six million square feet of it. Small bubble, twelve-inch, perforated, one hundred fifty-foot rolls. You see a promo sale for bubble wrap at a store, odds are good we're supplying it. I'll take you by warehouses 4 and 5 and show you. It's kind of cool."

"Why six? Why not just one?"

"It was way too good a deal to pass up. My grandfather would have laughed. The guys did. Earned my stripes with my first buy."

"You really like this job," he said, surprised.

"Love it. Warehouses fill and unload in a choreography of trucks, trains, and forklifts. I'm a good forklift driver — I've got a soft touch for the tight moves, as my trainer likes to say. And there's only one big rule for running this place — don't forget where you put something."

She pointed down the hall and led the way. She turned on her phone as they walked, and he realized she'd had it shut off for their drive. "Thirty-eight messages. Not quite a new record."

They entered what looked like a massive break room, a combination of kitchen and gathering room, with round tables, couches, comfortable chairs. She waved him toward the comfortable seating. "I'll get us cold drinks. What appeals? We stock everything."

"Root beer."

She skipped through the phone messages as she crossed to one of the four refrigerators and pulled out sodas, paused to listen to one message. She carried back two root beers. "Not much marked urgent." She turned her phone off again, dropped into a comfortable chair and opened her soda, tipped it toward him, smiled. "Welcome to Graham Enterprises. It doesn't look like much — warehouses, lots of gravel roads, miles of grass to mow, but it's an incredibly profitable company. It's hard to comprehend the volume that flows through here until you've seen it over a twenty-four-hour cycle. Busy days, we're unloading six trains with eighty cars stacked behind the engines. It takes high volumes, because margins in this business are measured in tenths of a percent."

Bryce wondered now why he had assumed she'd find it hard to step into her grandfather's shoes and run the business. She was comfortable here and spoke of it with the understanding of an owner. "I like your business, Charlotte. I like the fact you like it."

"Thanks." She set aside her soda with a smile. "You've politely listened to the Graham Enterprises spiel, but that wasn't why you made the drive. You came to see coins."

"I'm guessing because we came here and not to your grandfather's home, the coins are here."

"His house is up by Shadow Lake, and we'll swing by there later as I'm packing group three to ship and can give you a preview. But, yes, the coins I want to show you are here."

She tugged a lemon drop from her pocket and unwrapped it. "Bishop Chicago has an inventory floor for coins at about five hundred dollars on up, and your client list is the top five percent of coin collectors. You routinely handle multi-thousand-dollar coins. I want you to consider expanding down in price to the twenty- to three-hundred-dollar coins where most mom and pop coin shops do the bulk of their business, and where most coin collectors are looking to buy. I've got some nice coins to sell in that price range."

"Got an example?"

"A thousand Standing Liberty quarters in Extremely Fine to About Uncirculated."

"I haven't seen that grade in quantity outside a major dealer."

"The safe-deposit box I closed last week had twenty-five rolls. Besides the coins he had stored here, Fred had safe-deposit boxes at various banks across the country. I've been closing them as I can get to them." She considered Bryce. "I'll take the coins to Wyatt's in Ohio if you don't want to pursue it."

"I get a choice this time?"

"This one will be a bit of work. I've got a lot of coins to . . ." She paused as her two dogs entered the room. A tall, lanky man walked in behind them.

"Charlotte."

"John."

He crossed to one of the refrigerators, opened the freezer, removed an ice pack, opened a drawer and pulled out a first-aid box. He took the seat facing her. "Let me see that ankle."

She pushed off her left tennis shoe and put her foot on his knee. Bryce winced when he saw the large, dark bruise yellowing with time.

John shook out the Ace bandage to remove

the twists, then used it to wrap her ankle and hold the ice pack in place. "Stay off it for the next half hour."

"Can I have my hat back?"

"Are you going to listen next time Brad tells you to be careful?"

She crossed her heart.

He pulled the ball cap from his back pocket and put it on her head. It read *Boss*.

"I don't want to see you here at midnight. You call it a day by seven."

"I'll knock off early." She nodded to make the introductions. "John, Bryce Bishop. He came to talk coins."

Bryce found himself being summed up in a quick, penetrating glance.

John looked back at Charlotte. "A conversation not work-related? Good. Have a long conversation. Stay out of trouble." John got to his feet and tweaked the bill of her hat. "And quit climbing on chairs."

"Busted."

"The coins are now on your worktable. I hauled over more boxes." He pointed to Bryce. "Let him do the carrying."

"It's a shipping and transport company. I can snag a couple of guys to carry boxes."

"Which is what you said last time, and who was hauling them at ten p.m.?"

"I'll do better this time."

"Ankle's never going to heal unless you do."

"I hear you." Charlotte glanced at Bryce. "I'm going to take him over to see vault five."

John pulled a pen out of his pocket, picked up her hand, and wrote a number in her palm. "You miss-enter it twice, call me before you do it a third time. They rewired it in alongside the severe weather sirens, so this whole place knows a security breach happened and locks down."

"Too many false alarms and it's going to lose its effectiveness."

"Folks are hoping for false alarms. You're now paying every employee on the grounds a thousand bucks if they can lock this place down within five minutes of the sirens sounding."

"A thousand —"

"Cash gets people motivated."

"Gets me motivated to type in the numbers properly."

"It's tied into the security for the level-three vaults, unauthorized movement of equipment, and a few other things I've chosen to care about."

"How often are you going to 'accidentally' trip it?"

"Once a month. Different shifts."

"Give everyone a chance to earn some extra cash."

"Basically." John looked at the time. "The 73 is coming in at five thirty via the east gate. I could use you on the lift."

"I'll be there."

"Who drove?"

She pointed at Bryce.

"Better." John headed out, and the two dogs followed him.

She watched him leave. "That's John Key. He's head of security for Graham Enterprises." She came back from a reflective moment and looked over at him. Smiled. "So, lower-priced coins. Are you interested or do you want to pass?"

"Depends on the volume and the price," Bryce replied, still sorting out the dynamics he'd just seen play out. Those two were close in a way he'd rarely seen before, but he wasn't sure it was what he had assumed. He forced his attention back to the topic of coins. "The reason we don't handle the lower-end coins through Bishop Chicago is the high overhead costs of our location. Secure vault space is expensive, and the more volume you do, the more space you need for the pack and ship. So far I've concluded we're better off focusing on the high-end coins and limiting how much we try to press our facilities to handle."

"Then let's talk price. I'll show you what I've got available, and we'll see if you want to stay with that limit or get creative and go another direction."

"What do you propose?"

She tugged five folded sheets of paper from her briefcase and offered them.

He scanned the pages. Coin, year, grade, price. She was pricing the spectrum of coins, from Bust half-dollars to Buffalo nickels, in grades from Fine to Brilliant Uncirculated. "You're well below wholesale pricing on most of these."

"I'll make a good profit. And I'm hoping you can buy in volume."

"I've got no problem with your prices, Charlotte. I feel like a shark snacking on a naïve seller, but I'll be able to sleep at night — barely."

She smiled. "Let me get the keys, we'll head over to vault five, and you can select what you'd like to buy."

She unwrapped the ice pack and slid her tennis shoe back on.

"You need that ankle elevated and iced for a bit longer."

"I'll wrap it again this evening. It's not barking at me like it was a week ago." She put the ice pack back in the freezer, stopped briefly in an office to leave her briefcase, and to open a desk drawer and select keys.

She pointed to her own truck in the parking lot. She drove them past warehouses, keeping the speed down.

"How did you pay the estate tax on Graham Enterprises without having to sell the business or some of the property?" Bryce turned to see into one of the open warehouses. "None of my business, but I'm curious just the same."

"I had to sell a chunk to cover the tax bill. I sold forty-five percent of this place to a group of employees Fred had chosen — an insurance trust out of New York loaned them the money for the deal. After I've finish liquidating what Fred has in personal property stored around here, I'll likely sell them the rest. I'll keep part of the family land and Shadow Lake, sell the rest of the land to the trust for future business expansion. As much as I enjoy this job, Graham Enterprises is not my future."

"Art is?"

She glanced over at him. "I wondered if you knew." She shrugged. "I don't know yet. But I view this time as an interesting interlude — probably a decade of my life — from meeting my grandfather to wrapping up his affairs for him as he wanted them done. I'll move on once it's finished."

She changed the radio station. "To your original question, the estate tax matters are still ongoing. The lawyers reached a deal with the IRS. They would file an estate return, which valued the Graham Enterprise business, would make a good faith estimate for 'other assets yet to be located and appraised,' pay the estate tax, then have three years to find all the property and file an amended final estate return.

"I'm dealing with the tangible things Fred left behind while the lawyers sort out the more difficult ownership matters. It appears Fred and his father took ownership stakes in businesses in place of payments during the Great Depression and when the economy hit severe recessions since then. How do you value two shares of something called HM Construction when the paper-work is sixty years old? It's keeping the lawyers busy.

"This place is giving me the same kind of odd surprises. Last week we opened a stor-age barn we thought held two old farm trac-tors and discovered a plane — a 1970s crop duster — in apparent working condition. It's that kind of discovery that just baffles me about what to do with it. Oh — and eighteen canoes painted lime green. Let's not forget the canoes. I'm actually relieved when I find something like old coins, Mason canning jars, or thirty cases of imported caviar that went bad ten years ago. At least I have a clue what to do with it."

A fenced area with posted warning signs came into view ahead of them. Charlotte slowed and stopped at the security gate, entered a code to pass them through. Bryce saw more security cameras, and twice they passed men walking with dogs. "We pay a bit more attention to who comes into this part of the property, not only because the secure vaults are here, but because this part of the former military base was used as a firing range. We still occasionally find after heavy rains an unexploded shell we have to deal with."

She pulled to a stop in front of a single-story building that looked like it was built from concrete cinder blocks. "This is the doorway into the berm you see stretching for the next half mile. Most of the berms within this property are actually storage bunkers. The earth above keeps the temperatures steady."

She used keys to open two locks, opened the steel door, and turned on lights. They stepped into a small entry room. She looked at the code John had written on her palm, entered it on the security pad. The steel rods barring the next door retracted. She unlocked and opened the inside door. "After you."

Bryce stepped through. A hall went left and right. The air was still and dry. The lights overhead were bulbs surrounded by a wire mesh mounted every few feet, and they made the place almost too bright.

Charlotte headed left. They passed a series of gray metal doors, big rivets lining the metal frames. An ammunition bunker was the closest parallel Bryce could come up with, the doors able to absorb and contain a blast. Nothing was numbered or marked; it was just a line of identical gray metal doors.

"Here's vault five."

It was the ninth door they had passed.

She used keys to open the two locks on the door and switched on the lights.

The room was a decent size, probably twelve by sixteen, crowded with shelves and boxes. A table in the middle of the room, a row of cabinets with map drawers two inches high and twenty-four inches long on the east wall, two-by-two-by-eight coin boxes neatly stacked, six boxes high on the shelves.

She cleared the table of coin magazines.

"What would you like to see first?"

"The Bust half-dollars."

She scanned the cabinets, reached for a drawer, pulled it out and brought it to the table. "Here is a sample of them."

He picked up white cotton gloves from the stack on the shelf, pulled out a chair at the table. There were more than fifty coins in the drawer, and he selected three at random. He found an 1814 Very Fine, an 1807 Fine, an 1828 Extremely Fine. "Nice, Charlotte."

"I think you'll find a lot of pleasant surprises in this room."

She returned the drawer to the cabinet. "I know it can feel like being stuck in a tomb in here, but if you can handle it, I'll let you have some time to simply open drawers and look through what's here."

"It does feel a bit like a metal coffin."

She turned on the radio. "Phone service isn't great inside a berm, but the radio gets decent reception. And just for info's sake — emergencies within a berm are handled in a pretty basic way. Toggle the lights five times on and off — that pattern flips a circuit and makes the security board light up. They'll come get you."

"And if they don't see the distress signal?"

"When we entered the gate for this section I put in my code and our destination. If we don't exit that gate by end of shift, someone will come to physically check on us."

She sorted through her keys. "Let me show you the rest of vault five. This is just the entry room. It's actually six rooms."

She stepped out into the hall and went to the next door, opened it, turned on lights, moved down to the next door, and the next, doing the same. He looked into the rooms. Across the various rooms there were thousands of shotgun rolls of coins stacked neatly on metal shelves and coin tubes arranged in groups. He stepped into the third room and picked up a coin tube of Benjamin Franklin half-dollars, slid them out into his gloved hand. Full Bell Lines. He felt the sigh deep in his chest.

He heard Charlotte return and glanced over at her. "What did you think when you first opened this vault and saw what was here?"

She perched on the small table inside the door. "Fred showed me this vault the year before he died. His dad had passed it down to him. He said he didn't know much about coins, but that I could probably learn."

She shook her head at the memory. "I drove into town and found a bookstore that had a coin-price guide and tried to figure out what I was looking at. You get numb to it after a while. They're coins, Bryce. I've got a lot of things in my life I will enjoy more. But I understand their value. Fred slept better at night knowing he wasn't dependent on a bank not to fail."

"Who knows this place exists?"

"John. Myself. My grandfather never spoke of old coins to anyone I've met among his friends. He probably told his family, but he outlived the last of his family by ten years. The old record books for this section simply say *Graham* on the storage ownership, and the rest of this berm's units are empty. His security was silence. Even the coins at the house — you'll see when we stop by there — if you didn't know where to find them, there's no indication they are there."

She went quiet for a moment, then half smiled at a memory. "Employees know the Graham family kept a lot of stuff going back decades in these old bunkers, but when we clean them out, most are filled with trunks of old clothes, old machinery parts, farm tools, boxes of books. Lots of old books. My grandfather didn't live or act wealthy. He watched every penny of his business. It would surprise his friends to think he left a million dollars outside of the business, let alone the actual truth of what is here."

"He didn't want the distance wealth would create between himself and his friends," Bryce offered.

"Probably part of his thinking. He simply enjoyed running this place, had more cash available if he needed it, and never did." She slid off the table and went to the two-drawer file cabinet, opened the top drawer. "Feel free to mark this up." She handed him a stapled ten-page inventory list. "I pulled together all the inventory sheets I could find for this vault into one list. The handwritten notations are my counts. If it lists fifteen rolls, I've noted how many I counted. The grades have only been spot-checked, but the old inventory sheets appear roughly accurate."

He scanned the pages. "Thanks. It's a good place to start."

"I found it helpful." She glanced at her watch. "Let me give you some time just to look around. I'll come back at, say, six thirty? John wants me to help on a lift. I'll be on the crane for about forty minutes, with my trainer standing at my shoulder. It's taken six weeks of asking for him to give me an assignment, so I'll probably be lifting a pile of steel plate or something else non-fragile, but still, it's the big crane."

Bryce smiled. "Six thirty will be fine."

"I promise I'll return." She smiled as she said it, then disappeared out the door.

Bryce looked around the room at the rolls of coins, the list in his hand, softly laughed, then prayed, *Jesus, I was thinking something interesting would be coming, and this certainly qualifies. This woman just keeps surprising me. What's the wise thing to do here?* He headed to the last room, planning to work his way back to the first after a quick visual inspection.

Bryce heard Charlotte coming back and closed up the box he was inspecting, returned it to the shelf. He pulled off the gloves and took a seat at the table, found his pen and made a note on what he had just found.

She came through the door in a bit of a rush. "Returning, as promised. I'm only five minutes late."

He smiled. "How did the lift go?"

"Eight oversized drainage tiles. I set them down like a snowflake on a butterfly wing. Got a 'good job' from Brad, which is impossible to get." She grinned. "More than you probably wanted to know. So, coins. What do you think?"

"I'll take it all."

She pulled out the chair across from him, dropped into it, and just looked at him. "I underestimated you, Bishop. My apologies for that. I'll get an accurate inventory done for you this month."

"I'll take your preliminary count for what is here, and we'll square up the price if it is off more than five percent." He offered the inventory pages to her along with her price list. "Check my math. It's five million six."

She scanned the numbers, reached for the calculator and ran his tallies again. She nodded. "We've got a deal."

"I'll have the bank wire the money in the morning. You've got some very nice coins here, Charlotte."

She smiled. "Now you do. I'll lease you the space for a dollar a year. You can have the keys and set a new security code for this berm as we leave. I'll post a security bond for the five million six and put you on our insurance as a client. Your coins will be safe here until you can make arrangements to move them."

"You've thought of everything. Appreciate that."

"Group three is at the Shadow Lake house. It's going to seem anticlimactic after this vault, but do you have time to come

130

over and see a portion of what's there? I know it's getting late to do a five-hour drive tonight, and you still need to arrange a car."

"Phone reception is actually decent in here. There's a rental car for me now dropped off at the sales office parking lot, I've got a room at the Hyatt in Madison, and your Henrietta stopped at the mall for me after her hair appointment and picked up the basics of a wardrobe so I could stay a couple days."

"I would've liked to have overheard that conversation," Charlotte said. "I'll stop doubting your resourcefulness."

"Show me the group three coins, Charlotte. I'm curious to know what I'm going to be buying next."

"What are you going to do with these coins? Expand Bishop Chicago?"

"I don't know yet. I've got a friend who built a very good business in the fifty- to five-hundred-dollar coins, then sold it when she decided to become a cop. I'm going to go pick her brain for ideas on what to do. But for the next day or two, I'm simply going to open every drawer, every box, and take a photo of it. From those I can formulate a game plan for how I want to sell the coins."

She looked around the room. "I'm so glad

this is now your problem."

He smiled. She'd given him a very good deal to clear out her problem and make it his. But having seen the scope of Graham Enterprises, he was beginning to understand why she'd set him up to have this conversation. She had bigger concerns to deal with. She had a lot of coins to sell, and she wanted one buyer. He'd been in a position to say yes. Their business was about done. He was beginning to almost regret that.

He followed her through the berm, reset the code, and accepted the keys.

SEVEN

Bryce liked her grandfather's home on sight. The ranch-style house was built on a hillside near Shadow Lake, structured as three wings under a common roofline. She parked at the back of the house where a large porch and patio overlooked the lake.

Four German shepherds were on the porch. "Fred's dogs, and they still miss him. Hang back a moment while I say hello and get them settled." Charlotte walked to the porch, and the oldest of the dogs brought her a knotted rope. She knelt and played tug-of-war for a moment, then ruffled his ears and kissed him. She tossed tennis balls for the other dogs to chase. "Come on up. They're friendly, just rightfully cautious of strangers."

Bryce joined her on the porch and hunkered down to greet the older one.

"The dogs are content now living with the foreman, but I've asked if he would bring them out here when it's convenient for him so they can enjoy the lake and what used to be their home. He's fishing at the moment — that's his van and boat trailer down by the dock. He'll take them home with him when he's done."

Charlotte unlocked the back door to the house and turned off the security. "I'm in the middle of packing up the house. It's been hit or miss on my priority list depending on what else we've found to deal with, so some rooms have been emptied out, others I haven't touched yet. I'm currently working in what was previously the library."

Bryce followed her into a large room, where built-in bookshelves on two of the walls were now nearly empty. He saw the coins John had mentioned neatly lined up on a table in the center of the room. Several dozen more coins were stacked on the bottom shelf of one of the bookcases.

"What's here is the start of group three. I've packed the first hundred-plus coins" — she gestured to the boxes on the far wall — "but you're welcome to open the boxes and go through them. The ones here still to be wrapped will get me up to about two fifty, the rest I'm still gathering out of various safes. Fred believed in numerous safes, well hidden, instead of one general vault."

She glanced at the time. "I don't know about you, but I'm ready for some dinner. I'll go over to the diner and get something to bring back for us. Do you mind if I leave you here for about an hour? The trip is twenty minutes; the conversations that will inevitably happen with people are the other forty."

"I'll be fine here, Charlotte."

"There is surprisingly good internet access in this house. Feel free to check your email, call your office — whatever you need, the computer is on. The kitchen is fair game too, although I think I packed the glasses last week by mistake. There should be sodas in the refrigerator, and a stack of paper cups beside the paper towels. Help yourself to whatever you can find." She left with a smile, and after she left, the sounds of an empty house settled around him.

Bryce walked over to the table to look at the coins. Several caught his attention, but he stopped when he saw the middle set. The first of the Flowing Hair half-dollars he had seen in the collection. She had two of them. Only 294,000 ever minted in the year 1795, and she had two. He just stood and looked and let that realization settle inside. He'd never seen an estate like this one. He'd have a buyer at eighteen thousand for one of them, and probably get a bidding war for the other at twenty-six thousand.

He scanned the other coins on the table, ran the math. Three million, maybe three million two, if the rest of the coins in group three were like these.

He wished Charlotte had simply called him and let him do this work for her. She should have a staff of people helping her, and yet she was ordering her days to do the work herself. Part of it he was beginning to understand. She thought of the coins in the same way she thought of the hurricane lamps and the Mason jars — as responsibilities to sell for her grandfather. Because somewhere under the weight of this was the realization she was now very wealthy, and this wasn't a woman accustomed to being wealthy. How did you help someone accept wealth? Then again, he wasn't sure he wanted her to learn.

Bryce picked up the roll of tape and put together another box. He could at least help her pack the coins.

"Anybody home?"

"Back here, John."

The head of security for Graham Enterprises walked through the door of the library with Charlotte's two dogs trailing behind him.

"That the chair she was climbing on?" Bryce asked, nodding toward a dining room chair that was out of place in the room. Footprints with crushed white gravel road dust were still obvious on the chair seat.

"Yes. The safe in this room is built into the wall above the top shelf of the bookcase. She's too short to be trying to clean it out. Should have been smart enough not to try."

"There were some very nice coins in that safe."

"I thought so too." John picked up another roll of tape and taped together a box. He started boxing more of the books. "Know anyone who could figure out the value of old watches?"

"I can ask around."

"Shoebox over on the desk is the collection she's found so far."

Bryce wondered if that really was the topic on John's mind tonight. "I'm buying the coins in vault five."

John nodded. "Did the background check on you, concluded you were the right guy to handle them for her. You'll make some money on them. She'll be relieved to have them gone."

"A phone call would have been an easier introduction."

John grinned. "Now where would the fun

for her be in that? She's got her reasons for the store."

"I gather she's getting tired of selling stuff."

"We both are. Found five hundred tennis rackets this afternoon where there should have been crates of paving tiles. There's not a tennis court on this property — not that I've found yet anyway. I think some in the family had a bit of dementia in their later years. Fred was a sharp enough man at ninety-two that he wasn't the one. But he probably knew and decided to leave it to Charlotte to sort out all the oddities after he was gone. Not sure I wouldn't have pushed back a bit harder if I knew what he was leaving her to do."

"She could hire someone to handle this for her."

"Not her style." John taped the box of books closed, wrote on the end what was inside, and picked up another box.

"What kind of trouble did she have when she was twenty?"

John shot him a look.

"Paul Falcon told me you were her bodyguard for a couple years."

"Her business to tell, not mine."

"It's over?"

"Cops killed them before I got hired for

the job. Best I could do was punch a few reporters who invaded her privacy."

Bryce smiled at the way John said it. "Okay." Bryce took another look at the man Charlotte trusted. "Between the time being her bodyguard and taking over security for Graham Enterprises, what did you do?"

"Worked for the musician Brandon Yates for a few years. The singer Evelyn Hayes."

"That's where I've seen you before. The guy who tackled the guy —"

John smiled. "Got more famous than Charlotte for a few days. I can understand better why she dislikes the press as she does." He finished packing the books and hauled the boxes out of the room. He came back and sorted around the packing materials until he found a plastic sack. "Thought I would finish chasing down the golf balls tonight. Found some in the garage, the mud room, kitchen drawers. Since I haven't found any golf clubs, I think someone liked to sit on that back patio and throw them into the lake. You golf?"

"No."

"I'll find someone who does. One thing Charlotte is determined not to do is to throw anything away."

John left the room and the dogs got up to follow him out.

Bryce picked up the shoebox of old watches on the desk. Most were simply old, but two were gold, and one was diamond-rimmed. Fred Graham was the kind of guy he wished he had met at least once, so he could square what he was seeing now with the man he had been in life.

Bryce pointed to the fish in the sampler platter Charlotte had brought for him. "This is good." He reached for a napkin. They had settled at the kitchen table. "I figure most of tomorrow to get the photos taken, and then I'll head to Chicago and get a plan put together for how to sell the coins. I'll likely be back next week to begin hauling coins out."

She picked up her cheeseburger. "If you want boxes for shipping them, just let me know. Boxes and bubble wrap I can give you in abundance."

"I'll take you up on that. And that's it for coins tonight," Bryce offered. "Question. Why do your dogs seem to prefer John?"

Charlotte licked a smear of mustard off her thumb. "He's presently walking around with bacon bits in his pocket, as if I don't know he's feeding them. He's trying to get them to learn to bark on command, shake hands, and catch a Frisbee. Princess is cooperating; Duchess is just looking to mooch food. They are as much his dogs as mine. I'd say we share them. John's home is a little farther to the east around Shadow Lake. He's the person who gets called when something goes wrong anywhere at Graham Enterprises, so it's easier for him to live nearby. My place in Silverton is about twenty minutes north of here, though I've been bunking here while I get Fred's place squared away."

"You two have been friends a long time."

She slipped a finger around a chain she wore, tugged out dog tags and two worn keepsake medals. "He's a genuinely nice guy. Military — can be a very dangerous guy if he doesn't like a situation. I'd say I'm somewhere between a girlfriend and a kid sister, which means I am free to annoy him and tease, but I'm kind enough to know where his lines are, and I don't cross them if I can help it. He's done me a few big favors, and I've done him a couple in return over the years. John's the guy I called when Fred Graham showed up on my doorstep saying he was my grandfather. John would like to marry my best friend Ellie Dance, and I'd love to see that happen one day, but she's still thinking about it."

They ate for a while as Bryce absorbed

that answer. "Reading between the lines, John would like you to slow down a bit. This job of dealing with the estate doesn't have to be finished in the next few months."

"I'm not the kind who stops easily until a task is done. Then I will full stop for a long while." She ate a fry, considered him. "Do you like being a businessman? Managing employees? Deciding the business direction? Dealing with the finances and the profit and loss?"

"A company that isn't showing a profit is a charity."

She smiled.

"Sure. I like business," he answered. "I like putting all the pieces together to get to a sale or to get a product finished. And I like people as a rule. Business has lots of them. Customers, suppliers, employees. There's a sense of having accomplished something at the end of the day when you can open the doors of the store in the morning, buy and sell goods, close up at night, and most days have made a profit after your costs. It says you were a good manager. I like being good at something that matters to people — my employees like a steady paycheck and some job security."

"I wouldn't have opened my store had you said no."

He wasn't quite sure he believed her. "You went for the jugular, if you remember."

"I did. A necessity, but I'm not sure you'd appreciate why just yet." She pushed back her plate. "With art it was a private studio and one person, me, although most of my work was done outdoors — the high school track meet, the park, a restaurant opening. I like to sketch life happening. It was just me, and sometimes I would have John in that equation to consider, but life was mine. Now I've got more employees than I care to think about, and business on a big scale. They know what they are doing, and my job right now is to not get in their way and mess things up, but I've decided I don't like business. The responsibility of it."

"That's why you are pushing to get the estate sorted out and dealt with as soon as practical. You don't want to be responsible for a lot of other people's lives."

She nodded. "Pretty much. I'll sell the rest of Graham Enterprises to its employees once Fred's personal holdings have been dealt with." She pushed back from the table. "I need dessert. Want a pudding cup?"

"I'll pass."

She came back with a glass of milk and a tapioca cup. "I hope you can afford group three of the coins. I know I'm really pushing matters, given the size of vault five."

She didn't look that worried. He smiled. "I'll have no problem buying your coins, Charlotte. When you get the group put together, we'll find a price we agree on."

"If Fred hadn't walked around this house and told me where to look, I would have never found everything he had tucked away. The rest I want to gather together are in the den, I think, and a couple of the bedrooms."

"Fred didn't trust banks?"

"Not much." She leaned back in her chair. "I was going to work on the kitchen some more tonight, but my body is saying the day is done. I'll drop you by your rental car. Do you know how to get to the hotel from here? I can probably find you a map."

"I'm good." He offered the page he had handwritten while she was out getting dinner. "This is for you in case I don't see you tomorrow. The list you asked for, places to contribute, suggested amounts."

"Oh, excellent!" She read the list as she ate the last of the tapioca. "This is good. I can do the whole page."

"That's nice of you, Charlotte. Really nice."

She waved her spoon at him with a bit of a frown, looking uncomfortable. "If I give you the checks, could you deliver them or mail them, as the case may be?"

"Sure."

"I'll get my checkbook."

Bryce watched her leave. By her own words she didn't believe in God like he did, yet he'd just given her a list of churches and organizations that would preach the good news about Jesus and do acts of charity in His name, and she had said yes to gifts totaling two hundred twenty-five thousand dollars.

He knew she could afford the gifts, his total with her for the coins was now nine million two after vault five, but what he found remarkable was her willingness to give it, and to let him direct where.

Charlotte came back with her checkbook. She wrote out checks for his list, stacked them neatly, and handed them to him.

"Your money is going to help a lot of people, Charlotte."

"I think it will. You're careful with money, so it's going to be a good list. I do have two conditions, Bryce."

"What are they?"

"You can't tell anyone the money is from me. The checks are written from the Cleo Simm Trust, and unless you knew that signature said Charlotte Graham the best you would guess is Charles Something. I've actually paid people a hundred bucks to see if they could figure out the name and only one has come close to finding my name in my signature."

He laughed at that admission.

She smiled and added, "Cleo was a friend of mine. We formed the trust together years ago to invest in art we both liked. I left the trust open after she passed away as the anonymity has been useful to me. I've given some of my art proceeds away through Cleo Simm, and now some of the Graham estate. I'm not asking you to bend the line of the truth, just keep my personal involvement as the source of the funds confidential."

"Okay, I can do that. The second condition?"

"I need another page."

"Another — sure. I can come up with some more ideas."

"Thanks." She pushed back her chair. "Let me get a jacket, and I'll drive you over to Gate C and your rental car."

Bryce drove to the hotel, thinking back through what had been a very interesting day. The coins were a solid buy. He would figure out how to sell them efficiently. The challenge of that had his attention.

Seeing Charlotte on her own turf had

been fascinating. She was a woman comfortable running the business, comfortable dealing with the size of her grandfather's estate. She truly enjoyed parts of the job if her reaction to being able to train on the big crane was a snapshot — and yet she planned to sell the business and return to her art. It told him she loved her art with a passion that was more than just a first career. It was how she thought of herself — I am an artist — and that felt like a significant piece toward understanding her.

It was the charitable-giving list and her reaction to it that had him puzzled. There had been obvious relief when he handed her that piece of paper and a list of ideas. Her request for a second page had been genuine. She was a wealthy woman, yet he got the impression she didn't know what to do with it. She made million-dollar deals related to the coins and was at ease making those decisions. She was comfortable dealing with money, but not so much with having it. He felt the tug of an important fact buried in that observation. He needed to determine why that was if he was going to figure her out. And figuring her out was beginning to matter more with each day.

EIGHT

Bryce stepped off the elevator into the entryway of Paul and Ann Falcon's home in downtown Chicago. The fourth floor of the building had been in Paul's family for many decades, and it made for a spacious home. A sculpture of a horse and cowboy straight from the Old West dominated the entry space. "Ann, thanks for allowing me to drop by like this on short notice," he said as Ann met him.

"It's always a pleasure, Bryce. Paul just got home, but he's on the phone — there's been developments in a case, so he may be a few minutes yet."

"It's your advice I need."

"Oh?" She looked at the folder in his hand. "What do you have?"

He handed her prints of the photos he had taken of vault five and a copy of the inventory list. Surprise, then pleasure, crossed her face as she realized what she held.

"Come on back." She moved into the dining room and spread the photos across the table. "This estate just keeps getting more interesting. What did you spend?"

"Five million six."

Her gaze shot to him, and then she laughed. "You're killing me here, Bryce. I told Paul I was staying out of the business, but this is like catnip." She scanned the inventory list. "The market is good right now. No need to hold them hoping for a better price. I'd sell, and do it while the market can absorb this volume."

He pulled out a chair and settled in to talk strategy. "How would you handle it?"

"This many coins to sell and ship — simplify and standardize. Sell by the roll anything that prices below a hundred dollars a coin. That price point will push out the better grades of the draped and capped Bust coins, the large cents, half dimes and Barber halves — the ones where you'll want to sort and grade more carefully."

Ann thought for a moment. "The outliers — those hard to find rare dates and mints — are where you can get a nice surprise in a volume purchase like this. You can spend the time to look for them or you can deliberately not do so and price accordingly. I've done it both ways. With this kind of collection I'd say don't sort. Set the price for the rolls a bit higher and let random chance for whoever finds the semi-keys and keys bring more buyers to you. Word will spread fast that you've got fresh coins. You'll make close to as much as if you had found those outliers yourself, and do it with a lot less effort."

Bryce saw her point. "The buyer gets the advantage on the individual rolls while I get the advantage over the entire collection."

"Exactly. No need to get elaborate on the selling. Just the description and the price. Five rolls, Mercury dimes 1916 to 1931, Extremely Fine to About Uncirculated — ten thousand dollars. Put the list on the website, no photos, just your reputation backing the description."

Ann sorted through the photos and tapped one. "These coin boxes, the odd lots, you would be better to move at auction. Something low-key. Think a big room, a bunch of tables, with groups of coins laid out. Target the week of the national coin show since it's in Chicago this year, invite dealers to stop by and bid on the lots. Let the buyers do the work of figuring out the values. Close the auction after five days. You can always decline to sell a particular lot if you don't get a reasonable price."

"Everything you just said makes sense,

and it's the absolute opposite of what I would do for higher-end coins. I'm glad I never competed with you in this business, Ann."

She smiled. "Two different client sets, different goals. My clients were focused on completing a collection of every Buffalo nickel or searching to find the error coin in a dozen rolls of Wheat pennies. Most enjoyed the treasure hunt aspect of the coins as much as the value. High-end coins tend to be more about wealth preservation and rarity and are individualized purchases." She stacked the photos and handed them back. "You paid five million six. Given today's market, I bet you go back to cash at eight million and can be there within four months."

"You want the job of running the prep room? I'll find some space to rent nearby."

"I'm tempted."

"I'd love it if you would say yes. This is what I bought this week. I got a preview of the group three coins that are coming. My guess, that group is going to be another five hundred coins at around three million."

"Will that be the last of the coins?"

"I don't know."

She laughed. "You are having a good year, Bishop."

"A profitable one." He stored the photos in the folder, then hesitated. "Do you mind if I take this conversation in a more serious turn?"

"What's on your mind?"

"Charlotte Graham — I'm guessing it's not her real name. Do you know who she really is?"

"I've known for a few years."

"I wondered about that." He knew Ann was a cop who kept secrets, all the way up to those of the former vice president. She'd been the Midwest Homicide Investigator for years before marrying Paul. "If I wanted to escort Charlotte into a museum showing, a concert, something public, is there going to be a problem? Is the press going to recognize her?"

"A slim chance, but yes. In Chicago, a few of the more sharp reporters might be able to put it together. You shouldn't have a problem if you stay low-key, avoid the events that would attract the press." She leaned back in her chair, considering him. "I'm good for a plane trip, if you decide you want to take her somewhere else for an evening out."

He knew she was a good pilot; she'd paid her college tuition by ferrying planes around, then spent thousands of hours in the air with her job. "I may take you up on that, Ann. Charlotte gave some money to charity, took my advice on where to give it. I want to say thanks. She shrugged it off when I tried to thank her, but it matters. And she needs an evening off."

"It sounds like a very nice thing for her to have done — for you to do."

"It's odd, because she's said flat-out she doesn't believe like I do. But she's giving to churches and charities that are Christian, giving generously."

"I'd say that contradiction suggests there's a lot more going on than appears on the surface."

"She asked me for another list of places to give."

"Then I'd write her another list." Ann grew thoughtful. "Bryce, would you accept some advice?"

"You know I will."

"Charlotte's past — you don't want to know. I realize you're a man who doesn't like mysteries, and not having all the facts bothers you. And yet I'll say for your sake as much as hers, you don't want to know. It won't help anything. It will hurt something. If you go looking, she doesn't get the choice to decide if she wants to tell you. I speak from experience. If she doesn't want to talk about something, doesn't want you to know, do her the kindness of not asking and not looking."

"I'm beginning to guess, Ann. I met John Key."

Ann smiled. "I like him."

"Charlotte said he's a very dangerous guy if he doesn't like a situation."

"An interesting way to put it. She'd be right. Some people have jobs so suited to their person that you can tell they're exactly where God designed them to be. John's a bodyguard, a security professional. He doesn't accept that assignment for many clients, but when he does, he'll do what needs to be done to keep someone safe."

"Is there a threat still out there to Charlotte?"

"No. Cops killed the guys I would worry about. But I'm glad John's still around in her life. Help her with the coins, Bryce, and whatever else she asks. It's the right thing, the kind thing, to do."

Paul hung up his jacket in the bedroom closet. "I'm sorry the call ran so long that I missed Bryce. They picked up six guys at Willis Tower and fanned out to arrest another six, so it just kept rolling all evening."

Ann, sitting on the floor, pushed Black to turn over so she could brush his other side. "I could tell it was getting interesting."

"It looks like corporate espionage. A major airline is moving its headquarters, leasing thirty floors in the building, and these guys were trying to get the offices bugged before the company moves in. The place is swarming with our tech people right now, trying to figure out what they did. Looks like they were about halfway through with the job. The conference rooms were all bugged, and they were already ghosting most of the traffic on the internal network."

Paul tugged receipts from his wallet and change from his pockets. "We'll know more once we figure out who was paying to have it done." He put his phone on to charge. "I'm guessing Bryce also had interesting news since he asked to stop by."

"Charlotte dropped a nice bombshell on him. She showed him a vault full of coins. Bryce spent five million six on seventy thousand coins, and if he doesn't clear eight million inside four months, I'll be surprised."

Paul paused to process that news. "So it was a volume of coins. I wondered. She had called the first coins chum."

"They're the lower price range of coins

Bryce doesn't normally handle. This volume — I've seen some nice hoards and bought this big once or twice, but it's rare to find this range of coins at the price she was offering. Charlotte has quite the coin collection to sell. Bryce said there's also another group of the high-end coins coming, probably five hundred of them in the range of three million. He'll have a challenge finessing that cash flow, but, man, what a nice problem to have."

"I'm guessing Bryce was looking for advice on how to manage the volume."

"Simple answer. Sort, roll, and sell."

Paul laughed, took a seat on the edge of the bed, and offered to take the dog brush to finish the job. Ann handed it over.

"He asked me if I wanted to help with the coins."

Paul smiled. "Do it and enjoy it. You like the world of coins. You've handled so many you know what you're holding at a glance. You'd consider it more fun than work."

"A couple of months, maybe three. It's not an opportunity that comes around very often. I can take Black with me. A prep room is basically space with a lot of tables."

"He can sleep there with his head on your feet as easily as he does here. Call Bryce, tell him yes. I'll join you when I've got the odd hour free, and you can teach me about coins."

"I'd enjoy that."

"How's it going with Bryce and Charlotte? Can you tell?"

Ann smiled. "He's definitely interested."

Paul leaned over and kissed her. "Then it's an extra good thing if you help with the coins — you'll know what's going on."

"I think she's been dropping clues, and he hasn't picked them up. I suggested tonight he not go looking for information, but I'm beginning to think that was a mistake."

"Personally I think the more time they have without the past stepping on the present, the better off they're going to be. He'll learn the details soon enough. It's not like he can change what's old history."

"They'll make good friends."

"They will. And I'll be glad to see Charlotte back in Chicago if she decides to stay around once her grandfather's estate is settled."

NINE

Bryce settled on simplicity for emptying vault five. He started at the first room and boxed coins until he had enough to fill the SUV he was driving, took them to Chicago where Ann had accepted the challenge of running the prep room, then returned to box and haul more. He could hire it done, but he liked the privacy and security of doing it himself. And the drives back and forth between Chicago and Wisconsin gave him some much-needed time to think. The reason he needed time to think was currently headed down the hall to join him, her off-key whistle echoing off the metal walls inside the berm.

He hadn't seen Charlotte much the last couple of weeks, despite his hopes. He would have thought she was avoiding him, but a few passing comments from John had filled him in on her travels. She was busy hauling items to her various shops.

Charlotte appeared in the doorway of the third room, looked around, and perched on the table inside the door. "I see empty shelves. I'm impressed. You're making progress."

"Good progress," he assured her, finishing packing a box and taping it closed.

She held out a bag she had in her hand. Bryce slipped off the cloth gloves and took a handful of her M&M's. "How was Cincinnati?"

"Wet. It rained the entire time I was there. Sales have been good, though. They even sold the last of the cigar boxes." She nudged with her foot to get a better perch on the table. "I dropped off four hundred very old books, a dozen old mirrors, five cases of Christmas wrapping paper, a wooden barrelful of bows, and probably a thousand pieces of ladies' costume jewelry from every decade since there has been a Graham. The barrel itself is probably the most valuable item, oddly enough."

Bryce reached for more M&M's, and Charlotte obligingly tipped them into his hand. "To their credit, the two ladies I have running the store sorted through the items and said it would be no problem. They've hired four more staff so they can handle the volume. The store in St. Paul said there was a bidding war over Fred's old desk set from his father. I had a few more items of that kind boxed, so I took them all over to St. Paul, including four trunks of dresses that must be from the 1930s and '40s. I don't understand vintage clothes. They said the very old shoes were popular too, and I should bring the rest of what I find."

"Age brings character."

"Something. I will say everything was in excellent condition. They've been stored in a berm for decades that stays sixty-five degrees and dry. I've got three more storage rooms of clothes to empty out as my next priority."

"Any old toys?"

"An entire truckload — they're what I used to open the St. Paul store. They sold out in less than ten days."

"Admit it, Charlotte. You like selling stuff."

"I'm not any good at the customer face-to-face part, but I enjoy seeing items being put to use versus being thrown away. I'm getting more efficient. I used to agonize about what to take and how to price it. It's not such a big deal now, as I've realized the market will bid up the price on the few rare items, and the rest will sell if reasonably priced."

She slid back to her feet. "Could I get a ride back to Chicago with you? I need to fly to New York tomorrow and it's easier to leave from O'Hare than Madison."

"Sure. Going to see your sister?"

"No. Other business."

"I figure I'll leave about three, if that works for you."

"Appreciate it. I did get one useful piece of business done. The group three coins are now at my shop and priced. Stop by and tell me what you think. I'm at two million eight, but I'm flexible."

"I'll stop there first thing tomorrow morning. Is there going to be a group four?"

Charlotte considered him. "Would you like there to be?"

Bryce thought she was teasing, but didn't want to chance it. "I'd like to buy whatever coins you have to sell, Charlotte."

She smiled. "That works for me. Yes, plan for a group four."

Bryce settled into the drive that he had done several times now, familiar enough with the scenery to know the time remaining, the exits he would like to stop at, without having to refer to the map. It was nice having a passenger along, though a quiet one.

Charlotte had her sketchbook out. He was

content not to interrupt her as the hours of the drive passed. She drew with the concentration that said this was her real job. She finally snapped a rubber band around the pencils she was using and dropped them in the briefcase.

"What do you think?" She turned the pad to show him.

It was her dogs looking back at him from the page. "Nice."

"I know their faces so well, sometimes I dream about them looking at me."

She flipped the page. "Just a concept. I'll do the final sketch in color."

He glanced over at the pad and saw a misty fog over Shadow Lake, the trees faint silhouettes. "It's beautiful, Charlotte."

"Thanks." She paged through the sketches. "A couple of these have potential."

"How long have you been selling your works?"

"About fifteen years. I let Ellie manage the business side of the art for me. I just hand her the sketchbooks, and she decides what is worth selling and how to price it. She's got an extraordinary gift herself for the business side of art. That's rarer than most people realize."

She pulled out her briefcase and put the sketchbook away. "There's about an hour left in the drive?"

"Fifty minutes."

"I stay with Ellie when I'm in Chicago. I would appreciate it if you could drop me off there. She's on Bryston Avenue, just west of Porters Street."

"No problem."

Charlotte sorted around in her briefcase for a pen. "You mentioned you had another giving list for me?"

"The page is folded in that book on the back seat."

She reached over to pick it up, looked at the cover and said, "Andy Stanley, any good?"

"I'm enjoying it."

She tugged the page from the book. "Thanks for the list."

"I've jotted down some ideas for projects — a new dorm for an orphanage in Zhanjiang, China. Four deep-bore wells for clean drinking water in Sierra Leone. A vaccine distribution effort in Uganda. The equipment, supplies, and salaries for a health clinic serving the Mathare Valley slum area of Nairobi. Two agriculture projects targeting food transportation across Kenya. There's also some general suggestions for several churches I know well that have strong mission budgets."

She read through the page. "I can do your full list."

"Seriously?" He'd put together a list totaling eight hundred thousand, thinking a few items might appeal. It hadn't crossed his mind that she'd say yes to everything.

"My offer was to do your suggestions or tell you to scale it back. I don't mind giving this amount."

She got out her checkbook.

She was now at just over a million in gifts based on his recommendations. Bryce found the thought disconcerting. He'd put some care into the two lists, she'd asked for his best ideas and he'd given them, but the scale of it now began to sink in. *What did I miss here, Jesus? She's giving away a million dollars because I mentioned some places . . . this just doesn't happen.* He glanced over at her. *Thank you* didn't seem sufficient, and the best he'd done so far was treat her to fast food during the drive. "Thank you, Charlotte, from all these places that will be really helped by your generosity. And thanks from me for doing this."

She smiled. "Relax, Bishop. It's only money." She wrote the checks for his list, stacked them neatly for him, then pulled out the pad he'd seen her work from before, and she began to write checks to food pantries, addressing envelopes as she worked.

He realized she wrote two-hundred-thousand-dollar checks as easily as she did fifty-dollar checks, and took a moment to process that unexpected fact. "You send checks every month?"

"I prefer doing it that way. It's easier on their planning if support is a steady amount rather than lumpy with occasional gifts during the year."

"If you run labels for the addresses, it would save you time and you would know you didn't skip any place you intended to give."

She licked another envelope and sealed it. "That would fall in the category of a good idea that I haven't made time to do yet. Ellie would jump at it, she likes to organize things, but I try not to land everything on her plate."

"It really is a nice thing you're doing," he offered. Words were failing him just when he wanted something eloquent to say. *Jesus, what's an encouraging word here? She's doing something that truly matters. I want her to hear that.*

"I'm not particularly nice, Bryce. I've just got the resources to write some checks this year, and it makes sense to use some of the money this way."

He watched the stack of envelopes grow. "You said you don't believe like I do. What do you believe in, Charlotte?"

She gave him a long look, then signed a check before she replied. "I would call myself a struggling Christian. I was raised attending church every Sunday, baptized when I was ten. But I've got some doubts about God."

She'd addressed the topic rather than brush off his question, but Bryce sensed the conversation was going to be short. He chose to go to what mattered most to him personally. "God is all about grace, the same as you showed your brother-in-law. We repent, He forgives us, and we get another chance. We need a clean slate, and can't earn that new chance, so Jesus paid the penalty for what we've done wrong in life. It's a goodness we don't deserve, but need, and a magnificent act of grace. God likes to forgive."

"I know." She finished writing another check. "That's the problem. God is too good. He's too willing to forgive. He would have forgiven the men who hurt me."

The car swerved slightly right, and he put his attention back on the road. "Charlotte —"

"They're dead," she went on, "so it's theoretical now. But it also isn't. God meant it. He would have forgiven them if they asked him to. I don't know that I'm interested in a God who would give a second chance to the men who hurt me."

He breathed in very carefully over the pain in his chest. "What — ?"

"I don't talk about it. I'm not talking about it any further."

He literally bit down on his tongue to stop his words, afraid he was going to take a wrong step, say the wrong thing, and do real damage because he didn't know what he now *had* to know. "I'm sorry."

"Yeah. So am I."

Charlotte finished stacking the envelopes and pulled out her sketchbook again. She shut down the conversation like a wall, and Bryce let her have the silence.

Them. Plural. He felt sick. And she was right. God would forgive even the men who hurt her, had they repented and said forgive me. *Jesus, what happened? How do I even begin to find words to have a conversation with her about it?*

Bryce had rented as the prep area for the coins part of the third floor of the office building where Chapel Security had its

167

headquarters. He walked into the large room shortly before eight a.m. The boxes he had unloaded from the SUV the night before were stacked on a push trolley by the east wall, the top two boxes now open.

Ann was at the third table sorting silver half-dollars. The people he had hired to help her were not in yet.

Bishop pulled out the chair across from her. "Ann, I need to know."

She took one look at his face and set aside what she was working on. "Something happened?"

He nodded.

Ann took a deep breath. "Bryce, she's Ruth Bazoni."

Shock ripped through him, then grief, pain, and enormous sadness. Pity finally overwhelmed every other emotion in him.

She laid a comforting hand on his arm. "I'll get you some coffee."

Ten

Bishop could vividly remember, shortly after his college graduation, seeing a television interview with Charlotte's twin sister.

"Ruth and I were sixteen when we were kidnapped, initially held for twenty-four hours by two men in a van that just drove around. The older man had just returned with the ransom money. He tossed the duffel bag into the back of the van with us. 'Your dad paid this, he'll pay more. Only one of you is getting out of this van.' The words had no more than left his mouth than Ruth planted her feet in my ribs and shoved me out of the van. I fell onto the pavement. The guy slammed the door shut, laughing. It was the last I saw of my sister for four years.

"It was four years and three ransoms before the FBI found the two men, killed them, rescued her. Everything Dad had left to sell, my modeling income, a loan against my future earnings, even donations from strangers paid ransoms two and three. Though Dad and I thought she was probably dead, we just couldn't give up hope. She saved my life that day, at the cost of her own. She looked like a skeleton with skin when she was found. She was twenty, yet her gaze was of someone in her eighties. She's never said a word — to the cops, to her doctors, to her family — about those four years. She just smiled at me and said, 'I missed you.' "

Ruth Bazoni had disappeared from the public view, changed her name, and rebuilt her life. John Key had helped her.

Bryce closed his hands around the coffee mug Ann brought him, needing the warmth. "She talked about God briefly. It shook me. Now . . . now I get where she's coming from. She doesn't know if she wants to believe in a God who would be able to forgive the men who hurt her."

Ann traced a circle on the table with the cold soda she had brought over for herself. "I imagine, Bryce, that God broke her heart, that she couldn't trust Him to keep her safe. If He loved her, He wouldn't have let her stay trapped in that nightmare for four years."

"It's hard to comprehend, Ann. Four

years, three ransoms. She was just sixteen when it began. Just a kid." He tried to get that image in his mind to square with the woman he knew today, and he couldn't do it.

"It's a black eye to the FBI and the task force of local cops who worked the case. It shouldn't have dragged on that long," Ann said. "They finally found the two guys, killed them and rescued her, but it was four very long years. The fact she was found less than three miles from her home, had been there the entire time — there's a reason it's the most famous kidnapping case in recent Chicago history."

Bryce thought about all the media the event had attracted, even during the missing years, and then after she was found. No wonder John had been hired as her bodyguard to keep reporters away.

He looked at Ann. "I understand where Charlotte — I can't think of her as Ruth — is coming from. If those guys had asked forgiveness, God would have done it. Doesn't matter that it's only theoretical now, that they didn't repent. God was willing to forgive them, wipe their slates clean, and accept them into heaven. That's what Charlotte can't deal with. God meant it."

"Truly evil men rarely repent, even though

they are invited to do so."

"Charlotte said God is too good," Bryce said softly. "Implied if God loved her, He wouldn't have offered them the chance. Today, I almost agree with her." He taught basic theology at his church, had spent his life willing to put his time, money, and personal honor on the fact God was worth following — and right now it all felt off-kilter. "Ann, what am I going to do?"

"What do you want to do?"

"Make it go away."

"The one thing you can't do for her." Ann wiped the moisture off the table. "Figure out how much it's in the past, Bryce, and let her decide what, if anything, she wants from you. It's been years, and from what you've said up to this point, she's rebuilt a good life. I don't think Charlotte's nearly as separated from God as you would think. I think she's still wrestling with the hurt of what happened, but her charitable gifts are just one clue God still matters to her. She doesn't understand Him. But you don't wrestle with a problem when the answer doesn't matter to you."

"I wish I didn't know."

Ann nodded. "I know what you mean, Bryce. Where is she now?"

"Her flight to New York is not until noon.

She's probably still at Ellie's."

"Better to have a conversation today than several days from now."

Bryce got to his feet. "Thanks for telling me. And for the warning earlier that I didn't want to know. You were absolutely right. I wish I didn't."

Bishop rang the bell at Ellie Dance's home, expecting to get no answer even if Charlotte was still here. He didn't imagine she was going to want to see him before she left for New York. Especially when she found out —

Charlotte opened the door before he could complete the thought.

"Charlotte . . ."

He didn't know how to begin. On the drive over he thought he had worked out what he would say, but the words failed him as he saw her.

"Come on in, Bryce."

She stepped back to let him enter, walked into the living room ahead of him. She picked up the book on the couch to put it on the table, took a seat and pulled her legs up under her. "You know," she guessed.

"Ann told me."

"Why hadn't you looked me up and already known? I laid a bread-crumb trail right to the answer with the fact my sister

173

was named Model of the Decade. There's only *one* of those in a decade."

"It simply didn't occur to me, Charlotte. The background report had you being from Texas and the sketch artist CRM. It never crossed my mind that you were originally from here. I thought I knew who you were. I just hadn't asked you to confirm it."

She looked . . . he could see what John must have seen in those early days . . . the bruised emotions of a survivor. He walked over to the window to look out at the traffic.

A minute passed.

"I'm sorry, Charlotte, about what happened." He kept his eyes on the street outside, but he had to say it. He still felt sick with shock and grief, and neither of those emotions was going to improve matters with her right now.

"I don't talk about it. Never have. Never will."

He turned, pushed his hands in his back pockets. "I won't ask."

She shrugged.

It seemed important to say something else. "I remember when you disappeared. I was starting college. And I was graduating when you were found."

She didn't respond.

Bryce could feel the seconds tick by. *Jesus, give me some help here, please. I've known about this for only a couple of hours, and I'm drowning here, trying not to make it worse, but feeling appalled at the idea I'm supposed to ignore what shattered this woman's life.*

He glanced around the room, seeing a few pictures of Ellie and Charlotte, several more which included John. Friends. Family. He latched on to that thought and looked at Charlotte. "How about your dad? How's he doing?"

"He lives near my sister in New York. Had a stroke and thankfully doesn't remember those years. I go see him when I'm in town. He thinks I'm his nurse's niece and tells me how much he likes jazz. He gets agitated after I visit, like part of him is trying to remember, and the doctors have carefully suggested that maybe it would be better for him if I visited less often. He seems okay with Tabitha and the girls, so they have a meal with him every week. When Tabitha and I talk on Sundays, she's good about telling me how he's doing."

"You're not catching any breaks, are you?" he murmured.

"The name change confuses him. I changed my name after it happened, Ruth Bazoni doesn't exist anymore. I was Charlotte March until my grandfather showed up. I decided his family name was more appropriate and would lead to fewer questions, so I became Charlotte Graham when I moved back here."

"John knows. Ellie," Bryce said, trying to form a picture of those who knew.

"Paul does, and you've just said Ann knows," Charlotte added.

"She won't speak out of turn."

"Not a concern. I know her by reputation," Charlotte replied, "and we share some common friends. Don't treat me differently, Bryce. It will annoy me."

He nodded, but wondered just how he was supposed to do that. The knowledge literally hurt. "I'll go take a look at the coins for group three today, have an answer for when you get back. You need a lift to the airport?"

"Already covered."

"How long will you be in New York?"

"Three days, maybe four if business bogs down. Lawyers can be slow when they feel a need to explain every detail after I got the gist of it in the first five minutes."

He smiled. "I'll track you down when you get back. We'll talk coins."

She half smiled back as she nodded. "Maybe dogs too. Let yourself forget you know, Bryce. John has, enough it doesn't color how he nags at me." She studied him. "It's not fragile glass you're dealing with, Bryce. I survived. I shouldn't have. You want to remember something, remember that. I'm neither nice nor particularly soft."

He didn't understand her perspective on herself, but accepted that her comment originated in one of the many layers of her history. Nothing was going to be simple about this woman — nothing ever had been. But now he was understanding the reason. "Why doesn't John travel with you? Reporters have long memories, and you're still a story."

"I vetoed it years ago. I don't look like my sister, and she's the one whose photo is everywhere. I know John has security around me when he thinks circumstances warrant it. He's got my truck tagged. Probably Mitch or Joseph will be on the flight this afternoon. We've got an agreement that I won't ask so he won't have to tell me. He handles the security so I don't have to worry about it. But unless someone really tries to find me, they aren't going to link Ruth Bazoni to Charlotte Graham. Your background check didn't turn it up."

"You must have had some law enforcement help burying those name changes," he guessed.

She nodded. "For that, and a few other matters that keep my identity under wraps. They are inclined to do what they can — an apology of sorts for not being able to do more when they couldn't find me."

"One question, Charlotte, and I promise to leave it be. Did you know that you were only miles from your home?"

"I knew the street I was on, had guessed the house."

He closed his eyes. "Okay." When he opened them he met her gaze, and he knew what she meant when she said she was a survivor. She had known, and she had lasted four years.

Chapel Security had been fast. Bryce had three boxes of material to read regarding the Bazoni kidnapping, most of it from newspapers, along with four videos of prime-time television shows done about the case while she was missing, interviews with the FBI and local cops working the ransom demands, another six tapes of press conferences, fund-raisers, newscasts. Bryce spread it across his desk at home and went through it all late into the night, dug out his old video equipment and watched several of the tapes. He got to relive it, from the search for the missing girls, the initial ransom demand, the hope when Tabitha had been freed to the desperate realization Ruth wasn't going to be so lucky.

Four years, three ransoms, a reorganized task force, cops who burned out physically and emotionally, reward money for leads, fund-raisers to secure ransom money, and constantly the press — *what had happened to Ruth Bazoni?*

Bryce didn't try to figure out all his emotions. Instead he just absorbed the breadth of it, then shoved it back into the boxes and went upstairs to turn in for the night. All that activity and Charlotte had probably not known it was happening. She'd watched the days pass and wondered what her family was thinking, doing. Wondered if God was ever going to send her help.

Ruth Bazoni.

Bryce tossed his shoe into the closet, then hurled the other one after it.

Eleven

Paul settled beside Ann on the couch in the den, and she set aside the pages she was working on. "How did Bryce take it?" he asked.

"Not well. It shocked him. Then I think it was simply pity I was seeing, to go along with the pain."

"He'll get past it."

She nodded. "He's a good guy. He'll absorb the hit and shift to deal with it. It's just going to take time."

"I can feel your sadness, see it."

"She never gets a break, Paul. She carries deep inside what happened for the rest of her life."

"So do you, Ann, with your own experience. Not the same level of burden, I know, but similar at its core. Not your choice, and it will be there forever to deal with. But she's tough, like you. She copes. I admire that."

Ann turned on the couch to fully face him, resting her back against the armrest. "I think it might be a good idea for you and Bryce to play some pool, go running, put a few things on the calendar — give him a sounding board if he needs it."

"I'll do that." The only thing that was going to help Bryce and Charlotte right now was time, but eventually some conversations might be helpful.

Paul glanced over at the whiteboard leaning against the wall, looking for a change in subject, for there was nothing that could be done at the moment for Charlotte and Bryce. Ann had been working on the cold case. *Baby Connor. A kidnapping gone wrong.* She'd made three notes. We're looking for: 1. Murders in the area the year after baby Connor died; 2. A name for the voice on the tape; 3. A family in the area with financial trouble — maybe a couple of guys and a woman, maybe an older woman.

Before the case was solved, the board would likely be covered with notes and questions and ideas. He reached for the list on Ann's lap that she had been marking up. "Where did you decide to start?"

"Names of people in the pub the night the call came in saying baby Connor was dead. Cops looked at the people on the list to see if their voice was that of the caller. It wasn't a scientific audio comparison. The cops simply tried to find all the people on the list, have a conversation with them, write *not him* or *maybe* next to the name. For the possible matches cops tried to come up with a reason to get them in an interview room so a recording could be made of their voice and the audio guys could have two tapes to compare. Are there old tapes still in evidence so we could have the sound guys today take a second look?"

"I'll check. There probably are. I only asked for the files, not the physical evidence."

"Do you think we can solve this, Paul?"

Paul reached over and ran a hand down her arm. "I can tell you're sad when you're pessimistic about solving a case. You've dealt with harder cases than this one. We both have." He took her hand in his. "Let's take Black for his walk and then turn in. We could both do with an early night."

"I hope she's not having too hard a night."

Paul didn't have to ask who she meant. "Charlotte's a survivor, same as you. And you shouldn't count Bryce out. The man may surprise both of us for how he handles this."

TWELVE

Bryce Bishop pulled into the drive of Fred Graham's home and parked behind Charlotte's truck. John had said she was back. It was a gorgeous day and he made a guess, circled the house. Charlotte was sitting in a chair on the back patio, looking out over Shadow Lake, a sketchbook on the table beside her. He walked up the path to join her.

"I'm fine at two million eight for group three." She wanted to talk coins and dogs, he'd oblige her. He knelt to greet the Irish setter that came over, thought it might be Duchess. The other setter merely smacked a tail on the deck but didn't rise.

Bryce pulled an envelope from his pocket and offered Charlotte the check. He was beginning to get numb to the fact he was carrying checks with all those zeroes and *million* written out.

She smiled as she folded it and tucked it

into her pocket. "It's nice doing business with you, Bryce."

He walked to the edge of the patio, pushed his hands in his back pockets, looked out over the lake. It was peaceful here. She had mentioned there was good fishing. Maybe he could talk her into taking him out for an afternoon. He hadn't fished in more than a decade, but he might enjoy it. She might too. "How was New York?"

"Busy." She sent a tennis ball sailing into the yard, and Duchess took off after it. "If you don't mind simple, I'm having grilled cheese for a late lunch. You're welcome to join me."

He glanced back at her, surprised. "Sure. I'd like that."

"I saw a play while I was in New York." She picked up her sketchbook and led the way inside. "I would tell you about it, but I was lost within the first ten minutes. Something about two neighbors and a common love for birds."

"How did you happen to choose it?"

"One of those impulses where you ask the hotel concierge what tickets are available for that night. The fact they were unsold should have been my first clue."

Bryce smiled. "Business go okay?"

"I read a lot of paper, signed a lot of

paper. They are handling all the odds and ends of ownership that Fred had in companies. I've opened the last of the safe-deposit boxes, so hopefully there should be no more surprises to find on that end. Another few months to get it all signed and sealed, and I'll have to decide what to do with the rest of what they've found."

In the kitchen Bryce saw a card table where the dining room table had been. "The furniture is moving out."

"John laughs at me over my priorities. I like moving some of the more important pieces so I can see progress. I need to see some progress. I've kept the bed I'm sleeping on and the patio furniture."

She moved over to the refrigerator and pulled out butter and cheese slices, opened a drawer for bread. Bryce slid a folding chair out and sat at the table, staying out of her way.

Charlotte glanced over at him. "Do you regret the vault five buy? Now that you've got the group three coins to also deal with?"

"No regrets, Charlotte. The lower-priced coins are simply a different animal to sell. Different clients, different focus. Ann is good at managing them. We're selling rolls at a pace that will put us through most of the coins in about ten weeks. The rest we'll move by auction at the summer coin show."

"I'm glad, as I appreciate having vault five dealt with. I think we're getting a handle on the other stuff around Graham Enterprises. Fewer surprises are appearing when we open up storage units, just more of the same. There's still a lot of work to be done, but at least there seems to be ways to tackle it all." She turned the sandwiches in the oversized flat skillet. "Somewhere in the pantry there are probably potato chips."

He got up to find them. A few minutes later she brought over a plate stacked with grilled cheese sandwiches. They ate lunch sharing the bag of potato chips, sliding the container of chip dip back and forth.

"I'd offer dessert, but John finished the ice cream last night, and I had the last tapi-oca for breakfast."

"Sounds nutritious."

"I'm remarkably tolerant with myself over what I eat and when. Pizza's a pretty good standby even for breakfast." She picked up her glass of ice tea. "Let's find somewhere more comfortable to sit."

The living room still had two comfortable chairs, but the couch was gone, the glass display case, two of the tables. The stereo had been moved to the floor. Bryce took a seat while Charlotte wandered the room.

"I figure if I wrap something every time I walk into this room, I'll eventually get it cleared." She started wrapping the porcelain birds that had been in the display case.

Bryce smiled, but understood it. She was getting the job done.

He had no idea what to say to this woman. Four days of her in New York, his five-hour drive this morning, and he didn't have a grasp on it yet. But ignoring it wasn't going to make it settle. He squeezed the bridge of his nose, wondering at the wisdom of asking anything further. He finally said, "Can we talk about the after of it?"

She shrugged.

"Why Texas?"

"The press was predominately Chicago and New York, where my sister modeled. I didn't want the congestion of the coasts, and I didn't want to be cold anymore. The Keeler-Resse clinic has a branch in Houston, and the doctors encouraged me to spend a few months there. It helped, in its way. John tutored me through my GED and first two years of college. Then I started selling sketches and realized I already had a career I could enjoy."

She pushed the wrapped items around inside the box on the floor and closed it, taped it shut. She got to her feet. "I'm single for life, Bishop. Lots of money, lots of reasons for someone to overlook the baggage I bring. That's not going to happen. I don't need the pity. So I've built a life I like for myself. I'll go back to it full time once Fred's estate is dealt with. I like my art. I like my friends."

"John loves you."

"No. He likes me — rather a lot. He loves Ellie. Big difference."

"Are you afraid of the flashbacks?"

"This is not a conversation I want to have with you, Bryce."

"It's been eighteen years. You never had a choice, Charlotte. You do now."

"I was thirty before I kissed a guy by my choice."

"How was it?"

"Not something I've repeated."

"Charlotte —"

"Don't feel sorry for me, Bryce. It makes me mad."

"Actually, I was going to say something along the lines of practice would probably help."

She pushed hair away from her face. "Yeah. Probably. Not going to happen either."

She pushed the box over to join the others by the door. "I've been putting off dealing with the safe Fred pointed out in the master bedroom. It's behind a false wall. You want to see what's in it today?"

He felt like breaking something. "Sure."

Bryce lifted stacks of coins out of the safe and handed them to Charlotte to box. He'd given up trying to count, but it looked like a good portion of group four was going to come from this safe. He finally reached to the back of the safe and lifted out the last stack. "I've never seen anything like this estate," he said as he handed them to her.

Charlotte added the coins to the open box, glanced at the boxes of coins by the closet, then looked back at him. "Ellie, John and I — we had to decide on someone to buy the coins. That's why I pushed you that first day. I couldn't afford to give you a choice. You were the pick from a long list of names we had considered. It had to be one person. We couldn't let this estate become common knowledge."

"Apology accepted. But I did have a choice, Charlotte. Not a good one, but I could have said no and let you open your store. It would have been a character-building exercise to have had to compete with you in business."

She laughed. "I'm glad you said yes. I'll

bring these coins down to the storefront in a couple days, get them priced."

"You don't want me to just buy them here?"

"As minor as it sounds, I feel better taking your money when I know the coins are safe in the store next to Bishop Chicago."

He smiled. "Create your bubble-wrap balls for the coins and take them to the store. I'll buy them from you there. I'm enjoying this, Charlotte."

"You'll forgive me if I say I'm getting really tired of old coins? It will be nice to have them done with."

"I can understand that." He offered her a hand to help her up. They were going to be finished long before he would like them to be.

Bryce opened the display case in Charlotte's store to pack the last of the group three coins. He would take them over to Bishop Chicago for Devon to grade and Sharon to photograph. Kim was doing an excellent job getting them sold. They were running a solid thirty-percent profit on the coins sold so far. He should be thrilled, but he found it hard to find enthusiasm to match that of his staff.

Group three would be done today —

Charlotte would need the space for group four — and he'd head back north after he completed this task to retrieve more vault five coins for Ann's team. The work was getting done, and he was getting tired. "Tell yourself another fib, Bryce," he muttered, pausing to pour himself coffee.

The truth was, he missed Charlotte when he didn't see her at least every few days.

She had loaded him up with more coins and then disappeared again. She'd taken off for Ohio, then Texas, then taken a detour to close a safe-deposit box in Wyoming that had been overlooked. He hadn't seen much of her the last three weeks. It was hard to tell if she was avoiding him. Her schedule made it easy for her to find reasons to be gone, but he thought she might be. He did miss her. And what was he going to do about that?

He heard the back security-door chime. "Charlotte?" He put down the coffee and turned toward the back hallway.

"Yes." She came into the store proper, no dogs with her this time. Her tan had an edge of a sunburn, and her hair looked lighter, if only the illusion of being sun-bleached. She looked good, really good. His mood lightened considerably. "Nice to see you. How was the travel?"

"Hot. Texas was miserably hot. Wyoming was just having a heat wave. I'd love if that was the last plane I'm on for a while. Anyway . . . I heard you were heading north. I stopped by to see if I could get a ride with you?"

"Sure."

"Wait till I tell you the rest. I've got a problem I need to work around. I can't go until late tonight. I arranged to ship some art I had stored in Texas. It was supposed to arrive three days from now, only it shipped early and will be arriving at Ellie's between four and six today. She would cancel her own travel plans if I told her, so I'm just going to stay long enough to sign for it. Could we leave after six, seven at the latest? I'm dangerous driving that late at night, as I fight sleep, but tomorrow's John's birthday and I normally try to fix him breakfast on his birthday. I'd hate to mess up tradition."

"We can make it a late trip."

"Thanks." She settled into one of the comfortable chairs and looked around. "I still like this storefront. The remodel job came out nice."

"Going to let me take over the lease when you get done with the coins? Bishop Chicago could use an expansion."

"I've got some other plans for the space first, but one day." She dug into her pocket for a piece of candy. "I heard from my sister briefly this morning."

"Everything okay?"

"From what little she said, yes. The girls are having a musical recital next month. She said the girls were going to send me invitations, but she'd be relieved if I could come up with a reason to decline. There's been a reporter asking questions about me, and she's afraid he might think the recital is something I might attend. Tabitha said she'd tape the recital for me, so I could see it that way instead."

Bryce carefully closed the display case. "What are you going to do?"

Charlotte shrugged. "I won't go. That's Tabitha's call to make. But I'll find something better than a lame excuse for the girls for why I can't be there. It happens, the media. Every couple of years there's a reporter hoping to make a splash in his or her paper, the 'what happened to . . . ?' article with me as the feature. Tabitha can't avoid that publicity, modeling keeps her in the public eye, and she never could escape the media onslaught — that's one of the reasons I like her husband so much. Thomas is like John. He pushes back on the press and protects his family from it. But he can't stop it from happening. She's the door to someone wanting to find me, and reporters know it."

"I'm sorry for it, Charlotte."

"So am I." She offered a sad smile. "Figured I would send Tabitha flowers this time, maybe a box of chocolates. I'd send her a sympathy card but that would just be stating the obvious." She got to her feet, stopped by the display case, looked at the remaining coins from group three. "They're truly gorgeous, but I'm just going to bring you more."

"The coins have become work — for you as well as me, I think. But you don't have to be excited about it in order to do a good job. I'm glad you chose Bishop Chicago rather than Cambridge Coins out of New York to handle the coins."

She glanced at him. "I hope you still think that in a few weeks."

"Charlotte —"

She shook her head. "I appreciate the ride tonight. I'll see you at Ellie's later." She disappeared down the hallway, and he heard the door chime as she left.

They were four hours into the drive that night when the clock slipped past eleven.

194

The moon was bright, traffic was light, Charlotte was quiet, and Bryce was content with the silence rather than find music on the radio.

Not a bad ending to the day. He'd drop her off at Graham Enterprises tonight, catch a few hours of sleep at the Madison hotel where he was now greeted by name, spend part of the morning packing another shipment of coins from vault five to take back to Ann, and then maybe talk Charlotte into a couple of hours in a boat on Shadow Lake before he headed back to Chicago. Something different. Tomorrow had possibilities.

"Bishop."

"Hmm?" He glanced over, surprised she was awake.

She stretched in the seat, then settled back with a sigh. "I've got something I need to tell you."

"Okay."

"Best have your eyes on the road."

He looked back at the empty highway, where his vehicle lights were the only brightness in an otherwise dark night. "What have you got to tell me?"

"We think there are about sixty million in coins."

He would have closed his eyes, but he was driving.

"There are two vaults deep in the berm complex that make vault five look small."

He dropped the cruise speed. "And the individual coins you've been selling in groups?" he asked, surprised to find his voice sounded normal.

"You've bought fifteen hundred coins; group four will make it two thousand. There are eight thousand of them."

"Why are you telling me now?"

"You're about through the coins at the house. Another week and you'll be clearing the last room of vault five. And there's no good way to ease into this. You haven't flinched yet, but even I would flinch at that scale. I need to sell them."

"The sixty million estimate?"

"The number we paid estate tax on, the best guess based on the inventory sheets and a count of the rolls. The lawyers are simply hoping it wasn't too low. Can you scale what you are doing to increase the volume you're selling?"

He could literally feel his entire work life shift at the question. "The market gets soft even at lower-end coins if you push too hard. We can put that much into the market over a year and sell them, but we simply become the market price. Where it will hurt is the mom 'n' pop stores where inventory is now overpriced relative to these coin prices."

"It has to be done."

"Then I'll help you get it done."

"Thank you."

Miles passed in silence as Bryce tried to get his mind around the implications of what she had just told him. "Charlotte, how wealthy are you?"

Another mile passed.

"Too wealthy to sleep well at night."

Bryce tossed his overnight bag on the bed in room 413. He thumbed through the hotel guide. Having requested the same room the last three stays, he knew where the ice and vending machines were located. But he remembered passing a business office off the lobby and looked up the hours, hoping it was open all night. It had closed at midnight and would reopen at seven a.m. He glanced at the front page of the guide. The complimentary strawberry smoothie from the last trip had disappeared, been replaced with a "refreshing coconut ice drink." He doubted they had as many takers for the coconut. Room service also stopped at midnight.

He dropped the guide back on the table, took the ice bucket and some change, and headed out. He returned with a Snickers bar and an orange juice. The maid who had prepped the room had left him two mints on the pillow. Bryce used the juice to swallow two Tylenol, ate the candy bar while sitting on the bed, thinking, then the two mints. He tossed the extra pillows into the barrel chair, found his toothbrush and finished getting ready to turn in.

He set the alarm for nine a.m., figured trying for eight hours of sleep might get him five the way his brain was churning. He was meeting Charlotte at ten a.m. He shut off the bedside light and forced himself to close his eyes.

The business side of his brain was still running at a staggering speed. He sat up, turned the light back on, picked up the hotel notepad, and confirmed his math. He'd bought twelve million in coins so far. She estimated sixty million. So forty-eight million left to go.

He'd bought three groups of coins. He was looking at thirteen more groups. Vault five was coming in at more than seventy thousand coins. He was looking at, minimum, another two hundred eighty thousand coins. He shut off the light again.

How wealthy was Charlotte Graham? Too wealthy to sleep well at night. The perfect answer. He knew exactly how she felt.

Twenty minutes later, he turned the light on again and found the Bible tucked in his travel bag, opened it at random to the Psalms.

Jesus, I don't know what to say. Sixty million total — I need some room to breathe. Charlotte's been sitting on this fact since we met. I'm stunned. Between Graham Enterprises and sixty million in coins, she's extremely wealthy. I'd say she's at her capacity too, given her remark about not sleeping well. I need good judgment tomorrow in what I say and do. I've wanted to be able to do something to help her, and this is the definition of a need where I can be of some help. I can't afford to make a mistake.

Bryce prayed until the words finally felt all said, read the thirty-fourth Psalm open before him, the words familiar and comforting, then closed the Bible and shut off the light.

A thought crossed his mind as he closed his eyes. God definitely had a sense of humor. *You're bored? How about meeting Charlotte — ?*

THIRTEEN

"You told Bryce about the larger vaults," Ellie confirmed.

"Yes." Charlotte handed Ellie a teacup with her friend's favorite — hot lemon tea with just a little sugar. She'd fixed the tea when she heard Ellie's alarm clock. It was just after four a.m. and the dawn was barely beginning to lighten the sky. She had been up drawing, too restless to get more than a few hours of sleep herself.

The guest bedroom at Charlotte's Silverton home had always been arranged with Ellie in mind — the elegance of the room, the comfortable furnishings. Her friend had driven up early yesterday afternoon, long before Charlotte and Bryce had left Chicago. Ellie sat back down on the bed she'd been making and sipped the tea.

Charlotte settled into a comfortable chair by the window. "I'm glad you came north. John's going to be delighted to have you at his birthday breakfast."

Ellie considered her over the rim of the cup, offered a small smile. "Don't get your hopes up. I didn't come to tell him yes to his proposal."

"You came to go fishing with him. I saw the straw hat spiked with your favorite lures by the door."

"It's the other birthday gift he really wants." Ellie carefully put the teacup on the side table, piled the pillows, and leaned back against the headboard. "Back to Bishop. You told him."

"I'll show him the coins later this morning. The words don't mean as much as standing in the middle of one of the vaults and seeing it. Sixty million in coins is a breathtaking problem."

"How did he take the news?"

"Too calmly. He eventually asked how wealthy I am."

Ellie tilted her head. "How did you answer that one?"

"I'm too wealthy to sleep well at night."

"Good answer." Ellie picked up her earrings from the bedside table and put them on. "The plan always was to make the coins Bishop's problem rather than yours."

"He'll step up to the challenge. I'm getting to know him well enough to understand that."

"Good." Ellie smiled. "You like him, don't you?"

"He's a businessman, Ellie. He's such a serious man, and I don't think he knows the meaning of the word *relax*. But there's something likable under all that. He's turned out to be what we needed to find when we put together that list of names. I'm confident we chose well."

"Of all the decisions you have to make, at least Bryce Bishop was a right one."

"Yes." Charlotte got up from the chair. "Enjoy your morning with John."

"He hits the water at five a.m. I'm going to take along a thermos of coffee and a good attitude and be sitting on the dock when he gets there."

"It's going to be the best birthday he's had in years. I told him I'd serve him breakfast at Fred's around nine. He wants bacon and eggs. Would you prefer waffles? With fresh strawberries? I'm leaning that way."

"Sure."

"Try to have fun this morning."

"As long as I don't fall into the lake trying to step from the dock to the boat, I should be fine."

Charlotte laughed. "See you later, Ellie." She left her friend to get ready for the day.

Bishop stepped out of the passenger side of Charlotte's truck. They were in an older part of Graham Enterprises, near the boundary with the family land. Threatened rain had faded, leaving a partly cloudy sky. Charlotte pulled out a jacket from behind her seat. "John will be free in an hour — Ellie's visiting and he's seeing her off. But if you don't mind trusting my sense of direction, there's no need to wait on him. He knows where we'll be. He's in a good mood — this time I only slightly burnt the bacon for his birthday breakfast, and thanks to Fred, I gave him a very old autographed baseball, which he very much liked."

Bryce smiled. She was trying to keep a light touch to the conversation this morning, but he wasn't going to be much help on that score. "I'll trust you on it, Charlotte."

She tugged on the jacket. "It can be cool inside. Fred called this the blue berm, after the color of paint that dominates the walls." She opened doors and led the way into the berm, locking the doors behind them. It looked very much like the berm for vault five, except for the blue-painted walls rather than gray.

She stopped at the twelfth metal door and opened it, turned on lights. "We go down a level now."

She pushed aside two crates, and he helped her pry up a panel in the floor. A ladder disappeared downward into the darkness. She turned on more lights, and it became as bright as daylight below them. "There are easier but longer ways to the lower level. This is the most direct route." She took the ladder down.

A brightly lit hall ran both directions, and she headed left. She walked almost a hundred yards past a line of doors, then stopped and tapped on one. "Here's vault nineteen."

She unlocked the door and flipped a light switch. It looked remarkably like a room from vault five, filled with metal shelves, neatly stacked shotgun rolls of coins and tubes of coins organized by type. Only here Bryce couldn't see the far end of the room, only lines of shelves like a library.

"This room goes about sixty feet straight back. We're now under the next berm. John thinks this was actually a cold food storage room when this was an active military base. Old freezers and some of the cooling plant are still down here."

She turned on more lights. Bryce stopped

to count the rolls on one shelf, to multiply by the shelves he could see, and then simply stopped counting.

"This is vault nineteen. Vault twenty-two is a room roughly this size and looks very much like this. And then there is this." Charlotte opened a side door and switched on a light. "The fifteen hundred coins you've bought, plus group four at the house — these are the rest of them."

The shelves were lined with coin boxes. "You think eight thousand in total?"

"Yes. If I can trust the inventory sheets, one of the coins you mentioned you would most like to own, the 1838 half-dollar minted in New Orleans, is in here some-where."

He stopped by a shelf and carefully picked up three coins at random. A 1798 Small Eagle silver dollar in Very Fine condition, an 1804 Draped Bust quarter in Extremely Fine, and a 1853 half dime without arrows in Fine. Nineteen thousand dollars' worth of coins, pricing conservatively.

"This is all the coins, Bryce. No more surprises."

He smiled, wondering how she thought that might make this sit easier. He was look-ing at more inventory in coins than he thought might exist with any collector in the country. *I need wisdom, Lord, and good judgment,* he prayed, looking around the room. This was going to take every bit of his skill, knowledge, and expertise. He turned to Charlotte. "Let's go back to Fred's house. We need to talk."

Charlotte nodded. She turned off lights, relocked doors, and led them back through the berm to the surface.

She brought him a cheeseburger she'd fixed, along with fries, and took a seat across from him with a matching plate for herself. The card table wobbled a bit as her foot hit the leg. It was early for lunch, but he'd realized she was looking for an excuse to stay busy and said yes to the offer.

"You've been quiet," she noted.

"Just thinking, Charlotte." He picked up the cheeseburger. "You're firmly decided on selling them?"

"Yes. I want to sell the coins and give the money away."

He studied her, trying to gauge her thinking. "Because wealth is a threat?"

"My sister sees it that way. Money is a threat to her marriage, to her girls. I'm not that fond of it myself in quantities more than I need. It's a headache to manage. And it's a ransom waiting to happen for someone who knows I've got that kind of cash around, and given my history . . . well, I'm never going to sleep easily. I want to sell the coins and give the money away. The majority of it, anyway. I could use another rather large giving list from you."

He thought she looked overwhelmed. In control, trying to be confident, but just on the edge of overwhelmed. He didn't like the look of it on her. He guessed it had been a few months since she last stood in that large vault of coins and felt the full reality of what Fred had left her.

She'd worked a plan to this point with good tactics. From that first contact in Bishop Chicago's parking lot, that first group of coins, through each new group to now she'd laid a path to get him to this point and the answer she needed. He was beginning to seriously admire the woman even if he was the one being led to where she wanted him to go. "I'll talk to Ann on how best to sell them, and I'll get you another giving list, Charlotte."

She visibly relaxed. "Thanks."

"I like a challenge." And wasn't that an understatement? He added ketchup next to his fries. "Why did Fred leave them to you rather than equally with your sister, or to the charities of his choosing?"

"I think this was his version of an apology. That he didn't know he had a granddaughter in trouble, didn't know there was a ransom demand for my freedom. He felt guilty that he wasn't there when I was sixteen. My sister met him first — she was easier to find — and Fred mentioned he had family wealth. She refused to let him see her girls or name her in his will. She wanted nothing to do with the man who could have ended what happened to us had he originally acknowledged our mom, had he been in our lives when we were young girls. Tabitha's still angry with him, even after his death."

"Yet you forgave him."

"I forgave him. He was an old man, and reality couldn't be changed. I didn't want his money, Bryce, but I would have broken his heart if I had also refused. We're the last of his family. I'll keep enough that my sister and I won't need to worry about the occasionally costly problem that appears in our lives, but I'm not going to turn us into people who watch the money in the bank as our career."

"John could manage the cash for you."

"Already tried that. He said no, in rather more emphatic terms. Ellie is back and forth about it, but basically agrees there's no reason to keep most of it, so I might as well give it away now. She'll manage what I decide to keep, as she enjoys the bookkeeping, but I won't ask more from her than that." She dipped one of her fries into his ketchup. "You're in, Bishop? No matter how long this takes?"

"I don't know whether it's the best decision for you to make, but yes. I can get you through the process of selling the coins and giving away the cash." He leaned back in the folding chair. "One thing in return?"

"Okay. What?"

"Have dinner with me — my place — every week or so."

Her hand, reaching another fry for his ketchup, froze midair. Her gaze caught his. "Why?"

"Because I like you. Because you terrify me and interest me at the same time. Because this is going to get complicated in ways I can only guess at before it is over, and we'll need a regular time to talk it through. Because when these coins are finally sold you're going to be gone again to wherever you end up with your art. I'd like to seize some time with you while I have it."

She blinked. "You're thinking you can fix me."

"You don't need fixing. You survived.

You'll get things straightened out with God eventually, because it matters to you, matters to Him. And you'll sort out what you want in your future once you're past closing this estate."

"We might manage to become actual friends, Bryce. There won't be more than that."

"Maybe not. But I'm safe, Charlotte."

"I'm single by choice, Bishop."

"Choice or circumstances?" He shrugged. "Anyway, that's what I want. Dinner at my place every week or so. In return I'll help you figure out how to give away sixty million in a way that values every dime you give."

She considered him. "That's a lot more daunting problem than selling the coins."

"Oh, yeah."

She swiped more of his ketchup. "Are you a good cook?"

"Passable to good."

"I like food. Not much talent for it, but I enjoy it."

"Then we'll have evenings with some good food and some conversation. I'll make a list so I don't repeat the menu very often."

"Pizza, lasagna, a nice steak."

Bryce laughed at her hopeful tone. "I can probably manage those to start the list."

"Okay, Bishop. I'll do dinner occasionally. How do you want to start with the coins?"

"Silence has been the best security for decades. Let's try to keep it that way. I'll start with photos, make a trip back to Chicago to talk with Ann. She's the best secret keeper I know." He looked over, considered her. "But you would come in a close second. There are a few more days of existing work to wrap up," he went on. "I've got vault five to finish, and there's the group four coins you're gathering at the house. It makes sense to clear those first before we open this Pandora's box."

"I can give you some time, help in the vault."

Bryce smiled. "Thanks, but I formally give you permission to not think about coins for a while. You've got your hands full else-where. Finish up the storage units and odds and ends the Graham family tucked away around Graham Enterprises. John and I can work this project for a bit."

Charlotte nodded. "I'm going to accept before you change your mind. Give me darts, bowling pins, and two thousand skeet balls over coins any day."

Bryce laughed. "Are those the latest discoveries? Where did they find all this stuff?"

"Fred's dad — my great-grandfather — actually advertised himself as 'The last buyer you need to call.' Once warehouses started to be standardized with pallets, forklifts, and cargo containers, all the odd-sized berm storage units on the property just became unwanted space, too awkward for most companies to want to lease. The Graham family was happy to take them over for personal storage. This place is huge, and they put stuff everywhere. It turns out they just didn't feel a need to keep good records of what they stored where."

"You're sure there are no more coins?"

"Ninety-five percent sure. Fred was definite about the location of the safes, the vaults, the inventory sheets — he would repeat himself as if a list was running through his head that he had memorized. And we've opened all the units now, at least briefly. There are probably twenty percent we've glanced in, written down boxes and crates, and closed the doors to come back to it later. I've found some old logbooks that indicate Fred's dad bought a bunch of model trains. It's that kind of item I'm hoping to still find. But I don't think I'll find more coins."

"Then focus on those items, Charlotte, and let me worry about the coins."

■ ■ ■ ■

Bryce watched Ann sort through the pictures he had taken of vaults nineteen and twenty-two. There was too much cop in her, even after retiring, for him to tell what she was thinking.

"How much is she asking?"

"Thirty-two million for the eight thousand individual coins, twenty-eight million for the rest. That includes the first three groups and the vault five coins I've already bought."

"Sixty million for everything?"

"Yes."

Ann barely blinked at the number. "She's been underpricing the individual coins by, what, thirty percent, based on the three groups you've bought and sold so far?"

"It fluctuates around that."

Ann went back to thinking. Several minutes passed. "She's underpricing the rest of the coins by about fifty percent."

"Fifty — you're serious?"

She looked up, nodded, and tapped the top photo. "Do you know how rare this is? A truly untouched, very old hoard of common coins? They didn't even consider die errors to be worth collecting in the thirties. Nor did they care about where a coin was minted, just the year. It wasn't until the fifties that collecting every mint location became a serious focus for collectors. You're looking at a collection that could yield more keys and semi-keys per roll than anything that has come to market in decades."

She handed him back the photos. "The value of this purchase isn't in the individual eight thousand coins, as rare and valuable as they are. The real money is in common coins. I'd put fair value at forty-two million for the eight thousand individual coins, and an equal forty-two million for the rest. I think she's asking sixty million for what is an eighty-four-million-dollar coin collection."

Bryce absorbed that. "A sizable spread."

"Too large to be fair."

Bryce steepled his fingers, mentally running the numbers. "A twenty percent spread is more reasonable, so bring the purchase price up to sixty-seven million two. The critical factor being how underpriced she is on the rolls. How certain are you she's underpricing fifty percent rather than thirty percent?"

"There are no rolls in that inventory list dated after 1930. No silver Washington quarters, no Benjamin Franklin half-dollars. Silver was such a key store of wealth in the

Depression once gold became illegal to hold that there would have been an accumulation of at least Washington thirty-twos. Vault five had some Franklin half-dollars, some rolls from the thirties and forties. That is the newer hoard. This is the older one. And it's four times as large."

"Telling."

"Very. This collection was probably intact at the time of the crash of 1929, may have been bought as a single acquisition — a major coin dealer who had to liquidate. That would explain the wide scope of those eight thousand coins and the sheer size of the hoard."

Bryce nodded. "That fits what I know about this family."

"It would have been expensive, even at distressed prices. I don't know what inflation would imply running this back in time — maybe a few million in '29?"

Bryce started thinking out loud. "Maybe use a buyer syndicate for the common coins, but the higher-grade individuals — the eight thousand — I continue to buy in groups of five hundred every thirty days. Charlotte would make closer to seventy million, and I wouldn't need to raise as much cash, as I could use the cash flow as coins sell. I've bought the vault five coins for five million six, there's three million left in what I've raised so far, so I'd need to raise another twenty-five million."

"I've got a name."

"Who do you have in mind?"

"Kevin Cooper, retired shortstop for the Atlanta Braves, now The Pizza King for his nationwide franchise of pizza shops. This is right up his alley. It's an illiquid investment with a good return and solid management already in place. His floor on investments is ten million. Knowing Cooper, he'll do the full twenty-five if you let him. The coins are solid collateral. He'll take my word on the price being fair."

Bryce blinked. "I don't know what to say, Ann."

She smiled. "I'll set up a meeting for you with Cooper. Next Friday work for you? I already have plans with his wife for that day. He'll appreciate an excuse to step away from the office."

"And I thought the money raising would be the hard part of this."

Ann smiled. "With this kind of cache? You've got an investment that's a once-in-a-lifetime opportunity. Money isn't a problem."

"Can we scale what you're doing with vault five to handle this?"

"We hire eight to ten more people who are really good at coins, an equal number to handle the packaging, add some more space — we can multiply the volume. This quality of coins at these prices, you won't have a problem attracting buyers to take even this amount of inventory."

"You signed up for a few weeks. I'd guess this is going to take a year."

"I'll talk to Paul, but provisionally I'm staying in. I can manage the prep room without having to be on-site every day."

"Thanks, Ann."

"I'm going to enjoy this. What did Devon say about the individual coins?"

"He choked on his soda and asked me to repeat the number. Sharon laughed, then started to cry. I figure Bishop Chicago will be able to buy about twelve million to hold for its own inventory. I'll let Devon do that buying. Then I'm going to sell Devon and Sharon fifty-one percent of Bishop Chicago so that when this is done, I won't have to look at another coin for a few years beyond the ones in my pocket change."

"A wise man." Ann considered him. "What did you do to end up with a year like this? Were you praying for something in particular, Bryce?"

He smiled. Trust Ann to get to the heart

of it. "I was bored. I probably mentioned that to God a time or two."

"That's a rather dangerous prayer in my experience. You won't be bored now."

Bryce settled back in the chair, feeling much of the stress flowing away. With Ann continuing to help manage this, Devon on the individual coins, and if she was right about Kevin Cooper being willing to fund the purchase — the risks to doing the deal were fading quickly. "Charlotte wants to give most of the money away."

Ann smiled. "Good for her. How's she doing?"

"I'd say she's relieved her plan to hook me worked."

Ann laughed. "You didn't know you were swimming in chum the whole time."

"I thought vault five was the catch. It was in fact the bait." Bryce thought about that and smiled. "Charlotte's got me selling her coins and helping her give away the cash, which is the answer she wanted before we ever met for the first time. And she curved the path so it was my decision to opt in for both. I have to admire that about her. This was a carefully played plan from the start. So it begs the question — is today the end of that successful plan or just another chapter of it?"

"Think she would tell you if you asked?"

"No."

Ann smiled. "Then enjoy the present. If nothing else, the situation is interesting."

"Charlotte's interesting. The situation is kind of a hit-your-thumb-with-a-hammer-and-ask-did-that-hurt kind of moment. I have never seen so many, never imagined so many coins as are in those vaults."

Ann tilted her head. "I didn't see that, Bryce. That you're nervous. You're in deep water, deep enough to seem like it's over your head — so you swim your way out of this or drown."

"Basically."

"You needed a challenge, my friend. You just got one. You need this, Bryce, as much as Charlotte needs you to solve the problem for her. You won't be the same once it's over."

"I'll agree with you there. I'm not going to be the same after this experience."

FOURTEEN

Bryce was wiping off his hands when he heard the doorbell. Charlotte was early for their first dinner. He walked through his home to the front, pulled open the door to see her impatiently half turned away, a shopping bag in one hand and her phone in the other. He forced his smile to stay in place. "Welcome, Charlotte. Have any trouble finding the place?" He reached out and put a hand on her arm before she could walk back down the steps.

"None. Why don't you wave to John, who's pretending not to be tailing me? Your nine o'clock."

She wasn't annoyed at him. Bryce glanced over, spotted John's black SUV, and felt immediate concern. John didn't tail because everything was fine.

"As if I really need someone to make sure I don't get lost around Princeton Circle. My grandmother lived on this street."

Bryce ignored her complaint and eased her inside past him. "Stay put. I'll be right back." He closed the door firmly with her inside.

The driver's window lowered as he approached. "She's going to be in a snippy mood with you tonight for that last bit," John mentioned.

"She'll get over it. What's up?"

John simply handed him a photo. "Richard Sill. You see him, you plant yourself between the two of them. I don't know if he's in Chicago."

"Will do."

"Five aliases on the back, and it's probably changed again. He earned some reward money back eighteen years ago, giving cops tips on where they could find her. One of those tips indirectly led to them really finding her. I've never been satisfied — I don't think the FBI has either — about how he knew wrong information that was just enough right to be eventually useful."

Bryce burned the guy's image into his brain. "Okay."

"He's written her in the last month, care of her sister. A lot of mail has come over the years via that avenue, and her sister is smart enough to have a security firm simply intercept all the mail so neither of them ever sees it. They send it to me. Richard is looking for a thank-you for helping her out back then that suggests ten thousand today would be a kindness, as his luck has been rough lately."

"Charming."

"He's done this before. Last time he showed up in person at Tabitha's home, hoping to collect his thank-you money from her. The thing is, this guy has fixated on Charlotte for so long he's the one guy who likely would recognize her on the street at a glance if their paths happen to cross somehow. I don't like this guy's history of being lucky enough to be in that wrong place. Until someone I've got out looking puts eyes on him and tells me where he's at, she's got a close tail."

"You should tell her."

John shook his head. "Long ago Charlotte and I made a simple agreement. I say I've got an active threat, her mouth shuts, she does everything I say, no questions, no hesitation. Anything else that bothers me — that's less than that active threat — I deal with however I see fit, but without her. She can be as annoyed as she likes, spout off all she likes. We do our own thing. But you'll notice your front door still hasn't opened, and when she realized I was on a close tail, she was standing on your porch with her phone open in her hand and two numbers of 911 dialed. She won't willfully undermine what's going on. She'll just be annoyed that I'm being John on her again."

"What's an active threat?"

"I hand her a gun and tell her to shoot whoever walks through the door."

Bryce opened the front door of his home mentally braced for Charlotte to be waiting. The foyer was empty. Her shoes were in the middle of the rug, and the sack she had been carrying was resting on the bottom step of the staircase.

"Charlotte?"

She appeared from the direction of his kitchen. She was carrying the bowl of cheese popcorn. "You two were having a long chat."

"He's just being John."

She blinked, then laughed. "I use pretty much those exact words, but mine have a more exasperated air and tossed-up hands accompanying them."

"You're fine. He had a pho—"

She raised her hand to cut him off mid-word, wiped the back of her hand across her mouth to deal with cheese dust. "I'll ask if I want to know. I don't want to know. If I knew the problem, I'd just be bugging him for updates. He's already doing whatever he has decided needs to be done. After eighteen years of this, I think I've earned the right to stay in the dark."

"Okay." He took a handful of the popcorn from the bowl. "So how was your day?"

"I had this evening dinner appointment I was supposed to go to, and it threw off my concentration the entire day. I had to change clothes like four times."

He blinked, trying to catch up to the fact he was hearing humor, bad humor, but she was trying. "I like the final choice."

She'd found a striking dress that did a nice job of reminding him why she was dangerous, and a silk black ribbon to tie back her hair. The bare feet failed to tone down the impression of it.

"I've been wandering around. I like your house. It has furniture."

He laughed. "Rather too much of it I think at times, but all of it comfortable. Much of it has been in the family for a lot of years."

She nodded to the sack she'd brought. "I was told housewarming gifts were the thing to do. That's for you. I'd hand it to you, but no way I'm giving up cheese popcorn to give you a badly wrapped gift. I fail miserably at straight edges."

He reached for the sack and took out the

package, felt a picture frame under the wrapping paper. "Can I open it now?"

"Sure."

He tore off the wrapping paper and caught his breath. Bishop Chicago. She'd drawn his storefront from the perspective of across the street, caught Devon and Sharon walking hand in hand on the way in to work. The store display was accurate for last week's specials on early-date half-dollars. "It's wonderful, Charlotte."

"I have very few talents in life. But I can draw."

"How did — ?"

"I snapped a photo, worked from memory. It's a little flat — it lacks the smaller details that make a scene feel authentic — but I wasn't able to linger and see what else caught my attention."

"Quit criticizing," he murmured. He balled up the wrapping paper. "I'm going to go get a hammer and nail."

He decided the sketch deserved the attention of all his guests, so he took the drawing to the front hallway and stood by the front door to look around. He selected a wall, used approximate eye level as a guide, placed the nail so he'd be looking down a few inches, and glanced at her. She'd taken a seat on the staircase to watch him. "You can comment."

"I didn't say anything."

"Thought it."

"In the summer afternoons when you open the front door, the sun hits that wall. Your guests will see a beautifully reflected sunlight on glass rather than the sketch."

"Excellent point." He stepped back to consider other options. Chose another wall, looked at her for approval, and drove the nail. He carefully hung the sketch and stepped back to admire it. She really did beautiful work. "Thank you, Charlotte."

"You're welcome."

He glanced over at her. "I had in mind feeding you something better than half a bowl of cheese popcorn."

"I've still got my appetite. I missed lunch due to all the clothing changes required for this evening."

He reached for her hand, grinned. "You're not going to get me to say anything more than I like the results. You don't need more compliments at the moment; you need some real food. Come on back to the kitchen. Pizza is in the oven. I was working on the salad when you arrived."

He picked up where he had left off, cutting tomatoes. The pizza cheese was bubbling, and the kitchen smelled good.

"The photos are your family?"

He glanced over his shoulder at the refrigerator covered in snapshots. "Yes."

"Do they come here or do you go visit them?"

"Mostly I go. This house isn't very kid-proof. But someone tends to drop by every week or so, or I find excuses to drop by their homes." He shrugged. "When family lives in the area, it's just part of the flow of life."

She turned the vase of flowers on the counter. He watched her finger one of the petals but didn't say anything. Telling her they were for her would just add a layer to the evening she likely wasn't ready for. "Want to put those on the table?" he suggested. He'd decide later if he would mention she should take them home with her. "What else have you been up to today?"

She took the flowers over to the table. "The group four coins are now at the store. I'm at three million two."

"I'll write you a check."

"You don't want to go look at them first?"

"The first three groups are averaging a profit of thirty percent. I'm not going to quibble with your pricing."

He sliced the last carrot and used the knife to scrape it off the cutting board into the bowl. It added nice color. He'd gone skimpy on the cucumbers and mushrooms since they weren't his favorites. Pizza and a salad, brownies for dessert. He'd spent the better part of a week figuring out how to keep this evening simple and informal.

He refilled her glass. "The last of the vault five coins went up for sale today."

"So this is a celebration meal. You're ready to tackle the big vaults."

"It is. I've got the signed lease on my desk for more prep space, Chapel will have his security work done in a week, and I'm hiring people. First of the month I plan to bring the first shipment of coins to Chicago."

"Thanks, Bishop."

"Sure you don't want the other check today?"

A check for twenty-eight million was in his office safe, waiting his signature. He'd buy the large volume of coins, and she'd continue to sell him the individual coins in groups of five hundred every thirty days. Ann had been right about Kevin Cooper. He'd wanted to fund the entire syndication share himself.

Charlotte shook her head. "I'll take the check the week you start moving the coins. An earthquake might happen in the next few days and bury them."

He laughed. "Worrywart. Have you re-laxed at all since Fred told you about the coins?"

She half smiled. "Life was simpler before I had a grandfather."

"Check out the cupboards for me, would you? See what I've got for salad dressings and choose what you'd like. I bought new."

She opened the long cupboard, pulled out a ranch dressing and set it on the counter.

"I thought you were going to bring your sketchbook with you."

She looked over her shoulder. "I thought you were joking."

"I'm planning to eat pizza and watch a ball game. The only business we need to talk through tonight is what you want to do with the next thirty million. We can have that conversation during commercials."

She laughed. "Sure we can." She set a French dressing beside the other one. "I'd like to keep doing what we've been doing. You give me a page of ideas, I look it over and fund the page or not."

"You can't abdicate the decision making."

"I'm signing the checks, so I'm making the final decisions."

"Food pantries. Animal shelters. What else interests you?"

"Those are the core ones. I'll give you the

checkbook registry, and you can see what I've done for the last few years."

She set a third salad dressing on the counter, this one a Caesar. "I want to give so carefully no one even notices a wave. Existing organizations, not new ones, places with a clear mission statement and goals, a passion for their work, integrity in their finances, stable staffs."

"You've given this some thought."

"The broad strokes. How much to give, specifically where, and when, so the gifts are helpful but aren't being noticed as excessive — that's your problem, please. It's been a challenge to give away a few million quietly. I don't know how to approach doing sixty million in a year. I'd like you to figure that out. I don't want this to take three to five years. Sell the coins and give away the money."

He picked up his glass, drank half of it, considered her. "Do you like to give?"

"No. I just like to keep it even less."

"I actually understood that distinction."

"Where are the plates?"

"Second cabinet to your right."

The oven timer went off. He pulled out the pizza. "There's probably a sketchbook around here somewhere that one of the kids left behind."

"I'm a snob about paper. I like a nice, heavyweight, hot-pressed paper — something sturdy and smooth to the touch — and archival grade so it's not going to yellow in the next hundred years."

Bryce smiled. "You've got a favorite brand?"

"There's a place in New England called Traverse that stocks paper from different manufacturers, and you can buy for the year of production as well as the brand. The year the paper was made actually can make a difference." She carried two plates to the table. "Silverware?"

"Right-hand drawer next to the dishwasher."

She pulled open the drawer. "Arches makes a hot-pressed watercolor paper that's sturdy and forgiving — it's what I toss in my bag if I'm just walking around to see what I happen to notice that day. I love Stonehenge 2006 when I'm working at the drafting table — it's a bit soft for the surface, but I can make the details almost photo-like. The Strathmore Bristol Plate Finish from 2004 is my all-around favorite paper when I'm doing a sketch where I can take my time. It's the smoothest of the papers and it doesn't step forward and interfere with my pencils or pen." She

231

stopped, smiled. "Bet you're sorry you asked."

"A sketch artist who didn't care about her paper would surprise me more."

"I'm kind of the same about my pencils and pens."

Bryce laughed. "Expected that."

They fixed themselves their salads, lifted slices of sizzling pizza from the hot stone, and took the meal over to the table.

"I've not been over to the Dance and Covey Gallery yet," Bryce told her. "My apologies. I've been a bit busy, thanks to you. But I plan to change that fact soon."

"I think you'll enjoy it," Charlotte assured him. "You'll find hundreds of my framed sketches at prices that make me wince. Six of Marie's oil paintings, five on loan from their owners, one on display pending being priced for sale. I'm guessing Ellie will price it around eight million. Marie and I are an odd combination for a gallery's exclusive artists, but it works. The main hall show-cases whatever artist Covey has brought in to feature for the month.

"Ellie manages the business affairs for Marie and me for the art we create. Covey deals with the rest of the artists and the business of the gallery. It leaves Ellie free to do whatever traveling she wants, be at the gallery when she wants. Covey gets a partner to help keep the business profitable while still running the gallery as his. It's a good arrangement, has been a stable one for the last fourteen years."

Bryce got up for more pizza. "Why select a gallery in Chicago?"

"Just the way it happened to work out. We considered Texas, but both Marie's and my work is Midwest in its flavor. Ellie grew up about two hours south of here. The city is large enough it has a vibrant art community and can support a specialized gallery. Ellie knew Covey through her uncle. Covey's been in the business thirty-two years, and he's a guy with solid integrity. It works. This pizza isn't half bad, Bishop," she said as he slid another piece onto her plate.

"Not frozen, and there's no recipe, so don't ask me to repeat it. Every pizza I put together comes out different. But the sauce stays the same."

"I'm mildly impressed," Charlotte promised. "I'm not in Chicago very often," she continued, reverting back to the prior conversation, "and I'm rarely at the gallery. CRM is known as the artist who does interesting work but carefully keeps her privacy. Ellie has made that a feature rather than a drawback with collectors. Covey would recognize me, but I doubt his staff would know me by sight. Marie is the same — she's not one to make public appearances to sell her art. You can tell from the prices that it hasn't hurt her sales or reputation among collectors."

"You know her?"

Charlotte took another careful bite of the hot pizza. "I know her very well."

"Let me show you around outside while the evening light is still good." Bryce walked through the kitchen into the sunroom where he opened the French doors that led out onto the back patio.

Charlotte, carrying her glass with her, had stopped in the sunroom. She was looking down the length of the room with a stunned expression. "What is this, about forty feet?"

"They built the sunroom to run alongside the garage addition, so thirty-six feet by fourteen feet wide."

"Forget the room. I'm looking at all that gorgeous expanse of white wall and thinking of the art it's missing." She looked to the open French doors and the patio beyond him, laughed. "This just keeps getting better." She stepped out onto the paving stones. "This is like an oasis in the city."

"The woman who built this home bought

four lots. She planted the blue spruce trees around the perimeter knowing in twenty years they would create this sanctuary. Trees have been replaced over the decades as they age, but the concept has been kept. I get the benefit of her foresight."

The distant noise of traffic was a steady backdrop, along with some sounds of neighbors. But the backyard was white birch trees, some flowering shrubs, roses, against those year-round evergreens.

Charlotte rested her hand on the back of one of the patio chairs. "You must spend a lot of time out here."

"Not as much as it deserves." He nodded to the windows to their right. "But my home office looks out over the yard, so I get to enjoy the scenery. The birds consider it a safe haven and nest here in large numbers. I'm partial to the sparrows, oddly enough."

"This is why you bought this house."

"It is. The property will also appreciate in value faster than other homes in the neighborhood because of the yard and the oversized garage."

Charlotte laughed. "Always the businessman."

"I'm wired that way, so I'll say thanks for the compliment. I like the combination of practical decisions along with long-term thinking that drives most decisions I make. Life stays interesting that way."

Charlotte smiled. "I like that about you, Bryce."

Charlotte liked Bryce's living room. It was casual and well lived in, the couch and chairs chosen for comfort, the books on the shelves indicating the man probably read as much as he watched TV. She set her drink on a coaster on the coffee table and sank into the plush leather of a chair. "Good food, a comfortable chair . . . you're going to lose my attention."

Bryce turned on the TV and found the baseball game, set the volume on low, then took a seat on the couch. "You nod off, I'm not going to be offended."

"I won't, but thanks."

"There's a reason I want a few evenings of conversation with you," he mentioned, "and I was semi-serious when I suggested we could talk during commercials. I'd rather have you take a question, mull over your answer until the next commercial, and give me some depth to your answer, than simply give me the surface answer you think I want to hear."

"An interesting way to put it."

"So here's my first question. I need you

to think about the approach you want to take to your giving. Do you want a top-down approach with objectives, categories, and I find ways to give which express those objectives? Or do you want a micro approach, where the giving is lists of specific items to fund where the criteria are simply whether it's a useful gift?"

She picked up the paperweight on the table and idly shifted it from hand to hand as she considered him. "In order to ask me that question, you've already been thinking about how each approach might look. Can you describe what you're thinking?"

"The first approach is to focus on, say, three categories: extreme poverty, hunger in the U.S., supporting and developing vibrant churches. You would target funds to each priority through existing organizations that are already operating at scale. For extreme poverty relief, for example, ten million to Samaritan's Purse and ten million to World Vision. To address hunger, ten million divided up as five thousand to each of the existing major food pantry distribution hubs, and another ten million for program grants of fifty thousand each. To support and develop vibrant churches, ten million could go to the Willow Creek Association for developing church leadership worldwide, and another ten million spread across the hundred twenty-five evangelical churches averaging over a thousand in attendance. The sixty million gets deployed in ways that produces results but doesn't expand an organization or create a reliance on your continued funding."

Her hand holding the paperweight stilled. "I think I just heard your preferred plan for the cash. You've already thought this out."

"An enjoyable endeavor," Bryce offered. "It's one recommendation. It would take a few weeks to further refine the idea so the sixty million could be made even more effective. But the core approach is there. Your gifts would make a serious impact, and the decisions you would need to make are reasonably contained. I rather like it for its simplicity. But it's not necessarily the right approach for you."

His comment surprised her. "It's not?"

"Pardon me for saying it this way, but you're a single woman giving away a fortune. You might not need this cash yourself, but whether it's sixty dollars or sixty million, you're making a sacrifice in giving away the money. Thirty years from now, looking back, you might feel better knowing more about who you've helped. No matter the amount involved, this is a personal gift."

He pointed to the folder on the coffee table. "Option two is the micro approach. A food pantry in Denver needs eight thousand for a used van. A group called Clean Water Today is raising funds to drill a well in Nierra, South Africa. Micro is when you fund very specific needs. And if they need four thousand, you don't give them five. You find another specific need for the other thousand."

He considered her for a moment. "Charlotte, I can give you a businessman's advice and plan for what to do — nice, neat, organized, and it will accomplish a lot of good. Or I can give you specifics until the sixty million is given away. Either way, you should think like a treasurer, for that's what this is. A treasure to disperse."

She set the paperweight back on the table. "It would be an extraordinary amount of work to find sixty million in micro needs rather than allocate the funds to organizations and let them work down to the line-by-line decisions."

"It's more time, but a lot more personal. That's the decision I need from you. How much do you want this to be hands-on giving, Charlotte?"

She shook her head again. "If you're helping find the micro ideas, it's your time too, far more than mine."

"Your cash. Your decision."

She leaned her head back against the chair cushion. "Let's watch a few innings of the ball game. This is not an easy question, Bryce."

"Take your time and ponder it. The Mets are playing tonight, and it should be a good game." He reached for the remote and turned up the volume.

She took an hour to think about it. "I like the idea of knowing who was helped with the money."

He muted the commercial and turned to face her. "Then micro it is."

"Can you come up with that many specific needs to fund?"

"We'll find out." He reached for the folder of micro ideas. "There are a few ways to organize it. Let's try this." He handed it to her. "I'd like you to remove any ideas that don't appeal to you, put a check mark on pages you're okay with, and put a question mark on items you want to think about further. I'll check out the organizations' financials and staff before you make a donation."

She accepted the folder and flipped through the pages, nodded. "I can do that."

"Having a page of items to write checks from has worked well so far, so we'll continue to do that. I'll put together that page each week. It would be wise to order checks that can run through the printer so all you need to do is sign them. If the average gift is five thousand dollars, we're looking at twelve thousand checks over the next year."

"I'll mention it to Ellie." She found a pen and took the first page from the folder to read.

"You're welcome to take that folder with you to review."

"I'll do it now. I want to finish the game."

"I didn't know you liked baseball. I thought you were humoring me."

"Watching a Mets game — I'm humoring you. But when you see the sketches at the Dance and Covey Gallery, you'll realize I've probably watched more sports than even some sports reporters. You want a good penned sketch, give me a live sporting event."

"You don't like to be cooped up inside."

She shrugged. "I get restless. I like a crowd, and something to sketch. A friendly competition fits the need beautifully, so I gravitate to sporting events."

She started reading.

Bryce watched the game, occasionally her,

as she worked through the folder. She wasn't skimming items; she was reading and thinking through each possibility. He felt himself relax. He could give her good advice, options, but the decisions needed to be those she was comfortable with. She'd give him that.

The scope of what she had entrusted to him had begun to settle in over the last several days. Sixty million in gifts. He'd see to it that every dollar was given away with care and prayer. He owed her that, for the privilege of being able to be a part of what she was doing. She was giving the money away because she had concluded she didn't need it, wouldn't enjoy holding on to it, wouldn't like the responsibility of managing the wealth. He understood her reasons, but he admired the decision all the same. She had a generous heart. He tucked that knowledge beside the fact she was an artist.

He was slowly figuring out who she was when he looked beyond what had happened to her, and he liked what he was finding.

FIFTEEN

Bryce found the work took on a rhythm. He would make two trips a week to Graham Enterprises to haul pallets of coins from the vault back to Chicago, spend most of his day at the coin-sorting room working with Ann, stop in late in the day at Bishop Chicago to talk with Devon about the higher-priced individual coins, and then head home. Charlotte would meet him in Chicago every ten days or so for dinner, to review ideas he'd pulled together for places to contribute, to sign checks. She'd stay the night at Ellie's, then head to her stores in Cincinnati or St. Paul with another load of items to sell. She was emptying out the storage bunkers at a faster pace than he was getting through the coins, but they were both making progress.

Their fifth dinner and evening together, the baseball game was tied one to one going into the seventh inning stretch when Bryce followed Charlotte into his kitchen, by unspoken agreement both looking for something to snack on.

Charlotte opened his cupboard and looked at options. She was barefoot. He found it oddly fascinating to realize her tan ended in a nice U across the top of her foot. She wasn't one to wear sandals, but she apparently often wore deck shoes. "What are we having?"

She pulled out a bag of tortilla chips. "Nachos."

He got a bag of grated cheese from the bottom drawer of the refrigerator. "Chips, cheese, microwave, eat a layer, add more cheese, heat again."

She popped open the salsa jar. "We agree on the nacho recipe."

He fixed a plate of chips and cheese and put it in the microwave for a minute twenty seconds. She dumped the salsa in a bowl and moved around the counter to pull out a stool. She tugged the chip bag over and dipped one into the salsa while she waited.

The timer dinged. Bryce pulled the plate of nachos out and set it on a counter between them. She went for one with the most melted cheese and folded another chip over it to lift it. He worked from the edge of the plate toward the center. He'd forgotten how much he liked simple nachos.

He ate another chip and glanced over at Charlotte. The conversation he'd been thinking about for weeks needed to be opened and it seemed like now was the moment. *Jesus, is this the right time?* He thought the prayer quietly while he ate another nacho. Her fifth visit. She'd either shut him down hard or she would be willing to listen — he had no clue which it would be. He picked up a napkin. "Can we talk about God, Charlotte, and what you said in the car about God's willingness to forgive the men who hurt you?"

She shot him a look that wasn't encouraging. "Why?"

"Because I know the topic hurts you, and the only way I know to help is to bring it up."

"I didn't ask for your help."

"I know. But I'm not one to ignore a problem, and I'm a guy who considers God to be very important. I'm going to keep coming back to this subject until we can have a conversation. So it's to your own benefit to have it tonight so the topic doesn't keep coming up. I'm not asking you to change what you think, just to have the conversation."

She sighed and pushed away the plate.

"You know how to kill a good nacho plate."

"Sorry."

"Not as sorry as I am." She walked to the far counter to get the pitcher of raspberry tea. She brought a glass of ice and the pitcher back and settled onto the stool. "Ten minutes, Bryce. Because after that I don't want the topic brought up again unless I choose to introduce it."

"Fair enough." He glanced at the clock. She'd be literal about it.

He got himself a glass and ice and passed it to her to fill, then leaned against the counter, cradling the drink in his hands. "You said God was too willing to forgive. That you didn't know if you wanted anything to do with a God who would give a second chance to the men who hurt you. I'm remembering it correctly?"

She nodded, not meeting his gaze.

"I want to agree with you. My instincts, my gut, everything in me tells me you're right. God goes too far when He offers the men who hurt you a way out. They could have repented, asked God's forgiveness, and they would have received a clean slate and heaven, even after what they did."

Charlotte studied the glass in her hand. "I hear the *but* coming."

"Christianity isn't fair, Charlotte. That's

246

the source of your pain. Christianity isn't fair, but it is what we need. Grace so scandalous we can never get beyond its reach to forgive." She was listening, and Bryce was relieved she was offering him at least that.

"God's forgiveness wouldn't have removed the consequences of what they did. Repentance would have meant accepting responsibility, coming forward, pleading guilty, facing life in prison or even the death penalty if that's what the court deemed necessary. Forgiveness for what they had done to you would, however, have removed God's judgment from resting on them through eternity. Forgiven, they would have a place in heaven.

"I understand the pain and frustration you feel at that truth. They hurt you and yet they get that second chance. But the Bible says God doesn't want anyone to perish — to be eternally separated from Him. So He offers even those who do terrible harm the extraordinary grace of forgiveness if they will ask Him."

Bryce wished he could leave it there, for the rest of what he had to say was where the deep pain rested, and she was going to flinch when he said it, but he couldn't help her if he didn't open the door. He took a deep breath and exhaled. "And I know,

Charlotte, that's only the top layer of what's going on." He reached out and brushed her hand with his, wanting to offer the contact, wishing he could make this not hurt so much.

"God offered them that second chance because He loved them," he said quietly, and saw and felt her flinch. "That's the core pain you feel, as much as anything you've put into words. They hurt you. God shouldn't get to love both them and love you. He should have to choose. So maybe they do get forgiven, but He isn't supposed to love them. He's supposed to love you first and most. Yet Jesus loved the men so much He died to take their punishment on himself, and He held out to them extraordinary grace to fully forgive what they had done."

He reached over to carefully wipe a tear away. The emotion she was trying to contain devastated him. "I am sorry, so sorry, that evil touched you like it did when you were sixteen. But God never stopped loving you, Charlotte. He didn't choose them over you. To this day He loves you.

"God is good. Really good. But that good-ness means He has the capacity of offering a second chance even to those who have done evil. You need to accept that fact if you're going to find peace with God. We all do. It's part of who He is. God deeply loves you, Charlotte. Trust that."

She swiped a forearm across her face. "Do you . . . do you think you could stop talking now?" She took a broken breath as she fought fresh tears, then walked away toward the powder room.

Bryce leaned his head on the counter, then silently punched the silverware drawer, knowing he'd just made things worse. How many times had he run that conversation in his head? He'd mangled it.

"Don't hurt anymore, Charlotte. Please," he whispered, knowing the hurt tonight was going to be his fault. *Jesus, I need help with a heart I just busted. How can I help get it back together?* Was there anything worse than knowing he was the one who'd caused her to cry?

He dumped the remaining nachos into the trash. He had no answer for why God had let her awful tragedy happen. God loved her. He had allowed those four years. God could have stopped it. He didn't do so. Every statement true. Bryce couldn't reconcile those facts for himself and had no way to help Charlotte do so. She either accepted that God loved her and made peace with Him over the mystery of why He had let it happen or she would remain buried under the terrible grief of believing that because He didn't protect her, He didn't love her.

Bryce faced a painful fact about his own faith tonight, about his Christianity. It was easier to show that God loved the men who had done evil than it was to show God loved the innocent girl they had hurt. And wasn't that a mess? *I need to do better at the words, Jesus, for her sake as well as mine.*

Of everything he wanted to do in life, helping Charlotte heal was close to the top of his list. But all he'd managed to accomplish tonight was to cause her more pain and more tears.

Bryce slit the tape on the box of coins he'd carried over to the prep table, lifted out a dozen rolls of Liberty V nickels from 1883 to 1896. Ann had given him a searching look when he joined her but hadn't asked the question yet. He wondered if he'd chosen to work with Ann this morning precisely because he knew she would ask about Charlotte, and Ann was simply biding her time until they were alone.

He pulled on white cotton gloves and began to carefully open the paper on the rolls, laying the coins faceup for her. Ann sorted by date and grade, keeping pace with him, moving the coins to various display trays until there were fifty coins on a tray. She passed the tray on to the lady working farther down the table for the coins to be rerolled and the sort classification marked. The coins would be packaged five rolls to a box, listed for sale, and would likely have a buyer before the end of the day.

Bryce carefully flattened the paper to make sure no coin had been caught in a fold. "We're on pace to clear more than forty-six million on the common coins. At that total it's hard to imagine this, but do you think we're actually pricing too low? I'm never quite sure what to think when coins sell the first day they're listed."

"I know the feeling." Ann shook her head. "We're pricing for value, but not excessively so. Coins are flowing out at such a fast pace because fresh inventory is so hard to get. A couple months from now when we've saturated the immediate need, the pace of sales will slow. The sweet spot is a price that can sustain itself across the whole volume that's for sale. I think we've found it. We've got dealers repeat buying, so we're below market, but we're the ones who know the scope of what else is coming from the estate. We're going to be the market price in a few months. But we should be able to sell the entire group at these prices. That's going to maximize the overall total."

Ann pushed a coin his way. "This is why the buyers will keep coming back."

He picked up the nickel to see what she had noticed, realized he was holding a production error. The back had been stamped with a thirty-degree rotation from the front rather than aligned. "A five-hundred-dollar coin," he said.

"Yes." Ann slid it onto the tray with the others. "And someone's very welcome surprise when they look at the coins they bought."

"The value of not sorting out the specials. Everyone pays a bit more for each roll on the hope and dream they find that kind of surprise."

"And it's why you're on pace to clear more than forty-six million for the common coins," Ann told him. "You made a good buy, Bryce, for the syndicate, for Charlotte, and for every customer who orders coins. It's not often you can be fair to everyone involved, but this deal hit that sweet spot."

The coin sorting paused every two hours, a necessity in order to keep fresh eyes and energy on the details of the task. Bryce lingered by the coffee station with Ann, ate a donut just to have something in his hand.

"Everything okay, Bryce?"

"It will be when I fix it." He studied the coffee in his cup to avoid looking her direction. "I made Charlotte cry."

"Hit a raw edge?"

"Did it on purpose to get the subject on the table. But rather than begin to heal matters, I simply ripped the wound open again."

"You could try pink roses. Those worked for Paul with me."

He half smiled. "Charlotte might be the flowers type, but I don't know her well enough to know for certain. Bad mistake on my part."

"Have you called her?"

"She's on the road somewhere and turns off her phone when she's driving. I'm thinking I'll start with 'I'm sorry,' work my way to flowers and maybe a hot fudge sundae."

"That would work for me," Ann offered with a smile.

"Problem is, the conversation isn't over," Bryce said.

"Important subjects take time. I'm not going to ask which nerve you touched. The fact of the matter is you'll touch them all if the relationship is going to have a chance to become something serious."

"I'd like it to."

"Really?" Ann thought about that. "I'm

surprised."

"So am I. She's not my type, Ann. But I'd like her to be." He pondered the why of that and didn't have an answer. "We've spent several evenings together now — dinner, work through some giving ideas, watch a game — share a pleasant evening. She's even accepted those topics she would have preferred I never started. But she leaves at the end of the evening and it feels like I had only half her attention. She's preoccupied. I don't know if it's me or something else is going on."

"You haven't asked her?"

Bryce shook his head. "I've meddled enough in this woman's life. I'd rather not go pushing around into more corners of it for a while. I just want to apologize for the one I crossed into last night. I did it deliberately, I knew it would be painful, but I thought it would help. Instead it simply hurt her."

"Flowers. The *I'm sorry* will be better in person than on the phone."

"Yeah." He finished the coffee and wondered, not for the first time, if he was simply complicating his life. Charlotte wasn't the kind of woman to think in terms of a serious relationship. For her, a friendship was where this ended. But he couldn't move away from the fact he found her interesting. No one else had crossed that line before, and he wasn't willing to step back until he could see where this might go.

Sixteen

Paul pulled into the area where baby Connor's remains had been found and parked. Ann pulled out the pictures of the park from that day and offered them. "Doesn't look like it's changed much."

Paul studied the surroundings. "Trees have nineteen years more of growth, but the buildings are the same. A good place to bury a child if you had to select a spot. You could approach from any direction. They chose to move two stepping stones and bury the child, return the stones. It rained that next morning and most of the day, a steady drizzle, so before the pub call was made, Mother Nature had already returned the spot to unchanged. Had the man not called, it's doubtful anyone would have discovered the body for a good number of years."

Ann pulled out the picture of the missing cat from the pub's bulletin board, compared the hand-drawn map on the back to the surroundings. "The sketch is to scale. It had to be drawn from memory — someone doesn't bring a photo of a missing cat to this park, draw a map, and return it to the pub. Whoever drew the map and made the call had been here many times, knew exactly where the child was buried."

"Someone from the neighborhood, I think. When they thought 'We've got to bury this child without being noticed,' they thought of this park. This is familiar territory to them."

Ann picked up the street map. "The shopping center where baby Connor was snatched looks a good distance away, but when you see the routes in and out of this neighborhood, it's nearly a direct line to that upscale shopping area."

"A target of opportunity. Simply go hunt in a rich area of the city," Paul agreed.

"Paul, think about that. They pick a baby at random, they dash to the van and drive away. How do they know who to contact for the ransom demand? How do they know the name of the parents, the phone number, the address where they live? They have no idea who this child is; they know only that it's a baby boy."

Paul pondered the implications of that observation. "If this is truly a random abduction, they'd have to wait for the media to tell them who the child is and who the parents are."

Ann nodded. "So part of the delay in sending a ransom demand is waiting to see who's desperate to get their child back."

"Or they get proactive. They leave someone at the shopping center to watch the mother react to the fact the baby's gone, to listen to the information she's giving the officers, to listen to the questions they're asking shoppers," Paul suggested.

Ann wrote that down. "You know, it fits with the assumption a woman was somewhere involved in this. Leave her behind initially to gather information about the baby. She'll blend in as a concerned shopper at the scene. The investigators likely already pursued this idea, but it's worth reviewing the file again to see what they noted down about the people at the scene."

Ann studied the case summary. "The father made a televised appeal for the child that evening, so maybe identification takes part of the first day, but I'm still puzzled as to why they didn't provide that ransom demand in the three days when the baby was alive. In most abductions of an infant, the call with the ransom demand is within twenty-four hours, unless the child was taken for other reasons, such as replacing a child who died. The note in the stroller suggests money was the object from the beginning."

"They aren't sure how to pick up their ransom without getting caught retrieving the money," Paul guessed. "The shopping center is close to this neighborhood. Maybe closer than they realized. The cops fan out with road blocks and a canvass, their presence is going to be felt here. The abductors freeze up. They had a plan for getting their ransom money, but now they have to rethink it. So another two days go by. The snatch itself and getaway from the area suggests good planning. The burial was quickly planned but executed well. I think retrieving the ransom money is what got them hung up."

Paul started the car. "Anything else you'd like to see?"

"Let's drive around the neighborhood a bit just to see the area."

Paul took them on a slow tour of the streets. "I don't think the neighborhood has changed much in the last nineteen years," he said. "The Meadow Park neighborhood is what I'd call a borderline struggling community surrounded by more wealthy areas. It's got potential — middle school, high school, park. It's prosperous enough that the houses have grass, the kids have wide streets to play on, neighborhood businesses dot the community."

He pointed to the older home on the corner. "But houses need painting, some need repairs, a few streets show abandoned properties. It's not urban poor, nor is it city wealthy. It hasn't been gentrified and fixed up yet. It's just existing. If you were born here, it's the kind of neighborhood where your family continues to live, where you might also work and raise a family. People will have lived here twenty years and remember the baby Connor case well. We'll be lucky that way. If this were the comfort zone of those who abducted baby Connor, there are people still here who know the people we're looking for. People will talk to us. The question is, where do we want to begin and what do we want to ask?"

"Baby Connor is news in this neighborhood," Ann agreed, "and it's their news, the baby was found here. Memories of that day will still be fresh, handed down by the constant retelling."

"Exactly."

"I think we start at the park, then the pub. Then we find the community center or wherever folks hang out to share stories and coffee and play dominoes, and we start listening. People who were living here twenty years ago — the list can't be that long. We'll likely need to talk to all of them to form our own impressions of the neighborhood."

"It will make for some interesting weekend excursions," Paul said. "We can bring Black along as an icebreaker. Anything else you want to see while we're here?"

"I've got enough to make the baby Connor case tangible. We'll carve out some time next weekend to begin having those conversations." Ann stored her notes. "While we're in this area, let's see if the house where Charlotte was held still exists. I'm curious."

"Sure, I think I can find it." Paul pulled to the curb and went online, searched the archive file to confirm the property information and address. He turned to the north and drove along one-way streets paralleling the railroad tracks to a crossing point. He entered an older part of the city along the river.

He eventually pulled to the curb and pointed to a two-story house with attic dormers set back in a lot. The shrubs had overgrown the land, and the yard needed mowing. The house had weathered poorly, tan paint peeling in the sun, and the roof looked like it would leak with even a mild rain. "The uncle of the two men who were killed still owns the property. It was rented to an older couple last time the file had been updated, but it looks to be vacant now."

Paul rested his arm across the back of the seat, studied the house, studied his wife. He understood why she'd been curious to see this place. He had read the full Bazoni file now, the classified sections included, and he knew why Ann had encouraged him to look at how it had ended.

He had a kidnap victim skittish to the point she hasn't said a word about what happened. He had the two guys holding her shot and killed during the rescue. And he had ransom money found in a cop's possession.

Ann had known that fact and not warned him. Not entirely a surprise since her security clearance was higher than his, and he had enough on his plate. But she had known. He wondered who had told her and when. "She doesn't talk about what happened with good reason," he said.

His wife glanced over at him, realized he knew, and nodded. "I'm not sure I wouldn't have made the same decision in her place. Howard Benson, my boss when I worked with the Chicago PD, had history with this case and used to talk about it when we were traveling. I don't think he was ever comfortable with the outcome."

"I can understand why. It's not any cop. It's the hero cop of the story. Chicago cop, thirty years on the job, clean record. He gets a tip, he's the first guy through the door when they get to the house, he shoots and kills the two men holding Ruth, rescues her. He's the hero of the city. He dies in a car crash on the way to a television interview the next morning. A friend of his who goes from the hospital to the house to take charge of the dog finds twenty-five thousand from the third ransom in the pantry, in the dog food sack, wrapped in plastic. Was the cop framed or was he involved?"

Ann nodded. "*The* question. There's no way to tell if the money was there before or after the cop died. The house locks might have been picked. No prints on the money, and the cop had a solid alibi for the abduction itself. He could have been framed. Someone angry the cop shot the two men — possibly the uncle — decided to trash the cop's reputation after he died."

"Or just as likely, the cop *was* involved, and he made sure to be first through the door so he could kill his accomplices under cover of the law," Paul said. "He thought he was free and clear — instead a car wreck sends him to the hospital where he dies. The cop was either innocent and framed or he was guilty and we can't prove it."

"I'm glad you didn't think we should to tackle the Bazoni cold case," Ann mentioned. "Baby Conner is difficult enough."

"Given the size of the task force, if there was a lead to chase in the Bazoni one, it was followed. The men involved in the case are dead. Unless Charlotte is willing to talk with us, there's nothing else that can be done. And even then, the best we likely could do is fill in some of the corners."

"Maybe if she gets comfortable with Bryce," Ann offered, "if she stays around, there will be a day she decides to talk about it."

Paul could share the hope, but he knew reality. "She hasn't said a word in eighteen years. I doubt she ever does."

■ ■ ■ ■

PART TWO:
THE GIFT

■ ■ ■ ■

SEVENTEEN

Bryce added a band around the boxes on the pallet for extra stability, then marked it as ready to transport. John would be down to the vault around one p.m. with the forklift to haul the pallets out to the truck. Bryce glanced at the time. He had time to find Charlotte. She would probably be unloading a storage unit somewhere on the property, but he would start at Fred's place and make the circle looking for her truck if she wasn't at the house. He'd prefer to see her today rather than wait for their next dinner. She'd accepted the flowers and his apology and been embarrassed by both. He wasn't in the mood to wait to find out how severely he had complicated things with her.

Charlotte was standing on Fred's back porch. She'd been playing with the German shepherds, for she still held the tug-of-war rope, but the dogs were now chasing each other along the water's edge, and she was lost in thought. Bryce walked up the path, not sure if she'd heard him arrive. She glanced over as he came up the steps. He was relieved at the quick, if brief, smile she offered.

He stopped beside her. "I've been toying repeatedly with the idea of asking if you'd like to go out on the lake for an afternoon. Want to skip work and go find boat keys?"

"I'm afraid of the water."

The answered startled him. "Really?"

She looked over, and he glimpsed something he didn't understand, an old memory that for a moment was in the present. Then she blinked and it disappeared. "John would be glad for the company if you'd like to join him."

"You're afraid of the water, but you're going to keep Shadow Lake, some of the family land, when you sell the rest of the business."

"Yes."

He pushed his hands into his pockets, studied the lake she had drawn so many times in her sketches, the water she so often sat and watched. "You're going to give it to John."

"Did I say that?"

"Unspoken, but you did." He smiled.

"Nice gift."

"He likes the water."

Charlotte would see it as giving John a peaceful sanctuary, but Bryce also thought it was a way she could honor her family by placing the land in good hands for the long term. It was a smart option.

Bryce glanced at her, and took a risk. "You like music well enough to put up with a crowd? There's a concert in St. Louis this weekend. Ann and Paul are flying south for it. She invited us to join them. A private flight, Ann's the pilot."

"Instead of dinner?"

"Along with. I thought we might live dangerously and do a double this week."

She thought about that, half smiled, nodded. "Okay."

"Then I'll see you Friday for dinner and pick you up Saturday at four p.m. at Ellie's for the concert." He hesitated. "You okay, Charlotte?"

"Why do you ask?"

"A lot on your mind. There has been for the last month."

"Decisions to make about the estate. I'll need to fly to New York next week for a few days."

"Trouble?"

"No. Only a raft of details." She glanced

at him. "I'll probably have another few million to add to the pool of funds to give when they get done."

"If I ever get to the point I run out of ideas, you'll see me wince when you say that. For now the needs seem endless. Do you ever stop to think about how much good you're doing with these gifts, Charlotte?"

"Give Fred the credit for having stored his wealth rather than spent it. Being generous with what Tabitha and I don't need — it seems like common sense to me. God's going to hold me accountable for what I do with it."

"You don't have to earn His pleasure, Charlotte. But I think your decisions please Him a great deal."

"As long as He's giving you some credit for the work involved. You never say much, but I know the hours involved."

"It's for a good cause. And it gives me a great deal of satisfaction to see the needs being met."

"A celebration dinner?" Charlotte hesitated in the kitchen doorway Friday night.

Bryce smiled. "Spaghetti, homemade meatballs and sauce, not much of a celebration. But when you sign that stack of checks tonight, you will have crossed ten million, so I found the candles and bought some flowers."

"I appreciate the thought." Charlotte pulled out a chair and picked up the list on top of the stack of checks he'd printed out for her. "You've gotten due diligence done for nearly everything I've approved. When are you getting time to sleep, Bryce?"

"I don't mind the work, Charlotte. It's for a good purpose."

She pulled over the checks to begin signing them.

Charlotte was more quiet than usual, Bryce thought, as they ate dinner. He picked up the plates and cleared the table, brought back a platter with brownies. She had a sweet tooth, and he was inclined to indulge her.

"When you were fifteen, before life took its turn," he asked, curious, "did you see yourself as single or married when you were an adult?"

She hesitated at the topic change, leaned back in her chair, and smiled as she picked up one of the brownies. "I was married with five kids, living in a chunky two-story house with these beagle dogs and a husband who always had a car in the drive he was working on for someone in the neighborhood.

We took care of people because we liked being part of the fabric of the neighborhood, and we'd lived in that same house since we were first married, packed it with memories and fights and backyard barbecues."

Bryce smiled. "You dreamed in stories."

"The best kind of thinking about the future includes a good picture of what it will look like."

"What's the story become now?"

She shrugged. "I was going to be an internationally famous artist known for my watercolors, but that collided with the reality of my talent. So it became a different but more realistic dream. Now it's the freedom to travel, to sketch whatever catches my fancy, to see my life across the years in thousands of sketches of places I went and people I met. I'm not making plans for something else to reach. I've got my life. I simply want to keep it."

"I like the image of that. Mine's a bit in flux. When your coins are sold, I'm going to sell controlling interest in Bishop Chicago to Devon and Sharon and find a new challenge to tackle."

"Getting tired of coins?"

He smiled. "We'll have a real celebration when the last coin is sold, and I will close this chapter in my life and not even look at a rare coin for at least a few years."

"I'm going to feel guilty if you're burned out because of this estate."

Bryce shook his head. "I was bored and looking for a change even before you appeared. I'm looking forward to what will be next."

The silence between them had turned comfortable. Bryce went back to an old conversation. "Who did you kiss when you were thirty?"

She blinked, then smiled. "John."

"Why?"

"Curiosity."

"You could kiss me and find out what you think when you're — what, thirty-eight?"

"I'm not giving you my exact age that easily." She slid back her chair. "I'm going to find out what's on TV tonight."

Since the table was clear, and the kitchen could be dealt with after she left, Bryce picked up the plate of brownies and followed her into the living room.

Charlotte stopped by the coffee table. "What's this?" A stack of art books sat there with a bow on top. For the delight that crossed her face, he would have gladly bought her a library of art books.

"So you have something to enjoy while I

watch the Mets."

"Nice. But we're watching a movie to-night."

"I can live with a movie — I'll record the game. Find us something interesting."

Charlotte wasn't watching the movie. She'd closed the art book on her lap and was watching him. Bryce turned his head to hold her gaze. They were sharing the couch, and he realized with a bit of a jolt the direction of her thoughts. She was wondering about his earlier suggestion.

He smiled.

She thought for a while and smiled back.

"Want to see what it's like when you're thirty-eight?" he offered quietly.

"Maybe."

He slowly leaned forward, and she jerked back.

He froze. "Did I misread the situation?"

"Changed my mind."

He eased back. "You're allowed."

He tried to focus on the movie, managed it for thirty seconds. "Not my breath?"

She giggled, but he heard the nerves. He reached over for her hand, rubbed his thumb on the back of hers. "Because I can find breath mints somewhere in a desk drawer."

"Watch the movie."

"Yes, ma'am."

She was looking at him again.

"You're going to drive me crazy."

"Yeah, sorry about that," she answered absently.

He looked over and held her gaze. Nothing tentative about the woman looking back at him. She was in a serious mood.

"Would you kiss me, Bryce, carefully? I am curious."

He slid his hand into her hair to gently ease her forward, dipped his mouth to hers, and tried for a kiss so soft it would be a first she'd remember for what it wasn't.

Her gaze held his for a long moment, and then she put her hand on his chest and pushed herself up off the couch and to her feet. "You should take me home again tonight, so I don't have to drive. Ellie can drop me off in the morning to pick up my truck."

Bryce had been thinking concert to give the two of them an evening out without calling it a date. But an hour into their Saturday evening outing he realized he'd misjudged how the evening would flow. Charlotte chatted with Paul on the flight to St. Louis, talked with Ann during the quick meal, slid her hand into his during the concert and shared his soda, joined Ann in the cockpit for the flight home. Bryce accepted the shift, aware it was deliberate on Charlotte's part.

She'd settled in comfortably with his friends, so the evening had accomplished one thing he'd hoped for. He hadn't been sure how at ease Charlotte would be around cops, Ann being former Chicago PD and Paul head of the FBI office. But Charlotte hadn't shown much hesitation. She apparently didn't blame cops in general for not finding her. Bryce wasn't sure he would have been so generous if the situation were reversed.

It wasn't until they left the airport and he was driving Charlotte back to Ellie's that he had her undivided attention, only now she was fighting to keep her eyes open. He gave up on the idea of having a conversation and just smiled over at her. "Take a catnap, Charlotte. I won't mind."

"It was a nice evening. I'm glad we went."

"So am I."

He turned the windshield wipers on to intermittent as the drizzle began to accumulate. The trip to Ellie's was forty minutes even with the nearly empty roads of two a.m. It had been a good evening and useful in its own way. Charlotte was starting to relax with him. She'd genuinely enjoyed the concert.

They were nearing Ellie's home when Charlotte stirred in her seat. "Bishop, I've got something I need to tell you."

He took his eyes briefly off the road to glance over at her. Late-night drives were becoming dangerous for news. "I'm listening."

"Fred's will requires that I marry if I want to receive the full estate."

"The coins and Graham Enterprises aren't all of it?"

"No."

"By when?"

"Three years after his death."

"You don't."

She looked over at him, surprised.

"The one thing in life that should be a free and clear decision — you don't let anyone mess with that." He turned his eyes back to the road. "You decide you want to get married, you get married three years and a day after Fred's death." His hands flexed on the steering wheel. "What was the man thinking?"

She laughed. "Not exactly the reaction I expected."

"Ticks me off to hear about the stipulation. Any other strings you're having to deal with?"

"Nothing else as major."

"You don't need the money, Charlotte. Even if you did, or just wanted it, I'd still say the right answer is no."

"Thanks."

"For what?"

"That perfect response."

"Fred didn't know you very well if he was trying to force your hand with his will."

"He meant well. His generation, there weren't many women still single as they approached their forties. He liked John. He hoped I might marry him. A nice sentiment, even if flawed in its implementation."

"John knows about the will?"

"Ellie and John both have copies. I don't make decisions based on the document. But it has been useful to have their perspectives on it."

"Why did you tell me?"

"Curiosity. I want to see what you might decide to do with the news."

He had no idea what to do with the news she'd just given him. "Okay."

Traffic in Ellie's neighborhood and the increasing rain were enough that he had to focus on his driving rather than pursue the conversation.

Charlotte gathered up her things and pulled keys out of her pocket. "Thanks again for the evening and the concert. Don't get out." She ducked out into the light rain, then leaned back into the open door. "Saylor Chemical."

"What?"

"My grandfather's grandfather owned Saylor Chemical. Look it up."

Look it up. That wasn't such an easy thing to do, even with the internet. Her grandfather's grandfather had Bryce trying to find business records going back more than a hundred years. Saylor Chemical didn't exist today.

He made calls and searched out old chemical-industry trade magazines, looking for a reference to Saylor Chemical. He didn't know which state to focus on, so he searched old newspaper archives at random, hoping to find a mention of the company in the business section. It took him a few days to answer his first question. Saylor Chemical was not, had never been, a public company.

He tried approaching it from the other direction, looking for information about the man rather than the company. He finally managed to locate a birth record for Fred's grandfather. He had been born in Wyoming. The father on the birth certificate was a man named William Graham.

His attempt to find a birth record, a death certificate for William Graham, or any other information about the man hit a wall. A search of newspaper archives across Wyoming for any mention of Saylor Chemical came up empty. What else could he do with Charlotte's cryptic bit of information to get it to lead somewhere?

Five days after he began looking, he found a patent issued to Saylor Chemical in 1906 for a machine lubricant. Saylor Chemical was a company incorporated in Nebraska. He finally had a location to start the real digging.

William Graham sold Saylor Chemical to Park Oil in an all-stock deal in 1909. In 1914, Park Oil split into two companies, Park Chemical and Park Resources. Park Chemical merged with Tri-Ag Seeds in 1923. Bryce started a new page of notes following the various company splits, mergers, and acquisitions through the years until he reached the present day. He had found twelve public companies on his list downstream of the original Saylor Chemical sale.

If the family had held on to ten percent of

the shares over the years, the estate would be worth — he looked up the stock values and ran the numbers — eight hundred seventy million. Shock rippled through him. He checked the math on the share distributions and calculations. The numbers were right.

It had been 104 years, and plenty of reasons to sell the stock, including the Great Depression and two wars. Fred had given Charlotte sixty million in coins along with Graham Enterprises. He had tied the rest of the estate to her getting married. If the Graham family had kept one percent of the stock, the rest of the estate was worth eighty-seven million. Bryce circled that number on his pad of paper with a hand that slightly shook. After 104 years, one percent was reasonable. Charlotte was probably looking at a will provision worth eighty-seven million dollars and trying to figure out what to do.

He looked at the time. She was in Silverton. He found his keys and headed to his car.

EIGHTEEN

Charlotte's Silverton property was a two-bedroom home with an attached garage tucked in among mature trees and farmhouses, down the road from a new subdivision development. Wind chimes on the porch and the fluttering of a flag mixed in with the music filtering out from open windows. The dogs met him, leaning in against him on both sides, their coats warm from lying in the sun. He knelt to say hello, stroked their brushed coats, and rubbed their ears. She had beautiful animals. The dogs headed back into the yard.

Charlotte answered the front doorbell, her hands busy folding a bath towel, with another tossed over her shoulder. "Hey, Bryce. John called to say he'd given you directions."

"Glad he made them detailed. Your house number is faded."

She stepped back so he could come inside.

He smelled cinnamon in the air and ginger and what he thought might be chicken baking.

He looked around with interest. The house was neutral in colors, mostly tans and browns, with generous amounts of white. Large landscapes dominated the walls, vistas of terrain from the Southwest, deserts bathed in warm sunlight. Her shoes on the entryway rug made him smile. A laundry basket was perched on the living room couch. She stepped over to add the folded towel to the stack on the coffee table, then folded the other one from her shoulder.

"How much of the stock is left?"

She gave him a long look, then took a T-shirt out of the basket and folded it with a practiced hand. "All of it."

The music faded and the red shirt in her hand turned gray.

"Whoa!" He felt his arm being grabbed. "You're too tall to go falling flat on your face. I'm so sorry. This is not the reaction I was expecting, Bryce."

He sat down hard in the nearest chair. The sound of her voice surged and faded a few times as his body caught up to the fact gravity had stopped moving. "You really want to give me a heart attack, don't you?" He took a deep breath, fought off the dizziness, raised his head, looked at her. "They never sold a share?"

She sat on the coffee table, knees touching his, and studied his face. "Not a one. They did spend the dividends," she offered hopefully, trying to cushion the news.

He tried to laugh. *All of it.*

He attempted to swallow and realized his mouth was dry as dust.

She watched as he absorbed the enormity of what she had told him. "Eight billion seven as of this morning," she said softly.

"And if you don't marry?"

"It's not my problem."

It felt like someone had walloped his chest with a concrete grapefruit, and it was the oddest unpleasant sensation he'd ever felt. He wished she'd keep talking, but she just sat waiting as he got past the reaction. He rubbed the back of his neck, surprised to realize his hand felt cold. "Why did you tell me?"

"I am so sorry for this. I didn't intend . . ."

He stopped her apology with a shake of his head. He studied her face, perplexed. "Seriously. Why did you tell me, Charlotte?"

"Curiosity. What's the dollar amount when principles bend to reality? I don't marry for money, or do I?"

"I don't know how to even approach

answering that, given these circumstances."

She held his gaze and then gave an embarrassed smile. "And now allow me to make this an even bigger apology by admitting the question itself was actually theoretical, even rhetorical, rather than serious, as the decision has already been made. I just wanted to have the conversation, Bryce. So I walloped you for no reason other than the fact I'm an idiot at judging how you might react to the information."

He could feel himself being two steps back and out of sync with the conversation. He locked on to the only point that mattered. "What decision have you made, Charlotte?"

She patted his hand, apparently relieved he looked and sounded more like himself, and went back to folding her laundry. "I'm single for life, Bishop. I'm not getting married. It's just going to take three years for people to realize I mean it since that's the will's deadline. Fred left me very well off if I stay single. He just knew I shouldn't try to deal with that Legacy Trust if I stayed single. It takes someone to share the day-to-day reality of it, the weight of it. He thought I'd marry John. That's not going to happen. I don't want to get married, and John loves Ellie. And I'm not going to risk my relationship with Ellie for any amount of money."

Bryce absorbed enough of her answer and the information flowing at him to realize the woman really had made her decision. She'd told him the news because she was simply curious how he'd answer the question and had thought he'd take the information in stride and they'd have an interesting conversation. The embarrassment over having not taken the news in stride was beginning to set in. He handled money matters with regularity and skill and couldn't explain the instant reaction that had hit him.

The stock hadn't been sold. He unwound the last five minutes in his head. She was waiting on him to say something in reply to what she'd just told him, but he was moving back in time now and his brain was beginning to snap into gear. The stock hadn't been sold. "Tell me that amount again."

She shook out a pillowcase. "Ellie's text this morning: eight billion seven hundred forty-three million. She gives me the figure and in the next text gives me the weather forecast. And since she likes those chance-of-rain graphics, she's borrowed the idea and sends me a frowning face when it goes down and a smiling face when it goes up. It's been frowning the last four days."

"Okay." He took another deep breath and

blew it out. "Okay."

He pushed against his knees and got to his feet, relieved to find the odd sensations were passing. If anything, the lightheaded feeling was being replaced with the opposite, and objects around him seemed to be too acutely in focus. "Has John asked Ellie to marry him?"

Charlotte smiled. "More than once. It's my personal soap opera, watching the two of them." She folded the last piece of laundry and stacked it all neatly back in the basket. "Graham Enterprises, the coins, the rest of what Fred left me directly — I'm already wealthy beyond what Tabitha and I, and her kids, will need in our lifetime. I don't need the money, Bryce."

No one needed that amount of money. "How have you, John, Ellie been walking around treating life as normal when this is sitting out there?"

"We've had over two years to get past the shock of it. After a while you realize it's just money. We're already dealing with more cash than we know what to do with."

"It's *the* lottery ticket. And you don't want it."

She rested the laundry basket against her hip and just looked at him, then shrugged. "The will requires I marry. It's a nice checkmate move, because I'm not marrying, so the next question is irrelevant."

"You're sure."

"Yes." She set the basket in the hall. "I'm repotting some flowers on the back patio. Do you have time to help me haul around some bags of potting soil? They're in the back of the truck."

He looked down at the dress slacks he was wearing, the suit jacket and tie, took off the suit jacket, tugged at the tie. He wasn't going to be fit to do any other kind of work today with this news rattling around in his mind. "I've got time."

"I find gardening is a good antidote for stress."

He dropped his tie across her shoulder. "I think you just like to play in the dirt."

She smiled. "That too."

Bishop found John down by Shadow Lake, clearing away debris the overnight storm had washed into the inlet near the dock. "You should marry her, John."

"Who?"

"Charlotte."

John tossed another chunk of driftwood into the bed of the truck. "I gather she told you."

"She did."

John pulled a piece of soggy cardboard from the water. "She isn't married, this is over. About the time you finish selling the last of the coins, she'll have Graham Enterprises emptied of Fred's family possessions and have it ready to be sold to the employees. She'll have her life back."

"She could do a lot of good with the money, John."

"She could." John picked up the trash bag. "What's your point, Bryce?"

"There's nothing right about this."

"You expect life to be fair, you haven't learned much from Charlotte yet. She lost four years of her life. She still can't go see her sister without risking a reporter catching sight of her and destroying her carefully built privacy around a new name. Her grandfather shows up when she's thirty-two and upends her life again. Now she's doing her best to deal with the estate while protecting her sister and nieces from the weight of it. The will has strings — it's par for the course."

"Does her sister know the size of it?"

"Fred told her he had sizable family wealth, and she said a few swearwords even I hadn't heard before. Tabitha is a strange bird, Bryce. She's famous from the modeling, wealthy now in her own right from endorsements, has a husband who goes through money gambling, and she's terrified she can't protect her girls as they are now coming up on age sixteen. I won't say she's paranoid, but I would say she's severely stressed. Even though Charlotte bore the brunt of it all, she has healed from what happened a lot more than Tabitha has. I would guess Tabitha thinks Fred's estate is in the few-hundred-million-dollar range, and Charlotte, wisely I think, hasn't corrected that assumption."

"It should be theirs. Charlotte's and her sister's."

"Should be. That's not reality." John shoved the truck tailgate up. "I'm marrying Ellie, if the woman ever decides she wants to take a risk on marriage. She's got a darker past than Charlotte, so I'm not holding my breath for when she's going to say yes, but I'm not letting go of that ideal."

John pulled off his work gloves. "Charlotte should be married if she wants to be. She should have the money if she wants it. I don't think she wants to be married, and I know she doesn't want the burden of the money. But it's her choice. You want to consider it, Bryce, tell her you'll marry her. She could do worse. I'd tell her that if she asked."

"I'm no more into an arranged marriage than she is."

John smiled. "A problem of timing, not of interest. You've been thinking on the idea at the edges."

"Maybe."

"Her grandfather assumed he could box her into a corner with the money. He assumed wrong. She could do a lot of good with that cash, but she won't try to meet those terms."

"I heard that in Charlotte's answer. The certainty she'll decline it."

"She will. Even if I was inclined to pursue it, which I'm not, she wouldn't consider marrying me because of Ellie. She values that friendship at priceless. Charlotte will keep enough of the Graham money that she and her sister stay comfortable for a lifetime, give the rest away, and let the remaining estate go. I know her. Charlotte's made her decision."

"What happens to the money after three years?"

"The trust keeps rolling on, being managed by a law firm, which seems to exist primarily to support it. With no appointed successor, it will enter a slow liquidation. The firm will eventually dole out the money as it sees fit over the next fifty years to various medical institutions. Knowing lawyers, they'll probably find a way to slow even that process down so the trust is still feeding the law firm an income a hundred years from now. But it's no longer Charlotte's concern."

"How many people know?"

"The total size of the trust — about twenty people at the law firm and who knows how many at the IRS. That Charlotte is the possible successor trustee — four, best I can tell. Fred's personal lawyer, and the three people she's elected to tell — Ellie, myself, now you. The rest of the law firm is under the impression the trust has now entered liquidation, as no successor trustee was appointed when Fred died — the fact there is a three-year window for the appointment is being held as a sealed fact to protect Charlotte. If she accepts the terms and marries, becomes the successor trustee — the people who know her name will rise to six to eight at the law firm and hopefully be contained to that. They have no incentive to get removed as the administrators of the trust by sharing what's very privileged information."

"How's the security around her? Does she have enough?"

"She's got lifetime coverage, Bryce, whatever I think she needs. Wouldn't matter if she was married or not, and wouldn't exactly be her choice. Her grandfather paid me in advance. Mitch, Joseph, or I have been around her the last couple of years. Her decision changes, the situation with the press changes, I'll make adjustments."

"I'm glad to hear it."

"She's got enough to think about without worrying about security. Her sister's got the same; that was the one thing Tabitha was willing to accept from Fred. I've got a friend in New York managing it. Tabitha and her girls are as safe as common sense can make them."

"When you said Ellie has a darker history than Charlotte's — where did they meet?"

"The Keeler-Resse clinic in Houston."

"Is Ellie doing okay?"

"She learned being stubborn from Charlotte. She's fine," John replied.

"I like her. She makes Charlotte laugh."

"They're the sister each one needs."

"A perfect description of it." Bryce pushed his hands into his pockets. "What does Ellie think?"

"She wants Charlotte to accept the terms and get married."

"To you?"

John smiled. "To you."

■ ■ ■ ■

Bryce thought it through as he drove back to Chicago. There were no easy steps now that he knew the scope of the situation. He could see a different reality now that he knew what had really been happening over the last months. *Eight billion seven.* Charlotte, John, and Ellie had known that before he had ever been approached.

Charlotte had made her decision, and he could feel the fact she was settled, maybe even comfortable with it. John's interests in the matter seemed more aligned with simply keeping life calm no matter what the decision was. The man was relaxed enough about the cash already flowing around that he would adjust to whatever amount was involved without losing his equilibrium. Ellie. There was a conversation that needed to be had, and it wasn't with Charlotte.

God, I need Ellie to be honest with me, open and willing to talk about Charlotte, because I need the full picture of what's going on. Help me get the facts, as best I can, from those who know the situation. When I'm finally home, I want a pizza delivered in, a few cold sodas, and a conversation with you that is going to be deep and wide and long. I feel like I just got hit by a fastball I didn't know was coming at me.

He let the prayer linger in his thoughts as he drove into Chicago and headed first to Ellie's place. Bryce walked up the steps and rang the bell, not sure if Ellie would be home. She opened the door a minute later.

"Can we talk?"

"I've been expecting you, Bryce." She stepped back and let him inside.

Ellie led him back to the kitchen where she was washing up from what looked like a marathon cooking session. She handed him a dish towel and went back to scrubbing a cookie sheet. He picked up a muffin tin to dry.

He studied this lady who was Charlotte's best friend, the quiet, organized one keeping Charlotte's art and life flowing efficiently and safely by — and, he realized, the one protecting her even more than John. He set down the tin, picked up another one to dry. "You were the planner behind the approach to me. The introduction phone call, the store, the progressive steps to the breadth of the coins and what this really was. You were the planner, not Charlotte."

Ellie nodded. "I gamed it out for her."

"Charlotte accepted it as her plan, has added her own exquisite timing, but this was forty moves deep and from someone who knows me very well. Charlotte doesn't know me that well. I thought it might have been John's hand I was seeing, but he's too open and pragmatic in his thinking, his decisions. You had a background check of me?"

"Yes."

"What else? You had more."

"I know some people who know you. They answered a few questions for me."

"And the charitable giving? No ones knows, Ellie, but somehow you do."

"You told me."

"*I* did?"

"God didn't make you an astronaut, an explorer, like your younger brother; didn't make you comfortable with danger, a submariner with a heart for defending the country, like your older brother. He made you a businessman, able to earn money and enjoy the work, and gave you a heart to give. You want to be a good businessman and give generously. That's the legacy you want, have always wanted."

It actually sounded like him. "When?"

"You were teaching a class at your church. You talked that morning on the subject of God's faithfulness, and about the responsibility to be faithful in return. You answered a question from a lady in the back of the room. I asked you about being an artist, what was my responsibility to God for the talent I couldn't explain, and you answered me with your own story."

He absorbed that answer. "You're an artist too. Like Charlotte. You're not just in the business of art."

"I'm excellent at both."

"Why don't you exhibit your works?"

"I do. But that's a conversation for another time, Bryce, and not why you're here." She dried her hands. "Ask me the question you came here to ask."

"Why do you want Charlotte to get married? Why did you choose me? You did select me, didn't you, Ellie?"

"I want her to be happy . . . more than she is now. And I want her to have the money. It's eight billion dollars, Bryce. I think she'd be crazy to turn it down. The condition is one that for anyone else wouldn't be a reason to say no. I'm her best friend. The fact she says she's not getting married and means it breaks my heart. I want her to share her life with someone who can help her build new memories, so she isn't living a life still haunted by the past. I want her to have the choice to be married or not, to have the freedom to be able to make that choice in the present, not bound by the past. She should have the money if she wants it."

"Ellie, she's going to turn it down."

"Probably. Likely. But she needs the choice. As to why you — Bryce, that's simple. You're Mrs. B's son."

"Mom?"

"She's a wonderful teacher. Charlotte had her for fifth grade. I'd guess you got your interest in teaching from her."

He reached for a chair at the kitchen table and tugged it out. "I think I need to hear the story, Ellie, and hear the plan. The real one. The one you didn't tell Charlotte."

She considered him, then offered a rich smile. "I've done a few with layers when it's been necessary. But in this case — no other hidden layers, Bryce. Just a knowledge of your family, of the fact I would like Charlotte's world to have that kind of extended family around her. She has to make a decision if she's going to marry. She won't marry John even if I think that's best for her. And Charlotte — she isn't going to date if horses tried to drag her to meet someone.

"That left doors I could open, and coins was the door that had the most interesting possibilities. I could have used the land, but that would have led to lawyers or finance guys, and a certain level of . . . sophistication, for want of a better word, that just isn't where Charlotte would prefer to reside. I wanted a comfortable guy she could trust, and a way to cause your paths to cross. You were my choice. I found her a husband because she's my best friend and she would never go looking if I left it up to her."

He pointed to one of the cookies on the plate and she nodded. He took a bite of a sugar cookie and considered her, weighing her words. "You're a good friend, you know that?"

"I'm a best friend."

"People would say I married her for her money."

"People would be wrong. She married you for her money."

Bryce smiled, appreciating the distinction. "It's a lot of money, Ellie. I'm not sure what I think about it yet."

"There's a slap-in-the-face kind of reality to it when you sit down and try to write out all the zeros, then repeatedly divide it by two in order to reach a number you're comfortable with. It's six splits larger than I know what to deal with. Worse for Charlotte, as she prefers to wince at the twelve hundred dollars I charge for one of her sketches. I'd sell them for two thousand, which is where the market is at for her works, but she'd start tearing up more of the sketches than she does now because she'd feel like they weren't perfect enough for that price. She's ripped up fifty thousand dollars' worth of sketches so far this year. She's killing me. I'd like to be able to grab them out of her hands first."

Bryce laughed. "You're perfect for her, Ellie."

"I'm a very good manager of art and artists." Ellie studied him. "Charlotte needs you, Bryce, for a lot more reasons than the money. She's not comfortable being alone, no matter how much she tries to present that to the world. She's most comfortable when she's with people. She needs a world she can capture in that sketchbook, something that is more than strangers and the latest town she's decided to drive through. She needs the family home, the dogs, the people who stay in her life for decades. That's where her talent really lies. You want to see a genius-level sketch, ask her to show you her collection of sketches she's made of John.

"John made an agreement with her, back in the first days of being her bodyguard, that she was free to sketch him for practice. He'd even cooperate on helping her get a drawing right, if she would promise to never sell one with him in it. From his background in the military he taught her faces, how to see them, how to divide them down into parts, to notice the expressions and understand how they were conveyed in all the elements of a face.

"He taught her to see places, how to notice what was there and what was out of place, how to see people and understand what they were doing, where they were heading, what was on their mind — all from what was observable. He was passing on a soldier's attention to detail to locate the roadside bomb, the friendly approaching with a hidden intention, but he didn't bother to tell her that at the time. He just taught her to *see.*" Ellie poured two glasses of ice tea and carried them over to the table.

"Charlotte will be subtle about it, but she'll reach for what's real about a place. Her sketches are about interesting places, about people who catch her attention. But she captures *life,* and life can leave rough edges in its passing. You'll see the dropped piece of trash, the broken latch, the flower that's been stepped on, the board that has warped. The details. You can't mimic a sketch of hers, her style, even though many have begun to try — there's a quality in her work, a way she sees the world that is unique to her. She's become an artist with a voice. Her words are simply written with a line of pen or pencil."

Bryce took the glass Ellie offered and waited while Ellie took a seat at the table across from him. "Charlotte put a fingerprint on the Bishop Chicago window glass — the sketch she gave me as a housewarming gift," he mentioned. "An inside joke, I think. The print is inside the glass of the frame, but perfectly centered to the window in the sketch. Not an accident. I smile every time I see it."

Ellie smiled. "She'll be glad you noticed. That's the conversation, Bishop. The subtle one. If you want to listen to Charlotte, to really hear her, watch for the whispers, the small things that show up in her interactions with you. She's careful around people. Spontaneous isn't easy for her. She's quiet and deliberate about how she moves to different topics, what she decides to say when, but she's got a good memory that shows she's really noticed you, along with a wicked sense of humor if you're not careful."

"I've picked up on some of that a few times."

He turned the glass in his hand. "I understand why you think she's better off being part of a family than not. What else are you thinking about, Ellie, when you think Charlotte should be married?"

She was quiet for a long moment. "If she can handle being married," she said quietly, "maybe I can too."

He realized the simplicity of that, the depth of it, and nodded. "John would like to marry you. Charlotte's told me that. John has told me that."

"He's asked. I'm not ready to open that door yet."

"Do you think Charlotte is?"

"I think she'd like to be brave enough to at least crack it open, look at what's on the other side. But she hasn't had enough time yet to find the courage for it. She's busy, but she's thinking. That's why she's on the road so much when she could easily send others to take things to her stores. She's thinking. She sees the potential of the money, Bryce, the scale of what eight billion can do.

"I think it scares her, the idea of being responsible for something that large, and she's afraid of how her life changes if it's hers to deal with. But she has been thinking about it. I get messages from her when she's on the road, questions and research and what-ifs, the hypotheticals that show her mentally sketching out what could be done with it. She may have decided she isn't getting married, but the separate question of what she could do with the money — she's been weighing that for two years now. The door is open for three years after Fred's death, and she's going to live with her decision with her eyes wide open to what it means if she says a final no. There's courage in saying that no — as much as there is in saying yes."

"How difficult is this decision for her, Ellie?"

"I couldn't make it."

"How bad are her flashbacks going to be?"

She bit her lip and pushed back her chair. "Come with me."

She walked down the hall to the guest bedroom, turned on the lights. She tapped her fist against the inside of the door and he stepped inside, looked. There were two strong locks on the inside of the door.

He blew out a hard breath. "Okay."

"This is a house she's safe in, comfortable in, trusts. And she doesn't sleep before the locks are thrown."

"What happened, Ellie? Has she ever told you?"

She leaned against the doorjamb, and he watched her think about answering him.

"Ask me again after she agrees to marry you."

He rubbed his thumb on the lock, looked back at her.

"It's what you think, Bryce, but it's different too. Some things you just do not want to know unless you have to."

He moved his hand and slid it in his pocket. "Yet you think she should get married."

"I know Charlotte better than she knows herself. If she declines the money, if she doesn't marry now, she never will. The past she lives with will always control her life. If I didn't think this was the crucial choice she had to make, I would never have found you and sent you across her path. You're a good man, Bryce. She's got a safe choice. She just needs the courage to make it." She tilted her head. "But that's a decision for after you make yours."

"What you're asking isn't an easy question, Ellie."

"No, it's not. And it would be simpler to agree if the amount was a few hundred million. But it's eight billion seven. It puts your family at serious risk that what happened to Charlotte could happen to one of them."

"I wondered if you'd factored that in."

"Elliot Marks out of Atlanta has no family, and John and I debated it for more than a few weeks before placing him as our second choice. If Charlotte says yes, it's going to be because she wants to give the money away. There aren't many men I'd trust to handle that. They'd see the power of the money before they saw the potential of it. I think you see the potential of it first."

"I'm beginning to. Money is an awkward reason to marry, Ellie."

"Charlotte will never marry if her hand isn't being forced to some degree. That's the scar the past has left. She won't even think about it, even though I believe she'd be much happier married. In this rare situation, Fred's will is a good thing. She can't avoid the question."

"Did you have a conversation with Fred?"

"I wouldn't do that to her. But I wasn't . . . displeased with his decision. He loved her. He provided generously for her if she stayed single, and gave her a reason to marry. I'd say he did the right thing."

"Why didn't he just spend the money?"

"A question I've asked myself more than a few times."

"Find an answer?"

Ellie smiled. "The dividends are four hundred thirty-five million a year."

Bryce closed his eyes, then laughed.

"Yeah, I see the problem."

"Charlotte Graham is Ruth Bazoni." It wasn't his news to share, but he didn't withhold material information to a decision. Bryce turned to face his dad. "You know what —"

"I remember the case, son." His dad lit the charcoal bricks in the kettle grill and watched them flame. "An awfully hard thing, what she survived."

"Tied to her grandfather's will is money that requires her to marry. The one guy she should turn to is John Key, and she's taken him out of the equation. There's no one else. So she's going to turn down the money."

"You think she should have it."

Bryce could feel the weight that came with his answer. "I do." It was the only thing he was certain about — he thought she should have the money. "I don't know if she will say yes if I offer, but I feel like I need to make a marriage offer. I'm not marrying her for her money, but the money is the reason for the decision."

"I understand the distinction." His dad sat down in a patio chair and studied him. "You're seriously thinking of getting married to Charlotte Graham."

"I am. The will gives Charlotte three years after Fred's death to marry or lose the money, and that time is running out. Her best friend admits to having picked me out for Charlotte. She wouldn't go looking to find a husband on her own, so Ellie took the task on for her. That's why I ended up being asked to sell the coins. Ellie wanted Charlotte and me to meet."

"Are you asking my opinion or are you hoping for my approval?"

"Your perspective, I guess. I know this is too far off the path to ask for your approval."

"It's not what your mom and I have been praying for," his dad agreed. "Let's start with the obvious. It's more than a little money or you wouldn't be pacing my patio."

"That's true."

"You want her to have the money. Do you think she's better off with it?"

Bryce hesitated. "I don't know."

"A wise answer."

"I know a day will come when she will regret having turned the money down. I want her to at least have the choice, a real choice, before she says no."

"It's a noble sentiment, son."

Bryce took the seat next to his father. He was trying to talk himself into this as much as he was his dad. "God's not asking me to step forward and solve this problem for Charlotte. He's not nudging me toward this decision. But neither is there a cautionary note, a 'don't ask her' check in my spirit. A lot of prayer simply keeps giving me the assurance to 'do what you decide is best.' And I know Charlotte having a choice matters to me."

He leaned forward, rested his hands between his knees. The emotions of the last thirty-six hours had taken a toll. This wasn't the kind of marriage conversation he had thought he would be having with his dad. There might be no purpose to it. Charlotte had already made clear her decision to stay single and let the money go. But he thought that choice was to protect herself. He remembered the first time she'd mentioned the topic because it had struck him at the time as something so sad.

"I'm single for life, Bishop. Lots of money, lots of reasons for someone to overlook the baggage I bring. That's not going to happen. I don't need the pity. So I've built a life I like for myself. I'll go back to it once Fred's estate is dealt with. I like my art. I like my friends."

He hadn't known it at the time, but her words were about the Legacy Trust. It hurt knowing the past had left so much damage that Charlotte would avoid something good just to protect herself. And maybe his proposing marriage would simply cause her more pain as she again made the decision to stay single. He didn't want to cause that. He looked at his father. "The fact she's Ruth Bazoni is a reason not to ask."

"On the contrary, it's probably the one good reason you should ask. She's been hurt before. If she wants the money, she has to marry. She's going to end up in a business marriage, a legal agreement with a guy who takes X dollars and lives elsewhere. She'll probably see that as the only safe way to proceed, the only safe option she has to protect against being hurt again. She won't risk a real marriage because of what happened in the past. She deserves something better than that, son.

"You don't love her, because you would have led this conversation with that if you did, and that's going to be a problem. But she deserves a friend. She deserves at least a friend. If you get married, you won't get divorced. She'll have you, and by extension this family, for a lifetime. I'd say she needs it. There are worse reasons to get married than to provide a woman a safety net of a good family."

"I wouldn't be letting you down, marrying someone I don't love, at least not yet?"

"Are you going to be a good husband to her?"

"Yes."

"Then you'll have my blessing and your mother's."

NINETEEN

Bryce flipped on the TV and found the game, set the volume on low, then looked over at Charlotte. "I've got a new folder of ideas for you to consider and a stack of checks for you to sign. Why don't you look them over while I fix us some coffee? Then we're going to talk about the elephant in the room we've been ignoring all evening."

Charlotte glanced at the folder and checks, nodded, and reached for a pen.

Bryce took his time fixing coffee, trying to sort out what he wanted for the rest of the evening. He could feel the nerves skimming around the edges of his system. Dinner had gone well, the conversation had flowed easily due to the fact they'd both avoided the topic of the Legacy Trust money. He came back with coffee for both of them and took a seat on the couch beside her, placed her cup on a coaster on the coffee table.

She straightened the stack of checks she

had signed. "What does this bring the total to?"

"Twelve million, seven hundred and twelve thousand. There'll be no problem giving away the sixty million within a year." He settled back with his cup of coffee. "Tell me about the day Fred told you about the Legacy Trust."

She curled up in the corner of the couch, turning to face him, finally nodded. "I knew about Graham Enterprises from our first meeting, and Fred showed me the coins the year before he died. About six months before his death we were talking about Graham Enterprises and the arrangements he had made to allow the employees he trusted to buy it if I decided to sell the business. Combined, the coins and Graham Enterprises were worth over a hundred fifty million. His advice was to decide what I wanted in my life and for my sister, to keep as much money plus a safety margin necessary to have it, and then make a decision. The rest of the money could be kept intact for the next generation and passed on, or it could be given away.

"I was thinking I might build a house with a studio and gardens and settle here in the area. I like the Midwest weather, and Ellie was comfortable in Chicago. I was creating possible sketches of the place, and Fred was helping me refine the floor plan for the house." She paused as she drank her coffee, remembering.

"Fred said the decision about what to do with Graham Enterprises would be only one of the decisions I would need to make. His father had passed the coins down to him. His grandfather had also passed down the proceeds of a company he had sold."

Charlotte stopped, finally reached forward and set her coffee cup down. "Fred didn't tell me the size of it. He simply said it was large enough he was going to do me the favor of not making it my problem unless I chose to get married and have someone help me with it.

"I told him I didn't plan to marry.

"He said that was fine. His lawyer would handle the details for me whatever I decided. He'd leave the option open for three years after his death. He wanted me to know his own decision had been not to do anything with the Legacy Trust, and he'd understand if I made the same decision."

Charlotte reached around for the throw pillow and tucked it behind her. "That conversation, looking back at it now, was such a simple thing for what Fred had told me, and what I had decided and told him in reply." She half smiled. "It obviously didn't stay that simple.

"His lawyer sat me down about three months before Fred died and told me the size of it." She went silent, remembering. "Not the kind of news you wake up one morning prepared to hear. It was a week before I felt able to talk with Fred about it. Fred simply said the family had been good at business, and he'd been proud he'd been able to be the same. The money was there if he wanted to spend it, and he had decided not to do so. He hadn't wanted that life for himself. He'd seen his father wrestle with the enormous wealth, and it was a continual pressure. I could decide what was best for me, and he'd agree with it. Fred said he had lived the life he wanted and had no regrets. He wanted the same for me.

"After Fred died, I told John and Ellie.

"Ellie and I daydreamed for a while about what could be done with the money — things we could do, places we could go. But our dreams didn't come close to the value of the coins and Graham Enterprises, let alone the Legacy Trust. The only thing to be done with that kind of money was to control something big like a business the size of McDonald's or to give the money away through something like the Gates

Foundation, where there are hundreds of staff and major initiatives to fund.

"I'm a sketch artist, Bryce, and I like — need — my privacy. I'm glad Fred gave me a clean out. He could have simply left the trust to me, and I would have no choice in the matter but to manage it somehow. I do have a choice. That matters to me. The weight of this isn't going to fall on me unless I want it to."

She stopped, tilted her head. "You listen well."

"I'm trying to."

"It would be useful to me to know what you've been thinking."

Bryce blew out a breath. "I'm still caught by the enormous size of it, and further, what could be done with those funds. It doubles the size of Samaritan's Purse and World Vision, it strengths and builds thousands of churches, it tackles hunger in a serious way. It's a choice to do some serious good."

"The sixty million looks small against eight billion seven."

"Yes. Was what we've been doing merely practice, Charlotte? The sixty million? To find out if you could give away a large amount of money quietly?"

She didn't answer for a long moment. "Yes. It's been a learning experience to see what giving sizable sums away would be like. It's something I needed to know."

He set aside his cup, leaned back on the couch, and made his decision. "We could scale it. A combination of macro and micro giving, the same focus on having each dollar matter."

"It requires I marry."

"Set the condition aside. If it didn't exist, would you want the money?"

She looked away, and he turned her head gently back with a finger under her chin. "Simple question. Honest answer. Charlotte, do you want the money?"

Seconds ticked by.

"Maybe." The answer came out like an escaping painful whisper. "I don't want it feeding a law firm for the next fifty years. It was entrusted to me. I believe Fred wanted me to control the direction, the potential, of it. I would want to give it away." She shook her head. "If I so much as hint I want it, marrying John comes into play. Ellie knows me. She knows John is the only guy I trust enough to place in that role. Her friendship is priceless to me. No amount of money is worth risking Ellie and me."

"Consider marrying me."

He didn't like the pallor that appeared. "Spend your life with me like we've been doing the last several weeks, only layered with more. Nothing else changes but another last-name change, and you've already adapted to those before."

"You haven't thought this through," she whispered, "and I don't want a husband."

"You need one," he said simply. "It's okay to want the money. It's okay to know John isn't the answer. So put together the next plan, don't simply stop at what looks like a wall. Consider marrying me. Ellie will understand your choice. John will too."

"I won't."

He smiled and leaned forward, softly kissed her worried face. "Think about it."

Bryce hauled another box of coins to the pallet.

John pushed his box in beside it. "What did she say?"

"Not much. She's got two hundred forty-six days left. Knowing Charlotte, she'll use every one of them to think about it."

"For what it's worth, I'm on your side," John said. "It gives you time to convince her to say yes."

"You have any ideas on how to do that? Because I sure don't."

John thought for a moment. "Treat her like she has said yes."

"Basically ignore the question."

"Yeah. It's worth a try."

Bryce thought about it, remembered that pallor, and shook his head. "No, the problem is she's scared. The only thing to do is to talk about it so much it stops being scary." He taped together another box. "Why are you so comfortable with the idea of Charlotte getting married, John? Of everyone, I would have figured you would be the least likely to see it as a good idea, given what you know about her past."

"Maybe it's because I do know the details. She'd be in good hands with you, Bryce. The money — it can be a problem, a blessing, or just a fact. It's not going to ensure her happiness. The people around her are the influences on her being happy. Charlotte being married to you — it would be good for both of you. You'd have an interesting life. You'd do something good with the money, she'd have family around her, somewhere to be settled, and she'll be glad a few decades from now she didn't turn down the opportunity."

"You sound certain this would be a good thing."

"I am. I know Charlotte. I don't think you'll get her to say yes, but it would be nice if you could." John leaned against the stack of boxes on the pallet and studied the shelves being emptied. "Another two pallets, we'll begin to see empty shelves in each section."

"I see why Charlotte moved out furniture at Fred's place just so she could see some progress. Otherwise the job never seems to end."

John smiled. "I figure another two months at this pace to clear this vault, add another four to clear vault twenty-two. It's going faster than I thought."

"I hired enough staff for the prep room that they've been able to keep up with us. Charlotte packed another five hundred of the individual coins. Let's take them with us this trip, leave them at the store, so she doesn't have to make that delivery."

"I'll get them loaded to haul out. There's time if you want to go find her for an hour."

Bryce glanced at his watch. "Maybe."

"She'll be at the admin office. She was helping Henrietta chase down an errant payment."

"Why does she keep working like she does?"

"Think of Charlotte's work as therapy. It was how she dealt with the aftermath of what happened. She worked. It's ingrained now. The more stress she's feeling, the more likely you are to find her working at something until midnight. It's a distraction."

"I hadn't realized."

John shrugged. "She's got the money to hire people to do everything she's doing now, but that would take away the part of work she needs — the fact she can start a job and get it done. She's overloading her schedule, but not as bad as I've seen her do it in the past. Busyness isn't the problem. Feeling like she has no control in her life — that's a dark line I don't want to see her walk again."

"How bad did it get?"

John shook his head. "Not going to answer that one, even if you end up her husband."

"You're asking me to step into a role where I could badly hurt her because I don't know those answers."

"Yes, I am. You'll find a way to deal with it."

"I don't seem to have much choice. Neither you nor Ellie are inclined to say very much."

"Maybe because we know the truth and don't want to scare you off."

Bryce heard the humor along with the caution. It wasn't as bad as he could imagine, but it was not good. "Charlotte's going to tell me even less than either of you."

"She doesn't talk about it," John agreed. "I don't expect she ever will."

Bryce glanced at the time. "I'll take that hour and go find her. You've got keys to the truck?"

John patted his shirt pocket. "I'm set."

Charlotte had left the admin building. Bryce found her at Shadow Lake, walking along its edge, tossing the occasional rock into the water while the two Irish setters explored what had washed up to the shoreline.

"Mind if I walk with you?"

"No."

"I've got an hour while John hauls the pallets to the truck." He slid the work gloves he'd been using back on and accepted a fish carcass one of the dogs brought back to Charlotte. "Smells good, huh?" He ruffled the dog's ears, pitched the fish far into the lake. Charlotte skipped a rock across the splash where it landed.

Bryce thought she looked very tired. He'd postpone this conversation, but she was still going to be thinking about it. "You need to make a decision about the money that thirty years from now you can still live with."

"Yes."

"If you say no to the money, I want you comfortable with your decision. I don't want you saying no because you're afraid to say yes."

She studied him, finally nodded. "An interesting way to put it. I'll agree with the premise."

"So we need an agreement, you and I. I want you to consider marrying me. I want a serious conversation about the possibility of you saying yes."

"Bryce, this wasn't why I told you about the will condition."

"I got that."

She pushed her hands into her pockets. "I need to know why you decided to ask."

"You need a choice. By your own words, it was marry John or say no, and you settled on no. But John, by definition of who he is in your life, in Ellie's life, wasn't actually a choice. I am a choice. I don't have major strikes that say I wouldn't be a good husband for you."

"You're making a sacrificial gesture to give me a choice."

"I was thinking more along the lines of interesting lady, a bit dangerous but interesting, and I could see you as my wife. I haven't been able to say that about a woman before. I offered because if you want the money, you have to get married, and I'm a safe choice. I'd be a good husband."

"The way you said that, you see it as an objective to be met — be a good husband to Charlotte."

"You would prefer I be a bad one?"

She half laughed and kept walking, shook her head. "Good one."

She glanced over at him. "I've already made the decision. I'm not getting married."

"Then the conversation will simply make you more comfortable with that decision. I have no wish to pressure you into changing your mind. But I do want you to clearly see the options you have. I am an option."

Bryce stopped walking, and she paused too, though she kept her attention on the dogs rather than look at him. Bryce smiled, easily reading her discomfort with this conversation, but relieved to see she was carefully listening to his words as well. "Charlotte, it's a lot of money. If you don't honestly and seriously consider saying yes, you are one day going to look back on this time with regret, and I don't want that for you. I sincerely don't."

"I believe you mean that." She finally turned to look over at him. "Purely as a hypothetical, wouldn't it bother God that you're a strong believer and I'm at best a messed-up one?"

Her question surprised him, that the issue was one of her first concerns. "God asks me to marry within my faith. You told me early on you consider yourself a struggling Christian. If I didn't understand why you struggled, I would have a problem. But I do understand. Messed up is a far distance from having rejected the faith. That's where my line in the sand is. You haven't rejected God, you don't disrespect the faith. You struggle. You may struggle all your life. It makes me sad for you, but it's not a reason for us not to marry."

He tugged off the gloves. "Charlotte, you're going to be fine, we both will, whatever you decide. I want the decision you are comfortable with regarding the money. That's the first decision. Because the money and the proposal don't have to stay linked," he pointed out. "There's nothing that says I can't ask you again three years and a day after his death. We keep talking, Charlotte. That's what I want from you right now. I don't know where this goes, but I want to find out. Take the risk and give me that."

She finally nodded. "Okay, Bryce. We'll continue the conversation."

Charlotte set silverware and napkins on the table, brought over the pitcher to fill the water glasses. "If I say yes, someone eventually finds out I'm very wealthy and I'm a public figure again, not for something that happened in the past but for the ongoing present. I'm stalked by paparazzi everywhere I go because I'm now one of the wealthiest women in the country."

Bryce pulled out the glazed ham, slid the pumpkin pie into the oven in its place, and wondered why he'd tried to be so ambitious with the meal. "Not the wealthiest, not even top ten."

"In the top twenty-five."

"We should be able to quickly give enough away that you drop way down to the top fifty."

She leaned against the counter and reached for one of the extra marshmallows he hadn't needed for the top of the sweet potatoes. "I'm being serious, Bryce."

"I know you are." He handed her the bag of marshmallows. "You're doing okay giving away the sixty million. Having a lot more to give away isn't going to faze you after a while. The public attention is the real reason you don't want to accept the burden of this."

She nodded. "I can put up with nearly all the rest of it, but the press and public attention — I lived through that once, Bryce. Its intensity mentally destroyed me. I felt like I was having to hide from the world those first months after I was found. Like I was a prisoner again. If John hadn't been around, carving out some safe places and the freedom to breathe in those days, I'd be a recluse today. As it was, I still came close to tipping past that line. I don't want to go back to that. I don't want to go back to feeling trapped, having to watch out for the press, and being nervous about everyone who comes up to me."

"Wealth buys privacy."

"But by doing so it implicitly confirms the wealth is there — the private estate, the secure building, the security presence. I don't want footprints to our lives indicating the wealth is there. The cars we drive, the places we stay, the things we own — they say something about us to others. I need it kept a secret. For us to never appear wealthy."

He glanced over at her. She'd said *us*. It was progress, and he'd take any small movement he could get. "I need a job, Charlotte."

"What do you mean?"

"A cover. I need a job in philanthropy, where I can gather information we need to make giving decisions without my inquiries and interest in any way implying we're the

327

source of the funds. Maybe something with an existing foundation."

"An interesting idea."

"Worth thinking about."

He decided the corn was done and turned the burner to low. He took the sweet potatoes out of the oven. "The risk of the wealth becoming public comes from a few different places. Someone at the law firm reveals the information and your name. Intentional or not, that could easily happen. Or we make a mistake. Someone realizes a pattern of donations traces back to us and starts to ask questions about how much money we've been giving away and where the money's coming from. Given the amount to be given away, it's not only possible, but probable, someone eventually realizes we're giving away a lot of money. Also possible, we inadvertently tell someone who doesn't keep the secret. Remote, but could happen — someone puts together the information based on what's out there in the public record."

She grew more still as he finished his list. "The information is going to eventually get into the public domain."

He nodded. "For purposes of your decision, you have to assume it will."

Bryce accepted the plate she handed him,

stepped back so she could fill her plate first. "We can keep the fact of the wealth a secret for decades if we're fortunate. I have no desire to have money change who I am — what I drive, what I wear, where I live. I like my life, and I've earned the right to keep it. The money's not going to be obvious to people. But it's a random variable. The question is, are you comfortable with the contingency plan. If you can live with the contingency plan, it's a manageable problem."

"I see your point."

He slid two slices of ham onto his plate. "If it became public, we would use the wealth to buy us privacy. A nice-size home and grounds with good security. We'd add more security around my family. We'd hire staff to do the public errands and other miscellaneous tasks we used to do. Church would get tricky, and other public venues, but we'd manage the problem."

Charlotte pulled out a chair at the table. "If it were just me, I would change my name again, my appearance. I'd disappear and start over. It's the safe route."

"The escape."

"Yes. It's when someone puts together Ruth Bazoni and one of the wealthiest women in America that it gets really bad."

"You have to make your decision assuming that will happen." He brought over the fruit plate before he took his seat. "If it got horrible, Charlotte, I could see slipping you and Ellie out the back door for a vacation away from it. But once the wealth is publicly known, that cap never goes back on the bottle. The contingency would be to manage the situation."

"It's the reason I keep landing on no." She tried the sweet potatoes. "The weight of how the money changes every day of the rest of my life is the other reason for a no. Talk to me about the money. What's the plan?"

Bryce cleared the table, feeling like the conversation was spinning off into circles. He could understand why Charlotte had settled on no as the right answer, because the more they talked, the more complicated the problem of the money became. He'd change the subject to give them a break, but this first evening of conversation was too critical. If this evening ended with the impression saying no was the only safe choice, he was going to have an uphill battle trying to reverse it for the rest of the days until the deadline.

He brought over ice cream with strawberries since the pie still wasn't done. "Charlotte, if we're married, what do you want? In the simplest terms you can, let's start over with that question. I'll tell you the same. Give me a picture of what you want."

She pushed around the strawberries with her spoon. "You'll think it's silly."

He smiled. To get something she thought was silly also made it something true at a deep level. He'd been struggling all evening to get that out of her. "Try me."

"I want you to keep cash in my pocket, pay my credit card bill, and remember my birthday with a nice meal out somewhere. The money is your problem. We can talk about it, but I don't want to be pulled into the decisions, the plans, the weight of it."

He felt them turn the first corner toward an understanding. "A good and reasonable picture," he said softly.

"What's yours?"

"I want your shoes dropped in the hallway and your sketchbook on the coffee table and the clutter of you trying to cook in the kitchen. I want you to live with me and become comfortable with me. I want us to live in Chicago if it's possible, this house for now. If the press becomes a problem, we'll move, but stay in the area because of my family."

"I like your home, love the backyard, but Chicago is a risk."

"We'll deal with the risk. I want you to accept John's decisions on security. If he wants someone with you when you're here, when you're traveling — you can fuss about it all you want, but you stay within his lines."

She lifted her spoon and pointed it at him. "His security, his thoughts on it, you don't meddle and make it tighter because you're more worried than he is about something. And it goes both ways. He wants someone on you, you live with it."

Bryce nodded. "He's going to have someone stuck on us both if the news about the money ever becomes public."

"He will, and not give either one of us a choice. I've already lived with that. You're going to find it an experience."

"I'll adapt."

She thought while she ate her ice cream. "I'd want to give Shadow Lake and the family land to John, enough money to manage it so the land can stay undeveloped. I'd remodel Fred's place and give it to Ellie. It will give her a home near John, and it would be good for her to have a place out of the city. I'd sell the Silverton house."

"Anything that puts Ellie more in John's orbit, the better."

"That's what I was thinking."

Bryce weighed the risk and decided to see how far she'd take the picture. "I want you to let me decide how much is appropriate to give your sister, your brother-in-law, their girls, and when. What else we give John and Ellie, how and when. I'll do my best to keep peace in your world regarding the money, but you let me deal with the dynamics of it. You simply say, 'Talk to Bishop.' "

"Thank you."

"It's the one problem I believe I've got the skills to handle for you."

"You also give generously to your own family and friends; you accept it's your money as much as it is mine. Without the marriage there's none of it for either of us, and marriage is two people, two worlds of family and friends. You carry the burden of it, you carry the nice parts of it too."

He nodded, pleased not only with the perspective she had but that she was willing to follow his lead and fill in more of the picture of what might work. It was a long way from a decision, but the picture was a useful step to reaching that decision. "We'll tell the family there's some money," he said, "as they already know about the coins I'm selling for you. But we'll leave the impression it's in the millions. No one ever needs to know it starts with a *b*."

Charlotte was toying with her ice cream. Bryce pushed back his chair. "Let's shift this to the living room. Find your sketchbook, and I'll bring in more coffee."

"I don't want people to know it's not a normal marriage."

Bryce put the ball game on pause. "It will be a normal marriage."

Charlotte set aside her sketchbook. "We won't be sleeping together."

"That's something that will make for some interesting conversations between us, but it will be none of anyone else's business."

He couldn't read her expression, and he felt like he was stepping into quicksand. "It's our marriage. We'll do what makes sense to the two of us, and we'll reach those decisions with some kindness and patience behind the conversations. All I'm expecting out of marriage is what we have now plus another layer of more of the same — a friendship, we live together, and we figure out how to handle Fred's estate in a way that makes sense to us. To the outside world, family and friends, it's going to look like a content and happy marriage because that's actually what it's going to be."

She got to her feet. Before she could start

pacing, he reached for her hand to stop her. He stood, settled his arms around her, and linked them loosely behind her back. "Charlotte, listen. I'm not making any statements that imply I'm not interested in kissing you, holding you, and spending the night with you. I'd like all those things. But it's not a destination you're promising me or that I'm counting on to go with the fact we have a wedding. It's simply an assumption on my part that fifty years is a long time, and we might flow from being friends to something more if that happens to be the shift we both want someday. It's not an expectation. I'm going to honor what you want. You have my word that marriage isn't going to change your freedom to decide."

"It's going to be awkward in public."

"Not so awkward," he reassured. "There will be lines you can depend on me to honor. I won't kiss you in public unless you give me the sign it's okay for me to do so. Something simple between us. You can spin your ring around. Someone teases us to kiss under the mistletoe, you're going to get a hug and whisper that will probably make you blush, but I won't kiss you unless you clear it first.

"I'm going to reach for your hand, because I like holding hands with you. I'll put my arm around you and share your space, occasionally hug you, not unlike this. My family and friends are going to see that. They'll see the affection, because that is easy to share. I'm marrying you because I want to, because I care about you, because I asked you to marry me, and you said yes. I would be proud to have you as my wife, and people are going to clearly see that."

"I don't deserve that cover."

"You'll have it, Charlotte. We'll be friends, good friends, but I'll also be a good husband to you. I'll protect your privacy, protect what is between us."

He leaned back just enough to see her face. "Charlotte, a promise. I will never say the words 'I love you' in public before I've said them to you in private. And I'll never say them to you in private until I can say them from the bottom of my heart. That day comes, I want you to believe me. I will not say the words lightly. But I'm not going to be pressuring you to move beyond where you are comfortable with me.

"There are only four people in our circle who know the will requires you to marry — Ellie and John, my father, and because he knows, my mother. It's not something others need to know. My family and friends will simply assume we're marrying because we love each other. I'll handle any awkward situations that develop, smoothly get us out of them. That will be my job."

Her hand settled flat against his chest. "You're putting your family at risk."

"I'm not going to live my life in fear of what might happen. We're smart enough to take sensible precautions." He nudged up her chin so she would look at him rather than the button on his shirt, saw the wariness in her eyes. "It's okay to say yes."

"I'm too scared to say yes."

He tightened his hug just a fraction to acknowledge the soft words and then answered her fears by relaxing his hold and letting her step back. "Then maybe you should think about why you're scared and let us deal with that."

"Are you going to tell your family I'm Ruth Bazoni?"

He'd known the question was coming. He took his time on the answer. "My parents already know. I told my dad, he told my mom, and I had a long conversation with my mom a few days ago. She remembers you, Charlotte. Mrs. B, from your fifth grade class. The rest of the family will be your decision for if and when we tell them."

"Mrs. B?" She looked startled at the news.

"I hadn't realized. It was your mom who encouraged me to draw. She used to put a smiley face on my papers when I turned in one where I had doodled in the margins."

Bryce smiled. "That sounds like Mom."

"When your family meets my sister, they'll immediately put it together."

"That day's going to come when it does. But by then, they will know you as Charlotte. They'll hurt for you, but they won't see you as Ruth. And for the most part, they'll forget, because it's in the past."

"I don't want people to know for as long as possible."

"Agreed. Would you want us to fly to New York and talk to your sister about this decision?"

"No. She'll try to talk me out of it. And I would let her. It's a conversation that has to come after the wedding."

"I won't let you have that conversation alone," he promised.

She picked up her sketchbook but didn't start drawing again. "Will you regret marrying me, thirty years from now when the money is gone?"

"No. When the money is gone, we'll be just like every other couple who's been married for thirty years. Older and wiser and good friends. The thirty years after that will be the easy years of the marriage."

"You're more optimistic about this than I am."

He studied her face. *Jesus, what are the right words here? I can hear her doubts, see them, and I know fear is the emotion she's feeling. I don't think anything can remove that other than the experience of a good marriage.*

"Charlotte, please trust me," he finally said, trying to figure out how to sum up the conversation. "This will work. If I didn't believe that, I'd be wise enough to say so. I don't want fifty years of chaos for my life or for yours. I'm not asking you to marry me because of the money, while ignoring the rest of what would be our reality. I think we could have a good marriage if you want to say yes. That's what I'm asking you to consider. I like the idea of being your husband. If you want to say yes to the money, I'm a safe choice. We would have a good life together."

Charlotte unlocked the door to Ellie's home, glad to have the difficult conversation behind her.

Ellie came to meet her. "You had a long evening."

"And anything but a simple discussion."

Ellie studied her face, started to smile. "It

went well. You're actually thinking about saying yes."

"We squared the corners of the idea and talked about what it would look like. My mind is spinning." Charlotte walked into the living room, picked up the pillows on the extra deep sofa and sank into it, hugging the cushions against her.

Ellie took a seat beside her. "How's your heart?"

"Troubled. I'm not an arranged-marriage kind of woman, and that's what I'm talking about having."

"You'd run scared to death if he said 'I love you.' "

She half smiled, acknowledging it was true. "I can maybe do the friendship he wants, Ellie, but he's a businessman. He's not an easy man to sync up with. John, I could pretty much always understand. Bryce — he'll do a fine job with the money, and he'll be a good husband because he'll measure himself against that phrase, but it feels —" she stopped because it hurt to say it aloud — "it feels like he's taking me on as a job."

"He doesn't mean to leave that impression."

"But it's the truth of what is developing. He gets a wife who's more like a houseguest than a wife, and a job of giving away the money. It isn't worth this, Ellie."

"Is being single any better? Honestly?"

Charlotte bit her lip. "No, it's not great."

"I'm not saying marry him. Just consider the picture of it. There are parts of not being alone that would make your life much better than it is today. What's the downside?"

"Fifty years of disappointing him."

"If he treated you like he does now for the next fifty years, would you be okay with the marriage?"

Charlotte didn't answer for a long time. "Yes."

"There's also risk if you say no. You overworked in Texas, to the point John and I both worried about you. You were too alone in your day-to-day. I worry about you slipping back into that mode. The work that never ends. The sadness of saying no is going to be heavy. You'd be giving up not only the money, but a different life. One that I think could be better for you."

"Do you really think this is a good idea?"

"How many times have you wished life had taken a different turn when you were sixteen?"

"Too many times to count."

"Take this turn, Charlotte. He's a nice

man — in every way I can see — and you won't be alone anymore. You don't have to tell him about the past, you don't have to even mention it. You can relax and just enjoy spending your present life with someone."

"He referred to Mrs. B, and it clicked, the image of his mom. Why didn't you tell me?"

"I liked the idea of it being a good surprise you could encounter. He's got a good family. You'll like all of them. More than anything I want you to be settled for the next decades of your life. You'll fit in, you'll have a place, and he's the kind of guy you can trust. His kind doesn't come around very often."

"The money is prompting his offer."

"Is it? I think the offer is prompted by the fact he wants you to have a real choice. He likes you, Charlotte. He doesn't like the situation you're in. He's being just a bit of a white knight, trying to rescue you by offering to give you a choice. I think it says something nice about him."

"He mentioned that his proposal and the money didn't have to stay linked, that there wasn't a reason he couldn't ask me again after three years . . . which would take the money issue away. I don't think he meant it as a serious idea to explore, but it was part of his original comments about this."

"I think if you wanted to get married without the money, Charlotte, he'd be interested in having that conversation with you." Ellie searched her face. "But I also believe he feels that however it has happened, that money is yours, and he can help you with it."

"He could handle the money and do it well. Not many people I've met could do that."

Ellie nodded. "I see the money, the giving it away, as something the two of you can work on together, the common ground you might need during the first few years of marriage. It will be a safe topic if you don't know what else to talk about." Ellie reached over to squeeze her hand. "Charlotte, what do you really lose if you say yes? If you can answer that question, maybe the decision will become more clear."

Charlotte ceased talking about it. Bryce expected the occasional comment or question, but neither came.

He put his focus on the remaining work to be done on the vaults and selling the coins. He expanded the prep room and doubled the coin shipments. He finished clearing vault nineteen and opened vault twenty-two. Whatever Charlotte decided, yes or no, it would be useful for the coins to no longer be a matter to deal with after the will's deadline.

Charlotte, emptying more storage units, found the model trains mentioned in the old logbook. The break room in the administration building soon filled with guys during their off-hours, helping their sons build an elaborate track so a dozen antique model trains could roar around the detailed display. Charlotte named engine nine the Graham Express and could be found at odd hours racing it around the intricate track.

Bryce had a lot of time to think, and he began to understand the problem. The more he thought about what could be done with the money, laying out tentative plans of how it could fund projects around the world, the more apparent how life-altering it could be. He wanted the opportunity, the challenge, and the satisfaction of managing the funds, and he equally understood why she would be inclined to say no. Her current life had a known quantity to it that was very attractive in light of her past.

Their dinners became more sporadic as the weather turned from the brisk cool of fall into the full-on cold of winter with snow coating the roads between Chicago and Wisconsin. In some ways he was grateful, for the decision had to be one Charlotte could live with for the rest of her life, and it needed to be her decision. He worried about pressuring her decision even with good intentions. The money side of this mattered to him, more than he was comfortable admitting. He wanted a life that wasn't boring, and spending the next decades managing where to give a fortune was a solution. If she said no, he didn't know where he'd find something else as interesting and fulfilling for his future. He needed time to let go of that motivation.

He believed in a sovereign God. The fact the money had been left to Charlotte had been God's plan for her. That he wished it had been left to him . . . he imagined anyone hearing about it might wish the same thing. God, in His wisdom, had determined the money would go to Charlotte. Bryce wondered what God was teaching her, or asking of her, by doing so. For Charlotte wasn't reaching for wealth for herself.

As time passed, that reality became yet another fact Bryce deeply admired about the woman. She had the capacity to turn down enormous wealth. He couldn't yet say the same for himself.

TWENTY

Paul Falcon joined his wife in their home office on a Saturday afternoon before Christmas, unwrapping a candy cane. Their tree was decorated and lit, and Christmas music was playing in the background. He'd taken over the dining room table to finish wrapping his share of the gifts they would be distributing. He wasn't surprised to find Ann, headphones in place, working on the Conner case. Her gift wrapping had been complete for several weeks.

He picked up the list of names she was annotating. She was back on the core problem — identifying the voice of the Dublin Pub caller who said baby Connor had died.

His wife pushed off her headphones. "The audio guys have been through the last of the old physical tapes found in evidence. They've confirmed none of the men the cops questioned and recorded in a formal interview is a voice match to the caller. It shrinks the list quite a bit. But I noticed something today. Does our caller sound drunk to you, or like he had been drinking heavily?" She handed him the audio headphones and cued the call to replay.

Paul listened carefully. "No."

"Agreed. I'm not catching even a slight hesitation in his speech. I noticed something related and interesting in the list of names. Lynel Masters. He was at the Dublin Pub that night because the bartender called him to pick up his sister, who'd had too much to drink. I wonder who else was there that night to pick up someone, meet someone — not there to drink or stay, but just stopping in. I wish the cops had thought to collect the names of the women who were at the Dublin Pub that night. Women watch guys, remember them, and they could have been a good source to tell us if this list of names we have is complete. Maybe someone didn't stay but a minute — just long enough to make a call."

"A good observation. I wish we could have worked that idea at the time," Paul agreed. "We can track down Lynel's sister. And a few of the guys named on the list were at the pub with their wives. Maybe their wives can look at the list and tell us who should have been on it given who *was* there. Friends of friends kind of connections."

"It's worth a try." Ann looked at the page in her hand. "Either our caller is on this list of those at the pub that night, or he was there and his name didn't make the list because no one thought to mention him. I'm beginning to think no one thought to mention him."

"Maybe we'll get lucky this afternoon and add a new name," Paul said. There was too much snow on the ground today to walk around Meadow Park knocking on doors, but there were two holiday parties this afternoon they planned to attend, one at the community center and the other at a church, where neighbors were gathering and a few questions could be asked. Extended families would also be home for the holidays, and it would be a good chance to connect with people they otherwise would be unable to see.

Ann stuffed her working files into her flight bag to take with them.

Paul leaned down to rub the dog's back. "Which one of us is going to break the news to Black that he's not going with us today?"

Ann looked down at the dog. Looked up at him. "If I say pretty please, will you explain it to him?"

"Maybe we can put antlers on him and smuggle him in as a reindeer in disguise."

Ann laughed. "I'll call Kate and see if Black can visit. Holly will enjoy climbing all over him, and Black can go outside and sit on a snowdrift and play king of the mountain."

"That works." Paul settled his arm around his wife. "I like Christmas."

"It's the cookies. And the music. And the candy canes — those were for the kids."

"I used to be one." He dropped a kiss on her hair. "I'll add the dress you've got set out to wear on Christmas Eve."

Ann smiled. "I'm planning to turn your head. Your presents are wrapped?"

"All but the one for you-know-who. He would eat the wrapping paper to get to it, so it's left in the pantry."

"We'll cheat and let him open his first gift tonight."

Paul grinned. "I'm all for spoiling him. Call Kate while I get us our coats."

"You've been in a pensive mood tonight, son."

Bryce turned from the window where he'd been watching the snow fall. "Just wondering if this is my last Christmas alone." The family gathering would pack more than

349

twenty people into his parents' home, but it didn't change the fact Bryce would come alone and would leave alone. "I'm hoping it is."

"I'm growing more comfortable with the idea myself. You'd be a good husband for her, Bryce. I hope she accepts. Charlotte could use a family like ours around her."

Bryce would have invited her to the gathering tonight, but she had gone with Ellie to Texas for the holidays, along with John. She was at least out of reach of this snow. "You'll like her, Dad."

"It says something about her character that she isn't reaching for the money."

"It does." Bryce rubbed the back of his neck. "And it's a lot."

"I don't want to know the amount. You're nervous, that's enough to tell me it's large. But I know God has prepared you for handling even large amounts wisely."

"If she says yes, she'll want to give it away. She's already decided on that."

"A generous thing to do, and one you'll both enjoy. You're bothered by the delay in her decision?"

Bryce shrugged rather than admit he was. "She's got a very difficult choice before her. I would be a good husband, but she's got to accept being married. She's not inclined toward saying yes."

His dad smiled. "It's okay to admit there's a bit of pride on the line. You asked the woman to marry you. It's going to sting if she says no."

"More than I'm comfortable admitting." He could close his eyes, see himself married to Charlotte, and see something interesting. He liked the idea of being her husband. He liked the challenge of what life would be with her. He wanted to show her what it was like to relax and share her life with a guy day-to-day. He wanted to give her back some of the carefree days she'd missed during her teens and twenties. And wasn't that an interesting Christmas wish? "I'm just dreaming a bit, Dad, and hoping."

"Christmas is a good time for that kind of hope. You asked her in order to give her a choice. She has one now. It will be good if she says yes, and you'll survive if she says no. Now come help me with the tree. Your mom wants to bring out the last of her twelve days of Christmas ornaments tonight."

Bryce complied with a smile. He liked Christmas with his family and thought Charlotte would enjoy being part of this next year, should she say yes. He wanted a chance to share this with her.

TWENTY-ONE

The movie on TV had half Charlotte's attention; the rest was on the sketch coming to life. Butterflies were some of the most interesting creatures to draw — and some of the hardest to get the perspectives right. No two butterflies in the sketch were on the same plane, and their wings were tipped at different angles, some facing her, some nearly edge on, some in three-quarter profile as they hovered or sat on flowers. She loved Christmas but was equally glad the holidays were now past and a new year was unfolding. She was anticipating winter being gone and spring arriving.

"Want some popcorn?" Bryce asked.

She glanced up from her sketch. "Sure."

Bryce headed to the kitchen. She found the remote to put the movie on pause. She thought she had seen the film before. In the same vague way she was pretty sure Bryce had asked that question about popcorn more than once before she tuned in and heard him. She stretched her arms over her head and pulled against the stiffness in her back. Never before had she enjoyed regular evenings sitting with a guy simply to watch a movie, talk a bit, and draw. Sometime in the last few months she had come to realize these evenings were mini-vacations for her, and instead of finding reasons to push them off to a later date, she was at the point she preferred to say yes.

"Want butter?" Bryce called.

"Please."

He fed her, generated more ideas for giving, printed checks for her to sign, was curious about her day, and had stories to share about his family that made her silently regret her world was at its core only John and Ellie. He wasn't pushing at the question of marriage resting quietly but very much there on the table, hadn't even hinted at it. And that willingness to wait for her decision was more helpful to her than anything he could have said. He had made his case and was letting it be her decision.

The doorbell rang as Bryce came back with the popcorn. He changed directions to answer it. "John." Charlotte heard his surprise. "Please, come in."

"Sorry to interrupt the evening."

"In here, John." Charlotte recognized his expression and set aside pencils and sketchbook. "This isn't going to be good."

"How about a drive?"

She knew what he was asking and simply shook her head. "He can hear it." John would have said they *needed* to take a drive if what he was about to tell her was in the terrain of information she wouldn't later tell Bryce. She'd rather not have to repeat the bad news.

"I'm sorry I can't buffer this."

Charlotte nodded.

"A reporter is doing a book titled *The Bazoni Girls' Kidnapping*. The publisher approached him to time its publication with the twentieth anniversary of the crime, he thought about it, and said yes."

"We know him."

"Gage Collier."

Charlotte knew John and every nuance of how he handled trouble, had trusted him in crowds and when she was afraid. "That fact has you driving me home tonight and breaking the news, but you'd give me the few last hours of the evening to enjoy without knowing this." She braced with a deep breath. "Give me the rest of it."

He reached over and firmly took her hand. "Tabitha is cooperating with him."

She felt the punch.

And then she felt nothing.

She iced it over and left the emotions for later. "You're certain," she whispered.

"Do you want a flight to New York to try to talk her out of it? She's mailing her diary, your father's journal, the case file and notes your father had gathered, and once the package is postmarked we're going to be out of options."

Charlotte closed her eyes and thought of a lifetime with Tabitha. She opened her eyes and met John's gaze. "No. She's doing what she considers best for both of us." It was the wrong decision, horribly wrong in ways Tabitha did not know, dangerously wrong. But if she didn't trust Tabitha's motives, she had lost a relationship with her sister forever. To cooperate with a book — Tabitha needed to talk, needed people to hear her story, or she would have said no.

Charlotte could feel the nausea, knew the reaction was going to hit hard, and didn't want Bryce to see the shakes that were coming. "Would you take me to Ellie's?"

"She's on her way here. I want you north. Gage knows your name."

A reporter knew her name. It impacted like a bullet. Had she lost it all?

■ ■ ■ ■

A reporter was doing a book about the Bazoni girls' kidnapping and knew Ruth Bazoni was Charlotte Graham. Bryce immediately understood the implications, was thinking through it better than Charlotte was right now. "Drink this, Charlotte." He folded her hands around a mug of hot chocolate.

She did as he asked. Bryce was relieved some color was coming back into her face. John had stepped out to arrange with Mitch to take Charlotte's truck back. "A book publication is at least six months to a year away. There's time," he told her.

She nodded. "Gage is . . ." She stopped and looked up at him, the panic in her eyes nearly breaking his heart. "Bryce, he's the best investigative reporter in Chicago.

"At the hospital he used to send me homemade sugar cookies, movies, and these scrapbooks he had made on various topics — everything that happened in music the last four years, popular culture, world events. To help me get up-to-date. He wanted an interview like every other reporter, but he was nice about including a genuine get-well along with the request."

"Did you ever meet him?"

She shook her head as she sipped at the chocolate. "Talked to him twice, briefly, on the phone. John knows him." She handed back the mug when it was empty. "Tabitha didn't call me, Bryce. Didn't warn me."

He knew the deep pain that simple fact created. Tabitha likely hadn't wanted Charlotte to try to stop her from cooperating with the book, so she had not warned her. "I'm very sorry she didn't."

He heard the front door open and wished he had more time. "Will you call me later, just to talk? It doesn't have to be on important things. We can talk coins and dogs and what movie to watch next."

She smiled briefly, then began gathering her things. "If I knew how the rest of this night was going to unfold, I'd say yes. I'll be in touch, Bryce. I just don't know when."

"You'll be in my prayers, Charlotte."

She hesitated, then nodded. "Thanks for that."

Bryce hoped and prayed to hear from her that night, but the phone never rang.

John called him the next morning. "She's at Silverton with Ellie for the next few days."

"How's she doing?"

"Hard to read. Charlotte handles something like this by getting very quiet, which is why I wanted Ellie along. Over the coming weeks the rest of this picture is going to become clear — what Tabitha is thinking, what Gage is planning. If we can keep Charlotte's current name out of the book, that will be a good step in the right direction for her."

"John, is Gage Collier the kind of guy who puts together Ruth Bazoni, the Legacy Trust, and one of the richest women in the country?"

"He's not looking for it."

"But if he bumps into something that makes him wonder — he's the guy who would find it?"

"Yes."

Bryce pushed a hand through his hair. "It's a reason she needs to consider staying at no regarding the money."

"She hasn't mentioned the matter, but I'm sure it's crossed Charlotte's mind."

The odds had just risen significantly that Charlotte was going to turn it all down — marriage, the inheritance. And Bryce couldn't disagree with that outcome given the circumstances. "You'll call if there's anything she needs?"

"I will."

"Keep her safe, John."

"It's what Ellie and I do, Bryce. When it matters we're her family. I'll be in touch."

Charlotte walked alone up the steps to the two-story townhouse, rang the doorbell. She had declined John's offer to accompany her. She was on time and expected, and the door opened before the sound of the chimes had faded.

"Charlotte, thanks for coming."

"Gage."

He stepped back so she could enter. "I asked for twenty minutes of your time, and I won't keep you longer than that. May I offer you a soft drink or some refreshments?"

She thought she'd test how he wanted to approach this. And how good a memory he had. "Have any sugar cookies?"

"Straight up or with a glass of milk?"

She could survive twenty minutes talking with him. "Make it with milk." He disappeared into the kitchen.

Surprised at how calm she was feeling, she looked around his home with interest. He was working on the book here, it appeared. The living room was an office, the dining room crowded with four long tables neatly stacked with paper. Charlotte recognized her father's journal, two of the cloth-covered diaries Tabitha favored, the neat handwriting on the folder tabs — the material from her sister was on the second table.

The background report John had handed her on Gage Collier ran five pages single-spaced. Pulitzer Prize, weekend investigative pieces, scandals and crimes he had uncovered — his work had been admired and feared for decades, and he had a solid reputation as a cynic who didn't trust an answer he couldn't verify. That work history she expected and respected.

His personal information had been more useful. Gage Collier was a widower who had lost his wife and unborn son in a house fire. That particular fact was enough for her to accept she'd be able to find some common ground with the man. He understood personal pain in a profound way.

Reading the report hadn't completely settled her nerves, though. She was the fact-finding target of this man. He might be a decent man at the core — John liked him — but she had good reason to fear what he could do. She stopped the thought. She was here, it was her choice, and she could walk out the door to the car idling at the curb whenever she wished.

Gage returned with a tray holding two glasses of milk, a plate piled high with sugar cookies, and a stack of napkins. He placed it on the table between two comfortable chairs, took a seat and picked up one of the glasses. He dunked a cookie. "I haven't forgotten any detail of our short relationship to date. If you're willing to trust me with more, you'll find I don't forget those details either."

"A useful trait for a reporter," she noted as she sat down.

"You interest me, Charlotte. Which is one reason I didn't dismiss the publisher when they approached me about this project."

Charlotte reached for the glass of milk and a sugar cookie to have something in her hands.

"I wasn't the first one they asked — Ann Falcon turned them down — and I modified the terms to suit me before I said yes. This will be my first book, and it will be well researched, on par with the best journalism I've done in my career. The cops who worked the task force, both local and federal, have retired, and many are willing to now go on the record.

"I didn't expect your sister to cooperate with me. She's spoken on background for a couple of articles over the years, and while she's a polite woman in her dealings with the press, I expected her to decline to offer anything more than the same for this book. She instead agreed to sit for an interview concerning the day of your abduction and the twenty-four hours before you shoved her out of the van. She's provided me with what she had in written materials up to the day you were rescued — your father's journals, her diaries, the case file the family had built, notes about what the investigators told the family, what they thought had happened. She won't discuss her conversations with you or arrangements made after you were rescued. That's the background for our conversation now."

Charlotte nodded and picked up another cookie. "What do you want from me?"

"For you and I to reach an understanding."

Gage broke a second cookie and dunked it. "The book will stay with the name Ruth Bazoni. I will say you've changed your name and that you now live in Europe — or wherever you want it to say. There will be a disclaimer in the front of the book saying names and locations have been changed where necessary, so technically I won't be lying.

"I'm going to offer what I never offer, Charlotte. Read what I write as I develop the manuscript. Comment on anything you would like, or not, as you choose. You're welcome to review the materials gathered, go through the transcripts of interviews I do, treat this" — he gestured to the tables of materials — "as your own resource as well as mine. You lived through what happened, but I don't think you know many of the details of what was going on within the task force or with your family. If you want to go back and understand some of your own past, I'm offering you an open door to do so."

"I appreciate that," she finally replied.

Gage smiled. "I want your comments, Charlotte. I want whatever you decide to share with me. It's the only way it becomes an extraordinary story. As you see what's developing I think you're going to decide it's in your own interests to be part of this book, to offer your perspective." He dug in his pocket and came up with a key. "For you."

She didn't take it, too surprised by the offer.

"Take it," he encouraged. "A key to the front door. The alarm code has been set to also accept your birthday. I generate a printout of the current manuscript each Friday. The pages are marked by the date on the box and stacked on that far bookshelf. If you want to stop by at two a.m. and read, you'll probably find me at the desk. It's an open invitation. Come and go as you wish. I trust you. I trust you not to take something from this room or damage what is here. This is your story, Tabitha's. You should be involved."

"I don't talk about it, Gage. I never have."

"That's your choice. Read what I write. Then decide what you want to do with it. Give me that. You won't be blindsided by what's coming in the book, you'll know what I'm going to publish."

Charlotte accepted the key. "This isn't the conversation I was expecting to have with you today."

"I asked what I would want if our places were reversed. I can't give you control over what is going to be published, but I assure you I will listen carefully to your perspective on anything you see on paper. I can put you in the place to know what and why something is being written. If you disagree with what I've written and I'm not willing to change my words, I will promise to footnote it and give you space to reply as you like."

She nodded. "Thanks for that." She tightened her hand around the key. "I need John's name kept out of the book."

"I can give you that. John's the real difficulty for you, Charlotte, not Tabitha, a fact you both know. Reporters want to find you, they simply find John, and watch. It might not be common knowledge you've stayed friends, that he's in your life again, but a good reporter is going to find out rather than assume he's not. And while you may not look anything like your twin sister, you do look a lot like your mother. She was a beautiful woman."

"One statement we can agree on. How much time do I have?"

"I'm looking at a first draft to be finished in nine months. But I'll start having pages for you to read within a month."

Ann paused from wiping off the kitchen counter as the security panel lit. She saw with surprise it was Charlotte Graham in the lobby. "Please, come up, Charlotte," she said into the intercom. "Floor four." She keyed the elevator to release security.

Ann pushed bare feet into shoes, ran a hand through her hair, and went to meet her guest, somewhat nervous about the unexpected visit, and the reason for it. So few people knew this address that she guessed Bryce had to have been the one who passed it on. She met Charlotte at the elevator with a smile. "Welcome, Charlotte."

"I was in the neighborhood and thought I'd chance you were home."

"I'm pleased you stopped by." Ann picked up the rag she had dropped, gave a laugh, and grabbed the bottle of polish sitting on the floor next to the sculpture in the entryway. "You caught me on a cleaning day. I hide away for a week every month or so if I can — a much-needed chance to recharge. I try to leave Paul a clean house before I disappear. I'm inevitably disorganized about it. Would you join me for something to drink? Tea or soda?"

"Some tea would be nice."

Ann led the way to the kitchen, turned on the burner under the teapot.

"You turned down writing the book. I'd like to know why."

Ann pulled a soda from the door of the refrigerator, got out a cup and tea bag for Charlotte, and tried to get a read on her guest before she answered the question. Charlotte obviously knew about the book, so the bad news had already hit her. There were numerous ways to truthfully answer that question. Ann chose to take a very big risk.

"I was snatched too, Charlotte. Call it an odd form of kinship. I thought you deserved your privacy."

Charlotte visibly jolted. "You're the diary writer."

"Yes."

Charlotte could have said nearly anything given the shared terrain the news conveyed. She absorbed it, slowly nodded, then visibly relaxed. "And I thought I'd had it tough ducking the media."

Ann smiled, turned to pour hot water into the cup. "The form letter says, 'Thank you for the question, please see the press release and book for what I would like to say.' The firm handling my mail still sends out a few hundred of them a month."

"I can imagine."

Ann handed Charlotte her tea and gestured to the living room. "I gather you've had a conversation with Gage."

"He'll do an excellent job with the book, I'm sorry to say. It would be easier on me if it was going to be a sloppily written piece of fabricated true crime. I wouldn't wish a man to be hit by a bus, but I wouldn't mind Gage getting a job offer he couldn't refuse from some remote town in Alaska."

Ann laughed. "I understand the sentiment perfectly."

"He'll have to do the book without my help. I don't talk about it."

"I know."

Charlotte turned from looking at the artwork to look at her.

Ann simply nodded, indicating that she knew the reason. A cop had some of the ransom money. The cop was dead, but it was still going to be news to the public. "Gage will find the money trail because he's good at what he does."

"Figured that. Tabitha doesn't know," Charlotte said.

Ann understood a great deal more with that simple statement. "For what it's worth, it was a good decision to leave it unsaid, Charlotte. It's what you do for family. You protect them."

"You at least try." Charlotte looked back at the painting. "You have a fabulous collection of art."

"Paul enjoys collecting. Please, feel free to look around. Some are in here, some are in the office and den."

Charlotte accepted the offer and walked around the room. She paused at the painting titled simply *Quarter Horse at Work*. It was a vivid close-up portrait done in oil of a horse and rider chasing down a straying cow, behind them the vast wide-open land of Wyoming. The power and muscle, the determination and intensity of the task, were all captured in the movement of the scene. "You have one of Marie's works."

"You know the artist?"

Charlotte glanced back. "Yes."

"She's gifted with a paintbrush, just as you're gifted with pen and pencil sketches."

Charlotte smiled. "We live on different planets for talent, but thanks for the compliment." She looked back at Ann. "You're pretty decent with words. How long has the VP's biography been on the bestseller list now? More than two years?"

"I wrote a chapter in it."

"Rather fascinating chapter. Your O'Malley books were good. I'm partial to Lisa's story, if I have to choose a favorite."

"One of mine too. She's in town occasionally. We catch a ball game together, have a girls' day out. Maybe you'd like to join us sometime."

"I might take you up on that." Charlotte stopped in front of another painting, narrowed her eyes, stepped closer, then back, took in the full scope and smiled. "You've got a Sunfrey too. It's spectacular."

"It's not signed," Ann pointed out.

"Maybe not in the corner, but this is a Sunfrey. Not one from her published catalog either, or the coffee-table book of later works."

"You know her works well."

"Artists appreciate other artists' works with an intensity that borders on envy. I've been trying to capture her shift in greens from sunlight to shadows for years and still can't do it. She's making the brushstrokes flow in a curve when the light hits the shadow, rippling the effect of the falling light. No one had done it before her, and now everyone tries to employ the technique." Charlotte glanced over. "I get the feeling you know the artist."

"I do. I happen to know she's got a couple of your sketches above her desk. I'd say the admiration flows both ways."

"That I did not expect to hear." Charlotte chose to continue to wander the room rather than sit, paused to glance briefly at the papers Ann had gathered together on the table but not yet moved back to the office, walked over to the windows to see the limited city view from the fourth floor. "I need a favor."

Ann set aside her drink. "Ask."

"Whatever the FBI has that they aren't giving Gage, I'd like you to help arrange for him to see it. If the book is going to be written, I'd like it to be complete."

Ann slowly nodded. "I can talk with Paul. Something else back there, Charlotte?"

Her guest turned, held her gaze, shifted the question. "Whatever the FBI has. And if your friends at Chicago PD are willing, whatever they have in their files as well."

"I'll make some calls."

Charlotte nodded her thanks.

Ann wondered if the case was over or if it had just turned the page to a new chapter. The woman was a survivor. Ann had just glimpsed why. Charlotte was still holding the story, the real one, of what had happened.

Ann changed the subject rather than press the question. "Come over to the coin room some morning and I'll give you a tour of what's being done. You'd enjoy it, Charlotte, now that the coins are someone else's problem to deal with."

Charlotte smiled. "One of the more helpful things to have off my plate. I'm heading back to Graham Enterprises this afternoon. I've got a storage vault of old kitchenware to sort out, and we found crates of tools belonging in a blacksmith's shop, even a broken wagon wheel needing repair."

"The estate has been giving you a great deal of variety and history."

"It has. It's helped that I've been able to pass on to Bryce some of the major weight of the estate, selling the coins, and to have his help giving away the money."

"He's a man able to carry it."

"Is he running out of places to give?"

Ann smiled. "He'll find more. He's a good man, Charlotte. You chose well whom to trust."

"More Ellie and John's doing, I think, than mine."

"Maybe in the beginning." Ann picked up her soda, turned it in her hands. "If you ever want to talk, Charlotte — you'll find I'm a good listener. Bryce isn't bad either."

"I appreciate that." She glanced at the time. "I'm afraid I need to go. Thanks for letting me interrupt your day."

Ann wasn't surprised Charlotte didn't take up the opening to talk the first time it was offered. "Anytime." She rose to see her guest out.

"He's back this way. Let me show you."

Bryce heard Sharon speaking to someone out front, looked up at the tap on his office door and saw Charlotte. The relief he felt was intense. "Thanks, Sharon."

She disappeared with a smile.

"Have time for a walk?" Charlotte asked.

He picked up his keys and phone, reached for his coat. "Let's go down to the coffee shop."

She nodded and followed him out the back door of Bishop Chicago. He took her gloved hand as they joined the flow of traffic on the sidewalk heading north.

"I'm sorry I didn't call."

He shook his head. "It was an offer, not a demand. There wouldn't have been much I could do to help."

"Bryce, accept the apology. I should have called. I'm simply not used to having someone beyond Ellie or John when problems have to be sorted out."

He glanced at her, then smiled. "Apology accepted."

"There's not much that can be done about the book, but my present name will stay out of it."

"That's a big step."

"Gage and I have reached an understanding, I think. He's asked me to read what he writes, comment if I wish, or not, as I choose."

"Not what I was expecting."

"Nor I, but probably smart on his part. If he'd asked me for an interview, I would have said no, so he simply avoided the question." She glanced over. "I haven't spoken with Tabitha. I'm going to let her decide when and if she wants to discuss this."

"That's generous of you."

"She's got a right to say whatever she would like. She's the extrovert of the two of us. She processes pain by talking about it. I guess I'm only surprised she didn't do this years ago. Gage said she's not talking about the conversations the two of us have had."

"You're still protecting her, Charlotte, even in how you talk about her decisions."

"An older sister's prerogative." She pushed her hands into her coat pockets. "I came to tell you I'll be at Graham Enterprises for the foreseeable future. I need to get clear of the estate. I need to be mobile again, in case a problem crops up."

"I can accelerate the timetable for buying the rest of the coins and clearing the vaults."

"Where you can. I've still got storage units to clear."

"Are you going to change your name?"

"If it becomes necessary. I gave John a new one. Not Charlotte this time, so I'm hoping the step isn't required. I've grown accustomed to it."

"One of your first real decisions for yourself after it was over was your choice of a new name."

She glanced over at him, surprised he understood how important it had been, having that choice. "Yes. Helped more than a little by John's assurance that he liked the name Charlotte."

"A good friend to have." He put his arm around her, gave her a hug. "Are you okay?"

"No, but I'll figure out how to be. The publicity around the book will be a problem, not to mention its release."

"Ellie will come up with a plan."

Charlotte laughed. "A good one. I'm counting on her. John and Ellie make it possible to take a punch like this and still survive."

"Let me know how I can help."

"I will. Thanks for that, Bryce."

They reached the coffee shop, and he held the door for her. He'd help her get through this, however she would let him help. It was going to be a difficult book to read when it was finished. How much of it would be information he knew, how much would be new? The book would be facts, speculation, and whatever the reporter could get others to say. Her history, out there for anyone to read for the price of the book. It hurt, knowing that was coming. And he wished it was over rather than looming out there ahead of her.

TWENTY-TWO

The early signs of spring began to chase away the snow. Bryce hauled yet another load from the vault back to Chicago. The coins were selling at a price and pace that would make business for the last year the best in his lifetime. He was doing his best to enjoy it. His personal life might be on hold, but his professional one was coming together. The profits were strong, and the document for selling Bishop Chicago to Devon and Sharon was now on his desk.

The calendar days till the will deadline had fallen to ninety-two. He had resigned himself to the wait. John said Charlotte was still thinking about it. Ellie told him it had always been part of the plan for a contingency in case of a last-minute yes, that at thirty days left she would begin preparing for that possibility.

It wasn't Charlotte's style, though, to run things to a last-minute decision. Bryce had accepted reality. It simply might not be possible for her to get comfortable with saying yes. It seemed likely the time was going to run out with her decision remaining no.

Ninety-two days. When did the point of diminishing time indicate it was a no that would not change? Should he have a conversation with her again before they reached that point, or let Charlotte decide if and when the topic was brought up? He wanted to handle this with grace, and he wasn't sure what that might look like. God had taught him a lot about himself these last few months. He did not easily wait. He was learning patience above all else.

Charlotte was going to need a husband with a lot of patience, for much of what she needed to talk about if she was ever going to heal were events she had yet to say a word about. He wanted to help her heal — her relationship with God, the scars of what had happened. The patience to have the conversations when she was ready for them would matter more than anything else he might be able to give her. It might be five years, ten, before she ever gave him the first opening to talk about it — but he wanted to get them to those conversations. He wanted to help her heal.

The reasons he hoped she would say yes

to his proposal had been shifting over the months. He wanted her to have a choice regarding the money, and at a deeper level he wanted to protect her from getting hurt again, wanted to help her reclaim some of what she'd missed in life. But under those a richer level was forming now. He simply didn't want her to be alone anymore.

She had good friends in John and Ellie, but at the heart of it Charlotte was very much alone. Her family situation with her sister was ruptured and difficult to restore. She lived life alone, thinking that protected her best. Maybe it did. Maybe staying single was necessary to cope with what had happened. But Bryce ached at that reality.

He wanted her to say yes so she wouldn't be alone any longer. He wanted to help her deal with what had happened if she would let him. He wanted to be part of her life, and close enough to really matter. He hoped she would say yes, and couldn't help but worry she was going to say no. He had come to the same conclusion as Ellie. Charlotte getting married was in her own best interest.

Bryce accepted the change and the hot dogs and walked back to rejoin Charlotte at the bench by the fountain. She declined another one, so he ate them both. The park and ball diamonds were busy today. An early break in the weather and the taste of spring had everyone finding reasons to be outside. It was too early in the year for the kids' league to officially begin, but the boys were playing a practice game, and his nephew was in left field.

He was fascinated at the speed with which Charlotte formed a sketch. "Do you think about what you're doing or does your hand just move?"

"It's kind of like typing, when your fingers are moving as fast as your thoughts. The sketches are like that, simply motion I'm capturing as figures move around."

"But you get the image right the first time, the perspective, the details."

"I'm just drawing what I see. When you look across at the ball field, most of that image is a constant. The landscape, the sky, the ball field, the bleachers — all are a constant that don't move. Even the parents mostly stay in their chosen spots. The boys on the field are stationary until the ball goes into play. Once I see all the things that don't move, I simply focus on watching the few things that do."

"This is what you enjoy doing most in life."

She glanced over at him. "It's simply my day job, Bryce. I sketch. I'm fortunate enough to also make a decent living from it."

"That isn't going to change, whatever your decision. Money or not, married or not, the art will stay part of your days."

"I know. It's been useful to realize that."

Bryce watched her finish the sketch and turn the page. "Ellie said something yesterday that bothered me quite a bit. She said you'd see yourself being a failure as a wife." Her hand holding the pen stilled. "We don't need to talk about it, Charlotte, other than for you to hear from me that it would not be true. You'll be my wife. I won't let anyone, you included, qualify that. My wife. I'm the only one that gets to put an adjective with the title."

"Okay."

"I'm serious."

She looked away. "I've got an image for 'be a good wife,' the same as you have for 'be a good husband.' I'm not going to come close to being the person those words describe."

"I know who you are, Charlotte. I want the person I see, not the one you think you should be."

She didn't offer a reply. Bryce saw his

380

sister coming around the stands toward them. "Should I cut Josephine off at the pass? Redirect her — ?"

"There's no need. I like your sister."

Bryce rose to give his sister a hug, then let her share the bench with Charlotte. He walked down to the backstop as his nephew came up to hit. Jo had probably saved him from saying the wrong thing. He understood why guys didn't bring up the subject of marriage until they knew the lady would say yes when asked. This waiting for an answer was extraordinarily difficult. He forced himself to put his attention on the game. It didn't stay there. He glanced back to where the women were talking.

Charlotte was going to say no.

It was time to begin to accept that.

It was time to start planning the dinner for the day after.

Maybe it would be better if she did say no to the money so the day after he could ask her again to be his wife. He was content with the woman. The words *I love you* didn't seem to fit, but maybe it was for him the slow progress of time. She mattered to him, more than he could figure out how to define. Money or not, he was coming to the conclusion he didn't want her leaving his life.

But if a fortune couldn't convince her to say yes, how would he ever get her to say yes? He pondered that issue while he watched the boys play, and felt a sadness build. If she said no to marrying him, said no to the money, he would need more than a plan. He would need a miracle. The proposal in play was realistically the only chance he was going to get with her.

She's so scared of getting married, God, and what am I supposed to do about that?

He glanced back when he heard her laugh, smiled as he saw his sister lean over to give her a hug. His family adored her. *Just say yes, Charlotte, and put me out of my misery.* He wanted her to take a risk on him. He wouldn't let her ever regret that decision.

Boys cheered as a run was scored, and Bryce looked back to the game in play. It was going to be difficult to hear her *no.* He had to be prepared to handle it. He didn't want her memory of that moment to be *He took the news badly.* Bryce closed his eyes and then pushed the doubts away. He'd deal with whatever came, and he'd do it with some class. The deadline was looming. He'd have his answer soon enough.

TWENTY-THREE

Bryce pulled into his drive, watched the garage door open for him. He braked short of entering, sending the dry-cleaning bag on the hook behind his seat swaying. Charlotte was sitting on the front steps of his home. She hadn't said she was coming by. The tension coiled through him like a fist. He left his briefcase on the front seat, paused only to engage the locks, and walked around the sidewalk to meet her. He forced his voice to stay light. "I need to get you a key." He sat down beside her on the steps.

"I wouldn't have stayed inside today anyway — the weather's too nice. It's been a good day to draw."

She offered the sketchbook. He had caught the fact that when Charlotte offered the sketchbook, it was more than a courtesy. It was an invitation to share her day. Charlotte lived her life capturing the things she enjoyed on paper. If you wanted into her life, you wanted to see the sketches. He slowly turned pages, surprised to see most were flowers, a few were kids playing, the one he'd interrupted was a block scene — his block. He was still floored by the technical skill she had working freehand. "You've been sitting here awhile."

She inclined her head. "A little while."

He returned the sketchbook.

She slid it in her tote bag, then looked over at him. "I'll marry you, Bryce. I don't know if it's best for you, but I accept the reality that a yes is necessary."

He hadn't expected his relief to be so strong. "Thank you." She looked so incredibly serious, and he wondered at the weight of nerves she had wrapped in that calm, straightforward statement. He settled an arm around her shoulders and hugged her lightly. He had so braced himself for a no, it took a few moments for the yes to become more than a word. *She's said yes.*

He dropped a kiss on her hair. And felt her tremble just a bit. "I have something for you." He tugged the ring out of his shirt pocket. There were better places than the front steps to his home, but he wasn't risking the moment or what felt like a more than slightly fragile mood on her part. He reached for her left hand and slid the diamond ring onto her finger.

"It's lovely," she whispered, turning it so the diamond caught the sunlight.

"Tears are okay. I've got Kleenex stuffed in that pocket too."

She half laughed and wiped her eyes with both palms. "When did you buy it?"

"Before I asked you to consider marrying me."

"You were pretty sure of a yes."

"No, but I had a lot of hope."

She turned the ring and offered a slight smile. "You chose well."

She glanced at him, looked away, bit her lip. "I'm afraid I have one hard thing to ask."

He interlaced his fingers with hers, seeking to reassure. "One I'll accept," he promised. "What is it?"

"I want a church wedding, because it's important to me to be married before God. But I don't want anyone there. Not Ellie or John, not your family and friends. Just us."

The request surprised him. He thought about it and his smile faded. "I think you would like Ellie there, John, but can't ask that without being unfair to me. Do you want a private wedding because of why we are marrying? Or because eighteen years of staying out of the public eye means you don't want the wedding announced and known?"

"Both."

It saddened him to think about a wedding without his brothers as best men, without his parents in the first row, without his sisters and their families there.

"I know how difficult a thing this is I'm asking."

"I understand the reason for it," he replied quietly. She was embarrassed by the *why* of their marriage. She didn't want to have to pretend in front of his family and friends, their guests, that the wedding was because they loved each other. It was reality, and the first ache of many he would need to absorb.

He took a deep breath, let go of what he had hoped. This situation wasn't ideal, but he wasn't going to make it harder on her than it had to be. He gently traced his hand down her cheek, turned her face toward him. She'd said yes. The rest was going to be what it needed to be. "What I'd like is for you to marry me, Charlotte," he said softly, "with the people you know and trust, Ellie and John, standing with us, with a handful of photographs taken — you in a nice wedding dress and me in a tux that we can have on the mantel and I can have on my desk. I'll talk to my parents, explain there are some security concerns, that we want to plan a celebration for later, where friends and family can take part — maybe on an anniversary sometime in the future."

"They'll accept that?"

"They will because I ask."

She looked at him a long time, then said, "Thank you."

He ruffled her hair and deliberately sought to lighten the mood. "In a few years it's not even going to be something anyone remembers, how we chose to marry." He reached for both her hands and smiled. "This is a very nice day, Charlotte, one I plan to celebrate with you in a bit. Let's get a few things sorted out. Would it be possible to get the rest of the estate — Graham Enterprises, the coins, the items the New York people are handling for you — finished before we get married?" He loved the sound of that last phrase.

She visibly relaxed with the practical question. "I've got only twenty-three storage units left," she said. "The lawyers in New York are all but finished, and I've had the paperwork to sell the rest of Graham Enterprises to the employees on my desk for the last month. It's just waiting for my signature."

She was closer to having things concluded than he had realized. "I've still got about fifteen hundred individual coins to buy from you," he said, "and a quarter of vault twenty-two remains to be cleared. If you can price the individual coins, I'll raise syndicate money to buy them all now, then haul the coins from the vault. If I have to I can park a couple of trucks in secure storage until we're ready to unload the coins at the prep room."

"A good plan," she agreed. "It would be a huge weight lifted off me if the rest of the estate could be dealt with before we marry."

Bryce wanted that clean slate with her. "Then let's see if we can get that done. I'll also make arrangements to sell controlling interest in Bishop Chicago to Devon and Sharon. We'll both start our new life free and clear. We'll finish the estate, get free of obligations, then have a private wedding. I'd like to talk to you about your thoughts on a honeymoon, but before we get to that, can I have your evening? In hopes you would say yes, I've got plans for us in mind."

"Sure. I can go by Ellie's and change."

"You're fine. I'm the one who needs to get to casual for the night." He'd change and then he had a few phone calls to make.

Bryce didn't tell her where they were going that evening, simply suggested she could leave the tote bag with her sketchbook at his place. He pulled into a parking lot via the alley to keep the suspense another few minutes. He shut off the engine and put his hand on her arm as she reached for the door. "Before we go in, I want to have a conversation about something, Charlotte."

She turned to face him. "All right."

"After you hear what I have to say, you're welcome to ask me to drive around the block so we can talk about it a bit more before we go inside. I didn't mean to catch you at the last minute with this. If I'd planned it better, I would have brought it up earlier this evening."

She nodded and settled back in the seat. "I'll ask for more time if I need it."

He didn't want to break the good mood of the last hour's conversation, so he tried to choose his words with care. "The people here tonight will assume we're getting married for the usual reason of being in love. There are only four people who know the will requires you to marry."

Her smile faded. "We had this conversation last fall."

"What were words then becomes something practiced now. We're going to spend the evening together as a couple, and at the center of attention. I don't want to cross a line you're uncomfortable with —"

Charlotte interrupted his words. "I push back, Bryce. I start feeling crowded or uncertain about a situation with you, I'm going to push you back, probably do it deftly so it doesn't look like that to everyone else, but I guarantee you'll get the message. Try not to startle me from behind. Don't kiss me unless I agree to it first, and probably don't tease me or flirt too much." She met his gaze, looked worried for a moment. "This is going to be awkward. I'm sorry. Neither of us wants the facts behind our marriage arrangement to be known, and I'll do everything I can to keep up appearances."

He winced a bit at her last statement. "Charlotte, I'm celebrating tonight. I *want* to marry you. I'm *delighted* you said yes. I'm going to enjoy every minute of this evening, and I want you to be able to do so as well. I don't want to make you uncomfortable, and I know I unintentionally might." He was muddling this horribly. He reached for her hands and gave a rueful smile. "Relax with me. That's what I meant to say, and what I'd like you to be able to do."

He waited until he felt her hands relax. "This will be the toughest event for us to get in sync with each other, but once we're through this, it will get easier. I'm worried that I might cross your line tonight and make this difficult for you, and I don't want to do that. But if I mess up tonight, give me the benefit of the doubt. With some practice, I'll get it right."

Her hands tightened on his. "Okay."

He caught her gaze and realized she had turned amused.

"We're good, Bryce," she promised. "Let's go celebrate. And thanks for inviting our friends to join us. It's a nice surprise."

He smiled. "Stay put while I come around for your door."

He took her hand as they crossed the parking lot.

"What is this place?"

"Somewhere you and I will likely spend a lot of time after we're married."

Once inside, he took her jacket and directed her toward the corner table. The place was semi-packed, mostly with a neighborhood crowd. The smell of Italian food was rich in the air. "Charlotte, you remember Ann and Paul Falcon."

"Of course."

"Ellie and John will be here soon."

She was glancing around with interest. "We're playing pool?"

"Eating some food, playing a bit of pool. A little birdie told me you're good at the game. This place is called *Cues,* and it's a comfortable family-friendly place for spending an evening. I'm talking Paul into a rematch of darts since he won the last match. Devon and his wife, Sharon, are at the far table — I'll introduce you shortly. My parents will be by later this evening, along with my sisters and their families. We'll have the news spread before the night is over without making a big deal about it. Jackie is fixing us a special dessert. I told her we would head over to Falcons about eleven."

"This is nice, Bryce. Really nice."

"Just enjoy the evening. A low-key celebration. My preferred kind."

"Mine too." She squeezed his hand.

The two joined the family and friends Bryce had rounded up on the spur of the moment, and his quiet introductions of "my fiancée" drew smiles and friendly jests, laughter and hugs.

It was later, during his darts game with Paul, that he heard the first caution. His friend said softly, "You and Ruth Bazoni. Are you sure about this, Bryce?"

He let the dart fly, watched it hit the bull's-eye. "I'm sure," he said.

■ ■ ■ ■

Bryce held the door for Charlotte, reached around her to turn on lights at his place. It was after midnight and he could feel the pleasant tiredness after an evening with friends and family.

"The evening was good — really good." Charlotte let out a breath as she stepped out of her shoes. "But I'm glad it's over and everyone knows."

Bryce ran a comforting hand down her back. "The same. I'm getting us some coffee before I take you to Ellie's."

"I could use some." She came into the kitchen with him.

"We're going to have to come up with a different signal," he mentioned. "You turned your ring all evening — did it again just now."

She glanced at her hand. "I'm not used to wearing a ring. It's going to take a while to get comfortable with it."

"Can you wink?"

"Not well. We don't need a signal. I'll just say, 'Kiss me, Bryce.' "

He smiled. "That's clear enough."

She pulled over the flower vase on the counter and removed the blooms beginning to fade. "I enjoyed playing pool with you."

"John mentioned you were good. He forgot to mention you were *really* good."

"He taught me the game. He wanted me to get comfortable with a noisy, crowded room of guys — the definition of a pool hall — and still be able to keep my train of thought. The first several attempts lasted about ten minutes before I had to leave, and the others were pretty exhausting. He didn't know my coping skills would be to block out everything but my next pool shot. That I'm good can be chalked up to ten years of playing pool with him to get comfortable with that many guys, that much noise."

Bryce, reaching for the coffee mugs, paused. It was one of the more personal facts she'd told him about her past. It was painful to hear. But he could see John's logic. "Did the crowd bother you tonight?"

"No. It was actually nice to realize I was comfortable there. It's progress."

"Ellie likes to play pool too."

"She used to go with John and me, and she's always been good. Now it's their version of going on a date. I don't think she's into pool as much as she is into flirting with him. Who won your dart game — you or Paul?"

"I did. We go back and forth at the board."

"Ann said she encourages it — you and Paul hanging out together."

"She does, and I appreciate it. He's got family he's very close to, some good friends from work, but the job he carries has some heavy weight to it. Ann likes the fact I'm not going to be asking him about a case. I'm going to talk coins, sports, and occasionally hit him with a question about God that I might be wrestling with preparing for a class. I'm the normalcy of life Paul doesn't get in his day-to-day job."

"Is he your best friend?"

Bryce stopped, surprised, and gave it some thought. "Good question. I don't know that I have one, Charlotte. Paul ranks high up there as a good friend, as does Ann, surprisingly. She's hard to get to know, but I like her a lot. If I had to say best friend . . . I guess I'd still put my father in that slot. I trust Dad's advice and his perspective on things. My brothers and I are close, but we don't get to see each other often, given their jobs."

"I'm glad about your dad, Bryce. Ann and I could get to be pretty good friends. She's got that quality to her that says she listens well."

"It would be nice if that did work out. Ann and Paul would be good friends we could spend time with. The same with John and Ellie. We're both comfortable with them."

He brought over a cup of coffee, rested his arms against the counter as he held his. "I'm glad you said yes."

She gave a small smile back. "I'm starting to feel that way too."

"When do you want to get married?"

"I've been thinking about April the tenth, a Thursday evening. It's enough time to get the work done with the estate, so the only thing after we marry is the Legacy Trust. We'd still have a month in case something goes wrong and it needs rescheduling."

"Then April tenth it is."

She opened her tote bag. "If you don't mind an early wedding present . . ."

He took the ribbon-wrapped box she held out and, at her nod, opened it.

A 38-O half-dollar. One of only twenty minted in New Orleans in 1838. It was uncirculated, in stunning condition.

"Charlotte. I don't know what to say." She'd given him a six-hundred-thousand-dollar coin. She wouldn't think of that, just the fact it had been one of the two coins he'd mentioned he most wished he owned. She couldn't have chosen something more significant as a personal gift. He looked over at her for a long moment, offered a smile to go with the words he finally decided on. "It is absolutely perfect."

"I like to see you struggling for words." She grinned and rested her chin on her hand. "Pencils. Every anniversary for the next fifty years. Give me a nice new set of pencils."

"I could do that."

"Maybe birthdays too."

He laughed. "I won't forget." It was what was important to her — her art — as coins had been to him for the last decade. "They'll need to be expensive pencils."

"They are. You haven't walked into a good art-supply store yet. Good pencils are ridiculously expensive and they come in a couple hundred different colors."

He loved her return laughter and the way it lit up her face and reached her eyes. He wanted to kiss the woman. He wanted her comfortable enough with him he could lean forward and kiss her, for her to accept that. And the thought ran him smack into the reality of her history. It was going to be difficult, the first several years, remembering what this was. She held his gaze, and her smile faded. She reached over and ran her hand down his arm.

"I've been thinking about your honeymoon offer — anywhere I want us to go, and someone else makes all the arrangements," she said softly. "The idea of that sounds like such a luxury. There will be a day I want to take a trip like that. Go to London, or maybe Spain, with you — be tourists." She interlaced her fingers with his. "But I was thinking for our honeymoon I would really like to stay home.

"I'd like to get comfortable in this house, not have company or guests or things to think about, just some sleep and good food and time to decompress, for about five weeks. There will be legal matters we'll have to deal with. After all of it is finished, and life can be of our choosing once more — then I want that vacation with you."

He didn't mind her request; he simply answered the uncertainty he could hear. "We're going to have a good life together, Charlotte."

"Ellie says it's just early wedding nerves, but what would she know?"

Bryce smiled and tightened his hand. "Can I talk you into kissing me good-night on Ellie's front steps?"

"I'll think about it between here and there."

"You could consider it practice, in case you decide you want to kiss me on our wedding day."

"I haven't decided about that 'you may now kiss the bride' phrase yet either."

Charlotte wished she had said yes to kissing Bryce good-night. For days that moment had been running through her mind as an unanswered question. She kept seeing him in that quiet moment between when she had unlocked the door and when he had stepped back with a soft good-night. He hadn't crowded her, hadn't pushed. He'd simply stepped into her space, taken her hands, and given her time to think if she wanted to accept the invitation to kiss him good-night. She'd lost her nerve, given a small shake of her head, and he'd stepped back with that comfortable smile and quiet "Good night." The moment was haunting her. He wouldn't make the decision for her, and she didn't have the courage to say yes.

"You're thinking too hard."

She glanced over at Ellie.

The Graham Enterprises warehouses were busy, trucks lined up along the road, and Ellie waited for one to pass before pulling out of the administration building parking lot. "You've been thinking too much ever since you said yes to getting married," Ellie added. "Stop it. Life will be fine."

Charlotte smiled at Ellie's soft order. "I'll

work on it." She glanced back at the admin building and the still nearly full parking lot. The days lately had been so full there shouldn't be time to think. "I'm going to miss the guys more than I expected, and the job."

Charlotte carefully placed the farewell gift from Henrietta in her tote — Henrietta had given her a beautiful scarf and a framed photo of Fred from back when he was a young man. The older woman had become a true friend, and Charlotte would miss her even more than the guys. Charlotte knew Henrietta would keep the company running smoothly through the transition.

"They did a nice farewell party for you and for John."

"They did." Charlotte watched the traffic. She'd concluded the sale of the rest of Graham Enterprises to the employees that morning as planned, with John's resignation as head of security effective with the sale.

The guys who worked for Graham Enterprises had packed the admin building and the break room, told stories about her and her grandfather, had her run the Number Nine Graham Express for the last time around the model tracks, hauled out a massive sheet cake decorated with icing versions of catfish bait balls. She'd battled the need to cry even as she shared their laughter. "How 'bout one more forklift run?" one of them shouted, which got another round of laughter and eased her emotions.

Bryce had offered to be here, but there was only so much she could handle in this day. Saying goodbyes while handling questions about her upcoming wedding with Bryce was more than she'd be up for, so she had waved him off.

And the goodbyes had been very hard. Charlotte sighed, forced herself to close the door on what was now the past, and concentrate instead on the coming week. Only a few remaining items were in flux. She looked over at Ellie. "Are you going to accept Fred's house?"

"I think you should give it to John," Ellie replied, slowing to let a truck pass. "Guys who work with him will enjoy Shadow Lake. Give him Shadow Lake and the family land, Fred's home. The place would be ideal if he needs to tuck a client's family away from trouble for a month."

"Will you help him with the remodel job it needs?"

"I could do that."

Charlotte watched the warehouses as they passed, wondering if she'd be seeing them again. "I wish you'd accept the house, Ellie.

John loves you. You'd enjoy being up here at Shadow Lake, riding the trails John is talking about cutting through the woods, fishing with him on occasion, sitting on that patio watching Shadow Lake through the seasons of a year. I think you need to move up here, be near John, and seriously consider marrying him."

"You know it's not a simple decision."

"Neither was mine, but I accepted that a yes needed to be the answer. You can always give the house to John in a few years if you can't open that door. At least put yourself enough into his world so you can make a decision after seeing how it could be."

"You're tossing my own counsel to you back at me," Ellie mentioned, offering a smile.

"It was good advice," Charlotte replied. "Trust me on this, at least enough to let me give you the house."

Ellie finally nodded. "Deed it to me, and I'll see how much time I want to spend up here. You know John's not going to be around here much, not with you in Chicago, not with the job offers that are going to come his way. John is viewing Shadow Lake as a vacation property, a stopping-off point between jobs. He loves it here, but he's not inclined to stop working. Until you need him full time, he's going to be coming up with interesting things to do."

"The man doesn't know how not to work," Charlotte agreed. "But I think Shadow Lake is something fairly permanent he's ready for. He can handle Chicago for Bryce and me and be up here working on the land, be out on the lake, part of the week. He may surprise us both by picking up weekend assignments as part of someone else's security plan for a concert or a speech. Whatever it is, I do think he's going to base it around being back here at Shadow Lake during his downtime. I've watched him the last few years and seen the pleasure he gets being out on the water. He's ready to settle down, Ellie. That's the thing I've noticed the most. He really wants you to say yes, so he can build a life with you. The two of you would love living up here, and it's not so far from Chicago that you can't be back in the city whenever you want to be."

Ellie slowed as the Graham Enterprises security gate came into sight. Charlotte could feel one chapter in her life end as Ellie handed over their credentials and they drove through the gate, possibly for the last time. Life had just transitioned again in a major way, and this time it was her own decision. She was going to marry Bryce

Bishop and accept the Legacy Trust as her future. The decision was made. She just hoped neither she nor Bryce regretted it in a few years.

Charlotte glanced at her friend. "Thanks for all your help with the wedding plans. I know you've been carrying more than your share of the details."

Ellie smiled. "What are friends for? I do think you're going to be glad you're marrying Bryce. But I want to say one thing, as your friend. You get cold feet two minutes before you say 'I do,' if you change your mind, my guest room has your name on it. You'll come stay with me. I promise I won't question why you changed your mind. I'll understand, and I'll be there. John will be too."

"I won't change my mind. But it means a lot that you've offered."

Bryce walked into his house, skirted two boxes in the entryway, tennis shoes by the stairs. "Charlotte," he called, "I've got pizza if you're interested."

"Be down in a minute."

He slid the pizza in the oven to keep warm and went to find her upstairs. New art hung on the staircase wall, intricate watercolors, and he slowed to admire them. His home was filling with her collection of art to meld in with his furniture. He loved the results.

He found her unpacking. The bedroom suite she had chosen had good northern light, and the furniture she'd brought from her Silverton home fit it nicely. The door to the room's adjoining bathroom was open, the counter was cluttered with her things, and she'd changed the floor rugs. The closet was open and three-quarters full of T-shirts and jeans, the occasional really nice dress, an assortment of shoes. A line of porcelain figures followed the mirror of her dresser, and a new thriller was on the bedside table. Tomorrow this would be her home as well as his. His bedroom suite was two doors down on the other side of the hall. He found it notable — comforting too — that she hadn't chosen the opposite end of the house.

"Ellie said two locks on the inside of the door."

"I noticed. I won't often need to use them." She looked over her shoulder at him. "It's been eight years since the last serious crisis, but the locks are a nice safety blanket."

"What triggered it that time?"

"A party, loud music, a guy came up behind me and put his hand on my shoulder, shouted a question I didn't understand — just heard as a memory echo. Spent the next four weeks huddled at Ellie's trying to remember how to breathe."

"I don't raise my voice, never have, will be careful never to."

She nodded. "I noticed. I don't shake easily, Bryce. I'm not going to care if I hear footsteps in the hall, doors being closed, water running, voices on the phone. I'm too accustomed to Ellie and John being around. Noise isn't the problem. Startling me with a touch is.

"If I can't sleep, I'll throw the locks and try again to sleep. Sometimes my mind just needs that layer of control, of knowing my hand pushed the locks. I don't dream. I'm told I don't even snore. I sleep. But sometimes my mind is remembering without telling me what it's remembering. So I lock the door."

"I appreciate you telling me."

"Boxes downstairs are the last of my books if you've got room on your shelves."

"I'll make space. The sunroom — it will work as a studio?"

"It's perfect. It's one of the items that went in the reason-to-get-married column. I love that room and that fabulous expanse of wall. Good lighting, a beautiful view, and

I can push open the French doors and step outside anytime I want. That's ideal." She closed the suitcase and slid it into the closet.

"Do you have more items you want to bring over today?"

"This is the last of what I think I'll need. I told Ellie I'd be back to her place around eight tonight. She's out with John pretending like it's a date when I know for a fact she's got him helping her decorate the church for tomorrow."

"He'll enjoy being with her," Bryce said. "Ellie's enjoying this too."

"And I'm letting her. She loves to organize things."

Bryce carried the pizza box and paper plates to the back patio so they could enjoy the comfortable evening. Charlotte followed him with their drinks and napkins.

"Our last meal together before the wedding. What else do we need to talk about?" Bryce asked.

"I'm talked out, I think." Charlotte settled into a chair at the table and helped herself to a piece of the pizza. "But there are a few things left on the list. We need to talk about the money — the details and logistics of it. But while I know the information, Ellie is better at explaining it. Would it be all right if she came over sometime and walked you through it?"

"Sure."

Charlotte reached for a napkin. "She said the lawyer sent over the text formalizing what you and I discussed. Should something happen to both of us, the responsibility of the Legacy Trust will flow to your younger brother. Our estate outside the Legacy Trust will flow to your older brother, and my art will fall to Ellie. Should one of the three we've named be temporarily unable to serve, John will take the responsibility until they can do so. If the person we've named needs to permanently step aside, John will appoint someone from your family to take the role. And if John isn't available, your oldest sister takes his place."

"I'm still not entirely comfortable not naming your sister somewhere in the document."

Charlotte shook her head. "Tabitha can't handle the stress of it, Bryce. Nor can her husband. Your family is going to be fair to mine, I'm not worried about that."

Bryce considered that, and nodded. "I'll write a letter to be given to my family in case something happens. Something that will lay out my thoughts on the matter and your concerns, so they'll have our wishes spelled out. But I agree. They would take good care of your family, Charlotte, no matter what we said or arranged. It would be an honor thing, as well as simply the right thing to do."

Charlotte caught her napkin before the breeze carried it away. "I assume you've been thinking some more about the days after the wedding."

He nodded. "On the practical side of it, I'll be working from home, you'll have a studio here. I don't want to have an office someplace else unless it turns out to be absolutely necessary. I don't want our life to be one where I see you for breakfast and again at dinner. I'd like to be able to share our days if it's not going to disturb your work too much."

"I'd like that," Charlotte replied. "I'll be away from the house at times, wandering around to see what I find interesting to sketch, but when I'm in the studio I'm mostly sitting at the drawing board working on a detailed image. I don't mind interruptions. I can do eight to ten hours straight at the drawing board when I'm focused on something, so I need a reminder to get up and move around occasionally. I'll enjoy having you around." She reached for her drink, tilted her head as she studied him.

"You're going to need a secretary or assistant."

"I need to give away a million dollars a day just to stay ahead of the dividends, two million a day if I want to get through giving away the money in thirty years, so probably sooner versus later on the assistant. But I'm hoping I can recruit Ellie to help in the office when she has a few minutes to spare."

"It would be a nice gesture if you asked."

"I admire Ellie. She's incredibly good at what she does. Charlotte —" he waited until she looked over — "consider it a standing request that we have John and Ellie over as much as we can arrange this next year. We need friends who know what's going on, and John and Ellie are in that circle. I want the two of them comfortable walking in and out of our house without needing an invitation. It's important that they be part of discussions and decisions about what to do, that they become as integral to our lives as they have been to yours. They visit us or we go visit them. I don't want significant time gaps between times we see them."

"I appreciate that, Bryce. And I've been thinking we really should consider telling Ann and Paul about the Legacy Trust, along with your immediate family. You're going to continually feel the weight of the fact they don't know. It's not fair to you."

Bryce shook his head. "It's best if it stays with Ellie and John, at least for now. I can ask advice from my family about the giving without discussing our specific circumstances. The fact others in my family, other friends, don't know about the trust is something I'm going to learn to live with. It's easier if none of them knows. I'm not playing favorites that way on who we decide to tell, not tell."

She thought about it and nodded her agreement. He reached for his drink. "What else is on your mind?"

"The Silverton house," she said. "There was an offer on it this morning. I faxed my acceptance."

"Someone got a good deal with the price you put on it."

"They did. A family with two girls. They'll like the house, and the girls will love that yard."

"I'm glad." He thought through their to-do list. The coins had been cleared from the vaults, the last of the family-owned items emptied from the berm storage units. Charlotte had sold Graham Enterprises to the employees, and he had sold controlling interest in Bishop Chicago to Devon and Sharon. Charlotte had found buyers for three of her stores and finished up the final matters with the New York lawyers. "That leaves the storefront next to Bishop Chicago as all that's left to deal with."

"Yes. It feels nice knowing we'll start with close to a clean slate," she said. "At least for one day, the weight of the estate is gone."

Bryce smiled. "Enjoy the hours while you have them. You did a good job with what Fred entrusted to you."

"Thanks, I appreciate you saying that." Charlotte reached for another piece of pizza. "We haven't talked about the dogs, but I would like John and me to go on sharing them. They deserve to have the freedom to run around Shadow Lake."

"Princess and Duchess will be welcome in this house, Charlotte, whenever you want to have them here. I love your dogs."

"They aren't city dogs. Life for them is so much better when it doesn't have to be lived on a leash. Shadow Lake is where they belong most of the time."

He understood her decision, and decided not to press it. "Would you like apple pie for dessert? Mom brought it over."

"Sure."

He came back with a piece of pie for them both.

She considered him as she took the first

bite. "How is your family handling the fact they won't be at the wedding?"

"Mom and Dad understand. Mom especially. She said to tell you it was a wise choice. The others are disappointed, mainly puzzled. The current reasoning is you don't want to invite your sister to the wedding for some reason, but can't say that, so we're making it a private wedding with no family from either side to avoid creating problems."

"An elegant conclusion."

"I've neither confirmed nor denied the idea. My family will be fine." Bryce toyed with his glass. "Is Ellie throwing you a last-night-single party?"

Charlotte blushed and dropped her gaze.

Bryce laughed. "I see it's been rumored."

"Our idea is more along the lines of ice cream and girl talk. What about you?"

"I was able to successfully fend off most of it with a promise of a guys' weekend barbecue at a later time. Devon will be by later, Paul and Dad will call."

"That sounds nice."

She reached over and turned his wrist so she could see the time. "I should probably get going."

Bryce rose to walk with her through the house. "Enjoy tonight. Try to get some sleep."

"You too. I'll see you at the church, Bryce."

They both paused at the door, and she was the first to move, catching his hand to avoid a hug, then turning away even more quickly to head to her truck.

Bryce took his position at the front of the church near his pastor, John by his side. Four minutes early, the music Charlotte had selected filled the sanctuary. Ellie appeared first, stunning in a simple short white dress, carrying white roses. She walked the aisle looking both relieved and happy. John met her to escort her the last few steps.

Charlotte then appeared in the doorway, and Bryce took a deep breath and slowly let it out. For the first time that day he felt himself relax.

She was an absolutely lovely bride. She'd laughed about choosing a train that went on forever, and wanting the longest church aisle so she could enjoy it. She caught his gaze and they shared a smile. The gown was perfect.

The music changed. Charlotte began the slow walk down the aisle, carrying a bouquet of white roses wrapped in a red ribbon. Bryce took four steps into the aisle and met her to offer his arm.

TWENTY-FOUR

"Turn a little more to the left, Mrs. Bishop. That's it. Perfect."

Bryce didn't let himself look over to see Charlotte making the minor adjustments the photographer requested. They were forty minutes into the session he had hoped would take half that time, but it didn't seem to be the photographer. He and Charlotte were simply having a hard time getting in sync for the wedding pictures.

"Now can I have a smile?" The photographer went still to take the shot, hesitated, faltered, and finally lowered the camera. "You seriously don't like to have your picture taken, do you?"

Bryce broke pose to look at Charlotte. "We're done, Aaron. Thanks." He took her hands, found they had gone clammy. He stepped down a step and turned so he could be at eye level with her.

She gave him a weak smile. "Sorry. I don't

know if I'm suddenly hot or simply tired."

"Won't matter. We've got plenty of photos." He kept hold of her hands while Ellie gathered together the train, then helped her off the stairs.

"I'll help you change, Charlotte, and get you another bottled water," Ellie said, taking charge. "The lights are hot in here."

Bryce looked over at John as the women left the room. The man was frowning toward the doorway where Charlotte had gone. "That wasn't heat," Bryce said.

John met his look. "No, it wasn't."

Bryce pulled the car into the garage, noted Mitch pulling to the curb, and accepted the fact they were going to have security around for the rest of their lives. He understood Charlotte's decision to simply let John handle it, to not want to know. The two men John had introduced him to were both like their boss, former military. They'd been part of the security around Charlotte ever since her grandfather showed up in her life. Now they would be around the two of them.

"Home at last."

Bryce glanced over at Charlotte's soft words, shared a smile. "It feels nice."

Ellie had sent the roses and part of the wedding cake home with them, but otherwise pushed them out of the church with a hug and a laugh. She said she and John would handle the wedding dress and other final details. Bryce had wisely stopped for a low-key meal for the two of them on the way home, knowing Charlotte had been too preoccupied to eat much today, but would insist on helping if they were cooking at home. The dashboard clock said it was now twenty after nine.

"The luxury of not having the wedding on our to-do list anymore is its own form of bliss."

"I'm feeling the same." He came around to open her door, took the flowers, and waited while she retrieved the box with the cake. He unlocked the house door and reset security, still getting used to the upgrades John had installed. Charlotte walked through to the kitchen.

He tugged at his tie. She was looking for a vase for the roses. Bryce opened a cupboard over the refrigerator and got one down for her.

"Thanks." She arranged the roses and set them on the kitchen counter, smiled as she touched the white petals. "They should last a week or so."

"I'll replace them for you, if you like, when they begin to fade."

She looked over at him, gave him a thoughtful nod. "For a few weeks that would be a very nice gift." She took the rose he'd transferred from his tux to his jacket lapel and tucked it in the edge of the vase to reach the water. The rings she wore looked nice together. His bride. He felt more content at this moment than he had been in decades.

"I think I'm going to enjoy being Mrs. Bishop. It's a very nice new name."

"It sounds good on you." He gently tucked her hair back behind her ear. "You won't hear this suggestion from me often, Charlotte, even if I think it, but you're exhausted — let's save the conversations for tomorrow. It's been a long day for both of us."

"If you wouldn't mind, I am ready to call it a day."

"I'll lock up." He reached for her hand. "But first — wedding present number one."

She looked at the coin he handed her, then grinned. It was a production error, both sides of the quarter stamped with the face. "A two-front-sided quarter?"

"For when you want to flip me for something, but want to make sure the answer comes out your way. Use it sparingly, but well."

She considered that, nodded, and closed

her fist around it. "Thank you," she whispered. She tilted her head. "How many presents?"

He smiled. "Seven. I believe in quantity."

"As the recipient, so do I."

"They'll show up over the next week. Sleep well tonight, Charlotte."

"I will." She rested her hand on his arm, leaned forward, and softly kissed his cheek. "Good night, Bryce."

He stood where he was, absorbing that gesture long after she had gone upstairs. She'd scratched the line "you may kiss the bride" from the service, and he'd been glad, for the nerves she had been feeling had been visible by the end of the service. This . . . he looked to where she had disappeared up the stairs. This had been personal and not driven by nerves. He quietly smiled. Baby steps. He could go a long distance with baby steps if the time was measured in months and years.

He walked through the house to confirm everything was locked, the security set, precautions he intended to make a habit now that Charlotte was in his home. He was a husband. He already liked the role.

"Bryce."

He looked up from trying to unfasten his

cuff link. Charlotte was in the doorway only a few minutes after they had said good-night. "Hey, come on in. Solve this clasp for me, would you?"

She hesitated, then came into the bed-room, looked at his wrist and figured out how the clasp was stuck. When she had both cuff links in her hand, she turned toward his dresser, saw the collection. She smiled as she slid the links into an open slot.

"My dad gave me the first set of cuff links when I turned eighteen," he mentioned. "The card said, *A businessman should look businesslike.* They've been his gifts on birthdays ever since — cuff links or ties."

"I like your dad. Can we talk for a minute?"

He studied her face, catching the strain, feeling the importance that she'd decided to have a conversation tonight, but not sure how to ease the stress other than not to mir-ror it. "Sure." He sat down to pull off his shoes. Tossed one into the closet, followed it with the other. She glanced around, then cautiously perched on the edge of his bed.

"Charlotte, it's just a room. Get comfort-able in here. I don't have the habit of leav-ing the bathroom door open or walking around without being dressed. You want to chat for a few minutes, do me the favor of walking in, walking out, not worrying about it. I tend to watch the late news and read for a while at night. You aren't going to bother me if you want to toss a pillow against the headboard, sit for a while, and offer a conversation topic. I like talking with you."

"Maybe another chair."

"There are plenty around this place. Choose one and I'll move it in here."

He picked up the pillow on the floor, handed it to her, and pointed to the chair he had vacated. "Not the most comfortable place to sit but yours for tonight."

"Thanks." She curled up in it.

He tossed more pillows against the headboard. "You ever need to wake me up, I'm not quite as easily startled as you. I won't mind. But you might have to shake me pretty hard."

"You're going to regret offering that when I wake you up at two a.m. to go check on a noise I'm hearing downstairs."

"The ice maker. I can already answer that one for you."

He leaned back against the pillows and headboard and studied his wife. He did not know her expressions nearly well enough for his own comfort. "What's on your mind, Charlotte?"

"I realized something today, when we were saying the wedding vows . . . for richer for poorer, in sickness and in health . . . I forgot to have a conversation with you. I didn't mean to avoid it, not have it, I just tangled the subject with other things I don't talk about and didn't have it. So I came to apologize."

"Apology accepted."

She smiled briefly and said, "Maybe you should wait till you hear what it is." He simply waited, and she rested her chin against her drawn-up knee. "I'm an alcoholic, Bryce. I was sixteen, they were both drinkers, and I could get my hands on scotch, sometimes vodka. I would have preferred pills, but they weren't available, so I made do. I haven't had a drink in eighteen years, don't plan to ever have one, as alcohol is a trigger to memories I do not want to relive. I need you to help make sure the eggnog or the punch isn't spiked with something when we're at a party, even a bit. You definitely won't like the flashback that taste is going to trigger, and I probably won't walk away from the impact of it without a hospital stay."

"Okay. Apology still accepted."

"I'm sorry I didn't tell you."

"Charlotte . . ." He sighed. "That most

certainly is the kind of thing you're allowed to try to forget. Please don't worry about it. I can help with your request, and I'll be glad to do so."

She uncurled herself from the chair.

"Please stay." He motioned her back to the chair. "I don't want you going to bed on our wedding night with that being the last conversation rolling around in your mind."

She sat on the edge of the chair, looking surprised.

"I don't mind the hard news. But neither of us need it being the last thing we talked about today."

"Okay." She curled back up in the chair.

He ran his hand through his hair. Thought for a bit, shook his head. "Stay put. I'm going to go brush my teeth, because I don't have a single topic at the moment." He got to his feet, pulled two of the pillows from the stack, and dropped them in her lap. "That chair needs a few of them. How about socks for those bare feet?"

"I'm okay."

He nodded and turned on lights in the adjoining bathroom. He brushed his teeth, peeled off his socks and dropped them in the hamper. He checked the alarm clock out of habit, then made a point of shutting

423

it off. "I'd like your Christmas wish list. Husbands have a notoriously difficult time shopping for Christmas gifts, so you can take pity on me for the first year and give me a list."

"My Christmas wish list. In April."

He tapped the notepad on the bedside table. "I'll write it down."

She gurgled a chuckle, then full laughter peeled out. She wiped her eyes as she struggled to get control. "Thank you," she breathed, still smiling.

She rested her chin on her knee again. "I'd like a pair of shoes, please. Something red and shiny, so I have a reason to go find a dress I like that will match them. I take a size seven, or you can just have Ellie try them on — we wear and like the same shoes."

He wrote it down.

"And I'd like a puppy figurine, something to go on my dresser with the others I have, about three inches tall, and cute, with kind of solemn eyes."

"I noticed those." He added it to the list.

"I need a new tote bag, canvas preferably, something that can hold a twenty-four-inch sketchbook, with a pocket inside I can zip closed — the twin to what I carry now would be ideal if they still make it. This one has lasted four years and needs replacing."

When she didn't offer anything else, he simply waited.

"Could you find those cream-filled cakes, the ones with chocolate on the outside? And cookie-dough ice cream."

He smiled and wrote it down.

"That would be a nice Christmas."

"Thank you." He dated the list, added more numbers, then glanced at her. "Would you like my list?"

"No. Ellie and I like to shop. You'll like what we find."

He smiled at the way she said it. "Okay."

He set aside the pen. "Feel better?"

"Yes."

"You were more than lovely today, Charlotte."

"Thank you. I forgot the white slippers that went with the gown."

"I noticed."

She tugged a pillow up to cover her face, peeked around it. "Tell me Ellie didn't notice I was barefoot."

"Your secret is safe with me." He crossed his heart.

"If I had sent Ellie to get them for me, the service would have been late, and that would be worse."

"I'll have something to tease you about

for fifty years. And if that's the only thing that went wrong on our wedding day, it was a very nice day."

She wrapped her arms around the pillow. "I'm glad we got all the legal paperwork signed. But I'm sorry I asked that we do it at the church after the ceremony. It wasn't the appropriate place or time."

"The venue was fine, because it reflected reality. There was eight billion resting on you as soon as you signed that marriage license. If we'd had a car wreck on the way home . . . Signing the succession documents shifted the mood, but both of us were already feeling the weight of reality. To have not done those documents when we did would have been irresponsible. We got twenty minutes of a nice ceremony, and then got handed the world we're going to have to live in. I'd say it was appropriate."

"We're going to wake up with the responsibility of it."

Bryce nodded. "A few days from now it's going to get easier to breathe. It's not right now. I didn't expect to feel such a weight."

"Do you think we somehow bypassed the fun moment, the *Oh my, we're rich, really, really rich* moment forever?"

He smiled. "We did skip it. I think we'll learn to enjoy what we can do with the money when enough time has passed, when we get over the fact we're both staggeringly afraid of how much it is."

"I had a hard time deciding if a dollar was too much to pay for a soda yesterday. I just stood there looking at the selections, a twenty-dollar bill in my hand, and couldn't figure it out. Ellie finally put the twenty back in my purse, bought us a fountain drink to share, and then told me I'm supposed to call her when my brain freezes. I laughed and mentioned I'd forget that too if my brain froze." Charlotte held up her hand to show him her palm. "She wrote down her number. I've been afraid to wash it off because I might need it."

Bryce held out his hand. "Let me see."

She got up from her chair and came over to show him the neat numbers written on her palm. He picked up his pen and added his number beneath Ellie's. He curled her fingers across them. "A promise. You'll always be able to reach at least one of us."

Her hand quivered in his. "Thank you," she whispered. "I'm turning in for the night. I don't set an alarm, so you'll see me when-ever."

"Sleep well, Charlotte."

"I'll try."

■ ■ ■ ■

The house was quiet. Forty-two minutes after she left his room, Bryce heard her up again, heard the locks on her door pushed.

He tugged over a pillow and rested his arms across it. He had expected she would have trouble sleeping, this first time in his house, their house now. It still hurt to hear it.

■ ■ ■ ■ ■

PART THREE:
THE SECRETS

■ ■ ■ ■ ■

TWENTY-FIVE

He had a wife.

Bryce rested his hands across his chest as he looked at the ceiling and pondered that new reality. He had a wife who was currently treading lightly down the hall toward the stairs. He glanced at the clock. It wasn't six a.m. yet.

He was awake, she was on the way downstairs, but he didn't push back the covers to get up himself. A month from now he would have it figured out, how best to handle the mornings with her — whether she enjoyed company or needed her space, if she was a cheerful morning person or needed the silence and a cup of coffee.

He didn't think she was up early today because she was a morning person; he was pretty sure she was up because she hadn't been able to sleep. A new house, new room, a wedding ring on her finger, the inheritance weighing on her — he didn't have to wonder if she was feeling the stress of the changes. He'd stay out of her way for a while, let her have the peace and quiet of having the house to herself a bit. The calmer today flowed, the better it would be.

They were worth eight billion seven hundred million. The fact of it sat so heavy on his chest it took his breath away. It was more daunting than the reality of being married. He thought he could be a good husband. He wasn't nearly so sure he could make good giving decisions after the first five hundred million. Getting this right was going to matter. He didn't want her to ever regret her decision to marry him.

He turned his wedding ring with the pressure of his thumb. He'd watched his dad, and had a good role model for being a good husband. How these first few days together went were going to matter more than the months that would come after them. This relationship would form a strong footing right out of the gate, or it would struggle to find its balance for months. Today mattered. Each day of this week would be important.

He needed to help her get her studio together today. Most of the furnishings — the chairs, tables, shelving, drafting table — were now in the sunroom that would be her new studio. But having the pieces there was not the same as having the room arranged. Bryce remembered what John had said — she got stressed, she worked. So having the studio together, a comfortable place to work on her art, was a high priority.

Another priority for today was to choose a comfortable chair to drag into this bedroom, find another one for his office downstairs. He'd known Charlotte for over a year, and the three times she had dropped bombshells on him were late nights while driving, and late on their wedding day. He got the pattern of it.

He felt a deep sadness for what she had told him, but he had grabbed the significance of the conversation. If he wanted Charlotte to be willing to talk with him about hard things, he'd best give her a safe place to curl up, and encourage her to talk with him, preferably at night.

He wanted to understand his wife. If he wanted inside her head, into the things she'd never talked about, he needed to create the environment for it. Simple things to start with, such as how the day had been, but create the habit of it. And patience. He thought she'd tell him one day, at least pieces of it, if he was careful to hear what she was risking.

She'd given him eight billion dollars and

asked him to give it away. He was going to give her back something as valuable. He was going to help her heal. Her relationship with God, the memories she never talked about. If it took decades, he was going to help her heal in every way he possibly could.

He'd learn how to be a good husband — not just in general, but a good husband to Charlotte. He'd figure out a plan for the giving, he'd find the places which both needed the money and would spend it wisely. What he wasn't going to do was fail.

Charlotte was having scrambled eggs, bacon, coffee, and reading his paper.

"Good morning." Bryce tousled her still-damp hair as he passed and fixed himself a matching plate.

"I made the coffee too strong, so you might want to dilute it down before it crosses your eyes," Charlotte cautioned, "or better yet, throw it out and make new."

"Thanks for the warning." He took a sip and decided it wouldn't kill him.

"Ellie is coming over about ten to talk about the financial details, although I can push that back if you would prefer later in the day."

"Ten is fine." He settled in to enjoy breakfast. He offered her half his toast and slid over the strawberry jelly.

He read the paper with her, passing back and forth sections, while he ate. "Where do you normally start reading the paper?"

"The comics."

He lowered the page he held. "Really?"

"The rest is typically bad news."

"I see your point." He finished the sports section. "I'm going to attempt teriyaki chicken for dinner tonight unless you have a different preference."

"I've heard it's a favorite of yours. You know, I could probably do some of the cooking."

"Do you like to cook?"

"Occasionally."

"Then when you're in the mood, the kitchen is yours. But otherwise, assume I'll handle dinner. I rather enjoy cooking for you. I also know nearly every restaurant in the city that delivers."

"I like that idea. Grabbing a sandwich to eat at the desk works fine for lunch if my work is going well."

"I'm the same, and I'm not one to quibble if we eat dinner at six p.m. or ten p.m." He set aside the paper, content he'd seen the highlights. He glanced at the time. He'd normally be leaving for Bishop Chicago right now, in a suit, his briefcase packed. It felt odd to simply be sitting here in jeans and a T-shirt. He got up to get the coffee. "More?"

"Please."

He refilled hers, and she wrapped both hands around the mug. "Most mornings I'd go watch the dogs run around, or sketch the sunrise, or toss stuff in the truck and go to work. I didn't sit. I was only reading the paper today because it was there on the front step."

He smiled. "I was thinking something similar. I don't think breakfast is going to be our favorite meal." He stirred sugar into his coffee to get the extra kick. "You've been finished with Graham Enterprises for . . . what, about a week? Responsibility levels have drastically dropped. In about ten days you're going to be wondering why you didn't stop work months ago. But the transition is no doubt going to feel like a crash."

She finished the last bite of toast, reached for a napkin. "It already does. You're going to eventually feel it too with Bishop Chicago off your daily schedule."

"I'm feeling it. I miss the suit and tie, the cuff links, the briefcase. The business of it."

She rested her chin on her hand. "I like you in a suit and tie. And you're still going to the office, the commute is just measured in feet, not miles."

"I should go change?"

She smiled. "Why not? You'll feel more like yourself." She pushed back her chair. "I'm going to go tackle the studio, get the supplies in the perfect place, get the right location for the drafting board figured out, put together my idea board, think some about starting an ambitious sketch." She picked up her breakfast dishes and carried them into the kitchen.

He brought his plates to the dishwasher. "What's an ambitious sketch?"

"Something that takes a few hundred hours to draw, with layers of color, and intricately shaded figures. Think of drawing a horse and cowboy in the middle of a rodeo, or drawing a plane full of people, or trying to capture New York looking out a high-rise window during a rainstorm."

"You'll start work on an ambitious sketch so you won't be bored, so you'll remember why you chose art over keeping Graham Enterprises."

She rested her hand on his arm. "You're a smart man, Bryce Bishop."

"I am." He leaned forward and softly kissed her cheek. "Go to work, Mrs. Bishop."

She grinned. "Yeah." She selected an

apple out of the fruit bowl and went through to her new studio. He heard her push open the French doors to the outdoors and smiled, glad she'd have sunshine and outdoors as part of her new studio. He considered for a moment, then went upstairs to change into a suit and tie. She was right. He liked looking like the businessman he was.

Bryce answered the back door when the doorbell rang at ten a.m. "Come on in, Ellie. Charlotte's in her studio tacking up photos on a corkboard."

Ellie set the box she carried on the kitchen table. "She's working on her idea board? Already?"

"She was bored."

Ellie thought about that for a moment, and laughed. "I actually believe that."

Bryce tipped his head to indicate the studio, and Ellie walked through to the sunroom to see what was going on.

Bryce finished fixing new coffee, remembered Ellie preferred a vanilla-flavored coffee with a touch of cream. Laughter from the studio made him pause. It was a wonderful sound. Charlotte didn't laugh nearly enough.

Charlotte came into the kitchen with Ellie. "I've recruited Ellie to help me choose a theme for this ambitious sketch. It has to be something that when you hear the word or phrase, you think *perfect.*"

He handed them both coffee mugs. "Tell me about others you've done."

"*The Moon* was incredible. That one took you several weeks," Ellie offered.

Charlotte tugged out a chair at the table. "It was the most ambitious black-and-white drawing I've ever attempted. I like *School of Fish* for what it represented, the coral was beautiful. But technically it was pretty boring."

"*Lava Flows* from Hawaii still gets the most serious raves from viewers."

"That one I am rather proud of. Fire is hard to get right. And the shades of color in molten rock — that was sophisticated shading."

"So you're looking for a place," Bryce said, joining them at the table.

"Not necessarily. Just something that is bold when looked at in detail."

"Snowflakes."

Charlotte shook her head. "White is nearly impossible to draw well. The paper is the white, and you're drawing the place that is not your subject. It makes my eyes go batty."

Bryce ran back through his memory for

conversations lately with people who traveled, looking for an emotional connection to a subject. "The Great Plains, as seen from the air," he offered. "Ann describes that as her favorite vista. The patchwork of fields and rivers and pastures that stretch for miles against a skyline that also stretches without interruption."

Ellie stopped unpacking her box and looked at Charlotte. "Yes."

Charlotte looked back at Bryce. "Does she have pictures?"

"Pictures, video. She'll take you up for a firsthand view from the air if you like."

"Still photos are better for seeing what it could be as two dimensions. That's worth a call to Ann, and a look at some pictures."

"It could work," Ellie agreed.

Bryce picked up his coffee. "Now that I've given you that one, let me change my mind and give you another one. Glacier. Ice melting from a glacier and pouring down the crevices to the sea. The cold, blue shades of thick ice against the vivid blue of the ocean and the bright blue of a sunny sky . . ."

Charlotte started to smile as he gave his description. "One color pallet and scale. A really good idea. Cold is something fascinating to capture on paper, and technically little of it would actually be white." She looked to Ellie.

"Scaling it would be a challenge. You want the hardness of hundred-year-old ice, the grandeur of it. But pulling back from the surface to show you the size of the glacier costs you the details."

"It's worth some layouts. Two good ideas in twenty minutes. Very nice, Bryce." Charlotte was writing both down. "I'll develop a bunch of options for these and see what else we can come up with in the next few days." She looked over and caught his gaze. "Thank you," she said softly.

He smiled, understanding why work mattered like it did to her. "I'm good for ideas. Just don't ask me to draw them."

She held his gaze, nodded to Ellie, and he caught the signal. Charlotte would like not to be leading this next conversation.

"Ellie, Charlotte said you're better at explaining the financial details than she is, so I appreciate you coming over. What did you bring?" Bryce asked.

Ellie shifted to business mode. "Bryce, you need to know about four things to understand Charlotte's financial world. I'm going to give you the overview. The details you can take up with Fred's lawyer on Monday morning."

"That works for me."

"Start with the big and work to the small, Ellie," Charlotte suggested.

"All right." Ellie changed the order of the files in her hand. "First, the Legacy Trust." She opened the top folder. "Here's what the lawyer and I have been able to come up with."

Charlotte reached over and laid her hand on Ellie's. "I haven't heard any of this yet, Bryce — she's been saving it for a surprise, but I can tell you from experience this is going to be good." She looked at her friend. "So thanks in advance."

Ellie smiled back at her. "I hope you'll like what we came up with. Take a breath, Charlotte, there's no need to be so nervous."

"So says the lady who doesn't have her name on the money right now." But Charlotte smiled and complied.

Ellie looked at Bryce. "Give her a few months, she'll get used to this."

"Oh, I understand what she's feeling," Bryce replied, sharing a glance with Charlotte. His own nerves were rippling.

Ellie smiled. "I like the fact you're both skittish right now, but let me relieve some of the stress. Charlotte said she wanted simple. So this is for you." She handed Bryce a checkbook.

"Any check you write will clear. You could

write a check for two billion today and it would clear. The checkbook basically — actually is — a line of credit with the trust holdings as the collateral. Your signature on a check — or Charlotte's — is sufficient. Both your signature cards went on file with the bank this morning, so you can start using the checkbook today.

"The Legacy Trust owns shares in thirty-five companies, the most sizable positions being in the Saylor Chemical descendent stocks." She handed him a page with the list and the number of shares owned. "Any income earned by the trust — dividends, interest — is used to buy more of the same stocks. When there's a check to be cleared or a tax bill to pay, shares are sold. The Graham lawyer will handle those transactions. At the end of each month, you will get checking account and trust statements, showing the checks paid, the stock transactions, and the current trust holdings.

"The trust address — where all dividend checks, tax statements, and so forth, are sent — is presently the law firm. They will continue as administrator, generate the estimated tax filings, the annual tax return, et cetera. If you want to take over management of the trust, the majority of the shares reside in certificate form in a vault, with a working number of the shares kept in a brokerage account for convenience.

"There are no restrictions on the trust. You may use the money in any way you wish, buy or sell anything you wish. The current arrangement is simply one of many stable configurations." She handed him a brokerage printout from that morning. "Earned dividends have been buying more shares this last year. The current balance of the trust is nine billion, thirty-four million." Ellie closed the folder. "And that's it. That's the Legacy Trust."

Bryce looked at the checkbook he held, the page listing the holdings, then back at Ellie. He wanted to hug the woman for the job she had done. He settled for a chuckle. "I see your handiwork in the simplicity of it."

Ellie smiled. "I tried. You can put your focus on what to do with the money, where to give it, and let the lawyer handle the trust transactions. The firm is paid a yearly fee plus a nominal rate per hour for their services rather than a percent of the trust. For lawyers, their fees are actually quite reasonable and have been set for the next ten years if you wish to continue with this firm. The fact that they administer a trust of this size drives down brokerage costs for their other clients, so they keep this business relationship at close to their actual costs."

"A nice deal for us," Bryce said.

"Fred was thinking ahead. I've brought you a few boxes of the checks, including some you can feed through your printer. If you wish to make electronic transfers from the checking account, the phone number of the lady who will handle them for you is on the account summary. She'll set up onetime or repeating transfers and monitor that they're successfully made as scheduled."

"We're not going to have many questions to talk about with the lawyer. This is really nice, Ellie. I admire the simplicity of it."

"It's what I do well. But you will have questions. I have business cards for you with direct numbers — both office and home — for everyone involved with the trust, and I've noted their roles."

Charlotte shook her head when Bryce offered her the checkbook. "You keep it. I don't want to even hold that checkbook."

He placed it in front of him and glanced at it from time to time. Any check he decided to write would clear. His nerves were settling down, but the reality of it began to take serious substance. He looked at Ellie. "You said you had four things, Ellie. What else have you brought us?"

Ellie shifted the folders in her hand. "Separate from the Legacy Trust is the Cleo Simm Trust. As Fred's estate holdings were liquidated — Graham Enterprises, the coins, various minor ownership interests, and personal property — the money was placed in the Cleo Simm Trust. You've already been helping Charlotte give away those funds. I brought you more checks good for the printer, and this is for you." Ellie handed him another checkbook.

"Your signature is now good on this trust account too," she told him. "In a pinch, John or I can also sign as trustees. I currently handle the tax matters for Cleo Simm, and will generate the estimated tax payments and annual tax return for you. You're welcome to take over administration of it —"

"If you don't mind, I'd appreciate you keeping that role," Bryce suggested.

Ellie smiled. "Sure, I can do that. The current balance of the Cleo Simm Trust is just over one hundred thirteen million. The funds in this trust sit in cash until they're used, so you should consider giving from this account until the funds are down to, say, ten thousand, simply to keep the trust open for other possible uses over the years."

"Just a hundred thirteen million," Bryce said with a glance to Charlotte, feeling oddly more off-balance at hearing that number than the Legacy Trust total in the billions. Had Charlotte said no, she would have been able to give away sixty million in gifts and still have walked away with a fortune. Her decision to say yes to marriage . . .

Charlotte reached over and put her hand on his. "Breathe, Bryce. It's just money."

He laughed. "True." He held her gaze for a long moment. She'd married him not because of what she needed for herself — she'd been well set if she said no. She'd accepted the responsibility of what was entrusted to her and said yes because of what could be done with the money. He wasn't going to let her down. He looked over at her friend. "Okay, what else, Ellie?"

Ellie handed him the third folder. "Separate from the Legacy Trust and the Cleo Simm Trust, Charlotte has some personal property — the truck, some bank accounts — around two hundred ten thousand total. I pulled together the paperwork necessary to change the ownership titles from her name to joint ownership. You may find it simpler just to spend down the money and close the accounts rather than retitle items."

Bryce glanced at the documents and nodded. "Thanks."

"The last piece we need to discuss concerns Charlotte's art. It is owned by the CRM Trust. I'm presently listed as the administrator. It's a management vehicle, rather than a financial one, and controls the copyright for the art after her death. There are no tax returns or other forms to file each year. The income from her art flows through the CRM Trust to her personal name. I suggest we update the trust so the funds flow through to an account in your joint names." She offered Charlotte the paperwork to read and sign. "You'll see the funds as direct deposits into the account as her artwork sells."

"I hope you're not planning to retire in our lifetime," Bryce mentioned to Ellie, reading the page and signing it after Charlotte.

"I'm having too much fun to think of retiring," Ellie replied with a smile at them both. "Okay, that's the overview. I brought copies of the trust agreements for you, Bryce, copies of her last seven years of tax returns. And her passport is in the gray sleeve." She offered the documents to him.

"You haven't left much for me to do."

"The goal was simplicity and stability.

That I can manage. Giving the money away is your challenge."

"Now you see what a business meeting with Ellie is like," Charlotte said. "I listen, follow her advice, and I'm glad she's handling things."

Bryce nodded. "Ellie, this really is a remarkable piece of work."

"I've had three years to think about it. What you see as simple is the result of throwing out all the ideas that were complex until we figured out the definition of simple in Charlotte's situation. It took some time to get down to this. I think it will do the job for you."

"It will." Bryce opened the Legacy Trust checkbook, looked at the very neatly written amount in the front of the registry. She'd used the memo line to write out the full starting balance. He read the number and could feel the adrenaline kick in once more. "Would you like a job? When you're not managing Charlotte's and Marie's art, being her best friend, remodeling a home, thinking about marrying John, and having your own life? I could really use your help in the office."

Ellie laughed. "It's going to be fun, Bryce, over the next decade to watch you figure this out. I'll be glad to help when I can.

One of the joys of my days is walking into Charlotte's studio to see what she's working on. I'll stop by to give you some time, and keep an eye on her art. It will make an ideal day."

Bryce tugged a key out of his shirt pocket. "I had a copy made for you. You're welcome here anytime."

"I appreciate the key, but it won't be necessary."

Charlotte reached over and put her hand on Ellie's arm. "Think of it as insurance, in case I lock my keys in the car."

Ellie nodded and added the key to her key ring.

Bryce wrote down the current security code. She looked at it, nodded. "Rip it up, I won't forget."

Charlotte pushed back from the table. "A very good meeting. Is it okay if I escape to the studio?"

Bryce smiled. "Go."

Ellie watched her leave. "She looks happy."

Bryce heard the surprise in her voice, and chuckled. "You can relax, Ellie. I know you were worried, but Charlotte and I are going to be good together."

"I'll relax in a few months. I am very glad she married you, Bryce."

Bryce tapped the two checkbooks. "I'm

glad too, and for more reasons than the money, Ellie."

"You're a smart man." Her smile faded. "I owe you some answers, concerning what she's shared about what happened."

"Not today."

Ellie looked over at him, and he held her gaze. "Not today. We both get a pass from the hard things today."

Ellie slowly nodded. "She didn't sleep well."

"No, she didn't. But she'll compensate by putting her attention on an ambitious sketch and working until she can't see straight tonight."

"You're already figuring her out."

"My wife . . . my job to figure her out."

He picked up the box, the folders, the checkbooks. "Come back to my office for a minute, Ellie, if you have time. Let me show you what I've got organized so far. And I'd like your advice on a comfortable chair to move into the room for Charlotte."

She smiled. "Sure."

Charlotte tapped on his office door. "How's it going?"

Bryce stretched his hands over his head, sorting out the kinks in his neck. "Very well."

He pointed to the chair. "Try that one, see what you think. Ellie thought it might do as your chair."

"My chair?"

"We'll bring down a couple of pillows for it, get a sketchbook to rest on that shelf behind it, fill a mug with pencils — you want to come hang out with me while I work, you'll have a comfortable place."

She smiled and settled into it. "I appreciate it." She rested her feet on the footstool he'd brought in, nudged it a few inches closer. "This is very nice."

Bryce smiled. "Not quite as inviting as stretching out on a couch for a nap, so if I see you nodding off, I'll send you elsewhere."

"Deal. I came to see if you want to break for a late lunch."

He glanced at the clock, surprised to find it was after three. Ellie had left shortly after one p.m. "Sure." He pushed back from the desk. "So how is our first day going, Mrs. Bishop?"

"I'm glad it's Friday."

He laughed. "You know, I am too."

Bryce heard the music fade as Charlotte closed the French doors between the sunroom and the back patio. Minutes later he heard footsteps on the staircase up to the bedrooms. He glanced at the time. Quarter after five. He regretted not stopping to go see the changes she'd made to her studio before she called it a day.

He pulled another stack of checks from the printer. He clicked the spreadsheet column to check the tally for the day. Two million one. He'd call it a day and find her when these were ready for the mail.

The ball game he had been listening to concluded with a line drive and runner out at first. Bryce changed the radio station to background music. He labeled the envelopes, then started signing checks.

He heard Charlotte coming back down and found himself glad he hadn't added 'tightening stair treads' to the project list the last time he had carpenters working in the house. He could tell from her footsteps where she was in the house — kitchen, hallway, stairs. He figured she would be after food and drink and would head to the kitchen, but she turned into the living room. She didn't settle on the couch or turn on the television. She came on back to his office.

She tapped on his office door as he looked up. "Mind if I interrupt?"

She'd lost the shoes and was barefoot, her

hair was tied back with a ribbon, and he wasn't sure what she was carrying tucked under her arm. "I'd welcome it. Come on in. I'm just finishing up the food pantry checks for this month." He glanced at the address list. "We'll be sending out a hundred and six today."

"Nice." She leaned against the doorjamb. "Bishop, what do you know about precious gems?" There was just a hint of a smile in the way she asked the question.

He looked up from signing the check, studied her. Slowly set down the pen.

"The coins were just practice," she explained, trying to keep laughter out of her voice.

Precious gems. He closed his eyes as he sighed. "I can learn."

She came around the desk to his side and leaned against his chair. She opened the thermos she carried and poured a stream of diamonds into her hand. "My dowry," she said as he watched them glitter in the reflected light.

"My grandfather felt it was important I have something I could bring to a marriage — whenever it might happen during my lifetime — that said I was precious to him, that I should be precious to a husband. He settled on precious stones."

"How many?"

"Fifty million worth."

"Is that all?"

Her laughter bubbled. "Actually, that's just the diamonds. He bought some emeralds before he died too, and rubies, sapphires. He really fell in love with the sapphires. Coins were easier for me to understand, so I started with them."

He picked up a diamond from the handful she held. It looked similar to a stone in her wedding ring — a couple of carats, and beautiful. He looked at her. "That's why you kept the storefront next to Bishop Chicago."

"It would make a nice jewelry store. Custom-designed pieces, a choice of stones. The gems are in safe-deposit boxes. And in a couple of boxes stored in the bottom of my closet."

"If I had known I could have at least had insurance on them."

"Silence is the best form of secrecy there is."

"I'll learn about gems, Charlotte, enough to know the terrain. But it will be best if we open that jewelry store and let experts advise us."

"We could leave them sit for a while."

"The store is there and designed to be a

showcase. We can find the staff easily enough if we're willing to pay very good talent to move from where they're presently working. Better to have the stones sold and in circulation if we're not going to keep them. Do you like to wear jewelry?"

"I wear a piece on rare occasions, but not really. Ellie does. What about your family?"

"We can give a nice piece of jewelry to everyone in the family and it's still not going to use more than a couple handfuls of these gems."

"Hire good designers, have pieces made for your family, mine," Charlotte suggested. "They can be our first Christmas gifts. Everyone gets something custom-made and valuable, but no one gets singled out."

"A smart idea. Mom would get a kick out of a brooch and matching earrings."

Bryce put the diamond back with the others and circled an arm around her waist. "Any more surprises I need to brace for? You own an island? Half of Montana?"

"The gems were my last surprise."

"Fifty million dollars' worth of gems."

"Kind of a large surprise," she conceded.

He laughed as he watched her pour the diamonds back into the thermos and then tighten the lid. He marked his place on the checks and envelopes, set them aside for the day. He reached for her hand. "I'm fixing dinner tonight. Come sit in the kitchen and keep me company while I cook."

She nodded and followed.

"This is one reason you were comfortable giving away the money from the coins. You knew even if you said no to the Legacy Trust, the coins were just the tip of the items you had to sell."

"I could keep the gems tucked away for decades, sell a few as needed. But mainly my thinking was one thing at a time. Coins first, then Graham Enterprises, then deal with the gems."

She settled on a stool at the island counter, set the thermos by the flower vase, picked up an apple from the bowl of fruit. Bryce made a mental note since it was the second apple she'd picked up today. He put chicken strips into a hot skillet. "Tell me about your studio. What you like, what you think you'll want to change. I have a feeling that art and sports are going to be our subjects when we need to forget the money for a while."

"I think the lighting is excellent. Even late afternoon the direct sunlight doesn't come more than a few feet into the room, so I can stage the drawing table where I want. With the French doors open, the breeze ripples in. I'll make sure to keep the inside doors closed to keep flying visitors from coming into the house proper, so don't assume a closed door means I don't want company."

"Noted. But I need a signal for when you do want the solitude."

Charlotte thought about it, gestured with the apple. "If there's a red ribbon on the door handle, don't bother me unless it's a near emergency in your family or mine. If you're going out or something, just write me a note and leave it on the kitchen counter. What about you?"

"There are occasional phone calls with someone at church on a confidential matter, but otherwise there's very little you're not welcome to sit and hear. I'd like you to consider the door always open even if it's closed. If I'm on the phone, just curl up in your chair. I'll give you some idea of how long I think the call will be — you can decide if you want to wait or come back later, and I'll tell you if I need privacy for the call."

"Okay. Will it bug you if I decide to let you always answer the house phone? It's going to be telemarketers and political calls and people who have known you for years. I'd rather not have to tell a curious caller that I'm your wife and hear the shocked silence as they realize you're married and they didn't know — even worse, discover it was someone you once dated, or it's your great aunt I just shocked."

Bryce laughed. "No problem. I'd suggest you just turn off the ringer for the house phone in your studio and bedroom. I ignore the phone and let it go to a message when I've got company and will tend to do the same when we're having a conversation."

Bryce moved the rice off the burner to finish. "What would you like to drink?"

"Water is fine."

He filled glasses, and she took them to the table. She opened the drawer to get out silverware. He shut off the heat under the chicken and plated the meal. "My teriyaki chicken, with care not to let it get too dry."

She reached for the plate he offered. "It looks good." They moved to the table. She sampled it and nodded. "It's very good."

He tried his. "Jo's right. I tend to overcook the chicken."

She tried the rice. "I can do with you practicing then. I like this recipe."

Bryce felt himself relax as the pace of the day faded. "Grade day one."

"We survived it."

He grinned, nodded. "Not a bad grade then."

"Where did you put the two checkbooks?"

"Desk drawer, left side. The printer-fed version and extra check boxes are in the bottom drawer."

"Not the safe?"

"If an intruder wants me to write a check, I'm going to write a check."

"Good point."

"Ellie set it up well. The name and address on the checks is Legacy Trust with the address of an office in the building next to the law firm. She said to think of it as a correspondence hub for the trust. The law firm will keep a staffer there. As the confirmations for tax purposes start coming in, they'll track them. Any due-diligence materials about a particular organization I want to have mailed to me, I can use that address rather than this one. Newsletters. Correspondence. They'll forward on a box of mail every few days."

"It adds another layer of privacy."

He nodded. "Useful if we're traveling, or if we move one day. Nothing will need to change. You want wedding cake for dessert?"

"Absolutely. I was too keyed up to enjoy it the first time."

He brought over the cake and two forks.

"Did you make your two-million goal for

today?" she asked, slicing a fork through a red rose.

"I wrote four big checks, and another hundred smaller checks, so I took a short-cut."

"It counts. Is it going to be annoying if I ask that question every day?"

"Feel free to ask. It gives me an opening to mention whatever I found interesting about the recipients of the gifts."

He paused with a bite of cake on his fork. "Any more ideas for your ambitious sketch?"

"Great Plains. Glacier. Olympics. Kindergarten."

Bryce thought about them. "All four generate very vivid images."

"It's going to be a hard choice. It always is."

When they were done, he covered the rest of the wedding cake and put it away. "I'm thinking about a movie, then an early night. Does that appeal or would you rather go for a walk, find a book to read, like me to disappear for a couple of hours so you can have the place to yourself? Tonight I'm willing to be flexible."

"Let me choose the movie."

Bryce looked at the foot of space between

them on the couch and wondered how long it was going to take for her to want to sit beside him rather than just with him. He toyed with the ribbon around her hair, the movie not particularly holding his attention. For a first day, for the money and for being a husband, it would count as a good day. The gems were going to take some more thought. They were so wealthy fifty million in gems had lasted as a shock only about twenty minutes and he had moved on to fixing the chicken. The reality of that was beginning to settle in. Life had really changed.

Charlotte pulled her feet up under her. He needed to get her a pair of slippers to keep handy down here so her bare feet didn't get cold. The house did feel a bit cool tonight.

"Would you rather we watch something else?" She turned her head and met his gaze.

"No, this is fine."

"You're making me nervous, Bryce."

"Good or bad nervous?" He skimmed a hand down her hair. "You've got an interesting face." He eased his hand away and offered her another pillow from his end of the couch, patted his shoulder.

She hesitated, but shifted to sit beside him, rest her head against the pillow and his shoulder. He left his hand on the back of the couch. They watched the movie. She sighed.

"What?"

"Now you've got me bored with the movie."

Bryce smiled. "We're both unwinding from a very strange day. At least for me the house is familiar. You don't even have that."

"We are very wealthy."

"I was just thinking we should tuck one of those checkbooks in our pocket and get out of the house for an hour, go somewhere, buy something, just to have something to remember from our first day."

"Fancy car? Clothes? A pricey painting? For the right price someone would be willing to open their store for us this evening."

"If I spent more than ten bucks I'd feel odd."

"It would feel frivolous."

"A bit."

She shifted against the pillow, getting more comfortable. "I think my limit is five. Have you figured out how much money we earn every minute of the day?"

"Eight hundred thirty dollars per minute."

She thought about that and abruptly leaned back to look at him. "So that means we earn a hundred thousand while watching this pretty awful two-hour movie?"

"Sounds about right."

She dropped her head back against his shoulder. "I didn't want to be this rich."

He feathered her hair with his hand. "I'm beginning to realize I don't want to be either. Fifty thousand while we watch a movie — that's my upper limit."

She laughed and then sighed. "Give it away, Bryce. Good ideas preferably over bad, but give it away."

He dropped a kiss on her hair. "I will."

He watched the movie, trying to pick up the story line. He had no idea what it was about.

She was turning her wedding rings. He watched her for a bit, then took her hand. "Let's go buy a chocolate shake to split, then drive a loop out toward the airport and back to see the city lights at night. You'll sleep better."

"I'd like that."

"Find your shoes. I'll tell Mitch where we're going."

Her smile faded. "It's going to be like that whenever we go somewhere, isn't it?"

"Yes."

She settled back on the couch, deciding if she wanted to change her mind. He let her think about it.

He didn't bother to tell her he and John had an agreement. Didn't bother to tell her John had leased the house at the corner of the block, so security could have line of sight for this place. She didn't want to know, didn't need to know, the kind of security now around her.

"Are we paying them enough?"

"John is."

"Call Mitch. And I wouldn't mind splitting an order of fries to go along with that shake."

TWENTY-SIX

Paul studied the aerial photo Ann had taped to the whiteboard, the neighborhood neatly laid out as viewed from above — house rooftops, yards, trees, and streets. She had colored dots on various homes indicating those who had lived in the neighborhood back when baby Connor was found, more for those who had provided useful information. "Where do you want us to focus this weekend?" he asked.

"We need to know more about the Ryler family, and also the Yates family. Both families moved away soon after baby Connor was found. Both have sons who were in their twenties at the time baby Connor was kidnapped. Scott worked as an auto mechanic. Jeff worked for a landscaping business. Both boys had repeated trouble with the law since high school — fights, underage drinking. They liked fast cars, would steal one for a joyride. Both had burglary arrests in their background. I'm beginning to wonder if this wasn't so much a family decision to kidnap a child as two friends acting together, maybe add a girlfriend, wanting fast cash."

"Start with their former neighbors?"

"Yes." She tapped the map and an orange dot. "Mrs. Willis told me both families were embarrassed by their boys and the trouble they were getting into, said the cops at the time asked her if she knew where Scott and Jeff had been the day baby Connor disappeared. Maybe the detectives were on to something."

Paul picked up his phone and keys. The baby Conner case had been left on the back burner over the winter, while Ann helped with the coins, but the weather was nice now, a drive sounded appealing, and it was time to pick up where they had left off. Paul leaned down to ruffle Black's fur. "Ready to go on more interviews, Black?"

The dog pushed at him to move him toward the office door. Paul laughed. "We probably won't solve the case today, but it's going to be an enjoyable Saturday afternoon being outdoors."

Ann slid her hand into his as they headed downstairs and walked to the car, Black tugging to lead the way. "Remember our first weeks being married, being back here after the honeymoon?"

Paul smiled. "With some detail."

"I was thinking some this morning about Bryce and Charlotte," Ann said, her answering smile brief and her words turning serious. "I got the impression from Bryce they weren't planning to travel for their honeymoon. Probably wise, given how busy their schedules have been recently, and all they'll have to deal with early in their marriage. When the time is right, you should give him a call, go running together or something. I'd like to invite her over, if I can do so without sounding pushy about it."

"You're worried about them."

Ann lifted a shoulder. "Concerned, maybe. Like you, I was surprised when Bryce asked her to marry him, even more surprised when Charlotte said yes. I don't want to see the experience of marriage turn out to be a disappointment for either one of them."

Paul opened the door to the car's back seat, and Black dove in, tail wagging. "Bryce made his choice knowing what they'd be facing. I'm going to guess they end up with one of the strongest marriages among our friends, given the work they're going to have to put into it. This wasn't a quick decision for either of them."

"I just wish for a calm, comfortable transition, and I'm afraid if it goes badly they won't have people around to talk with. You and I at least know some of the terrain they'll be dealing with."

"We'll have them over for dinner," Paul suggested. "And I'm ready to get back on the track to do some running. I'll give Bryce a call in a few days."

TWENTY-SEVEN

Charlotte straightened Bryce's tie. "You look very nice in a suit. Very much the boss."

Bryce set his coffee aside, amused. "A boss with no staff." They no longer tried to have breakfast together, but they did often pass each other in the kitchen in the morning. She favored a toasted bagel with cream cheese, and he gravitated to oatmeal with raisins and brown sugar. He was up earlier than she was most mornings and made a point to leave the office and come join her in the kitchen for a refill on his coffee and a few minutes of conversation when he heard her come downstairs.

"We really should hire you an assistant. The stacks of mail to read are growing."

"I'm fine for now. Ellie is good at keeping my office organized, and I don't want to give her any reason to stop helping me out."

"She likes being over here."

"She likes the excuse to hang out with

you." Bryce caught her hand and interlaced his fingers with hers. "You both need that time together. I've never heard two women giggle as much as you two. What was it yesterday, the ball of rubber bands that set it off?"

"We're easily amused."

"More like a few decades of inside jokes you aren't sharing with me. She's looking more relaxed."

"She thought I might marry John. She was dealing with it, but the idea scared her."

He gently tucked her hair behind her ear. "I'm glad you didn't."

"Had it come down to ten days before the deadline, and it wasn't going to work with you, maybe John or I would have changed our minds. But I like to think we would have stuck with no. John loves her."

"Let's invite them to dinner — John and Ellie. Our first official guests. We could put something on the grill."

"I'd like that, but a few weeks from now. John's been tugging at her to come north and get started on the remodeling, and I don't want to give her an excuse not to go."

"Ellie told me she wanted to see you safely married before she thought about getting married herself."

"Did she?" Charlotte thought about that

and smiled. "I'm going to have to double dare her or something to get her to say yes."

Bryce laughed. "You'll find the right words when it's time." He ran his hand lightly down her arm. "Have you decided the theme for your ambitious sketch?"

"I'm leaning toward Florist — a lady in her shop, surrounded by the flowers she has to sell. Pretty vases, finished arrangements, common and exotic flowers. It gives variety, beauty, color, and lots of textures."

"A good challenge. I'll keep you supplied in a steady stream of flowers if that's the direction you decide to go."

"One good reason I might choose it. I'll come find you for a late lunch if you don't find me first."

"I'd like that."

Charlotte settled into her chair in his office, a glass of ice tea in her hand. "Your mom and I are going shopping about two, then meeting up with your sisters for coffee and pie."

He slit open another letter. "You'll have a good time."

"Expect so. I like your mom."

Bryce glanced over at her, thought she looked both rested and content, was pleased by both, and returned his attention to the letter. She joined him in his office for a few minutes most days, to listen to part of a ball game, to talk about her morning, to share a cup of coffee. He missed her on days she didn't come by. She put aside the tea, picked up her sketchbook and a pen, drew for a few minutes, then put it back on the shelf.

Bryce finished the letter. "Want to go for a walk? A short one since you're going out."

"Maybe. I'm just restless. I feel oddly guilty I haven't asked more than the occasional question about what you've been doing."

Bryce smiled. "I haven't done much yet, just put out a lot of inquiries for information. I have a list of places where I send a check every month. A second list of prospects — organizations we might support on an ongoing basis after I know more about them. And, finally, a folder of projects being done around the world I'm considering for contributions."

"Simple. Elegant. I like it."

"We need that monthly list to include about twenty-five thousand entries. It's currently —" he checked the database — "six hundred eight-two organizations. I'm giving an initial gift equal to ten percent of what the organization had in income the prior year, then making monthly contributions to give that amount again over the next year. It's enough to be helpful, but not so much we make any place dependent on us for funding. With every organization that gets through the due diligence and is added to that list, my job gets easier. A year from now we'll be giving away tens of millions in monthly support. Think of it as a big snowball. It starts small but keeps building in scale."

"Are you funding specific projects outright?"

"If I like the project and it's ready to go, I'll fund whatever remains to be raised. If it's early in the planning stage, I'll give five hundred or a thousand, depending on the scope of it, and simply monitor the progress. I'll give the bulk of our donation when the project is ready to launch."

"It's a good and wise approach." She studied the glass she held, glanced back over at him. "Bryce, I know I asked you to keep the burden of the money off me, and you've been doing that. But I feel like I should be helping you more than I am."

"Do you want to?"

She thought a moment and shook her head. "I really don't, I just feel like I should be. I know how big a task this is, Bryce. I watch the hours you spend working on where to give and it makes me feel guilty I'm not helping you any."

"Charlotte, why stress on it? I'm doing fine, and if I need an occasional extra hand, I'll let you know. Enjoy your studio time, some relaxing afternoons shopping like today. This time try to buy something besides dog rawhide bones and a book for me."

"It's hard to find something I want. I'm a wanderer when I shop, not necessarily a buyer. Is there anything you need for me to pick up?"

He tried to come up with something, finally shook his head. "No. I'd say a package of Strawberry Twisters, but I don't need to be eating them."

She smiled. "See the problem?"

Her phone rang. Charlotte dug it out of her pocket. "Hi, John." She reached for a pen. "Give me that item number again." She wrote a note in her palm. "Sure, tell Ellie I can pick it up for her." She got to her feet, covered the phone with her hand. "I'm going to have John drop me by your mom's. I'll be back about six."

"Have a good afternoon, Charlotte."

It was after ten p.m. when Bryce lightly

tapped on the studio door and stepped into the sunroom. The patio doors were open, and he could hear the faint sounds of traffic, of music drifting in from the neighbors. Moonlit shadows kept the backyard from being a fully black oasis. He frequently found Charlotte curled up on one of the couches, simply watching the night.

She loved to live visually. She'd filled the long room with comfortable seating, tables, art books and magazines, loaded the long wall with art — some finished pieces she had collected, others her own works.

Tonight she was at her drawing board positioned halfway down the room. She'd turned on lights around it, the bulbs chosen to produce the natural spectrum of sunlight so her colors would not be distorted when the sun was down. She was surrounded by the tools of her craft — trays of pencils angled so she could see at a glance every shade of blue, green, yellow, and red across the rainbow of colors. Tonight the browns were in first position as she developed a clay-pot design she might use on the flower shop counter.

Bryce settled into the comfortable chair near her, stretched out his legs, and opened the book he had brought with him.

"I'll be finished soon."

"No hurry, it's a new book. One you bought me."

She laid in a line of color, switched to a lighter shade of brown, glanced at him. "I probably just lied. I may tinker with this for another hour or two. I'm not particularly tired. The coffee with that pie wasn't decaf."

"Good thing it's a long book."

"I was politely trying to let you know you don't need to wait up for me, Bryce."

"Got that. Since I choose to stay awake until you come upstairs, I might as well enjoy your company."

"This is a *be a good husband* kind of thing?"

He shrugged but faintly smiled.

"It's kind of nice."

"Finish your pottery design, Charlotte."

She picked out a handful of pencils across the yellow and reds and held them out. "Choose your favorite color."

He selected a deep red. She frowned at it for a moment, then smiled and added the red around the shadow cast inside the pottery.

She bought him books. He bought her shoes. She hung sketches in his office. Shipments of her favorite drawing paper arrived with a ribbon around the box, and sketchbooks showed up in every room, easy to reach, with mugs of pencils in all shades finding their way to various tables.

They walked the neighborhood when they both needed a break, strolling east to stop at the coffee shop, west to wander through the card shop. He started mailing her cards — funny ones, thoughtful ones, blank ones that he filled with simple notes. They played pool. He taught her to play darts.

Movies began to gather on the coffee table, and evenings sharing the couch, sometimes her head resting against his shoulder, became common. Life began to fit together.

And Bryce started to fall in love with his wife.

TWENTY-EIGHT

Bryce slipped off his suit jacket as he entered his bedroom, moved to the closet to hang it up. He heard Charlotte join him and turned, smiled, as he tugged off his tie. "A nice evening. I'm glad we went."

Charlotte slipped off the emerald earrings she had tried as a favor to him. "I enjoy spending time with Ann and Paul."

He offered her the box for the earrings, and she carefully put them inside, thought for a moment, then shook her head. "Beautiful, but no."

"Okay." He set the box aside to return to their shop. He'd try something different. So far she'd chosen to keep only one piece of jewelry out of all he'd asked her to try. But he was enjoying the process. The precious gems to work with were diverse, the designers good, and his wife was a challenge. She would have a dozen pieces of jewelry she loved before he was done. The store would have no problem getting a very high price for the pieces he commissioned that she decided not to keep.

She undid the cuff links for him without him asking. When they were going out for an evening, she'd been selecting whimsical cuff links rather than the more proper ones for him to wear. These happened to be a tiny pair of running shoes.

She'd enjoyed the evening, but she'd been quiet, enough that Ann had given him a couple of concerned looks. Bryce didn't have to ask Charlotte what was still lingering on her mind. His wife had spent the weekend reading what Gage had written. The sadness was real. Even as she tried tonight to focus on the conversation with Ann and Paul, Charlotte had struggled to stay engaged.

Bryce took a risk and held out a pillow. Some nights she would decline with a smile, but sometimes she would curl up and talk awhile. Charlotte curled up in her chair.

He tossed more pillows against the headboard.

"I think I need to talk to you about the book."

He glanced over at her, then gave his attention to the clasp of his watch. Her words were tentative enough he knew she was already thinking of changing her mind. "You know I'll be glad to listen if you do." He put the watch on the dresser, his billfold, made a point of taking his time. She'd wrapped her arms around her knees. He didn't need a clearer visual reminder of how difficult this terrain was for her. She was trying to hide.

He sat down on the edge of the bed and took off his shoes, tossed them one at a time into the closet. She gave a faint smile but didn't comment. He settled against the pillows and forced himself to relax. "Gage is doing a good job?"

"Too good."

Bryce could see the sadness, hear it. He quietly waited.

"The book is going to reveal that a cop had some of the ransom money."

He felt the punch of the news catch him like a jab under the ribs. A cop with ransom money . . .

Charlotte's gaze held his. "Tabitha doesn't know."

And in those quiet words he heard her dilemma. Charlotte had been protecting Tabitha from the truth. And because she hadn't known, Tabitha had opened a door Charlotte had deliberately left closed for the last nineteen years. "You've known that news for a while."

"It's one of the reasons John took me to Texas as soon as I could travel." She rested her chin on her knee. "He's dead, the cop involved. He's the guy who came through the door first, shot and killed the two men holding me. He died in a car accident on the way to a television interview the next day. Gage is going to say the cop had financial problems and took some of the ransom money after I was rescued as a crime of opportunity. It was theft, a spur-of-the-moment decision, and only a theft."

Bryce only needed to see her face to know that wasn't all of it. "Is Gage wrong?"

Seconds ticked by, her eyes focused on her hands as she carefully smoothed out the folds in the fabric of her dress. She abruptly got to her feet. "Good night, Bryce."

He simply nodded and let her go.

Not all of it. Not even close.

He'd wondered if she would ever talk about what had happened, now wondered if she ever could. A cop had some of the ransom money. He closed his eyes and prayed for his wife. She was carrying a grief, a trauma so deep that God was the only one who could help her figure out what she could safely share.

■ ■ ■ ■

Bryce searched his desk for his planner. He remembered having it that morning after his dad called, but couldn't remember where he'd left it. He heard Charlotte in the living room. "Charlotte, do you see that brown leather-covered planner I carry around?"

"It's in here."

He left the office for the living room. She was sitting in her favorite chair, sketching variations of a flower arrangement. Charlotte held out the planner. "You use this a lot. What do you keep in it?"

"Notes of things to do, my schedule."

"I see you write in the back sometimes. Your to-do list?"

He hesitated because he never talked about it.

"That's okay, sorry I asked. I didn't look."

He heard his words echoing in his mind. He never talked about it . . . they mirrored hers. He sat on the arm of the couch. "I write my prayers in the back of the planner. The middle has my prayer lists. I find it easier to figure out on paper what I want to pray, then I read it to God, maybe consider it a letter to Him.

"The bottom shelf in my office holds the planners I've carried through the years. It lets me look back at my prayers. I put a checkmark beside those He answered, and write *no* beside those He didn't. Or leave blank the ones He might answer sometime in the future. It's useful to me to see my history with God."

"What are you praying about me?"

He opened the planner to her page and held out the book.

She hesitated, changing her mind about seeing it.

"It's okay." He put it in her hands. He'd written a Scripture at the top of the page under her name, followed by a list of specifics he wanted to pray for her.

She didn't make it past the Scripture. He held out the box of tissues from the side table, but she shook her head, scrambled up and left the room. He heard the bathroom door shut. He closed his eyes at the pain inside that was creating those sobs.

The Scripture was from the Song of Solomon: "You are beautiful, my beloved, truly lovely."

He waited for her as the minutes passed, finally heard the bathroom door open, and her steps in the hall.

She hesitated in the doorway. "You see me

that way?"

"Yes."

"I'm broken," she whispered.

She was breaking his heart. "You won't always be," he said simply.

She wiped her arm across her eyes, came back into the room and curled up on the couch. "Could I read the full page? And could you ignore the fact I'll probably cry some more?"

Her tears made his chest hurt. He gave her the Kleenex box, then again opened the planner to her page and handed it to her.

Is Charlotte at peace with you? If not, you know her questions and what troubles her heart. Find words to comfort and encourage her, lead her to the truth and help her be able to accept it so that she might be at peace with you.

Is there any hurt in Charlotte which has not healed that you wish to heal? If so, please ease her pain, repair what's damaged, erase the scars, restore what's been lost, help her forgive, help her forget, make her feel new again — heal her completely.

You've gifted her to draw and to enjoy

the work. Has she been able to experience that gift to the full extent you've envisioned for her? If not, please encourage, mentor, guide, direct, and inspire her today with her art.

Has everyone you would like to buy one of her sketches done so? If not, would you prompt, encourage, and remind them to buy one, and do so persistently, until they have done so?

She wiped her eyes, pulled another tissue. She hesitated, then looked over at him. "May I look through the rest of this?"
"Yes."
She turned the pages. She stopped on the page he had written for himself. He knew the words on the page by heart, for he had prayed them many times.

Please grant me a humble and teachable heart.

Please make me into a man Charlotte can safely trust.

What have I said today that bugs you, that you would have me apologize for and never repeat?

I wish to do your will today, not less than your will, and not beyond it. Allow me to accept the limits and boundaries and lines you see as best for me, while living fully within them for my joy and your glory.

Am I the husband Charlotte needs me to be, and the husband you want me to be?

Is there anything happening in the world today which is not in your will? If so, would you please stop, frustrate, interrupt, cause it to fail, or prevent it from happening, so that your will might be done instead?

Charlotte slowly closed the planner, ran her hand across the leather, and then held it out. "It's breathtaking, Bryce."

"God made me a businessman," he said as he accepted it, "gave me a desire to give, made me comfortable teaching. But I've never thought of those as the center, the way you can say 'I'm an artist,' or Ann can say 'I'm a writer.' Maybe God made me comfortable with prayer. I haven't talked about it with anyone. Maybe this is normal after being a Christian for decades. I simply know I'm supposed to pray, and I find life is better when I do so."

"I think it fits." She wiped her eyes one more time. "You pray nice things about me."

"God will answer them. I like praying for you, Charlotte."

Bryce thought the tone of things between them changed, softened, after she read the planner. She seemed more willing to simply chat with him about her day and what she was thinking. She started leaving him thumbnail sketches stuck to his coffee mug of a morning or slipped into his planner.

He tugged this morning's missive from its perch on the coffee maker and smiled at the image. He was in a suit and tie with baby ducks playing tag under his feet. He'd invested in a livestock program through World Vision the day before, bought ten thousand baby ducks. Not for the first time, he thought Charlotte was more comfortable indicating what she thought with a picture rather than words.

He took his coffee and headed back to the office. She had made a walk through the house sometime late last night because the books and papers she'd been working on were gone. He liked a neat house, preferred the order of it, but thought she probably was further along that spectrum than he was. Every few days her things disappeared and visual order returned. She was easier to sync up with than he had expected. Other than the fact she slept a fraction of what she should and their tastes didn't overlap much in music, there weren't many friction points. He added the thumbnail sketch to the growing collection he kept in his top desk drawer.

The early morning sunlight was just beginning to cross his desk surface. Rather than turn on the computer and look at the information flowing in overnight in response to his inquires, he simply sat and drank his coffee.

Buying her flowers for her Florist sketch had turned into something of a small delight between the two of them. She liked the surprise of what he would have delivered and what the card would say. He liked the opening it gave him to tease her a bit, and compliment her, and find things to say that would bring a smile. He had a feeling she'd been keeping the cards like he kept her small sketches. He'd continue the flowers after her artwork was completed. She needed the words. He didn't think she'd heard nearly enough of them over the years.

She was laughing with him more, mostly

over the Saturday morning cartoons he insisted on recording so they could watch them together on Saturday afternoon. She wasn't much for watching sitcoms, and shied away from anything that was a law-enforcement drama. She watched sports with him, or movies, occasionally the news.

She rarely slept without eventually getting up to throw the locks on her door. She was still skittish in ways that bothered him. He'd made the mistake of tossing a pillow her way from the couch, which made her cringe. Twice she'd checked throwing a fist at him when he made the mistake of startling her in the laundry room. He'd grabbed her arm to stop a fall on the steps and she had froze under his touch and then nearly panicked. She had triggers near the surface, and he kept brushing into them. She tried to down-play those moments when they happened, tried to ease the embarrassment she felt and wave off his apology, but they were taking an emotional toll. She was trying hard to adapt to him always being around, but she was certainly having a harder time of that than he was.

She was embarrassed by her quick emo-tions, both happy and sad — she cried over movies and books, and often he'd catch her struggling with some tears after her Sunday afternoon calls with her sister. But in some ways he was glad for those tears. Marriage had changed more than her name and where she lived. It had put her in a permanent place. It was safe to feel emotions here. For the first time he thought she was letting her emotions show without the buffers of always having to be in control. It was a good sign. It told him in small ways she was continuing to heal, was accepting him as her husband, and trusting him to see the emotions.

Those whispered words *I'm broken* told him everything he needed to know about his wife's perception of herself. She was wrong. She'd survived. If anything, that fact showed she was too strong to be broken. He desperately needed to change the way she saw herself.

He had another hour before he expected to hear her stirring. He needed a plan to court his wife. An old-fashioned word, but one he thought suited matters. He was going to be in love with her long before she got near that point with him, but he was a patient man when it mattered. She was simply nice to live with, and he wanted the rest of what marriage would give them. He was married to the lady he wanted to spend a lifetime with — now he just had to win her heart and get her comfortable trusting him.

She had to trust his love to be strong enough to deal with her past, strong enough to hear the truth and still accept her. She was his wife. His beloved and truly lovely wife. He wondered how long it was going to take before he could get her to see herself as he saw her. Patience was a good virtue, and never more necessary than now.

Bryce tightened the laces on his tennis shoes.

"Where do you go to run?"

He glanced over to see Charlotte coming into the kitchen.

"The university track. It's one of the perks for the alumni — we're free to use the track during hours it's not being used by the university." He wasn't getting much done in the office, he needed a break, and a few miles around the track would chase out some cobwebs.

"I wouldn't mind coming with you as long as we don't try to run together. Our strides are too different."

"Yeah? I'd like that."

"Give me five minutes to change." She lightly ran upstairs.

Bryce added extra water bottles to his gym bag.

When they reached the track he put the gym bag on a bleacher bench and began to stretch.

Charlotte looked around the large track and smiled her appreciation. "I can see why you enjoy this place. Let me know when you're ready to call it a day. I run like a tortoise, so I expect you'll lap me a few times." She put on earphones, turned on the music, and took off at a slow and steady run.

John walked over. "You can safely leave the wallet, keys, and phone. I've got some phone calls to return, but I'll be around. I told Ellie we'd swing by and pick up the dogs on the way back from here. I would have brought them with me, but she insisted they deserved a visit to the dog spa for a shampoo, hair and nail trim after a few weeks running around at the lake."

Bryce smiled. "We'll enjoy having them. Charlotte hasn't said, but I know she's been missing them. Sure you don't want to run with me?"

"I'll pass for today."

Bryce nodded and hit the track with a plan to do twelve laps for three miles. He waved at Charlotte the first time he passed her, the second time he slowed to run with her for a bit, the third time he ran backwards a few steps until she laughed and pushed him on. He settled into a steady run and felt himself relax.

Bryce looked back to the track, where Charlotte was still steadily running. He and John had been talking for almost an hour. He'd done his three miles and cooled down. She was at more than five miles now even at her slower pace.

"She'll go until someone tells her stop," John mentioned. "She's a natural marathoner; she just doesn't like the crowds at the events." John stepped into the track as she came around the curve and gave her the cut-off signal.

She tugged off the earphones.

"Cool down, Charlotte."

"How about a race, four laps?"

"Nope."

"Chicken."

John laughed.

"Two laps."

He picked up a towel and tossed it on the track.

"Time me then. Two laps." She took off.

She did two laps at speed, then slowed and walked half a lap, jogged back. "I like this track. It's got a friendly surface, a bit of spring, and not much slant."

"You were zoning out with the music," Bryce observed, handing her a towel.

"Best way to run. Start your feet moving and think about something else."

"How many laps did you do?"

"No idea. Enough I got some kinks out and enjoyed the run. We should do this more often, Bishop."

"We should. I enjoyed watching you."

She laughed and tossed the towel at him.

Bryce brushed his teeth and then shut off the bathroom light. One of the dogs had curled up on the rug beside the bed. "Hey, Duchess." The tail slap on the floor told him he had guessed right. He knelt to rub the dog's coat. One of the dogs would join Charlotte, the other would join him. He still had to watch them for a moment to tell them apart. Princess was sleeker, had a narrower face, and a more deliberate walk. Duchess was a little heavier, had more inquisitive eyes, and liked to bound from place to place in a hurry. He liked having them around.

"I wondered if she had retreated up here."

He glanced to the doorway to see Charlotte had joined him. "She's good company."

"Princess is asleep by the couch downstairs." Charlotte was carrying a handful of cookies and held out her hand to share.

He took two. "Thanks."

He moved to the closet. He set out his choice of suit and tie for Sunday morning, checked to make sure his shoes were polished, added breath mints and cough drops to the pocket, the routine of small things he did on Saturday night before he taught.

Charlotte curled up in her chair.

He glanced over at her, curious about what was on her mind. He poured a mug from the carafe he had brought upstairs, added honey to the hot tea. "You sure you don't want to try this? You might like the taste."

"No, thanks. It keeps your voice from growing hoarse?"

"Maybe at the margins. It's more habit than anything."

"Do you need to review your lesson for tomorrow?"

"No. It's nearly memorized now." He settled against the pillows against the headboard, drank the tea, set aside the mug. He folded his hands across his chest and let himself relax. She was awake, on the edge of restless, and he was glad she had chosen to join him. He didn't try to break the silence, simply shared the time.

She drew her legs up in her familiar fashion, resting her chin on her knees. "I think I want to tell you something, but every time I get to the words I hesitate."

"You can wait until you're sure."

"I'm just giving myself a headache chasing the idea around in circles. If I tell you, will you keep it to yourself?"

"Yes."

She still hesitated, and the quiet stretched between them. He didn't know how to make this moment easier on her. As the silence lengthened, as she started to speak and stopped, he expected her to shake her head, get up and leave, unable to take the step.

Her arms around her knees suddenly tightened, and she looked over at him. "There was a third man. He whispered, 'I'm a cop. I will kill your sister if you mention me.' The next day cops broke in, shot the two men, and rescued me."

The silence in the room absorbed the words and made them unsaid again. Bryce didn't feel much like breathing.

"Maybe he lied about being a cop," she whispered. "Maybe he was the cop in the wreck, and he's dead now. Or maybe someone else is still out there who does carry a badge. It was only the two of them in the van with Tabitha and me. The third man showed up at the house later. I don't know when. Sometimes I think he was always there. Sometimes I think it was just before the end." She was crying now, silently, her dripping tears turning a spot on her jeans dark.

He moved, he risked her retreating from the conversation, but she couldn't take much more of this memory. Bryce rose, picked up the blanket folded at the foot of the bed, and draped it around her, hunkered down beside the chair and mopped her face with his handkerchief. Her gaze caught and held his. The simple misery in the depths of her eyes broke his heart. He brushed her hair back from her face. "Tabitha is safe. John has excellent security around her."

"I know."

"And you are safe with me, Charlotte."

"I know that too."

She was a sketch artist. If she could remember a face, John would be drowning in sketches of the man. So she had only a voice and the memory of what he had said. And without knowing for certain the man was dead, was no longer a threat, she had no choice but to keep silent.

"Let the book say whatever it's going to say. You don't talk about it. You haven't in the past. You don't now. You can't take the risk."

She nodded. "That's what I've always concluded. I don't talk about it."

He eased open her clenched hand. She'd lived with that decision as the only one she could make for the last nineteen years. He would have read about the cop in the book, but not heard the rest of it. She was risking the rest of it with him. He felt physically sick at the news, and she didn't look relieved to have shared it.

"John's always known, but I haven't told Ellie much of it. Tabitha has no idea."

"Why did you tell me?"

"A lifetime together is a long time. I think it's easier on me if I don't have to carry the added weight of you not knowing."

She was offering a great deal of trust. He carefully brushed back her hair so he could better see her face. "Thank you for telling me."

"You're going to regret knowing. And I don't think I can say anything more than what I just told you."

"I'll never regret you trusting me, Charlotte. What do you say we go downstairs for an hour? We can start a movie while you let a couple of Tylenol kill that headache. There's no need trying to sleep while this memory is clouding your thoughts."

She wiped her eyes again, nodded.

Before he let her up from the chair, he made her a promise. "Charlotte, I won't ask. But I'll listen. Whatever you want to say, whenever you want to say it, I'll listen."

The movie he had chosen finally ended.

"It's one a.m. You teach this morning," she whispered.

They were sharing the couch, Charlotte curled up beside him, still chilled despite the blanket he'd brought downstairs and tucked around her.

"I'll be fine. John's driving us in the morning. Close your eyes, Charlotte. Trust me enough to give me that." He found another movie.

He felt it when she finally drifted to sleep.

He lightly brushed a kiss against her hair.

He needed to talk to John. And Paul. And do it without going beyond his word to Charlotte.

Bryce joined John in the kitchen for coffee while Charlotte was still getting ready for church. "John, how close are you to identifying the third man?"

John finished stirring cream into his coffee before he looked over. "She's talking about what happened."

"A little."

"I didn't think she'd take that risk with you until she'd been around you for a few years." John leaned back against the counter. "Charlotte can't give me a face. She tried for years after it happened, trying to get her memory to cooperate. She's only got a voice for this guy, and his words."

John took another drink of his coffee. "The cop who died in the wreck had several trial depositions I could access. I put together a tape, a couple minutes of his voice, and that of a dozen other cops giving similar depositions. Charlotte didn't pick his voice out. I had her listen to the tape a few times over a couple months' period. I'm convinced it's not him."

"This guy claimed to be a cop."

John nodded. "Could be a lie, could be true. She's never reacted to the voice of any cop she's met, and over the years I've arranged repeated conversations with the cops on the task force, ones who I thought were close to the investigation, or from the precinct that covered that neighborhood where she was held. She would have reacted if she heard that voice again."

John set aside his mug. "I can tell you, Bryce, no trace of the guy showed up at that house where she was held. No sign of him showed up in the phone records of the men who were killed. Whoever he was, he knew when the end was coming and carefully covered his tracks.

"This third man warns her not to mention him, twenty-four hours later the other two are dead, and he has disappeared like a ghost. It had been four years and she was dying. She wouldn't have lasted another month. I believe he made the choice to let her live and called in the tip himself. It ended on his timetable. I think he's still out there. My best guess, he left the area the day before the raid went down. I think he left and fully intends to never come back."

"She's never told the cops a third man was there."

"Her choice, but I didn't try to change her mind. She's got a voice, his words, the fact he was there, but nothing else to give them. Cops were already looking for evidence someone else had been involved, they were collecting fingerprints at the house, in the van, going through phone records, interviewing people, and creating lists of anyone those two cousins had been seen with during the four years they'd held her, doing what they could to trace the ransom money.

"Bryce, I hate the fact he's out there. But I'm a realist. Charlotte telling the cops someone else was there would simply put more pressure on her to remember, and in the first years after she was rescued, that was the last thing she needed. Security around Tabitha and Charlotte is there to insure he will never again be a threat to either one of them. I want to find the guy, I keep pursuing what is possible to do, but I'm not particularly worried about him. If Charlotte remembers more, I'll get him. It will be my pleasure to do so."

"You don't think he's a threat to her being in Chicago."

"I think he's staying as far away from Charlotte as he can. He got away with his part in the crime. Why risk coming anywhere near her and chance getting caught? I'll lay money he was gone the day before the raid and has never been back."

"The cops think this case is closed. That's a big problem."

"Bryce, understand her perspective. Charlotte protects her sister. She shoved her sister out of the van to protect her, and paid for that decision with four years of her life. Someone who said he's a cop has threatened to hurt Tabitha if Charlotte talks about him. Silence is the only decision she can make.

She's going to protect her sister. She's not going to talk to the cops. I'm relieved she's told you, but she's not going to take this further."

"When did Charlotte tell you about the third man?"

"After I learned a cop had been found with ransom money. She told me what the man had said, and I made arrangements that day to transfer her to the clinic in Texas."

Bryce heard Charlotte on the stairs. "Don't you think it's important to get the FBI looking into the case again?" he asked, his voice low.

"I'm not sure what they could do, but you've got my blessing as long as you keep Charlotte out of it. The book might create an opening you could use."

"I'm running with Paul this afternoon. I'll see what I can come up with without breaking my word to Charlotte."

Paul was waiting for him on the university track Sunday afternoon.

Bryce set down his gym bag on the bleacher bench, pulled out a bottle of water. "What do you want to do today, four miles, six?"

"I'm thinking four since I've missed a

couple weeks," Paul replied.

Bryce nodded, drank down half the water, began to stretch in preparation for the run.

"I'm glad you and Charlotte came over. It was nice to catch up."

"We enjoyed it."

"Marriage looks like it agrees with you."

Bryce smiled. "It does."

They hit the track at a steady pace, working through the miles. Running with Paul was always an interesting experience, for Paul chose a pace and tried to hold to it from the first of the run until the last. The workout became intense in the last mile if the pace had been set too fast.

Bryce waited until they were cooling down. "Charlotte doesn't want you to get blindsided by the book," he said, mopping his face with a towel. "Gage has the fact a cop had some of the ransom money."

Paul grimaced. "We figured he'd find it. I don't know what to tell you. Cops looked at him, Bryce, from every direction. I've looked at him. It's as likely the cop was framed as it is he was involved. The money may have been planted in his house after he died by the uncle of the two cousins killed. We just don't have enough to say one way or the other."

"Useful to know."

"How's Charlotte handling it?"

"She already knew about the cop."

"Ann thought she did. I know Charlotte's got a good reason not to trust any kind of cop, given the circumstances. I know she's never said a word about what happened. But she married you. She obviously trusts you. Has Charlotte talked to you about what happened?"

"She's talked to me." Bryce zipped the gym bag closed. "I told her not to talk with you."

Paul stopped. Bryce simply met his searching look. Paul slowly nodded. "That tells me something."

"It should."

Bryce headed back to his car. He'd told Charlotte he would stop at the Mexican restaurant they favored and bring enchiladas home for dinner.

Ann arrived first. "Where do you need me?"

"How far did they get tracing the ransom money?"

His wife sorted through the dates in the Bazoni case file, found the first section after Ruth was rescued, and pulled out the reports. "Bryce told her not to talk with us."

Paul nodded. "There's only one reason I can come up with that he says that to her.

Charlotte is worried about someone who is very much alive, and not just someone. Probably a cop."

Paul spread out the forensic reports on the table. "Charlotte wasn't talking, the two men who held her were dead — investigators had a limited amount to work with to answer their questions. The house was dusted for fingerprints, looking for anyone else who had been involved, the same with the van the two men drove."

Paul scanned the reports. "They lifted hundreds of prints. Most were matches to the two men who held her, or Charlotte's own prints. Thirty-eight prints were other people. Magazines, envelopes, a casserole dish — transfer prints from being handed something. Three family members, two known friends of the cousins, six people in the neighborhood. Only four of the prints remain unidentified — taken from a beer bottle in the trash, the side mirror of the van, and two prints from the underside of the kitchen table where someone might've gripped the edge to push a chair back. I'll get them run through the databases today. Hope we get lucky."

"John would never let her be near Chicago if he thought a threat was still here," Ann said.

"Even more to the point — if she had seen someone, there would be a sketch. She doesn't know who it is or John would have long ago dealt with the matter. She overheard a conversation, I think," Paul replied.

"One cop had ransom money, maybe more than one cop involved?"

Paul nodded. "Find out how much ransom money wasn't accounted for and maybe we get a sense of it. If someone else was involved, they'd want their cut of the money."

"Charlotte was quiet at dinner, a lot on her mind," Ann said. "I put it down to the fact she'd read what Gage had written. Bryce mentioned it when he and I were in the kitchen. I wonder if she was debating talking to us."

"Maybe. She's talking to Bryce. I'm going to guess for now that is as far as she goes."

Ann opened another folder. "Bryce is level-headed. So is John. The fact Bryce still has her in town, John does, the fact their security hasn't tightened up even more — she told them something, but it's not a recent detail."

Paul's two closest friends in the bureau, Sam and Rita, arrived. Paul didn't bother to ask if he'd interrupted a date. He'd heard the same music in the background of his call to Rita, then to Sam.

"What's up, boss?"

"The Bazoni case. The two guys holding her are shot dead during the rescue, a cop is found later to have ransom money. The task force did a thorough look for other people involved and didn't identify anyone. Cops had a suspicion their uncle was either involved or knew something — the cousins killed were often at his house during the four years Ruth was held — but they couldn't prove it. I want to know if the task force missed someone else."

"New evidence?"

"For now just an urgent question. There are four fingerprints from the scene never identified. We'll start with those. Ann's looking at how much of the ransom money was able to be traced or recovered. Focus on people the cousins might trust. High school friends, work buddies, neighbors they grew up with, family. Then widen it to people who could have been involved — the cop who died being a perfect example. He was there. Who else can we list that was there?"

Rita pulled out a chair and slid over a file box. Sam took the printouts.

Bryce took the stairs down quietly Monday morning shortly after six a.m. so as not to wake Charlotte, put on coffee, then walked back to his office. He liked the early morning starts to the day. He didn't have to wonder if the work he did mattered. Lives were being impacted by the decisions he made. There was a blessing in simply being trusted with the work, and every day he crossed the threshold of his office, he felt it. He often thought he now had the best job in the world.

At the right time, in the right amounts, funding made an organization flourish. Money was the easy part of the equation when it came to ministry. A clear vision and plan, well-trained leaders and staff, enthusiastic volunteers, opportunities to meet people's needs — those were more vital to the success or failure of a ministry than the funding, and he was the last part of the puzzle. But he and Charlotte could partner with them and make a difference when the time was right.

Bryce turned on the lights in his office.

A large sketch rested in the center of his desk, a cookie in cellophane resting on top of it. He opened the cellophane wrapper. Chocolate chip. He smiled, tugged it out, and took a bite. Charlotte had discovered his weakness for chocolate chip two weeks ago and bought him a fresh-baked cookie when she was passing the bakery.

He lifted off the sheet of tracing paper she had placed to protect the drawing. His mom, his sisters — smiling, eating pie, having leaned together for a photo.

He gently traced the edge of the paper. At least sixty hours of work. He'd watched Charlotte build these photo-like sketches. She'd humored his mom and removed the gray hair, given his sisters the earrings they'd be receiving at Christmas. His mom had her hand resting on Josephine's, and their wedding rings were lightly touched by the sunlight flowing across the table. Charlotte would have a snapshot on her phone of the three of them, had been able to transform that into this. The gift she had for drawing was truly remarkable.

A year ago he hadn't realized how much he was missing from life. Sharing the days with Charlotte made life enjoyable in a way that he couldn't have imagined or easily put into words. The real gift she'd given him was not the money; it was having her as his wife.

He placed the sketch on the credenza for Ellie to frame for him. Charlotte had drawn eight family sketches for him now. She was beginning to know his family and love them, and it showed in her sketches. He wondered if she realized it or if the family dynamics had gradually absorbed her, and a year from now she'd look back and realize with surprise they were now her family too.

The family had extended and made her welcome as his wife, created her a place. If there was something this marriage could offer her that mattered, it was his family and that absolute acceptance that came with it. She was one of them.

Out of habit Bryce glanced at his calendar. There was another birthday in the family tomorrow. Rose was turning six. He'd have a reason to go shopping with Charlotte this afternoon. They had a common love affair with toy stores, so it would be a laughter-filled couple of hours. Courting his wife by finding reasons to hang out with her and make her laugh . . . he liked the simplicity of it. One of these days she was going to laugh, turn and hug him without even thinking about it. The baby steps were adding up slowly and taking them somewhere.

He finished the cookie with his coffee, smiled as he glanced again at the sketch, then turned and started his workday.

TWENTY-NINE

Bryce was glad they had planned a trip north to Shadow Lake. Charlotte dozed during the five-hour drive, wrapped up in his jacket, her tote bag with an extra sketchbook at her feet. The dogs were asleep in the back seat. She needed the rest. She'd told him about the third man, and now seemed to struggle to push back the memories that went with it. She was getting up in the night to spend a few more hours at her drafting table, working on the final details of the Florist sketch. Bryce wanted to break the pattern but wasn't sure how.

Bryce drove to the lake, taking the road from the east so as to avoid Graham Enterprises and all the reminders of what she had left behind. He crossed the river that fed into the lake, then turned south around the lake past John's home to arrive at Fred's house. Ellie was there to meet them before Charlotte stepped out of the car.

He eventually left Charlotte with Ellie, surrounded by paint strips and carpet samples, talking about cabinet choices for the remodeled kitchen. Ellie would help her relax more than anyone else could. Bryce walked with the dogs down to the lake.

John had built out the dock so a couple of fishing boats could comfortably tie up, built a small boathouse to store fishing gear, and right now was in the process of putting in an outdoor sink and work surface as a convenient place to clean fish. Bryce thought it was the perfect addition to the property, and only regretted Charlotte didn't enjoy the water so he could take her for a boat ride while they were here.

John finished storing tackle. "You made good time."

"Traffic was light. Joseph had a woman with him in the tailing SUV."

"Kimberly Beach. I'll introduce you next week. She's going to be the new security with Ellie and Charlotte when they're out shopping. Easier for her to blend in than one of the guys."

Bryce nodded. "Appreciate that thought."

John pulled out cold sodas for them from the refrigerator next to the bait cold-storage box and handed one over. "I got a call from Ann Falcon yesterday, checking in on Charlotte, asking me to think back on the kidnapping and what Charlotte might have said about the two men killed — who they spent time with, who they trusted, had Charlotte ever discussed what or who they spoke about. I'd say you tipped over a pretty determined hornet's nest with whatever you said. I didn't have much I could give her, but she was asking the right questions."

"Interesting that Ann called you and not Paul."

"Not so surprising. Ann's been a friend for a long time." John offered the dogs each a biscuit. "Don't get disappointed when they hit a wall, Bryce. Cops have looked before."

"If that's what happens, I'll deal with it. Charlotte's having trouble sleeping."

"I can imagine, given she read what Gage has written. You don't stir those kinds of memories without it causing her problems. Charlotte's memory . . . it's not memories, Bryce, not like you think of them. She described it once as a 'black suffocating blanket.' She doesn't want the details. The emotions of it are hard enough. It simply takes her time to build a distance again so she's not feeling that during her waking hours."

"She's blocked out most of what happened?"

John shrugged. "It's there. But she remembers as little of the specifics as her mind can get away with. She'll sleep easier when this isn't so close to the surface."

"Does anything help?"

"Work. Time. She'll get past this, Bryce. She always does."

Bryce leaned against his car and watched the moon rise over Shadow Lake. The evening breeze had picked up. He glanced over as Charlotte joined him, bundled in his jacket.

"Ellie is making good progress remodeling the house. We had fun."

Bryce smiled and opened the passenger door for her. "It looked like you two were having a good time." John had cooked out at his place for the four of them, hamburgers and hot dogs, and they had lingered on his back patio until the sun went down, watched the water reflecting the colors of the fading sunset in the clouds. Charlotte had spent another few private hours talking with Ellie while he and John watched a ball game. "We can stay the night in Madison if you prefer not to make the long drive tonight," he told her.

"I'll let you make the choice since you're

driving. I'm fine either way."

"Then let's go back to Chicago tonight. Traffic is light, and it's a beautiful night." Unspoken, he hoped the long car ride would help Charlotte sleep for a few more hours. He found a station playing her kind of music and turned it on low.

"If Ellie would just marry John, life would be really good right now," she said, leaning her head against the headrest.

He smiled. "I'd say they're figuring out how it might work. She was finishing some of his thoughts, and he was directing her help on the meal preparation without having to say much."

"I noticed. She's comfortable with him."

"Will you tell me one day about Ellie's history, Charlotte?"

"No. She may tell you herself. It's darker than mine and did more damage."

"I'm very sorry for that."

"So am I. She was five." Charlotte frowned. "I try not to mention even that, so forget I said it."

"I like her, Charlotte. Whatever her history, it's not changing that."

"It's not that. It's just her story to tell, not mine."

Bryce let a long moment pass, then decided to risk a question. "Are the oil paintings hers? Is Ellie the painter *Marie*?"

His wife turned her head to look at him. Bryce hadn't expected to see sadness. There were emotions there, deep and dark, swirling in her eyes. And sadness was dominating. "I can't answer that," Charlotte said softly.

"Last month there was a trace of oil paint on the back of Ellie's jacket sleeve," he offered quietly. "And walnut oil has a faint smell, but it's distinctive. There was the whiff of it when she walked into the office last week."

"You observe well." Charlotte reached over and rested her hand on his arm. "Let it go, what you've seen. It's not a simple answer, of using a different name to keep some privacy. The truth is far more complex than that. She'll tell you one day. She likes you, and that's a large part of her decision. She eventually told John. She'll probably tell you."

He accepted that. "I won't mention it."

Charlotte nodded her thanks and closed her eyes with a sigh. "To think I used to run a full day at Graham Enterprises and have energy left over. Those days are gone."

"They'll return once you get some decent sleep for more than a night or two."

"Hope so." She gave him a tired smile. "It

was nice, Bryce, being their guests. I'll invite Ellie and John to come to dinner next week and return the favor."

"I'd like that." He made the turn that would take them across the river that fed into Shadow Lake. "Neither one of them ever mentioned the money."

"Did you expect them to?"

"No. I just realized that fact and find it interesting. The only two people in our lives who know about the size of the wealth didn't find it significant to mention or ask a question about it."

"You're enjoying giving the money away. They can see that when you talk about your days. I'm enjoying having a studio again and a chance to get back to some detailed drawings. They saw that too. They'll be happy to help if there's a problem, but otherwise it's just our life now."

"Anything you would change about that life?" Bryce asked, curious if she'd answer.

Miles passed by.

"I think I'd like to kiss you good-night sometimes."

"Okay."

"I heard that smile."

"Did you expect me to say no?"

"I'm just thinking about it."

Bryce glanced over. Her eyes were closed

519

and she was drifting. He smiled, and didn't break the silence. He was thinking about it now too.

Bryce checked the time and then the upcoming exits. They were four hours into the drive home, and he decided not to take the last of the exits they occasionally used when they stopped for gas or food. It would be better to simply get home. Charlotte was watching traffic pass by in the opposite lanes. He'd break the silence with a topic for conversation but wasn't sure what would help. He was beginning to recognize the distant expression she got when the memories were pressing on her.

"I need to tell you something, Bryce. Something that is going to be very hard to hear."

"I'll listen, Charlotte."

"They kidnapped a child the third year. A boy, a few months old. I can't stop hearing his cries."

He took the car off cruise and dropped their speed.

"They were going to get a nice ransom from his family. Three days later they shook him to death because he wouldn't stop crying. I tried to intervene to stop it. They broke my wrist. I was nineteen, and an infant died because I couldn't get him to stop crying."

Bryce kept his silence by strength of will. If he interrupted, she was going to stop, and she desperately needed to say the words.

"I grieved for the child. I stopped eating. I gave up. I'm not really a survivor, Bryce. The cops simply found me before I died."

He reached over, wrapped his hand around hers, felt her struggle not to pull away — and then she turned her hand, interlaced her fingers with his, and held on tight. "I can't stop hearing his cries," she said, her voice breaking.

She shielded her eyes when he turned on the kitchen lights. He eased her out of the jacket. "Go lie down on the couch, Charlotte."

"I'm going upstairs."

"I'm not letting you cry yourself to sleep behind a locked door. Stretch out on the couch, or take my bed and I'll sit in your chair. Don't ask me to listen to you cry and walk away. I won't do it. I can't do it."

She changed directions to the living room.

Spare blankets were in the hall closet. He pulled out a couple of them.

Charlotte moved to the couch, and Bryce brought a chair over. It took an hour and half a box of Kleenex, but her breathing finally turned deeper. He watched her for a few more minutes. She looked so incredibly sad. Tomorrow was going to become the second most difficult day of their lives together. He reached over and shut off the end-table light.

"You're not designed for that chair."

He opened his eyes and sighed.

She was up, showered, dressed, and sitting on the couch facing him. He lowered his legs that had stiffened overnight. He'd stretched them over to the armrest of the couch sometime during the night.

"I called your name. Tried coffee. Did everything but punch you."

"What did it?"

"The phone rang. You barely flinched the first few rings, then your eyes kind of flickered. The machine caught the call, something about a dentist appointment reminder. I hoped you would finally surface."

"Surprised I slept. Glad I did." He rested his head in his hands, scrubbed his face, gratefully accepted the coffee she offered. He could remember seeing the dawn.

"We need to talk."

"Now or later?" he asked quietly.

She carefully unfolded a newspaper clipping and handed it to him.

He didn't have to ask if this was the child. The newsprint was yellowed and fragile. He read the article, an obituary for baby Connor Hewitt alongside an update regarding the kidnapping case.

"It's my butterfly pin on his blanket."

He studied the photo of the infant, then carefully folded the clipping and handed it back. "He was a beautiful child, Charlotte."

"Connor's father, Henry Hewitt, came to see me late one night at the hospital about a week after I was rescued. He opened his hand and showed me the butterfly pin. He asked if it was mine. I started to cry. And he . . . he thanked me for trying to help his son.

"If you think I cry now, Bryce, I bawled that night, so hard I about cracked my ribs. It's probably what saved my life, that crying jag, and the fact the boy's father didn't blame me. I started to recover after that, slowly.

"There's a tape. A call made from the Dublin Pub telling Henry where his son was buried. The caller wanted some cash in return for the information. Henry played it for me that night at the hospital, and I recognized the voice. Whoever it was who called to say where baby Connor was buried also whispered to me he was a cop and threatened my sister.

"Henry asked me not to tell the cops. If I said my abductors had also killed Connor, cops would close the case on his son and he'd lose his leverage to keep them searching to find this man who'd made the call. Even without his request, I had no intention of giving them any information about the man because of the threat he'd made against Tabitha. Henry used to walk the streets of the neighborhood, encouraging conversations, simply so he could check a voice against that tape. We never expected it would be years and this man still wouldn't have been found.

"We have the man's voice on tape, so it's not just based on my memory. Cops have looked for him over the years in order to solve the baby Connor case, while John has looked for him over the years to solve who else was involved in my case. We both want the same man. We just haven't been able to find him."

"Charlotte, why did you tell me?"

She looked up from the folded clipping, met his gaze. "You deserve to know who your wife really is. You'll try to fall in love with me, because that's what a good husband is supposed to do. I couldn't live with you doing that while not knowing this."

He was already in love with her, but it would scare her to hear those words right now. He simply nodded.

"I'd like to show you his grave."

He slid his hand around the back of her neck, nudged her head toward his shoulder and wrapped her in a hug. "It will be okay, Charlotte."

It was a beautiful gravesite. The family stone was a pale gray granite, neatly etched cursive writing showing three people were buried here. Connor, age three months. Dana Hewitt, his mother, died three years after her son. Henry Hewitt had died two years ago.

"Henry died still hopeful the caller would be found one day. He handled the long delay better than I did." Charlotte knelt and laid flowers on the grave. "I knew the child for only three days, but I loved him, Bryce. With everything in me I wanted to protect him. And I failed."

Bryce wrapped his arm around her waist.

"I'm angry at God for what happened to me, but the real sharp pain . . . it's knowing God didn't answer my prayers to keep baby Connor safe. I watched him be killed, and there was nothing I could do to stop it."

Bryce didn't try to find words. There weren't any. He simply listened and hoped she would keep talking. She'd been silent too long. When her words turned into only sobs, he wrapped his arms around her and held her.

"You could use a drink. Sorry it's only strong coffee."

Bryce tossed aside the piece of split wood he was holding and took the mug John offered. He'd hoped restacking the firewood beside the garage might provide something to occupy his time for an hour. But he'd spent most of the time staring off across the yard, lost in thought.

"There was no way to warn you, no way to even prepare the ground for what she was going to say. I'm sorry for that."

Bryce accepted John's apology with a nod. "I can see that." He used his fist to check a chunk of the firewood. The last of the wood purchased five years ago was beginning to go soft with decay, while the wood from this year was still hard and filled with sap. They'd be able to have a good fire on winter evenings. Charlotte would enjoy sketching it. "She's so incredibly angry, John. It's a crippling pain. God let it happen, and she is extremely angry at Him."

"The men who hurt her and killed the child are dead — being angry at them doesn't get her any relief," John noted. "The third man who threatened her sister, who called Henry to tell him where his son was buried — she'd be angry at him if we could find him and give her a name. We have his voice but have never been able to identify him. That leaves God. You stir up the memories, the pain returns, and with it the anger. All the unanswered turmoil and the *why*'s about what happened get directed at God."

"She should have been talking about this over the last nineteen years."

John shook his head. "She would have never survived if all this had become known. She blamed herself for not protecting the infant. She grieved, gave up, and willed herself to die. Baby Connor's father broke some of that guilt. Ellie got through to her in Texas, enough to break some more of that pain. Time has helped her come to terms with the truth there was nothing she could have done to prevent Connor's death. But she lives with it. She's just beginning to accept it. I'm honestly surprised she told you."

"She didn't want me falling in love with her, not knowing this about her."

John considered the words, gave a half smile. "Boy, does she have you pegged wrong. Put it down to the fact she doesn't think someone could or should love her."

"I'm beginning to realize it. It's a difficult thing to live with."

"Her silence gave her space to come to terms with what happened, and her silence was useful in its own way. She did what Henry asked — it was the only thing she could do for him — and it steadied her a bit to be able to do so. The baby Connor case stayed open, cops focused on finding the caller. The work was pursued aggressively. No one expected the years to pass without someone identifying him."

"Can he be found, John?"

"I don't know. I'll play you the tape so you know his voice. The cops had been looking for the caller for over a year before Charlotte was rescued. They had gone through the neighborhood around the Dublin Pub in a systematic way. So I started looking from the other direction, looking at cops and those related to the investigation, working in toward the neighborhood.

"I'm afraid Henry and I missed our opportunity of finding him. Someone in the neighborhood would need to hear the tape and say that's so-and-so, give us a name, for us to catch him. We never found that person. More likely the person who could answer the question was more terrified of the man than the reward money we were offering could overcome. I think the man was gone the day before Charlotte was rescued. Our window to catch him closed. He's out there somewhere, but the odds of putting a name to that voice have faded with the years."

"What happens if he's never found?"

"She goes on with her life." John set aside his own mug. "For much of the last ten years she had moved on. The book has stirred it up again. She'll push this back into the past, just give her some time. It wouldn't hurt if you were to create reasons for Ellie to be over here more the next few weeks. If Charlotte will talk about something, she'll often trust Ellie first."

Bryce nodded. "What if Gage finds out about baby Connor and puts it into the book?"

"He won't find it." John rose. "Call if you need me, Bryce."

"I will." He set aside his mug. "John?"

The man stopped and turned.

"This is all of it?"

John hesitated. "Maybe. The cop having ransom money, the third man's threats against Tabitha, baby Connor's death — she hasn't hinted something else of that size is back there. But I know there's more she hasn't told me. She's reached that line and backed away too many times for me not to understand it's extremely painful. She's talked some to Ellie. But it's also probable she simply hasn't talked about it to anyone."

Bryce nodded and John left.

It was a significant assumption on John's part that the reporter would not discover the link to the baby Connor case. The more Bryce thought about it, the more he understood why John was certain the connection would not be made. Gage didn't have a single thread that could reach into the truth. The only pieces of evidence that the two cases were linked were a butterfly pin, Charlotte's witness to what happened, and her memory that the third man's voice matched the Dublin Pub caller.

Bryce returned to restacking wood, needing something to occupy his hands while his mind whirled with the facts, assumptions, and enormous unknowns. He could see Charlotte at her drafting table when he stepped past the corner of the garage. She was doing her best to get lost in work as well.

He took off his work gloves, rubbed his eyes. He was in love with someone who considered herself broken, who carried the burden of a child's death she could not prevent, who didn't know how to handle the fact God loved her and yet had somehow permitted all of that to happen.

He'd talk with her, but he didn't have the words to offer yet.

What he wasn't going to do was let this present reality become their future. He would figure out, one by one, the steps to help her heal. He was grasping the terrain she was wrestling with now. She had paid a steep price for far too long. He'd find the words he needed, the actions. She wasn't going to be bleeding inside another day without his help to get those wounds closed and healed.

They had to find the guy. Every road led to the need for that answer.

He didn't have to wonder if John had pursued every avenue to date. Bryce wondered if it would be worth praying for Charlotte to be able to remember the man's face, to be able to draw it, but he soon set aside that idea. He did not want her having to live with the image of that third man for the rest of her life. There had to be some other way to generate a new lead, something none of them had thought of yet. He tossed another piece of wood onto the restacked pile. He'd pray for that, and not give up until they had it.

Bryce sat down on a bleacher and changed into his running shoes.

Paul jogged over from the track, finishing his warm-up. "You look like you had a bad night."

Bryce glanced up, but he wasn't going to touch that comment. "Just things on my mind." He stretched in preparation for their run, jogged part of the track and back.

"Ann and I," Paul said as he capped his water bottle, "and a couple of people I trust have been looking over the Bazoni case file on the off chance Charlotte might like to have a conversation one day."

Bryce nodded. It seemed years since he had hinted to Paul there was a third person still out there.

"Bryce, can you give me something to work with?"

"I can't. Let's do six miles today." Bryce took to the track and set the pace. He appreciated the feel of the track under his feet. And as he ran, he felt his mind begin to clear. For the first time in days he pushed away the problems he was wrestling with, the pain his wife was in, and simply ran. He didn't want the six miles to end, even though they were both pulling in air and fighting quivering muscles as they passed the last lap.

They cooled down with a half-mile jog, then walked.

Bryce offered a water bottle to Paul, drank down much of a second one himself. "How's it going with that cold case you and Ann were working on?"

"Baby Connor?"

"Yes."

"It's coming along."

"Good. You should solve that case." Bryce pushed his water bottle into his gym bag. "I appreciate the run. Give me a call when you want to meet again."

Ann paused from icing a cookie. Her husband had retrieved a soda from the refrigerator but was simply standing, holding it, the refrigerator door still open, his attention obviously far away. "What is it, Paul?"

"I can't be one hundred percent sure," he said thoughtfully as he closed the refrigerator, "but I think Bryce implied this morning that the Bazoni case and baby Connor case are linked. It was deliberate, the way he said it. A six-mile run between my question and his comment, but he was responding to me. I heard him make the connection."

She put down the knife.

Paul opened the soda. "I mentioned the Bazoni case and asked if Bryce could give me something to work with. He said he couldn't. A six-mile run later, he told me I should solve the baby Connor case. It's just hit me — it was deliberate, the way he said it. The way he paused, looked over. It wasn't a casual comment."

Ann trusted Paul's instincts. "Then we pursue it as if they are connected and see where it leads us." Ann put down the cookie and reached for paper, quickly graphed out the details she remembered on each case. "They were in the same general area, and the time frames overlap."

Paul leaned against the counter to watch the outline develop. "The baby Connor case gives us a possibility of two men. The Bazoni case gives us two men shot dead. If they *are* connected, it's the same two men."

Ann connected them on the sketch.

"Bryce told her not to talk to us about what happened, which suggests there is someone out there Charlotte is still worried about today. We've got a caller never identified in the baby Connor case. Same person?"

"The simplest answer is typically the right one. The same person. Someone Charlotte is worried about, and we have his voice on tape."

"If the cases are linked, we know more about him now. We know he was friends with the cousins who were killed. If Charlotte is afraid of him, he was in the area during those four years. He had information about where baby Connor was buried. He likely had, and eventually spent, some of the Bazoni ransom money. He received ten thousand from Henry Hewitt."

"Someone the original cops had on their list and passed over. Or more likely someone the original cops did not have on their list," Ann guessed. "It's now a process of finding names and eliminating names."

Paul drank his soda and looked at the diagram. "Two cases. One group of guys behind both."

"At least three guys, two of them now dead," Ann agreed. "We are looking for a man in his forties or fifties now, who knew the two men who held Ruth Bazoni well enough to be involved in that crime, who was considered a local resident to the customers at the Dublin Pub, and who may or may not be a cop. We have his voice on tape, know he probably left the area about the time the Bazoni case ended."

"A good, workable summary," Paul said.

He tapped the page. "We passed over an obvious point. Charlotte can identify the voice on the Dublin Pub tape. Maybe not his name, maybe not his face, but she can say 'I know that voice.' It's interesting that she hasn't said that in nineteen years."

"She needs cops to be looking for that man, can't risk saying 'I think he's a cop,' so she doesn't say anything. That leaves the baby Connor case open. Nice tactics when you think about it. She has the cops looking for the man without saying she needs us to find him."

Paul thought about it. "I'll buy that."

Ann studied the picture and sighed. "Paul, it's Charlotte's butterfly pin on the blanket. She was the woman involved. It has to be. Her medical records — she broke her wrist about a year before she was rescued. It healed wrong. She tried to protect the baby from being shaken to death. The timeline on the injury fits too." She bit her lip. "This is more than you catching a hint of something from Bryce. I think Bryce knows they are linked. I think she told him what happened. We need to talk with her."

"We ask, she'll give us a variation of no comment," Paul replied. "Better to have the conversation when we have something to offer that's more than speculation. First we identify the voice on that tape. *Then* we talk to Charlotte about baby Connor."

"Bishop. Come see the sunset."

Bryce set aside a letter and went to join Charlotte. She made a point to sit on the front steps and watch the sunset nearly every evening. He took a seat beside her, braced with his hands behind him, and stretched out his legs. Thin lines of clouds cut across a wide swath of the blue sky, and the angle of the setting sun had begun to change them to pink. "It's pretty tonight."

She nodded, her chin on her crossed arms as she watched the clouds change colors. She hadn't brought her sketchbook out this evening, which was a bit unusual.

"God's an artist," Charlotte said quietly. "He makes sunsets change every evening, created everything from a walrus to a zebra to a parrot, designed dozens of different breeds of horses and dogs, even the leaves on trees and shrubs are in hundreds of different shapes. God is creative and artistic. That's the one reason I am still willing to wrestle with figuring Him out. He does beautiful work. He doesn't have failed designs."

Bryce realized she was opening a door to a topic she rarely discussed. She was right.

God didn't have failed designs. "You're seeing glimpses of Him through His work all around you. I think you're an artist because He wanted to share that joy of creating something with you, and He specifically gave you art as a gift so you could share something with Him that those of us who aren't artists don't understand."

"Probably." She was silent for a minute. "I can't believe He created me and then blew the design by letting evil tear it up. I still hold out hope that He can pick up the pieces of me and make something beautiful one day."

Bryce sat up and rested his hand on her back, rubbing his thumb lightly along her shoulder blade. "You're still His masterpiece, Charlotte. God's been fixing broken people ever since sin came into the world. Give Him time. He's not done. God promises He will work for the good in all things. What happened to you isn't beyond His ability to recover."

"I know you keep praying for me, but I don't find it easy to reconcile what I see about God all around me with what He let happen."

Bryce understood her dilemma. "Christianity is hard, Charlotte. Men have free will. Men choose to do evil, from Adam and

Eve on through time. I know God loves you. Trust what you see. God's designs are all around you. This is who God is. The fact evil exists speaks far more about man than about God. The Bible says God hates sin. He did not want you to get hurt."

She nodded and didn't say anything more. Bryce didn't know how to help her. She was asked to accept and reconcile a nearly impossible set of two facts — God was good, and she had been badly hurt.

It seemed like the flaw in life, that God had given men the freedom to do good or evil. And yet that freedom, a true free will, was at the heart of what he believed about life. Driven by love, God had created people with a free will, had given people the freedom to decide what they wanted to do, so God could know who wanted to freely love Him back. Most people rejected God and the world turned evil. But in the midst of that, God was still good, He still acted in love in every situation.

Jesus, is there anything else I can say right now that will help? The prayer circled through his thoughts, but as hard as he listened — hoping for a Scripture to come to mind, some words that might comfort — he heard only silence. Old hurts, as deep as this one, were the kind mere words didn't reach. *Help Charlotte feel the fact you love her. The only way she heals is if she gets held by you until the pain fades.*

Bryce slid his arm around her shoulders and sat with her until the sunset faded and the breeze picked up. He reached for her hand. "Let's get some dinner."

She let him pull her to her feet. "I was thinking I might like to go to the zoo with you sometime. I always get a kick out of watching the kids when they see a giraffe for the first time or when a goat at the petting zoo bumps them to get fed."

Bryce smiled. "We'll plan a day of it. I'd love to see the sketches that come out of that excursion. What sounds good to you for dinner?"

"Italian, I think. Maybe spaghetti and meatballs."

She set the table while he fixed the meal.

"It smells good." She paused beside him. "Why do you cook for me like you do?"

He blinked at the unexpected question, hesitated before saying what he had guessed some time ago. "Because they made you cook for them."

She held his gaze for a long moment, then softly smiled and moved to get out the loaf of French bread. "You're a very nice man, Bryce Bishop."

■ ■ ■ ■

"Bryce."

"Hmm?" Charlotte was curled up on the couch, her feet pulled up under her, with two pillows and his shoulder for a cushion. He pulled his attention away from his book. The movie she'd turned on after dinner had gone to commercial.

"Do you miss life as it was before?"

He thought about it because she asked it as a serious question. "Not a bit, actually."

"Not even Bishop Chicago?"

"Devon has it well in hand. I used to have ten people depending on me to make good decisions. Now I've got around ten million. Using the money wisely matters. I enjoy the job." He studied her, curious. "Why the question? Are you missing Graham Enterprises?"

"No. I just realized I'm not. I needed the studio. I didn't realize how big that hole was until I was at the drawing board again. It feels good to be working on the intricate drawings."

He waited to see if she'd offer another comment, but she fell silent. She was turning her wedding rings. He was learning to read that small tell. "I don't regret marrying you," he said quietly.

Her hand on her rings stilled. "We're simply living together."

"We live together very well." He tucked a strand of hair behind her ear. "Do you want us to be doing something more than that?" He knew the answer, but found it interesting she didn't respond right away.

She finally shook her head.

He dropped a kiss on her hair. "Relax. We made a deal, Charlotte. You can try baby steps before you decide what you want. Hugs and kisses are free gifts. No expectations they repeat. No questions about how they are. They just get to be good moments."

She wrapped her arms around him and hugged him. "I married a really good guy," she whispered.

She didn't pull back from the hug. He could feel the nerves in her and ran his hands lightly down her back. "I like the perfume. You smell good."

She giggled a little shakily. "You're a very solid man."

"Mostly bone. Like a big old fossil."

She laughed and turned her head to rest it against his chest, sighed. "I like not being alone."

"So do I. I love sharing my life with you,

Charlotte."

She toyed with a button on his shirt. "Would you kiss me, Bryce?"

He shifted how he held her and kissed her, the one he'd had planned for their wedding, the one he'd thought about when he watched her laugh with his family, and wished for when he told her good-night. He let the kiss linger. Nothing overwhelming, just her, and the feel of her, and the perfume he liked.

She had closed her eyes. He waited until she opened them, smiled.

Her hands slid up toward his shoulders. "I'm going to tuck that into the think-about-it part of my brain and finish my movie," she whispered.

"Okay."

She didn't move away. He simply waited. She leaned forward and kissed him back. "Thank you."

"My pleasure," he replied softly, and let himself add the word *beloved* only in his thoughts.

She moved back, but not far. He returned her pillows, picked up his book, found his page, started to read, but nothing registered. The emotions were still shifting on him. If he said *I love you,* she would freeze up on him, but the words were waiting to be said.

He settled his arm around her again. They needed time, measured in weeks and months. An untimely step, moving too quickly, could easily put them all the way back to the beginning. He gently hugged her, then turned the page in his book. Patience was turning into a very good friend.

Paul nudged his wife to the side of the whiteboard so he could read the notes she'd added on the case that day, look at the map. "You've been busy." He settled his hands on the back of her shoulders, felt the tension, and rubbed out the knots in her muscles, gently worked his thumbs along the back of her neck.

"That feels wonderful." Ann sighed with the pleasure of it and tipped her head forward. When his hands finally stilled, she laid aside the marker and turned to wrap her arms around him with a soft smile. "Welcome home. Workday go okay?"

Paul thought of the meetings, the headache he had fought all day, and simply rested his head against hers. "I've had better. Another political bribery case bubbled up to the surface, this time in the department of transportation. I'm losing two key guys who specialize in counterfeit drug imports to a multistate task force. We've got a credible lead on where to find Carol Boxx and her daughter, Tina. It will be nice to have that case off our plate. Best part of the day was leaving to come home."

"You need some dinner. Want me to cook?"

He kissed her for making the offer. "Tell me where you're at first," he said. "Then we'll eat and maybe go out for ice cream, have a mini-date."

"I'm in favor." Ann turned to look at the whiteboard. "When you overlap the Bazoni and baby Connor cases, you get a much bigger geographical footprint as the focal point. It encompasses where the Bazoni girls lived, the house where Charlotte was held, to the park where baby Connor was found buried. It's a three-mile area. We've been focusing on Meadow Park. The three miles now include Meadow Park, Sterling Heights, the private high school and private college near where the Bazoni girls lived, then northwest to the river and the Lakeview neighborhood."

"Our caller was farther out than we were expecting."

Ann nodded. "I think so. The Dublin Pub guys considered him local, so maybe someone with family in Meadow Park, but he lives in this outer circle. We can talk about how to broaden use of the tape — maybe start identifying business owners who have been at their location twenty years, see if someone in that larger group recognizes the voice."

She marked two items off the list. "I've given up trying to trace the ransom money in the Bazoni case since the two cousins liked to gamble. The holes I'm finding in the recovered money could be another partner getting his cut of the money or could simply be bad wagers. The four unidentified fingerprints are still a mystery — none generated a match in the current database. Did you bring home the year-books?"

"The box with my briefcase. Have an idea?"

"Rita suggested we work on a list based on who went to school the longest with the cousins. You do a crime like this only with someone you seriously trust not to give you up to the cops for some reward money. I'm thinking someone they knew from grade school through high school would fit the bill."

"The cousins were into sports in general, football in particular, cars. Look at sports first. It's the most common way bonds get built."

"I'll start there. Let's find some dinner while I tell you the rest of it." Ann headed to the kitchen. "Jackie's lasagna okay with you? I was just trying to scare you with the cooking offer."

"Sounds wonderful."

Ann pulled out the dish to reheat. "I had an interesting conversation with Gage this afternoon. A couple of things. The uncle of the two men who abducted Charlotte died recently. His sister went to the house, saw the porn magazines and videos the man had, and doesn't want to be the one to clean it all out. Gage made a deal with the family. He will throw out the offensive materials he finds, and in return he can search the house and business for anything related to the cousins. We know the two men spent time at the uncle's home during the four years Charlotte was held."

"Long odds something is still there, but it will be useful to have it searched. The uncle was always a wild card about what he knew. What's the second thing?"

Ann got out the salad and held up salad dressing options. At Paul's nod she set out French dressing. "The house where Charlotte was held is going to be sold, as no one in the family wants to touch it. Gage thinks John is going to step in, buy it, and demolish it."

Paul got out glasses and filled them with ice water. "That's the best news I've heard in a while. I wonder if he'll tell Charlotte before or after he takes a bulldozer to it."

"It might be good therapy to be the one sitting in the driver's seat of that bulldozer."

"Pass on word to John — if he needs some help getting the title cleared, the permits to destroy it authorized, whatever bureaucracy needs to be moved, I'll lend a hand."

"I'll do that. I'm having lunch with Charlotte tomorrow. I'm not planning to mention baby Connor, but I might bring up the house, see if she comments. We're going shopping to find a birthday gift for Bryce. She's thinking something baseball as he enjoys the game."

"He'd enjoy the movie *Moneyball* if he hasn't seen it yet."

"I'll ask her. The coin sorting room is going to finish work next week at the pace they're going. Charlotte is going to dovetail Bryce's birthday evening with the 'last coin' celebration. I thought we might make a symbolic purchase of the last coin, then give it to them framed as a late wedding gift. A memento of how they met."

Paul smiled. "A very good idea. Mention it to Devon and see if he can help us out with the arrangements."

The lasagna was good. He'd been rushed all day, and it felt good to sit down for a leisurely meal. Paul had seen his wife in a lot of moods, recognized the thoughtful one she was in tonight. "What else is on your mind?"

"Do you think God nudges on small matters like the cold case you chose to bring home because He knew this was the year the baby Connor case could be solved?"

"I don't think God wastes our time any more than He does His own. There were dozens of cold cases to choose from, but the details of this one sounded interesting to me. I'm as willing to accept that God was involved in that choice as not. I'd prayed about which cases we should tackle together, and this one got selected."

"I'm praying we have this case solved soon."

"We'll find the caller. As Bryce likes to say, a lot of coincidences seem to occur when you pray. If we don't already have what we need to solve this, I'm sure it will turn up. I'm guessing it's now a matter of months, possibly only weeks, before this is solved."

THIRTY

Bryce shut off the desk light and called the workday finished. He walked through the living room and headed to the kitchen. The house was quiet — too quiet for what he had discovered was his preference. He had grown accustomed to Charlotte's music in her studio or her favorite show being on television, and found himself listening to them during the day. But she'd gone out with Ellie for the evening.

He put chicken strips into a hot skillet, raided the refrigerator for salsa and the cupboard for tortilla chips. The doorbell rang, and he turned off the heat under the skillet, walked through the house, checked who it was, and opened the door.

John. Behind him Paul. Bryce knew with one glance there was trouble. He stepped back to let them enter. "What's happened?"

"Charlotte isn't home?" Paul asked.

"She's out with Ellie this evening. Kim-

550

berly Beach is with them."

"I'll warn Kim to give us a heads up before they return." John was already pulling out his phone. "We don't need Charlotte walking in on this conversation."

Bryce watched John walk away to make the call. "What's happened, Paul?"

"Another photo of your wife has turned up. Gage brought it in to the FBI this afternoon. We've confirmed it's authentic."

"*Another* photo. This isn't the first."

"There are four others that I know of, recovered from the house in the days immediately after she was rescued — likely proof-of-life photos they didn't use. They're sealed under a security tag to keep them out of the general case file."

"Where was this one found?"

John rejoined them, closing his phone. "The uncle of the two men who abducted Charlotte recently died," he said. "Gage got permission from the family to search his home and business. A box was found that looks like personal belongings of one of the cousins. The photo was found tucked in a magazine."

"Besides the time gap, why is this one significant?"

"The hand on her shoulder is not one of the men who was killed," Paul replied. "The photo proves a third man was involved in her case. Is there anything you can tell me now, Bryce?"

Bryce looked at John.

"Tell him," John said with a nod.

"There was a third man. Charlotte said he whispered 'I'm a cop, I will kill your sister if you mention me.' The next day cops broke in, shot the two men, and rescued her."

Paul winced. "No way that's a coincidence. Anything else you can tell me?"

Bryce looked to John, back at Paul. "I'm sorry. I can't say anything further."

Paul looked between them, then to John. "If I state it's Charlotte's butterfly pin on baby Connor's blanket, will you confirm it?"

"She was there," John replied.

"The voice on the Dublin Pub tape?"

"She confirmed the caller was the same man who threatened her sister."

"What are the odds I can get her to say any of that for the record?"

"Very slim to none."

Bryce stepped in before Paul went further. "You said Gage found the photo. Is he going to use it in the book?"

"He's assured me he will not," Paul replied, "but he doesn't need to use the photo. He's already realized it confirms a third man was involved. It's a disturbing photo, Bryce."

Bryce took a deep breath and let it out. "I need to see it."

Paul took an envelope from his pocket, offered it. Bryce slipped out the photo. He felt the impact of it as a physical punch knocking his breath out. He put his hand across the photo to block most of the image. The man's hand on her shoulder was a right hand. The third finger was missing part of the final joint. An old injury, well healed. Bryce felt the muscles in his chest tighten as a whisper of a memory took hold. "I've seen that injured hand before."

John was studying the photo equally intently. "I had the same feeling. You've seen it, not just read about it?"

"I've seen it, and almost identical to this photo, a hand on a shoulder."

"Not the case file pictures," John said, "I know them too well. Somewhere in a video?"

Bryce moved to his office to get the boxes Chapel had sent him, what seemed like a lifetime ago.

He set up the old video equipment in the living room and put in the first tape. The press conference tapes, the newscasts, the community fund-raisers. He played tape after tape, searching for what had triggered that fleeting memory.

He stopped the fifth tape. "There."

Tabitha had spoken a few words to the gathered guests at a fund-raiser for the family, was coming down the steps from the stage to talk with the gathered reporters. A man from the stage had joined her. The way Tabitha turned, smiled at him, leaned into his space, all spoke of an easy comfort. He put his hand on her shoulder as she turned to face the press.

John saw it and visibly flinched. "Anybody but him."

Paul held the photo near the screen. The hand injury was the same.

"Who is it, John?"

"Christopher Caleb Cox. Tabitha had quite a crush on him when she was eighteen, nineteen," John said, his voice not quite steady. "A recent graduate of the private high school, private college that technically was in their neighborhood by a fluke of geography but economically was a world away. He showed up in Tabitha's life when she was sixteen, in the days after Charlotte pushed her out of the van. Sporadic at first — 'How are you doing, anything I can help with?' Then as the modeling developed into more travel to New York, he'd help with travel arrangements, business details. He's five years older than Tabitha. Christopher helped Tabitha with the public events, recruited many of those who came to donate. She trusted him, depended on him." John looked physically sick. "It's going to destroy Charlotte and Tabitha to hear this."

"He put himself in the middle of what was going on," Paul said quietly. "He tracked the family, the investigation, and probably extended how long this went on by what he learned. What better way to be in the center of things than recruit the other sister as his inside source for developments in the case."

Bryce had seen enough. He moved away from the screen.

Paul was studying the video. "Play it. Let's see if we have his voice."

There were two brief exchanges with the press where Christopher's voice was faintly captured. "The odds of getting an audio match with that weak a sample are small, but we'll try," Paul said. "It's at least contemporary audio to the phone call. What else do you know about him, John?"

"This was thought to be a good guy. Well-respected family, honors at college, president of the class — a clean, attractive image. Most of what I know comes from having read the father's journal, Tabitha's diary. They wanted me familiar with the details so I could help answer Charlotte's questions about what had happened with her family during those four years.

"Christopher's father was a lawyer, a partner with a downtown firm. Christopher went out to California to get his law degree, get away from his father's shadow, started a firm out there with a couple of friends from law school. He made a name for himself as a defense attorney.

"After he left for California," John continued, "Tabitha eventually let go of the idea of the two of them having a future. Thomas was the guy she had met in New York, and as the modeling took off and the press intensity grew there, Thomas was the one she began to lean on. Eventually Tabitha married him. But Christopher was her first crush, her first love."

John ran his hand through his hair. "I can check with Tabitha, do it casually, but I don't think she's heard from him in the past decade. And as far as I know, he's still in California."

Bryce could see the line of dominoes lined up to hit his wife, knew she wasn't ready to absorb this. "Paul, don't tell any of this to Charlotte tonight. You can't show her the photo. Not until this is verified."

"I agree," Paul replied. "At a minimum I want an expert telling me that hand injury is the same, and I want a voice confirmation that our pub caller is in fact Christopher Caleb Cox. I want to have eyes on where he is today. We'll have the conversation with Charlotte after we have those facts."

"Charlotte's going to want to protect her sister," Bryce said.

"They've been victims once, Bryce, I'm not interested in making them victims again," Paul said. "We'll take this one step at a time. John, I want your word — you don't act on this. You don't track him down. You don't have private detectives working his name five minutes after I leave here. Give me a reasonable amount of time. I'll keep you both in the loop."

John looked at Bryce, back at Paul. "Forty-eight hours."

"I can work with that." Paul pulled out his keys. "I'll get out of here before Ellie drops Charlotte off and notices my car. If this is confirmed as the guy, you're going to have to be prepared to step in with both Charlotte and Tabitha. And I'm likely going to need Tabitha in Chicago for a conversation."

"We'll be ready," John promised.

■ ■ ■ ■

"You're quiet tonight."

Bryce stirred as Charlotte joined him on the couch. "A lot on my mind." She invaded his space, and he welcomed her into it. He liked holding her, and he no longer felt just that slight flinch at the first touch. "Have a good evening with Ellie?"

"We ended up at a bookstore with a stack of art books on the table going back and forth between us. She talked me into buying two; I talked her into buying six."

Another night he would have at least chuckled. "You did good." He feathered his fingers through her hair, held back a sigh. She'd had a good evening and he didn't want to disturb the calm.

"I figured out part of my problem with God."

His hand stilled.

"I don't know what I can trust Him to do. I was sitting across the table from Ellie tonight and it just struck me. I know what I can trust Ellie to do in a situation, and I can't say the same thing about God. I thought I could trust Him to keep me safe, and He didn't. I thought I could trust Him to answer my frantic pleas to save a baby's

558

life, and He didn't. I don't know what I can absolutely trust Him to do."

He felt her dilemma deep in his chest. The sadness in her voice was layered with her history. "I don't have answers for you, Charlotte."

"God is good."

"The Bible says He is good, holy, and perfect."

"I don't understand His decisions."

Bryce put his other arm firmly around her to complete the hug. "You want to understand and be able to predict God. It can't be done, Charlotte. You simply have to trust both that He loves you and that He is making the right decisions."

"I need it to make sense, Bryce."

"We would all like that, and it likely will make sense one day, from the perspective of eternity." He rested his chin against her hair. "You weren't forgotten, Charlotte. Explanations, reasons, would be nice to have, but the more important question is simply was God paying attention? He was, to every moment of those four years. He didn't treat your prayers lightly. He didn't dismiss your words. I can't explain His decisions, but I can say 'trust Him.' You weren't forgotten."

"Trust seems so easy for you, Bryce."

"Not easy. Anything but easy."

"I have a hard time praying like you do. I start the conversation with God, and all the stuff that hurts comes jamming into the conversation, wanting answers. And with that comes the feeling that God let me down. It takes about two minutes for my frustration level with God to get too high, and my only option is to stop praying and go do something else. I can't seem to get past that."

"I think God would rather have those honest two minutes with you than an hour where you gloss over what's really on your mind." He turned toward her. "What brought this topic up? Did Ellie say something?"

"Not directly. It was a quiet remark she made about John, the fact she could depend on him. Made me think how I can depend on you, followed by how I wish I could depend on God."

"You can. That's one of the things about Him I'm sure of, Charlotte."

"It's just hard to get comfortable with that. God will make decisions that are hard for me to accept. It's something I know from firsthand experience."

"God's more dependable than I am, Charlotte. Maybe it doesn't seem that way, but it is true. Keep wrestling with that fact until you realize it's true."

"God is probably tired of all my doubts, but I'm trying. I want a comfortable relationship with Him, Bryce. I see what you have, and I wish that was my relationship with Him too."

"It will heal. He loves us the same. Your journey is just different from mine. There are wounds and scars from what happened. Choose to trust God, even before you fully understand. There will be a day where you know you can love Him without reservation."

"I hope there will be." Charlotte suddenly leaned back. "Other news. I think Ellie's going to tell John yes. She's pretty quiet about that kind of big decision, but I think she's made it."

"Yeah?"

"I know her. It was in her voice when she mentioned they'd been out last night. I think she's decided to marry him. She hasn't told him yet, but it's like she's ninety-five percent decided that she will. It's going to be so much fun helping her plan a wedding."

"You'll enjoy every minute of it."

"Keep an eye on John for me, would you?" Charlotte asked. "As soon as it's official, I'm going to so enjoy teasing him. It will be a pleasure to see him settled. He's probably already chosen an engagement ring for her, but I was thinking we should offer to design the wedding rings if they would like. And I want to do a tiara for Ellie to wear with her veil. Something elegant."

Bryce smiled. "I'm now hoping this isn't going to happen too soon so you two can spend the next few months giggling over the wedding plans. She's a good friend to you, Charlotte."

"The best. They both are." She curled her feet up and shifted around to get more comfortable. "Are you okay staying up a while tonight? I'm wide awake. I wouldn't mind even watching a Mets game to fill some time."

He reached for the remote. "I'll find us something to enjoy. Tell me what else you did this evening." He listened as she gave the run-through and wished he could give his wife a month of these enjoyable evenings before she learned about the photo and what it meant. Once more she was going to feel deep pain, and he couldn't protect her. That's what was so agonizing to him about what was coming. He listened to her happy chatter and made a memory of this night, knowing it might be the last easy evening for a while to come.

■ ■ ■ ■

Bryce worked because he didn't know how else to fill the time, reading through financial reports, completing due diligence on organizations, evaluating projects being developed. He got through the mail, and he waited for Paul to confirm a name that was going to rip his wife's world apart once more.

John called midafternoon on the third day. "Paul just phoned me," John said quietly. "He's got confirmation. Christopher Caleb Cox is the man we've been after. He's the man in the photo with Charlotte, and he's a voice match to the baby Connor call."

"Find Ellie, Charlotte's going to need her, then tell Paul to come over."

"Expect us within the hour."

His wife was sitting at the back patio table, her sketchbook open and her focus on the birds visiting the feeder. Bryce stepped outside first. "We've got company, Charlotte."

She looked around, saw Ellie and John behind him, and a smile lit her face. Bryce knew Charlotte was hoping to hear the best kind of news, a wedding, and ached because he had no way to cushion the shock that was coming.

Her smile began to fade as she saw Paul behind them. She put aside her sketchbook. "What's happened?"

John took a seat in front of her, leaning forward, hands clasped before him. "Remember how I said some news you hear and then later feel? I need you prepared to do that now."

She slowly nodded.

"A photo has shown up of you from back then. A man's hand on your shoulder. It's proof a third man was there, Charlotte."

Her hand still holding a pencil trembled violently. "I need to see the photo," she whispered.

Paul offered an envelope.

Bryce squeezed her shoulder gently, steadying her, took the envelope from Paul, and handed it to her. She pulled out the photo, flinched, then went totally still. She studied the image carefully, thinking hard. "I don't remember the photo being taken, or the man." She looked at John. "I don't remember."

"Okay."

She rubbed at her forehead. Shook her head. "I don't remember." She pushed it back into the envelope and returned it to Paul.

"We've identified him from the hand injury, Charlotte," Paul said quietly. "His name is Christopher Caleb Cox."

She lost even more color. "Tabitha's Christopher."

"Yes."

She pushed out of the chair, then surprised Bryce by moving into his space, securing a tight grip on his hand. "Tell me the rest of it."

"He is wanted in California in connection with the homicide of a young woman who worked at his law firm," Paul replied. "The FBI also wants him for the theft of five million dollars from an escrow account controlled by the law firm. He's been missing for nine years now. It's believed he arranged a new identity for himself using the expertise of one of his criminal clients and disappeared. He's never resurfaced."

"You can't find him."

Bryce heard the faint panic ripple into her words. "Easy," he murmured, trying to reassure, wishing she could accept a hug right now so he could do a better job of it.

"Give me a few days to better evaluate the search that has been done before I try to answer that, Charlotte." Paul said.

"You have his photo, John?" Bryce asked.

"Everyone around Charlotte and Tabitha knows what he looks like."

Charlotte studied the paving stones, her jaw working as she fought to keep the emotions in check. She finally looked over at Paul. "You can't tell Tabitha he was using her. That the man she trusted, had a crush on, was involved in this. It destroys Tabitha if you say that. You'll make her his final victim."

"I've got people looking at the homicide case and seeing how strong it is," Paul said, "someone looking at the embezzlement case. If we can put him in jail for life on those crimes, we can leave this photo in the secure files and not pursue it as a trial matter. But Gage has the image. He's the one who found the photo. Christopher Caleb Cox is on video with your sister numerous times. Gage will figure it out, eventually find a name the same way we did."

Charlotte rubbed her eyes. "I can divert Gage from using it." She looked back at Paul. "Gage leaves the specifics about the third man out of his book in return for an interview about what happened to baby Connor."

"It's your butterfly pin."

She simply nodded.

"I'd like to hear those details as well," Paul said. "It's doubtful Gage will take that deal."

"It's worth asking him. Could you prosecute Christopher for his part in the baby Connor case, for his part in mine, based on what you have today?"

Paul thought about it and finally shook his head. "Not without your testimony, and even then the evidence is thin."

"Then please file the photo and don't pursue it. There are reasons I don't talk about what happened. My sister leads that list. I can't testify."

"Let's take this one step at a time. We find him. And you find out if Gage will keep the information quiet."

Charlotte looked over at John. "Christopher changed his name, he disappeared. But I bet he left at least one person alive who knows something about his new name or where he is, who might talk for the right dollar amount. Bryce can write some very large checks."

"I've already got tickets to California," John said. "I'm hopeful, Charlotte. But this isn't going to be quick. You need to brace for several weeks of waiting, if not longer."

"I know how to wait." She glanced around the group. "If that's all, I'd like to take a walk with Ellie." She took Paul's nod as agreement, then left with Ellie.

Bryce showed the last of their guests out, then locked up the house and reset security. He noted two more security personnel now visible on the grounds, the first of a wave of tightened security John had warned him was coming — around their home, his family, Charlotte. He would have to call his parents tomorrow, figure out something plausible for an explanation.

Bryce took two mugs of hot chocolate upstairs with him. Ellie and Charlotte had walked for over an hour before Charlotte had returned and headed upstairs. It had shaken his wife more to realize she couldn't remember the photo than the terrible memory of what that day must have been like.

He tapped on her door and leaned against the doorjamb. She was painting her toenails. He recognized the concentration of a woman trying to focus on the totally mundane. "You could have been drunk, Charlotte. That's why you don't remember. It might not be anything worse than that."

"Do you believe that's all it is?"

He wished he could lie to her. "No." The truth was probably something much more ugly.

"Neither do I." She rose to come get the mug. "Thank you for the hot chocolate."

"Do you want to call Tabitha?"

"I can't. She would hear in my voice that something is wrong. Best case, Tabitha never hears even a whisper about this."

"They will find him."

"The one thing I am certain of," she replied, trying to smile, "is that the FBI wants him, so do the California cops, and it's personal with John. I pity the man in a way. John isn't a man you want coming after you." She carefully sipped the hot chocolate. "You knew about the photo. You weren't surprised when John told me."

"They've had it for a couple of days while they verified its authenticity and who he was."

She absorbed that news, nodded. "Thanks for giving me some days without having to know it was out there."

"Sure." Bryce could feel the politeness of the conversation, knew it was the last thing they needed, but didn't know what he could say that would get her to shift to give him more. "Charlotte, I wish I could make this go away, not have it be part of your history."

"That makes two of us."

"You want to talk awhile?"

She tipped her head toward her nightstand. "I'm planning to finish that book and then turn in. I'm tired enough that sleep is not going to be a problem tonight, Bryce. It feels like I got punched. I just need the time to wear it off."

"This is going to be over — fully over the first time in nineteen years."

"You know, I believe it will be." She set aside her mug. "I'm going to go see Gage in the morning."

"Want company?"

"For the drive over. It needs to be a private conversation."

"I disagree with Paul's assessment. I think he'll take the deal."

"We'll know tomorrow."

His bedside table clock said two a.m. Bryce added a sweatshirt to the jeans, put his phone in his pocket, slipped on socks. He went downstairs to find his wife.

"Scoot over." He made room for himself on the couch and wrapped his arms around her. She had come downstairs so he wouldn't hear her crying. "I love you," he said.

"Don't say that," she whispered achingly.

"It's an explanation, not an expectation. I love you, and I have chosen to spend my life with you. I don't want to be somewhere else. So as hard as life gets for you, as tough as the emotions are to deal with, you and I are okay. I don't need you to try to keep up a good front for my sake. If you need to come apart, if that's the fastest way through this grief, then loosen that grip of control you're trying to keep, and let the grief come. It won't last forever, Charlotte, and life will be better on the other side. You and I will be fine. Trust me on that."

She was already on the edge of losing it, and his words intensified her struggle. He kissed her hair. "Do me the favor of going ahead and crying until you can't cry anymore. Okay?"

She curled herself into him, and sobs shook her whole body.

Bryce refolded the cold washcloth he'd gotten to rest across her eyes. "Better?"

"Getting there."

He shifted to make it easier for her to stretch out on the couch.

"I want to love you."

His heart skipped at her soft words. He brushed back her hair. "That's the nicest thing you've ever told me." He smiled. "You'll love me one day. I'm a pretty loveable guy."

She half smiled back. "I'm numb, Bryce,

even for me. This is survival mode. Emotions ice over for later. Tears aside, it's hard to feel much right now."

"It will pass. Once they find him, you'll start to breathe again. This will be fully over for the first time."

"I need it to be." She was silent for a long time. "I don't remember him," she whispered. "The photo being taken. The man."

He heard the fear in her voice. "If you ever do, we'll deal with it." She couldn't take any more tonight, and he desperately needed to yank her out of the past for a while. He ran his hand down her arm. "Hungry?"

"Maybe a little."

"Poached eggs and toast with strawberry jelly would do you a world of good right now."

"Better start with just the toast."

"I'll be right back." He kissed her forehead, then went to get them some breakfast.

Bryce thought life entered a kind of limbo while they waited. Ellie came over every day, tugging Charlotte into conversations about her sketches, the gallery, the direction she wanted to head next with her art. They started discussing the logistics of a wall-sized image, fitting together various sketches like a patchwork quilt into one mosaic. The idea absorbed a few days of Charlotte's attention, but then was set aside as something she didn't want to attempt this year.

Bryce started taking Charlotte running every morning, letting her steadily run for an hour on the track before waving her in to cool off. They both struggled with trying to ignore the more visible security around them everywhere they went.

Charlotte threw him a birthday party and final coin celebration, inviting his family and friends over. Paul and Ann brought a gift of the final coin, framed, in sequence with a set of wedding pictures they'd arranged with Ellie's help. Bryce hung it in the entryway near the housewarming-gift sketch Charlotte had done of Bishop Chicago.

Bryce enjoyed the party more for the fact it gave Charlotte a distraction than a celebration that he was a year older. For one of her wedding presents he had bought her a custom-made pool cue, and she'd named it *Elizabeth* since the ivory in the cue was engraved with English ivy and roses. She now returned the favor for his birthday, giving him a pool cue with a pattern she'd sketched that melded together his favorite cuff-link designs. They had played an hour's worth of pool together to try out the gift, both content to end the play when the score of games won was tied.

They talked briefly about her upcoming conversation with Gage. The reporter had agreed that if Christopher was charged only with the California crimes and the FBI didn't pursue the photo, he would keep Christopher's involvement in the Bazoni case out of the book — on the condition Charlotte talked with him not only about baby Connor, but also would discuss her thoughts about that first day and her impulse to push Tabitha out of the van. Charlotte took the deal to further protect her sister.

And they waited for word that Christopher Caleb Cox had been found.

Charlotte tapped on his office door. "Want some help?"

Bryce saw in a glance the restless energy that refused to let her stay with anything for very long. He took a stack of checks off the printer. "Why don't you sign for a while?" He offered her the checks and a pen. He'd automate the signature process eventually when the sheer number of checks became an issue, but for now he liked this hands-on final step.

She pulled her chair up to the edge of the

desk and began to neatly sign checks. "How much money is left?"

Bryce realized it was the first time she'd asked. He clicked over to the account balance of that morning. "Eight billion three hundred eighty-nine million."

"We've still got some work to do. At least you do," she offered.

He smiled. "A little." He slid checks into envelopes. "Let's go to the gallery for an hour this evening. Ellie is putting *Florist at Work* on display, along with *Lava Flows*. We should go enjoy how they look in a gallery setting."

"Maybe tomorrow. I think I want us to go for a drive tonight."

"Anywhere in particular?"

"Let's find an all-night diner with great cheeseburgers somewhere. I'd like to just people-watch for a while, have some time to clear my thoughts."

"We can do that."

The drive home was peaceful, music on low, the conversation drifting into long stretches of silence.

"I love you, Bryce."

His heartbeat skipped. He looked over at her.

"I don't know what that means exactly, if

anything can change, but I wanted to say the words," Charlotte said softly.

He reached over and took her hand in his. "The words matter. A lot." Emotions were rising so quickly they were overwhelming him.

"I was going to wait until we got home to say it, but it seemed easier when you're driving and I don't have to wonder what you will do in the next few minutes." She gave a sad smile. "I'm sorry about that."

Her words tempered the joy he felt, but only at the edges. "It's okay, Charlotte." He smiled and rubbed his thumb across hers, feeling her nerves. "Take a breath. Relax. One day it's not going to send nerves skittering around to say those words."

"I still can't sleep with you."

He gave her hand a gentle squeeze. "Do you trust me?"

"I'm working on it."

"Trust me to understand this road we're on. I love you, Charlotte. Over time we can go a very long way with small steps. Tonight is going to be like last night, tomorrow night will be the same. But you can give some thought to kissing me good-night. Why don't we start there?"

"I don't know where the triggers are going to be."

"You don't need to be afraid to find them. We both know they are there. We'll deal with them together when they appear." He looked over. "Relax. Life just got less complicated, not more."

"I'm afraid it's done the opposite."

Bryce smiled. "Trust me. You'll see."

Paul answered a call shortly after midnight, listened, leaned over and turned on the bedside light, reached for a pad of paper. "Thanks, John." He hung up the phone.

Ann rested her chin on his shoulder.

"John has a name. Simon Legard. Possibly Seattle."

"How much did it cost him to get that name?"

"Five million."

"Bryce will consider it a bargain."

THIRTY-ONE

Bryce moved the phone toward the front of the desk. "Go ahead, John. You're on speaker. Charlotte's here."

"He must have heard we were looking for him. He left Seattle in a hurry. My guess, we missed him by less than an hour. Fingerprints confirm we've got the right guy. The FBI will soon be running his photo on the national news, along with a hefty reward we're putting up for information. I'd rather you didn't watch it, Charlotte — you'll hear directly from me when there's something that is new."

Bryce glanced over at her, curled up in her chair. "We'll avoid the newscasts and wait for your call, John."

"We assume he's running under a different name, and odds are good he headed from here north into Canada. We'll either have him within the next twenty-four hours or this could take another detour and take a few more days. He tried to burn the papers he didn't take with him, but he was short on time. There will be emails and phones to trace and documents to work and people who know him as Legard — he won't be able to run for long. They're locking down accounts under the Simon Legard name, and even with other cash he can get to first and move, there's going to be a trail."

"You've put a name and face to him once, you'll do it again," Charlotte said confidently.

"I will," John promised. "Hang in there, Charlotte. Bryce, I'll give you a call when I have more. Expect an update in about three hours."

"We'll be here, John."

Bryce hung up the phone, looked over at his wife.

She got to her feet and restlessly paced the room. "I think I'll go for a walk. Come with me?"

"Sure." Bryce picked up his phone and keys. "This is going to take a few days, I think. An hour head start is substantial when he already had a plan in place for running."

"I've been waiting nineteen years. I can last a few more days."

"You're practically climbing the walls," he

said lightly, draping his arm around her shoulders.

"So it might be a kind of *wired* few days."

Bryce laughed. "Come on, Mrs. Bishop. I might even be talked into buying some ice cream, so we can make this a longer walk than normal."

"I'll take every distraction I can get."

Bryce bought her ice cream, and they perched on the empty bleachers of the high school football field to enjoy the cones.

"This was one of the things I missed most during those four years. A sunny day outside. Ice cream."

Not sure if it was simply a comment or an opening to a conversation, Bryce elected to leave her remark alone for now. "What do you want to do when this is over?" he asked.

"Celebrate. A party at Cue's maybe, or Falcons. Good food. Friends. Laughter. I may let you drag me home at two a.m."

Bryce smiled, nodded. "I can put that together."

She finished her ice cream and her smile faded. "I used to sit near a window in the house where I was held, look at the thin slice of the river I could see, and pray for a day in the future that would simply be one where I could wake up and go on about life and not have to care about who these men were or what their mood was going to be or what they would do when they wanted —" She abruptly stopped. "I've wanted this day for nineteen years. To wake up and not have to think about someone out there who could hurt me or my sister."

Bryce grieved over that sliver of memory she had just offered. She needed to give him a hundred more of those slivers if the pain was going to fade. "It's going to be over — in days, maybe weeks. It's not going to take years now to get this finished."

She looked over at him. "I'm scared to death that if I'm asked to see him in person, do a lineup, that I'm going to remember more. I feel at times like I'm living in two worlds."

"You're safe, Charlotte. Your mind is finally starting to accept the layers of what that means, to relax its grip on the past. Some of it you may have to remember in order to get closure."

"I'm so afraid the memories will drag on for years."

"You can't heal to some kind of schedule; it happens a piece at a time and on its own timetable. Expect this to take as much time as it needs to take. I'll listen, Charlotte. Whatever you want to share, whenever you want to talk, I'll listen. I can do that much for you."

"Thank you for that."

He reached for her hand.

She sighed. "You've gotten the difficult side of this marriage."

"That misses the fact that being part of your life is worth a great deal. I like that we're married," Bryce replied. "I like it a lot. I can't imagine life without you around. I'd like you to let go of the idea you have to get better on your own. We do this together."

"And if five years from now I'm still where I am today?"

He smiled. "I will have enjoyed those five years with you. Baby steps, Charlotte. We're building a very good marriage. Rushing forward to be somewhere by a certain date just topples what we've already built. You need to enjoy the process more. I like sunny days sharing ice cream with you."

"I'm impatient."

He shrugged. "It's not a bad trait to have. You want to move forward. Just choose your steps and risks carefully and see what the terrain is like. I promise to catch you if you fall. I think the next twenty years are going to be a good journey. I just think you need more time than you're giving yourself. You don't have something to prove. You're a good wife."

"I am?"

He laughed. "Yes, you are. You are so hard on yourself." He tugged her hand. "Come on, let's walk. It's a beautiful day and I want to enjoy more of it with you."

"Go ahead, John, we're both here." Bryce set the phone on speaker and placed it on the kitchen counter.

"This is going to take a few days," John said. "We know he headed east out of Seattle, but we lost the trail about a hundred miles out. I don't think he's going to hunker down quickly. I think he's going to run fast and far, then stop and burrow in somewhere under a new name.

"The FBI has his friends from the California days well covered, and they're working the ones who knew him as Simon Legard in Seattle. Paul's going to focus in on his family's ties in Chicago. I'm going to spend a few days here to see if I can find a source for his new name. If I can't find it in a few days, I'll head back. Christopher is going to need ready cash to keep running. He'll make contact with his old life somewhere. I'm betting he goes back to his old friends in Chicago."

Bryce looked at his wife. "It will be good

to have you back here, John."

"Charlotte, John and Ellie are here," Bryce called.

Charlotte didn't let John get more than two steps into the house. She reached him at nearly full speed. John caught her with a laugh and a very long hug.

"Thank you," Charlotte whispered.

"You're welcome."

The man had spent the night flying from Seattle and looked in need of some sleep and a good meal. Bryce could understand his urgency to get back.

John finally set Charlotte in a chair, since she wouldn't release her hold on him, knelt and studied her face. He smiled. "We know the name he's running under now is Allen Crimson. It's only a matter of time before they locate that name on a rental car, a bank account, or spot it at a border crossing. All it takes is one call from a hotel clerk who says 'I checked in someone who looks like the guy you're looking for' for us to have him."

John glanced over at Bryce. "Nice touch, by the way, to have his photo run at the top of every hour on all three networks with the reward for information and phone number posted."

Bryce shrugged. "A lot of money can buy a lot of airtime."

"He's going to find it very difficult to hide."

"Thank you for meeting me, Charlotte."

"I appreciate you being willing to let this be a private conversation, Paul. I'm meeting with Gage tomorrow, so I'm considering this discussion as practice for it." Charlotte watched John take a seat on a bench by the fountain. She could feel her growing nerves threatening the calm she had struggled to achieve. "Would you mind if we walk while we talk?"

"No." Paul matched his stride to hers as they took the path around the park. "Does Bryce know you're here?"

"He thinks I'm shopping, which I will be when I leave here."

Paul slipped his hands into his pockets. "I'm glad to hear Gage accepted your offer and will leave Christopher out of the book."

"Baby Connor is too big a story for him to pass up. Gage can mention he believes a third man was involved in my case without naming him. It will protect Tabitha — that's my priority."

"Christopher Cox is going to be found, and he'll be tried on the California matters before I ultimately decide what to do about his involvement in your case and in the baby Connor case. Hopefully he gets life in prison and the question is moot."

"Thank you for that."

They walked in silence for a minute. "Charlotte, I'm going to ask the hardest of the questions first. Did they hurt anyone else? Is there another baby Connor out there? Another girl like you and Tabitha?"

"No. My memories are fragmented, but I have to think that if there was someone else, I'd remember with the same vivid clarity that I do baby Connor."

"We've searched the records for cases from those four years and didn't find something that looked like it might be an overlap."

Charlotte felt some of her tension ease away. "Thanks again."

"Two men grabbed you, a third man whispered to you. Was there anyone else you can remember being involved?"

"I only remember the three of them. But I can't remember that photo. I don't know for certain, Paul."

"When we locate Christopher, do you want me to pursue the question with him? He would be in a position to know if anyone else was involved, and he's the kind of man who would go for a deal in return for a lighter sentence."

"I'd rather he never know he's been connected to my case unless you have to bring it to trial."

"Understood," Paul said. "Christopher met the two cousins during a six-month window he spent while going to public school during the seventh grade. His parents separated, he went to live with his mom who didn't have the money to continue a private school, he met the two cousins during the most turbulent six months of his life, and fit right in with them. His father had to do a lot of cleanup to keep an otherwise serious juvenile record from being built on Christopher. The parents got back together before the next school year, and he returned to the private school. But he was still seen with the two cousins at the Dublin Pub on enough occasions that people in the neighborhood considered him a local."

"I didn't know how they had met. That's useful to me." Charlotte looked over at him. "Gage writes that the task force nearly found me the first week after the abduction."

"We were working a tip you had been seen by the river, officers were canvassing homes, knocking on doors, looking for two men that fit the description from Tabitha. The address where you were held was on the list. A bad car wreck at the train crossing that day pulled officers off the canvass to help with the injured. The next day the first of several news specials on your case ran, and the tip line flooded with sightings. Manpower got diverted to work them. You were two addresses away from an officer knocking on the door. I can't tell you how sorry I am it didn't end that day for you."

"Life would have been so different if it had." Charlotte pushed her hands into her pockets, mimicking his. "I know cops did their best over the years."

"Did the cousins talk about planning a kidnapping in the days before they took baby Connor?"

She shook her head. "They didn't plan the crime. They went out to buy some beer, four hours later returned with a screaming baby boy bundled up in a blanket. They were yelling at each other, making the baby cry even louder. They thrust Connor at me and a sack of things they had bought and told me to make him be quiet." Charlotte went silent. "I thought that first evening — the cops are going to be searching for this baby, they'll find the boy and they'll find me at the same time, and so much hope welled up inside at that thought. I already loved that little boy, but I thought he might also be my way out of the nightmare."

"I'm so sorry he wasn't, Charlotte."

"After he died, I gave up. I stopped eating, stopped caring, grieved. I willed myself to die too. Baby Connor had escaped their grip, not as I hoped with his freedom, but with his death. I figured maybe it wouldn't be so bad being dead compared to what reality was." She looked over at Paul. "They were going to try again. I could hear it in their voices, see it in their frustration over not getting the ransom money they wanted. They were going to snatch another baby like Connor. I couldn't go through it again."

"I'm glad it took a different turn, for your sake, Charlotte, but also for every cop involved. You being found alive was the one bright moment in the case."

They walked in silence.

"How much of this have you told Bryce?" Paul asked.

"Enough."

"You can trust him for whatever you need to say."

"I know. He's a good husband, Paul."

"Ann and I know in a small way the terrain you're on. Her abduction lasted eight days, broke some bones, caused some medical complications. She still has trouble sleeping. If you want someone to talk with, you can trust my wife to keep your confidence."

"I appreciate that. You'll talk to Bryce if he needs a sounding board?"

"Of course."

Paul shifted his briefcase to free his right hand as the elevator doors opened on the private fourth floor. Black was waiting for him. The dog promptly sat, lifted his paw. Paul grinned and took the handshake. "You're getting fast at the greeting," he whispered, and slipped the dog a piece of jerky. Black headed at speed toward the living room with his reward.

Ann appeared, smiling and shaking her head. "He's not going to need dinner if he keeps this up. He got a double out of me, added a flourish of shaking hands, then rolling over and playing dead." She took Paul's briefcase, leaned in to share a welcome-home kiss. "I gather Charlotte kept the appointment."

"We took a thirty-minute walk, and she answered every question I asked."

"Anything else we need to worry about?"

"No. We find Christopher Caleb Cox, we

can safely consider the baby Connor case closed."

"How's Charlotte holding up?"

"From her body language I'd say she's a bundle of nerves. She has an identity for that third man now, and she needs him caught."

"Anything on the tip line that sounds promising?"

"Sightings are all over the map, most on the West Coast, a couple from here, a few for New York. You want to come in with me tomorrow, read through them? Fresh eyes are always useful."

"For an hour or two. He's going to need cash. John thinks he comes back to this area, returns to family and old friends."

"I tend to agree. And it would be appropriate if what began here could end here."

THIRTY-TWO

Bryce straightened his tie as he joined Charlotte in the kitchen for lunch, saw she was holding the pitcher of tea. "I'll take a glass of that while you're pouring."

She looked over to him from the television screen, blinked, looked down at her hand. "Oh, sure." She reached for another glass.

"What is it, Charlotte?"

"A boy was abducted on the way to school this morning. It led the noon newscast. They'll be giving an update after this commercial." Bryce watched the news with her. Samuel Gibbs, twelve years old, had been abducted while riding his bike to school. There was an urgent appeal for anyone who saw the boy or a blue sedan with tinted windows seen leaving the area to come forward and help police with what they saw.

"The cops will find him, honey."

Charlotte bit her lip, nodded. "I just hate when it's a kid."

Bryce rested his hands on her shoulders, rubbed at the tension. "John is coming over. You're welcome to join us."

"I've heard as many details as I can handle for a while. I'm going to go work in the studio if you don't mind."

"What's the latest, Linda?" Paul checked his watch as he took the call. Samuel Gibbs had been missing for four hours and ten minutes.

"The note left taped on the bike's handle-bars said *We will be in touch.* I'm set up for an incoming call. The father has given us more than forty names of individuals who might have done this. He's had some arbitration cases where neither side was happy with his ruling."

"Jacob need anything?"

"The canvass around where the boy was taken is wrapping up. He's got a partial plate on the sedan from a parent who saw the car turn out of the alley and into traffic ahead of him. Jacob's working it, and he's tasking people to check out names on the father's list. It's not common knowledge the boy rides his bike to school and even less that he takes that alley behind the diner as a shortcut. It's possible the boy could have been a target of opportunity — grab the first rich kid who comes along."

"Are the parents cooperating?"

"Yes."

"I'm a call away when you need something. Keep me updated."

"Will do, boss."

Paul looked again at the time as he hung up the phone. If the boy was fortunate, a ransom call came in soon, they had the money delivered by six, and Samuel Gibbs was home by nightfall. But life was rarely an ideal world.

Bryce selected a book and joined Charlotte in the studio. She was working on a playground scene with dozens of kids enjoying recess. What had been a large, blank piece of paper that morning was now a working sketch with swings, a climbing platform, a slide, rocking horses, and kids playing on all of it.

John came in to join them. "Bryce, Charlotte, I've got Paul on the phone." He set the phone on a tray of pencils. "You're on speaker, Paul."

"Charlotte, I need you to listen to something. Ignore the content of the call, just listen to the voice."

"Okay."

"Play the call again, Linda," he instructed.

"I have your son, Samuel. He said to tell you breakfast this morning was a poached egg and he forgot his math assignment on the kitchen table. I want three million, in black gym bags, left at the Haverford Street railroad crossing north of Meadow Park at three p.m. today. Deliver the unmarked cash, non-consecutive numbers, and the boy will be home unharmed tonight. Miss the deadline, the price goes up, and it's at least another day or two before you hear from me again. *If* you hear from me again."

Charlotte's face tightened as she listened. "Paul, that's the third man."

"That's what I thought too. Christopher Caleb Cox is back on his home turf, needing to raise some fast cash. He grabbed the son of a man he went to college with. Knowing who is holding the boy gives us a lot to work with. Thanks for the confirmation, Charlotte."

"Paul, we can source you that ransom cash, and do it in the time you've got," Bryce offered.

"You sure?"

"Yes."

"I'll take you up on that, Bryce. The father

is trying but doesn't have this kind of cash accessible."

John picked up the phone and took it off speaker. "Paul, where do you want me to bring it?"

Bryce counted stacks of hundred-dollar bills to reach three million, and John packed them into black gym bags.

"I didn't know we had that much cash lying around."

Bryce glanced up as Charlotte joined them at the kitchen table. "There are safes now tucked all around this house. I learned from Fred. You never know when you might need money in a hurry."

"For Samuel's sake, I'm glad you have it available. John, would you put this with the cash?" She offered a folded piece of paper.

John opened it, scanned the words, looked at her. He nodded and added the paper to a stack of the bills.

Bryce looked between the two of them, but didn't ask.

Bryce met their guest at the back door. "Ann, thanks for coming by."

"My pleasure, Bryce. Paul thought it might be helpful to hear an update with some of the details in person."

Bryce was slow to close the door, caught off guard by the increased security presence on the property. John had added security dogs. His quiet comment earlier that day, "This changes things," had been more layered with meaning than Bryce had realized.

"The boy is back safe?" Charlotte asked, walking into the kitchen from her studio.

"Young Samuel Gibbs walked into the police station in Evanston fifty minutes ago," Ann confirmed. "He picked out Christopher from a set of photos as the man who took him. His family is on the way to him now."

"Thanks for that very good news."

"I wish I had more to offer than just that. We lost the chance of trailing the ransom money to Christopher. He used the Madoni family to pick up the ransom. He knew what he was doing in that respect.

"Think of the Madoni family as running a cash exchange for hot money," Ann explained. "You tell them how much money you want to bring into their network, they tell you where to deliver it, you pick up clean cash less their fee at a different location. They've been doing this for at least sixty years. The dollar bills that enter their network end up in Mexico, some in Dubai, where it's not going to matter if the serial numbers on the bills are being traced."

"So the money we delivered isn't the actual cash Christopher received," Bryce clarified, thinking about Charlotte's note.

"The Madoni family doesn't normally release funds in less than forty-eight hours. They want time to make sure they aren't accepting counterfeit currency, want to confirm the amount. If Christopher didn't want to wait around, they would simply transport the bags and hand off the contents for a steep fee. Given the elaborate depths of the transportation shell game they put together, I'm guessing they simply passed along the contents of the bags to him minus their fee."

"How did they move it?"

"An ambulance with two men dressed as paramedics picked up the ransom money. The tracking signals on the money went dead, either dumped in water or stomped on. Then they started pitching black duffel bags out the passenger window every block, and the bags were snatched up by passing cars. They pitched out a lot more duffel bags than they had picked up. The money could have been moved then.

"The ambulance then pulled into the parking garage at Shore Mall. Within minutes a caravan of white vans exited the parking garage. The final count on them was twenty-two. The money could have moved to one of the vans or an entirely different vehicle in the parking garage.

"The ambulance then pulled into Bayfield Hospital, parked, the two men walked through the hospital and exited the front doors where they caught a cab. The ambulance owner didn't even realize it had been stolen for the hour and a half it was gone. Somewhere along the way, probably at the mall parking lot, Christopher was handed the ransom money."

"The priority always was getting Samuel back unharmed, so it was a good day," Charlotte said.

"It was," Ann agreed. "If Christopher is still traveling under the name Allen Crimson, this is going to be an easier search than if he's changed his name again. But even with the ransom money, it's going to be hard for him to hide for long. His photo is widely distributed now, and the fact he made this kind of desperate move means he has lost access to any cash reserves he might have built up. I think he's in the last days of his freedom."

"Charlotte turned in?" John asked.

"Half an hour ago. Today really took it out of her," Bryce replied, getting them both cold drinks. "It shook her more than I expected, having Christopher behind another kidnapping."

"He's running because we're chasing him, so indirectly Charlotte feels responsible for whatever he now does."

Bryce raised an eyebrow at that, but nodded. "What's going on? Charlotte writes a five-million-dollar check for cash, I figure it's for an interesting reason."

"We now own the house where she was held. I've been working on the demolition plans."

"She's appreciated seeing them," Bryce said.

John pulled a page out of his pocket. "This is the text of the note she asked me to slip in with the cash."

I remember what you said. I'll pay you five million more if you leave my family alone. I'll put it in the place you know.

"Interesting gambit on her part. Think it will draw him out?"

"He's running so short of funds he risks kidnapping a child? I think Christopher will stew about the money and try to figure out a way to determine if it's really there. He scared her so badly she kept silent for years. He'll know it's a trap, but it'll nag at him till he has to find out if the money is there and if the note might be legit.

"I had to scramble today on the off chance he tried for a lightning grab of the cash as soon as he found the note, which is why I didn't bother to go through the details earlier. I wasn't sure we could get it put together in time. But we're set up now, and the money is still in place."

John turned on his laptop and went into the security feeds. An image of the house and grounds where Charlotte had been held appeared, taken from above. "We'll know when the man turns up. This view comes from a thermal camera mounted on the old analog television tower. There are several other layers of surveillance that should work regardless of the weather. None of which is going to be visible to a person trying to decide if it's safe to approach the house to pick up a payment."

"Where did you put the cash?"

"The upstairs bedroom closet shares a wall with the bathroom. While she was held there, Charlotte figured out she could move the built-in shoe rack in the closet and get into the space behind and under the tub.

She used to hide things there. He knows the spot exists."

"Let's hope he takes the bait."

"If he doesn't, Paul will find him. It's hard to run very far when your photo is everywhere and the reward is large enough it's worth someone's time to call and turn you in."

"How long, John?"

"Probably weeks rather than days. You'll need to keep her occupied, and her mind off of this."

"Easier said than done. She's already working to the point of exhaustion trying not to think about it."

He was watching Charlotte mentally living in two worlds as the memories intruded, split between the past and present. The art, the work, kept her anchored in the present. Get this man caught, get the past truly finished, then he'd see how Charlotte was reacting.

Part of him was braced for the possibility she might crumble and get all the memories back in a tsunami wave of relived details. It would be the fast way toward healing, but traumatic. The opposite concern was if she told herself it was finished and tried to deny the memories the time they needed. He hoped for a smooth center path that gave her the ability to absorb and cope with the memories, share them, and be able to move on with her present.

She couldn't predict what was coming, and she was so nervous about it that she didn't know what to do to cope. At least it gave him a clear job — help her get through the days ahead with minimal turmoil.

Bryce turned the conversation to the topic that had been on his mind all evening. "Where are you at with security? I've noticed the changes."

"It's going to be stiffening even more in the hours ahead, around you and Charlotte, Tabitha's family, and yours. Since she was able to send that note with the ransom payment for the boy, Christopher knows now that she's somewhere in Chicago, that she's closely involved with law enforcement and the search to find him. That ramps up the security equation.

"There are limited ways Christopher can find out her current name, the fact she married you, and where she is. I don't think a direct threat from Christopher is any more tangible today than it was a month ago. That's why I'm not insisting you both leave town right now. But you'll both see and feel a lot more security until this is over. I'm also adding tightened security around the

603

reporter Gage Collier, as he knows too much about Charlotte not to cover that base, and also around Ellie."

"I want Charlotte out of here, John, before there's any additional concern," Bryce said. "All it takes is you saying this is an active threat, and she'll stop arguing the point and pack. We could be anywhere in the world rather than here."

"The situation changes, I won't hesitate to say go," John agreed, "but we're not at that point yet. And I think it's important that Charlotte be here to see this end. I think it will help her in the long run to have confronted this head-on, which is why I let that note from her go out in the first place. Christopher isn't winning this one. That matters."

Bryce understood his point. "I want another discussion on this every few days. Taking her away from here is the one thing I can do."

"Agreed," John replied. "Get a trip planned, a vacation, pack some bags, so if you need to go on short notice, it's already arranged. I'm not interested in taking a risk, Bryce, I just know how costly — and I don't mean money — it can be to take her out of her routine. I don't want to ask her to pay that price unless it's necessary. But this gets any more tangible, I will tell you to leave."

"Let's hope for both our sakes Christopher hits that house sooner rather than later," Bryce murmured. "You'll call, John, whenever there's something to know, no matter how small?"

"You'll be my first call, no matter the hour," John promised.

THIRTY-THREE

The phone woke Bryce. He listened, turned on the bedside light. "I'm on my way, John."

He paused outside Charlotte's bedroom door but heard no sound. He walked downstairs. He would leave a note rather than wake her. It had been a month and there'd been two false alarms already.

"I'm coming with you." Charlotte stepped into the kitchen from the sunroom.

"I didn't know you were up."

"I was on the couch, watching the moon." She pulled out a chair at the kitchen table to put on tennis shoes.

"John said there was movement around that house."

Charlotte nodded. "Even if it's another false alarm, I'd still rather go than wait here wondering."

John had an office at Chapel Security, with the ability to monitor their home, their vehicles, and now the house they would soon demolish. Bryce parked in the side lot, came around to open Charlotte's door, walked with her to the back entrance where he used his security card to enter the building. The security personnel who had driven over with them melted out into the shadows.

Bryce had finally figured out one mystery. When he had originally ordered a background check on Charlotte Graham the day he'd first met her, he'd unknowingly asked it of the firm that provided her security. When Charlotte's grandfather had paid John in advance enough to keep Tabitha and Charlotte safe for their lifetime, John had used some of the funds to become Chapel's silent business partner. The company had been providing John tech support and resources for the last seven years. The background report Bryce had received from Chapel had been all true, but very carefully worded.

Bryce and Charlotte joined John in his office.

"There's someone now in the house." John pointed out the movement on the screen from the thermal camera. "He's been inside about two minutes. He spent the first twenty just walking around the area outside the house."

"How did he arrive?"

"He came by car, parked to the east."

John picked up the radio. "Mitch, let's disable the car. Something simple but effective, like the distributor cap."

The thermal camera showed an image moving toward the car. John tapped the screen. "This one is Mitch, this one is Joseph."

The image in the house was walking around, entering various rooms, but moving at a leisurely pace. "This doesn't look like a man trying to get in fast and get out. It looks like someone finding a vacant house for the night to sleep in," Charlotte observed.

"We've had two such guests over the last month, so it could be. But this one drives a nice car, and the plate numbers come up as a rental." John picked up a handful of pecans. "The nice thing about whoever it is, he's stepped into my world."

John paused as another image appeared from the direction of the river. "That makes sense. Send in a decoy with your car, let him check the house, see if alarms go off, cops come in." John reached for the radio. "Mitch, Joseph, you've got one coming from the east near the river. Sit tight. We don't do anything until the money moves."

The two images met up near the front door of the house. Then the first man walked away, heading toward the railroad tracks. "Let him go by," John told Joseph. It looked on the screen like the man walked within ten feet of Joseph as he left.

"Mid-twenties, sandy hair, a jacket three times his size, carrying a bottle of scotch," Joseph radioed back.

The man in the house wasn't wasting time. Within minutes the dot tracking the money began to move.

"Mitch, Joseph, he's got the bags. Let him get out of the house, get back to the car. Let him think he's getting away with this."

The image was moving fast now, tracking a man who was running. He reached the car, got in. Time passed.

"He's realized his car isn't going to start," John said. "Now's the interesting question he's wrestling with. Did the guy he paid to help him just turn on him, or does he have worse problems, and the cops are there? He's on foot with his money. He has no chance if he tries to take it all with him; it's too much weight and size. If he leaves the money behind and runs now, he has a slim chance."

"He'll carry some of it, what he can pull out of a bag," Bryce guessed. "Will we lose the tracker on the money if he does?"

"He would have to open the plastic-wrapped bricks of cash, find the tracking chips, and do it in the dark. He won't find them all." John smiled and pointed. "There he goes with a bag of money heading to the river, probably thinking he can try to drown the tracking chips. Won't work with these — they're waterproof and nearly indestructible."

John radioed Joseph, "Let him get to the river."

John glanced back. "Charlotte, do you remember why you're afraid of water?"

"Yes."

"Should I repay the favor?"

She watched the man as he hurried toward the river. "I'd rather you just end this."

"Take him, Mitch."

Two images merged, and the man stopped moving.

John put the photo Mitch sent up on the screen. "Now that's not what I was hoping to see."

"That is not Christopher Caleb Cox," Bryce agreed.

Charlotte leaned her head against Bryce's chest and wrapped her arms around him. He had to get her to ease her grip so he could lift her chin and see her face. She was silently crying. He wiped her eyes and wrapped her back in a hug. "It's time to call Paul, John, see what the cops can convince the man to say. He knew where the money was at, so he's at least been in contact with Christopher."

"Don't get your hopes up. I recognize him. His name is Bill Davidson, and he used to work for the uncle who owned that house. His criminal record runs for pages." John reached for the phone. "Do you want to put the cash back in the house, reset the trap?"

Bryce looked down at Charlotte's bent head, then to John. "Return the cash to the house."

John nodded and turned his attention to the phone. "Paul, we've had a bite on the cash. But not exactly the one we wanted."

Bryce took Charlotte home.

John called shortly after seven a.m. Charlotte nodded to the studio and escaped the kitchen rather than listen to the update. Bryce watched with concern as she disappeared. "Yes, John."

"Paul's been able to get some answers. Davidson got a call from Christopher and an offer. In exchange for information about where the uncle had hidden some money, he would retrieve the money and pass on half of it to Christopher via the Madoni family. He thought he was recovering some of the original Bazoni kidnapping ransom."

Bryce refilled his coffee mug. "Interesting pitch."

"Caught me by surprise," John agreed. "Davidson called Christopher from the house to say the money was there, sent a photo, and was told to get on the Interstate heading south and call Christopher again in one hour for instructions on where to take half the cash."

Bryce winced. "So Christopher knows Charlotte's note was good, knows there was cash at the house, and also knows since Davidson didn't call him back in an hour that he's either been double-crossed or Davidson has been picked up by the cops."

"The number Davidson was to call is no longer being answered," John confirmed. "Christopher knows there's trouble and will assume the cops are involved."

"What would have stopped Davidson from simply running away with all the cash?"

"Christopher told Davidson there were three stashes of cash, and if Davidson wanted in on the other two, he would honor this first deal to the letter. Davidson believed it."

"I'll give Christopher credit for offering a good story. So what now? The money is back at the house, but it's highly doubtful Christopher will expect it to be back there or that he will try for it again."

"We're at a dead end. Paul has some phone numbers to work, but otherwise I think this attempt to draw Christopher out is over," John said. "This goes back to the tip line, Christopher's photo circulating everywhere, and cops searching to find him."

Bryce was tired enough he would leave sorting out the implications of what had happened for another day. "Thanks for the update, John. I'll give Charlotte the news."

With each passing day Bryce could see the increasing toll on Charlotte. She needed this to be over. Up to this point she had buried herself at the drawing board and with her sketchbooks for hours, but that had changed. She was no longer drawing. He would find her curled up with a book, or in the kitchen baking muffins or bread, but her sketchbooks remained closed. He was worried about the shift, about what it meant.

A week passed. The phone numbers gave the FBI leads on where Christopher had been, but opened up nothing on where to search next. A flurry of calls to the tip line and a number of sightings in the Detroit area looked promising, but turned out to be merely a man with a similar appearance to Christopher Cox. The search grew quiet again.

Bryce reached over and turned on the light at his end of the couch. Charlotte was sitting beside him, watching a movie, but not much of her attention was on the film as she didn't bother to forward through the commercials. Bryce stroked her hair, and she turned to glance up at him. "What's on your mind?" he asked quietly.

She didn't answer for a long moment, then sighed. "He's going to kidnap someone else, Bryce. Christopher wasn't sure if the money was really there or not, so he sent someone to check it out. Now he knows I was telling the truth. He's not going to walk away from five million dollars. He'll do what he knows, and he will snatch a child."

Charlotte reached over and intertwined her hand with his. "If he snatches a little girl, calls the FBI, and tells me to send the five million to him to get her back, he knows I will do it. I've set someone else up for heartache with my foolish attempt to draw him out. I should have never sent that note.

I've put something in motion that can only end in tragedy. And I don't know what to do."

Her scenario was one of a few John already had gamed out for what might come next. Christopher was an unpredictable man, but with a pattern of kidnappings that had proven profitable to him. Bryce hadn't talked about them with Charlotte, because talking about the what-ifs only set her up for things to worry about outside her control. But he should have, he realized now, as she had been doing so on her own, coming to the same point.

He shifted and encouraged her to lean against him so he could put his arm around her. "Charlotte, he might, and if he does it's going to be a hard day, but we'll deal with it together," Bryce told her, keeping his voice matter of fact. "If something happens, at least we have the means to end it quickly. For now, we pray he gets caught. That is something we can do."

"I've been praying that for the last month, and it's become urgent this last week. My heart is going to break if God doesn't answer this prayer."

"Pray for what you want, Charlotte, and trust that God hears you. Then step off a cliff and trust His answer. I don't know what God is going to do in this situation, but I trust Him and what He decides."

"It's really that easy for you?"

Bryce thought about it before he answered, "In this case, yes."

She finally nodded. "I wish I had your confidence."

Bryce hugged her. "Borrow some of mine."

Three nights later John walked through the back door with Paul Falcon behind him. Bryce was fixing dinner.

"There's news," John said. "Where's Charlotte?"

"Right here, John." She joined them from her studio, a magazine in hand.

Bryce turned down the heat under the skillet and reached for a towel to dry his hands. "There's trouble?"

"Some good news, some bad," Paul replied. "How are you doing, Charlotte?"

She shrugged. "Wishing this was over."

"Let's see if we can now make that happen," Paul said with a smile. He looked over to John. "Your conversation, I think."

John nodded, tugged a letter out of his pocket. "You've got mail, Charlotte, sent to you via your sister's address. It's from Christopher Cox."

She pulled in a breath as she paled. Bryce held out his hand, and she willingly took it, moved into his space. Bryce rested his arm comfortably around her shoulders and turned his attention to John. "Not something I expected to hear. What does it say?"

John opened the letter and pulled out a single page, laid it on the counter for them to read as he summarized. "He's threatening to snatch a child unless you deliver the five million to him. He wants the money taken to the bus depot in Wilmette. It's a known Madoni family drop-off location. The good news — Christopher hasn't snatched anyone yet. The even better news — this is an interesting move with some risk to him. His greed is making him vulnerable. He's playing a bluff without the leverage of a missing child."

"The bad news?" Bryce asked.

John and Paul looked at each other, then John said, "A warning about no cops this time, and he wants Charlotte to deliver the money."

Bryce felt Charlotte flinch.

"He's messing with you, Charlotte," Paul said quietly. "The whole point of using the Madoni family to move the money is the fact Christopher doesn't have to be anywhere in the area where the cash is first delivered. He takes delivery of the cash somewhere else in the city. He's simply manipulating you."

She blew out a hard breath. "He's doing a good job of it. He could be watching from someplace to see if I show up, though."

"He doesn't know what you look like. Beyond a woman of your age, he won't know if it is an undercover cop delivering the money or if it's really you. It's been nineteen years since he last saw you. It would be nice if he was there, watching the delivery, as it gives us a chance to spot him and catch him. But I doubt that's going to be his play."

"He's not asking for her to do something when she gets there? Take a phone call, follow directions to somewhere else?" Bryce asked, not liking where this was heading but trying to figure out the layers of it.

"No, just deliver the bag of cash as checked luggage on a bus trip," John answered. "Paul's people have confirmed the supplied ticket is one where the barcode and the text generate different data. It's how this particular bag will get misrouted to the Madoni family out of all the bags being loaded. The one thing we've been weighing is the possibility Christopher could have a security question in place, something only

Charlotte would know how to answer. Answer the question right, they accept the bag. Don't have the answer to the question, the delivery gets rejected."

"That possibility is handled easily enough by having an undercover cop wired for audio both directions," Paul put in. "If she needs to know the answer to a question, you feed that answer to her over the audio earpiece she's wearing. We need your assistance, Charlotte, but we do not need you delivering the money. Just for you to be someplace in the loop and listening to what's going on."

Bryce, watching her expressions change, realized the impact this was having and tightened his hold. Fear was fighting with an equal resolve to face doing this. She looked at him. "What if he asks something I don't remember?"

"You say that," Bryce replied.

Charlotte looked between Paul and John, focused her attention back on Bryce. "What do you think?"

"He's toying with you, Charlotte. He wants the money. Who delivers it is immaterial. He's just got a chance to manipulate you again, and he's using it."

She sighed. "It feels that way too." Charlotte looked at Paul. "All right, so you use an undercover cop, and all I need to do is be there in case you need an answer that would be unique to me."

"Yes."

"I can do that," Charlotte agreed.

Bryce knew that was the right answer, but one that would give her many uneasy moments in the days ahead. Bryce shifted the conversation away from Charlotte. "Assume the money is delivered by someone standing in as Charlotte. The Madoni family then delivers the cash to Christopher. Where does that get us? Christopher is in the wind again. Can we pay the Madonis enough they would tell us where that hand-off is going to take place?"

"That's the real play," Paul replied. "Having Charlotte — our stand-in — delivering the money to the drop-off point is a distraction Christopher is using to tie up resources. He knows we'll have to put cops on the ground around the delivery site on the slim chance he might be there watching. The place we have to focus on is where the Madonis take the money and where they hand it off. We can attempt to follow the money to that point, which can be nearly impossible, or we figure out how to get them to tell us where that hand-off location will be."

"You're thinking a hefty enough payment

might get the Madonis to tell the cops where that hand-off will be?" Bryce asked.

"They might be willing to sell the information to John," Paul said. "They are in business, and Christopher is a liability to them right now. They don't turn down customers, but neither do they want the scrutiny that being involved with a high-profile fugitive brings. It risks too many of their own people being arrested as the money is moved around."

"Will Christopher actually be there to take the hand-off or will he have someone else picking up the cash on his behalf?" Charlotte asked.

"My personal guess, he will have someone else pick up the money," Paul replied. "He would want one more courier in the loop before the cash reaches him. My guess is he'll want to be outside the Chicago area the entire time this plays out."

"So the real plan is to follow whoever picks up the money from the Madoni family," Bryce said, "and hope he leads back to Christopher?"

"Yes."

"When is this supposed to happen?" Charlotte asked.

"It's an open-dated ticket for a weekend bus route between Wilmette and St. Louis.

The next window for making that delivery is this Friday night."

"When you get the five million from the house, John," Charlotte said, "we should think about putting another note in among the cash. It wouldn't hurt to lay the groundwork for another reason Christopher should be in touch with us after this, on the possibility this attempt to catch him fails."

"A good idea, Charlotte." John folded the letter and slid it back into the envelope, handed it to Paul. "We've been waiting for another break in the case, and we just got one."

Charlotte nodded and attempted to smile. "At least it's only a threat rather than another actual kidnapping." She turned to Paul. "Whatever happens, the priority has to be to make sure either Christopher gets his money or that he's caught. Something that leaves him free but doesn't get the money to him only raises the real likelihood he will grab a child to demand his five million in ransom."

"We see the situation the same way," Paul agreed. "This is a defensive move, paying him now to try and keep anyone else from becoming his victim. We won't lose sight of that larger objective."

Bryce looked at John. "Make any offer you

think is necessary to get the Madonis to co-operate."

"I'll call you with the number," John said.

The police van smelled of sweat and stale coffee. Charlotte leaned back in the chair they had assigned her, wanting to stretch, wanting to get up and pace. Bryce caught her eye and offered a reassuring smile. He was watching security monitors to help canvass the people coming and going from the bus depot, looking for any sign Christopher was watching events unfold. John was out in the crowd, standing near the pillar that demarked the baggage claims area for those arriving. There was no sign of Christopher Cox. But the tension in her back was knotting her muscles.

Paul joined them in the van. "We're about ready to deliver the money. Any concerns?"

The FBI agents monitoring the surveillance indicated all was a go. Paul took a chair beside Charlotte. "Whenever you are ready, Rita."

Charlotte watched the agent with the money head into the bus depot and make her way through the crowds, join the line to check-in and drop off the bag. The video feeds were good, and the audio strong enough they could pick up the conversation of the couple next to Rita in line as if they were standing there in person. The van was quiet during the five minutes it took for Rita to reach the front of the line. She offered the ticket that had accompanied Christopher's letter. The clerk scanned the ticket barcode.

The bag of cash was hoisted onto the scale, and the clerk generated a baggage barcode with the destination and weight. "You'll be on bus seventeen, leaving from lane five, departing in twenty-four minutes. Your ticket has an extra item checked that you'll be traveling with an infant. For the boarding records, I need the name of the child."

Paul touched his mic. "Rita, use Connor Hewitt."

The agent said Connor Hewitt.

The clerk typed it in, then reached down to the printer, retrieved two boarding passes, handed them to Rita. The bag of cash disappeared on the conveyer belt into the back of the bus depot. Rita took the boarding passes and headed toward the departing passenger waiting area.

"That's it?" Charlotte asked, disappointed.

"The money is delivered," Paul replied with a smile. He pointed to the next screen. "Watch the tracker in the baggage. My guess, the bag leaves the building in the next two minutes."

Paul's phone rang.

John, on video standing by the pillar, lifted his phone as he looked toward the security camera. "Paul, Phil Madoni just called me. The hand-off is happening at the Gorum airfield outside Winetka in two hours. It's a short-runway airport serving small planes."

Paul got up from his seat. "The money is now officially in play."

"Christopher is going to fly the money out of the area?" Charlotte asked.

"Sounds like it. We need to shift surveillance to the airport."

Rita rejoined them in the van. "There was no sign anyone in particular was watching for me or watching where I went."

"We thought this would simply be a distraction, and it was," Paul said.

"He wasn't here." The realization began to calm Charlotte's nerves. A hand settled on her shoulder, and she glanced back to see Bryce had moved to stand behind her. She met his gaze and half laughed. "I was a basket case the last few days for no reason."

"You had a good reason," he said, his hand squeezing gently.

"There goes the money," the agent monitoring the bag said. He merged the tracking data with the security camera and pointed to a white van exiting the back of the bus depot. "That van. And now our trackers just went dead. They probably tossed the bag in a lead-lined safe as they all blinked out at the same instant."

"Keep a car on that van. Let's stay with the money as long as possible."

John entered the van. "What's the plan from here?"

"It's likely Christopher will be using a courier to pick up the cash and fly it to where he is," Paul said. "A small plane can land nearly anywhere if you ignore FAA regulations on what makes an appropriate runway. We'll watch the money be delivered at the airport and follow the plane by radar and a couple of aviation assets of our own to track where it goes. The delivery is in two hours, so add another two to five hours to that for it to be handed off by the pilot somewhere."

"Paul, we don't need to be involved from this point on," Bryce said. "I'll have John drop Charlotte and me off at the house, then he can join you at the airport."

"That would be best. I'll keep you apprised as this unfolds."

Bryce followed Charlotte into the kitchen.

"Are you disappointed?"

"I had gathered my nerves to have Christopher do something, want something. It feels strange to have the evening end like this."

"Christopher wants his money more than he wants to come after you — a fact for which I'm very relieved. He's a threat to you and Tabitha, but one we can still contain."

Charlotte walked over and hugged him, rested her head against his chest. Bryce was startled enough by the move it took a few seconds for him to raise his arms to encircle her, and then he simply closed his eyes and enjoyed the moment.

"I was afraid this letter, this request, was going to be the first move of an obsession," Charlotte whispered, "that he would be there with a need to see who I was today, that he'd take a dangerous risk just to see my face. I was so scared someone would see him in the crowd."

"He played on your nerves, but he wasn't there."

Charlotte nodded. She finally stepped back, smiled at him, and looked at the time. "I'm going to go stretch out for a few hours, force myself to close my eyes and try to sleep, to see if I can shake this headache."

627

"I'll wake you when there is news," he promised.

Bryce tapped on Charlotte's door, carrying a mug of tea for her. She had stretched out, but it didn't look like she had been able to do more than intermittently doze. "They're still tracking the small plane. It left the airport heading northwest."

She set aside the brush she was using and glanced at the dawn lighting the sky. "Where is it now?"

"Near Fargo."

She walked over to accept the tea. "Wide open spaces, a couple decent highways. Once daylight breaks, a pilot can tell from the air if there's a cop car in the area," Charlotte guessed.

"The pilot will be able to land, hand off the cash less his cut, and be back in the air within fifteen minutes," Bryce confirmed. "Christopher has a decent plan for getting the money delivered to him."

"The cops will be too far away to see and track Christopher's vehicle."

"I think the net that closes over the area once the pilot lands is going to be tight enough to catch Christopher," Bryce said, more confident than Charlotte about what would unfold. "A remote location also means not many vehicles are out on the roads."

"Where's John?"

"In a plane about two miles behind the one being tracked. Weather is good. John will be able to see and track any vehicle leaving the area of the exchange. The pilot should have landed while it was still dark if he wanted to better protect the hand-off." Bryce thought she still looked a bit bruised from the emotions of the last few days, so he changed the subject. "Care to come join me for breakfast? You should try to eat something."

"Sure." She followed him downstairs. The newspaper had arrived, so while they ate bacon, eggs, and toast, they passed back and forth sections of the newspaper and filled another thirty minutes.

Bryce's phone rang. He pulled it out of his pocket. "You're on speaker, Paul."

"The pilot landed on a country road south of Fargo, North Dakota. We're now tracking a blue pickup truck leaving the area."

"Any hope it's Christopher?"

"State cops are closing the roads in the area and boxing him in. We'll know within the hour."

"Thanks, Paul."

Charlotte pushed away her breakfast plate.

She got up to load the dishwasher, then ran water in the sink to wash the skillet. Bryce joined her and picked up a towel.

She was struggling not to cry. "Take a deep breath," Bryce whispered.

"I'm shaking at the idea he gets away again." She swiped an arm across her eyes.

She finished cleaning up the kitchen and then restlessly picked up a deck of cards and sat at the kitchen table, building a house of cards.

Bryce's phone rang again. Charlotte started and knocked over her card house. Bryce gave her a small smile and answered, "We're both here, Paul."

"Christopher Caleb Cox is now in the custody of the North Dakota state police."

Charlotte put her head down, laughed, then hiccupped. Bryce circled the table and knelt beside her chair. "Paul — thank you, from both of us. Let me call you back."

She was struggling with streaming tears, her hands shaking as she used her palms to wipe them away. She pulled in a deep breath and tried to smile at him. "Bryce, I prayed God would put him in a blue pickup truck and have the state cops arrest him."

The comment so surprised him, it took Bryce a moment to answer. "A blue truck and state cops — so you'd know if God was answering your prayer rather than mine," he said, smiling. "I don't think God minds dealing with specific requests like that."

He wiped at her tears, and she laughed again. "I'm so happy I'm bawling — go figure. Oh, this news feels so good." She leaned forward and wrapped her arms around his neck. Sighed. "I need more sleep. Then a celebration once John is back."

He wrapped his arms around her. "Ellie called earlier. She wants to know if she can ice cookies to look like jail bars, or if that would be tacky."

Charlotte laughed. "I love her. She's making me a cake too, something with lots of icing, and chocolate."

Bryce rubbed her back. "It's over now, Charlotte."

She leaned back just enough to see his face. "You weren't praying for a blue truck and state cops?" she asked quietly.

"I was praying for lightning to hit the guy."

She blinked, smiled. "I wish I had thought to pray for that."

"We have what we need, Christopher Caleb Cox in custody. This is over. Completely, finally, over." He kissed her forehead. "Go get some rest, please. You're running on fumes. John will be home in a few hours and then we'll celebrate."

Her smile was without shadows for the first time since the photo of her had turned up. "Thank you, Bryce."

He didn't dare follow through on what he would like to do right now — really kiss her. That would simply overwhelm her. He turned her gently toward the stairs. "Rest." He had some calls to make. She needed a good party, and he and Ellie had been making some plans.

THIRTY-FOUR

Bryce took Charlotte home at two a.m. from a celebration that would have gone until dawn if she had been the one to decide.

"Did you see Ellie's engagement ring?"

"Several times." She started to undo his cuff links for him, got distracted by his tie and trying to figure out the pattern in the random lines. Amused, he stilled her hands, and turned her around. "Hold still." He worked to undo the knot she had made of the ribbon in her hair. She'd been tugging on it while she played pool and had turned it into a hard knot. "John looked like a man very content with life. You teased him mercilessly tonight."

"He didn't mind. Besides, if I distract him enough I might win a game."

Bryce got the ribbon to finally ease open and slid it off. "There you go."

"Thanks." She shook out her hair, and it cascaded across her shoulders. "What did

Paul have to say? You two were having a long conversation."

"He's closing your case and the baby Connor case. Christopher is going to trial here for the kidnapping of Samuel Gibbs, then to California on a murder charge and federal court on embezzlement. He'll get life in prison without the possibility of parole. There's no need to mention his role in your case. It's over." He tucked a strand of hair behind her ear. "It's completely over."

She grinned. "And it feels wonderful."

She undid his cuff links and stored them away. Bryce hung up his suit jacket.

"Ellie brought the albums over from Texas," she said. "We used to dream up these elaborate weddings." Rather than her chair, Charlotte tossed pillows against the headboard beside his and spread the albums out around her. Bryce took off his shoes, tossed them one at a time into the closet, debated taking the chair. She was not going to be sleeping tonight, he concluded. He settled against the pillows on his side of the bed, looked at what had her attention. She handed him the thickest of the albums. "Can the gem designers maybe do something like this sketch for Ellie's headpiece?"

Bryce realized instantly the sketch wasn't

one of Charlotte's. This was a different artist. "Ellie drew this?"

"Marie did. She prefers oil paints, but she's not bad with a pen."

"I'd say not."

It was a princess design, something out of a fairy tale, the crown and veil a latticework of lace and gems. "I think the designers would love to try. Gold or silver on the curve?"

"Gold, I think. With silver loops on the earrings."

She turned pages in the album. "Here's another sketch of it. Maybe one of the sapphires here in the center, and diamonds in the lattice, then lace from there."

"It will look spectacular. Can I look through this album?"

"Sure."

She told him about the images as he turned the pages, laughter in her voice as she talked about meeting Ellie and the places the two of them had gone in Texas during their college years. On another page he found sketches of John. He looked even more like a military man in the early days after he left the service. Bryce tapped a sketch. "Who's this?"

"One of the doctors at the clinic. She's a nice woman. Heather Ollen."

He realized for the first time he was seeing her history, as close to unfiltered as he was likely going to get. When he finished the album he pointed to another and she handed it to him, describing the people in the sketches while he turned the pages. Her doctors. Her college classmates. Her neighbors at her first apartment, first studio. John, several more of John with Ellie. Bryce picked up the next album, taking his time. He didn't have to ask as many questions now as he began to recognize people in the photos.

Bryce stopped on a photo taken of Charlotte in her Texas studio. The sunlight was streaming into the room, and she was barefoot on a stool, sitting in front of a long drafting table, a large sculpture visible over her shoulder. She was in the early hours of creating *Lava Flows,* the finished artwork he had admired at the gallery. On the drafting table he could see one of the molten hot lava streams sketched in.

"Did you ever try to work in oil paints?" Bryce asked, curious.

Charlotte didn't answer.

He glanced over.

She was asleep. Her eyes had closed where she sat, her chin had dropped forward, and her breathing had turned steady.

She'd literally run past her ability to stay awake. Bryce picked up the albums and closed them, set them on the floor beside the bed. He didn't try to move her, just lifted the comforter around her. He settled in beside her quietly. She'd retreat to her own room as soon as sleep took the worst of the exhaustion away and she jerked awake to find she was here with him. But he'd take the hour he could get, for it felt like a good step. She'd never before let herself be this vulnerable.

The biggest challenge she faced was getting past the instinctive recoil when she was surprised by a touch, and he'd been puzzling over the last weeks on how to approach it. She was embarrassed by her reaction but couldn't defeat it by willing it away. It would only fade with time as unnecessary.

Bryce rested his hand over hers. She'd probably fall off the bed, scrambling away before she was awake enough to realize where she was at and who he was, but he could at least hope she would laugh about it rather than cry. He watched her sleep. She was so incredibly beautiful when she relaxed. Words couldn't capture how much he loved her. He had married very well.

Charlotte was awake, solemnly watching

him. He could see the light of dawn against the drawn window shades. He ran his hand lightly down her arm. "You stayed the night with me."

She leaned forward and kissed his chin. "You sound pleased."

"I'm extraordinarily pleased. It's a pleasure to wake up with you."

She traced a finger lightly down his rumpled shirt. "You snore."

He grinned. "So do you."

She laughed and got up on her side of the bed. "I'm fixing us breakfast."

He rolled over and acquired her pillow. "I need more sleep."

"You can have an hour before I notice. Bryce?"

"Hmm?"

"I want to go on vacation with you. Paris, I think."

"Am I going to see anything other than the inside of an art museum?"

"Maybe for an hour or two."

"Then I'll take you to Paris."

"We can stop in New York and see Tabitha on the way."

Bryce opened one eye to look at his wife. She looked as calm as she sounded. He closed his eyes again. "I'd like that. We can offer to take her girls with us if you like."

"Just us this trip. Breakfast will be warming in the oven if you sleep more than an hour."

"Thanks."

Charlotte had fixed cinnamon rolls, scrambled eggs and bacon, hash browns. Bryce filled a plate, poured a cup of coffee, and carried it with him out to the sunroom. "This is a nice way to start a morning."

Charlotte laid her pencil down and stretched her arms back. "I was hungry."

Bryce leaned over and kissed her good morning. He didn't warn her, kept his hands full, calculating that the risk of startling her was worth the possible reward. "Thank you for breakfast."

She nodded and didn't say anything. Her color was high. He settled into the chair he favored. "What are you working on?"

She reached for a thumbnail sketch on the side of the drawing board, fumbled a bit picking it up. "A larger image of this as a wedding present for Ellie and John."

Bryce studied the swift sketch she had made at the party last night. She knew her friends well. Even quickly drawn, the portraits were exquisite. "It will be beautiful, Charlotte."

"They love each other."

"They do." He handed back the sketch.

He ate a piece of the bacon. She was fiddling with her pencil, looking anywhere but at him. He watched her, smiled. "Going to say it, or should I say it first?"

He set aside his plate, wiped off his hands, and reached over to take the back of her chair, rolled her his direction until she was in his space. He rested his arms lightly across her shoulders. "Good morning, Mrs. Bishop."

Her color was remarkably high. "Bryce."

"I love you," he said quietly. He brushed her hair back from her face, watched her blush come and go, the pallor come and go. "You've got lovely eyes. No more surprises today, just a nice memory to share. It's easier to kiss you good morning than goodnight. I get to enjoy it for longer."

She lifted her hands and rested them on top of his. "I made you a Valentine's Day card. It's either very early or very late."

He grinned. "Did you?"

"I love you too, Bryce."

He could feel his eyes growing damp. "Would you like to go on a date with me, Mrs. Bishop? Maybe go see a movie and have ice cream afterwards?"

"Yes."

He turned his head and kissed the inside

of her palm. "Six p.m. I promise to have you home by midnight."

She laughed. "You should go to work so we can go have fun tonight."

"I should. So should you." He slid her chair back to the drawing board, then picked up his plate and mug. "We're going to have a good next fifty years together, Charlotte."

"We will."

He paused at the sunroom door. "Can I ask a favor?"

"Of course."

"John's going to demolish that house tomorrow afternoon, take a wrecking ball and bulldozer through it. It's kind of an odd date, but I was thinking we could go watch it get flattened. Kind of a ceremony of sorts."

"I would like that."

"I'll mention to John we'll be there."

Bryce left her to her work.

Her oversized Valentine's Day card was on his desk. She had sketched him in silhouette, writing in his planner, the simple pen drawing breathtaking for its accuracy. He opened the card and color burst out — a sprawling oak tree with their names etched inside a heart on the tree trunk. Her dogs were asleep under the tree, and in the background his family was playing baseball, his parents drinking ice tea and acting as the cheering section. The sky was turning a brilliant sunset.

He lifted the card closer and laughed out loud. The bases were coins, the bat was wrapped in hundred-dollar bills, and the ball being hit was a diamond. She'd placed him as the runner on third base. She was at bat. Shimmering in the dirt around home plate were the words *I love you, Bryce.*

"Very nice," he said softly, tracing the words.

"You think so?"

He looked up to see her in the doorway. "I do think so."

She looked visibly relieved. "If you want to make it an evening with some music instead of a movie, I found a very nice dress to go with the red heels you bought me."

"Jazz or country?"

"Surprise me."

"All right. We're going to start a list, Charlotte. Favorite dates."

She came over to his desk, opened his planner to a blank page, neatly wrote numbers one to ten, and solemnly handed him the pen. "Will you teach me to flirt with you?"

He closed his eyes and laughed. "You'll

kill me, but yes."

"And let me practice kissing you good-night?"

"Yes."

"I'll look forward to our dates."

"So will I."

She disappeared from his office, and he set her card on the corner of the desk. He realized she'd signed the front sketch *Mrs. Bishop.* She was going to make his next year interesting. He was looking forward to every minute of it.

ABOUT THE AUTHOR

Dee Henderson is the author of eighteen novels, including *Jennifer: An O'Malley Love Story, Full Disclosure,* the acclaimed O'MALLEY series, and the UNCOMMON HEROES series. Her books have won or been nominated for several prestigious industry awards, such as the RITA Award, the Christy Award, and the ECPA Gold Medallion. Dee is a lifelong resident of Illinois. Visit her at DeeHenderson.com.

To view the video trailer, read the extras, and join other readers to discuss this book, visit:

www.unspokennovel.com
www.facebook.com/DeeHendersonBooks